The Perfect Murder . . .

Dr. Jessamyn Quilter has committed the perfect crime, murdering her abusive husband in cold blood. No one will ever know what she did. No mortal, that is. But her evil deed has unbalanced the cosmos. And the balance must be restored.

Desperate to leave her old life behind and make a fresh start, Jessamyn books a long sea voyage aboard the container ship *MV Andaman Pearl,* to contemplate her future.

After an auspicious beginning, her journey goes terribly wrong. As her life unravels, a series of chance encounters convinces her the evil she has unleashed will destroy her unless she confronts it. But how?

The answer lies with an indigenous tribe deep in the Amazonian rainforest. Her quest for healing and purpose involves an unlikely assortment of jaguars, *jinn*, witches, cannibals, shamans, pink dolphins, teacher trees and the guardians of the cosmos, Grandmother *Aya* and Anaconda Woman.

Advance Reviews
for
Transit

"A woman struggles to begin afresh after committing a heinous crime in Malin's thrilling latest novel. Dr. Jessamyn Quilter has done something terrible, and she must set things right. ... Suspense and tension are in plenty, and the secondary cast is fully realized. Diabolical plotting, swift pacing, and meticulous worldbuilding come together with Jessamyn's affecting first-person narration to create maximum suspense and propel the story forward. Jessamyn's journey to completing the dieta and medicine ceremonies under Grandmother Aya, the jaguars, and the teacher plants' guidance leads to an intriguing narrative turn ... a riveting final act and a satisfactory ending. The plot stands out for its tightly-wound tension during the beginning and the delicate bond shared between the main protagonists in the second half. It's a thrilling journey from start to finish." —*BookView Reviews*

"A physician trying to escape her old life embarks on a sea voyage in Malin's novel. Dr. Jessamyn Quilter methodically plans her professor husband's "accidental" death. He not only emotionally abuses her; he bullies his students and has even incited a gay man's suicide. Rid of him, Jessamyn happily moves on to the next chapter in her life, beginning with a two-month ocean excursion. In between docking at such beautiful places as Manila and Singapore, Jessamyn reinvigorates her sex life: Several people onboard catch her fancy, including Lovely Bayani, the captain's much younger daughter. Menaces abound as well, including individuals who may prove to be more dangerous than her late husband. Jessamyn has vivid recurring dreams of jaguars and later hallucinates one in particular—it's apparently a sign of a "great evil" she harbors inside. Jessamyn then goes in search of someone who can guide her on a vitally important spiritual quest. The author dives deep into the psyche of her protagonist

in an illuminating first-person narrative. Jessamyn isn't cold blooded; while she feels justified in killing her repugnant husband, regret and guilt slowly seep into her mindset. She's surrounded by engrossing characters like the youthful Èlia, who "carries herself with preternatural dignity," and a band of mercenaries engaged to protect the ship from pirates. The novel's latter half focuses on Jessamyn's quest to find herself and address her presumed spiritual affliction, unfolding in a lush rainforest and involving a physically demanding ceremony. Despite the potential presence of spirits, the story feels grounded and authentic. This absorbing story of self-discovery explores redemption and female sexuality."
— *Kirkus Reviews*

"**Offers a rich tapestry of diverse characters,** each with their compelling backstories ... The narrative is dynamic and contains a myriad of twists, ensuring that readers remain on their toes. ... It encapsulates the complexities of human relationships, cultural diversity, and personal discovery. Highly recommended for those seeking a read that interwines suspense, romance, and cultural exposition."
— *Literary Titan*

"**A twisty, satisfyingly unpredictable speculative fiction tale** ... In Malin's latest novel, an emergency physician struggles to prevent her past from sabotaging her present. After killing her abusive husband, Dr. Jessamyn Quilter knows she must restore balance and embarks on a long sea voyage aboard the container ship, MV Andaman Pearl. Soon, she begins to have strange dreams. ... As the tension rises and suspense mounts, readers will eagerly anticipate how events will unfold. ... Part suspense thriller, part speculative fiction, and part coming of age tale, the novel offers both thrills and chills while exploring the subjects of self-realization, identity, freedom, sin, regret, and redemption. A gripping story of friendship, human connection, and healing."
— *The Prairies Book Review*

" A newly liberated doctor launches herself into a high-seas journey of self-discovery in *Transit* by Marty Malin, a smart and scintillating read about taking control of your own story. When Dr. Quilter boards the MV Andaman Pearl in Japan, she is hoping for excitement, but multiple love interests, a tragic murder, rebel pirates, and some disturbingly feline dreams end up spinning her onto a much different and more dangerous adventure. Her particular skill set makes her both an asset and a target, while the ship's eclectic cast of travelers makes this dauntless doctor's dream vacation more exhilarating and enlightening than she could have imagined. A visionary read that is at once action-packed and cerebral, the novel totally defies any expectations of genre, resulting in a story that is continually surprising and intellectually audacious."   — *Independent Review of Books*

Kudos
for
Grandmother's Devil & Other Tempting Tales

"In a world that puts too much value on youth, [*Grandmother's Devil*] is a refreshing anthology. ... Stories are original and unconventional. ... Sometimes odd but always highly interesting and compelling. ... Highly recommended."   — *Readers Favorite International Book Awards*

"The author composes with literary flair and has a knack for description while being efficient with words—the mark of a strong short-story writer. ... Readers who prefer story collections with a quirky edge will find much to love in *Grandmother's Devil*."
— *Writer's Digest Self Published Book Competition*

"One of the best indie books of 2021."
— *Finalist, Next Generation Indie Book Awards*

Books By Marty Malin

Grandmother's Devil & Other Tempting Tales

Transit

TRANSIT

A Journey
of
Transfiguration

ISBN: 978-1-7343827-8-5
Library of Congress Control Number: 202391499

Published by Canyon Rose Press
Benicia, California
email: info@canyonrosepress.com

Book design: Jan Malin

Images: Adobe Stock

TRANSIT

A Journey
of
Transfiguration

Marty Malin

At present we know only that the imagination,
like certain wild animals, will not breed in captivity.

GEORGE ORWELL

The Prevention of Literature

CONTENTS

The Journey

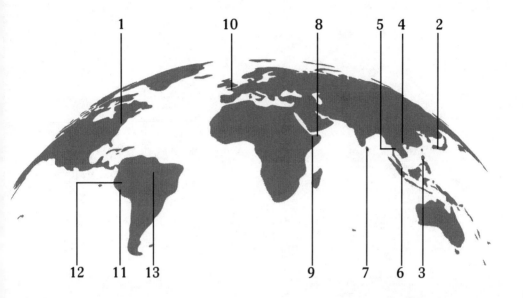

1	*WESTBURY, Massachusetts*	*February 17*
2	*YOKOHAMA, Japan*	*June 28*
3	*MANILA, The Philippines*	*July 7*
4	*HAIPHONG, Vietnam*	*July 11*
5	*KOH SICHANG, Thailand*	*July16*
6	*SINGAPORE*	*July 21*
7	*COLOMBO, Sri Lanka*	*July 30*
8	*CALUULA, Somalia*	*August 3*
9	*DJIBOUTI*	*August 3*
10	*PARIS*	*August 6*
11	*LIMA, Peru*	*September 14*
12	*IQUITOS, Peru*	*December 22*
13	*MANAUS, Brazil*	*December 24*

PART ONE

MV Andaman Pearl

Tell me, O Muse, of the man of many devices,
who wandered full many ways.

HOMER
The Odyssey

1

Premeditation

O nce I decided to kill my husband, it was just a matter of the details. I'm very good at details. As a physician, it's important to get the details right. And I do. I always do.

He's not the poster boy for abusive husbands. Not the creep who traffics in black eyes and broken bones, whose handiwork I encounter all too frequently in the emergency department.

He's a different sort of creep. A remorseless spirit-killer who bedevils the vulnerable and lays waste to their souls.

He's no more abusive to me than anyone else he meets, but his other prey can avoid him. His students move on or quit. His colleagues don't associate with him except under duress.

The owner of the Chinese restaurant we patronize thinks he's a laughable prick. She smiles and pretends not to understand him when he bitches at her, then flips him off behind his back. Even the cat hides when he hears his car pull into the driveway, lest he risk being booted out of the way.

Now we can add DeShawn Livingston to his roster of soul murders. DeShawn was one of my husband's mentees, a gifted math/philosophy double major and athlete at Upper Valley University where my husband is an associate professor who will never make full. DeShawn was a polite, animated young man. I liked him very much on the occasions when he

1

came to our home for a weekend dinner or to discuss his research with my husband.

The university was advancing his candidacy as a Rhodes scholar until he made the mistake of coming out to my homophobic husband. He did a number on DeShawn, and the university dropped him from consideration a couple of weeks ago.

"Nasty little faggot," he fumed. "The last thing Oxford needs is another queer. I suggested he do the world a favor and kill himself."

So, he did. Last Saturday DeShawn got drunk and went to sleep on the railroad tracks north of town. I couldn't bear to have his remains brought to the morgue in my hospital and asked the sheriff to divert to Holy Cross a few miles away.

"Good," my husband muttered when he heard about the suicide.

I was furious and I told him so. He laughed and said he expected as much from an ugly bull dyke like me. Not the first time he's called me that since the early days of our marriage when I disclosed a brief fling with a female college classmate before I married him.

No matter. He can yell at me all he wants, make ignorant remarks about my body, and berate me. It's water under the bridge.

I've gotten used to living with this man. I try to get along, appease him. But my husband's unvarnished joy at the annihilation of DeShawn Livingston is a bridge too far. I can't allow him to continue destroying other people's lives or my own.

I've had it with him. I'm fed up with his bigotry, his churlish behavior, and his lack of compassion. Tired of his abuse, entitled arrogance, and contempt for anyone he considers a lesser being, which is everyone he encounters.

It's a little thing compared with DeShawn's death, but I'm also tired of our bedtime routine, worn thin after thirty years of marriage, being treated to the same performance by him each evening in our en suite bathroom. Pee splashing into the water. A few squeaky farts surreptitiously loosed into the bowl while he clears his throat to cover the noise. The hiss of air freshener.

Paper unrolls. The toilet flushes. Always twice. He stands and pulls up his boxers, snapping the elastic into place. I've asked that he put them in the hamper while he's in the bathroom, but I might as well be talking to the cat.

I hear him gargle and spit. What I don't hear is evidence he's washing his hands. How can anyone past the age of five not wash his hands after using the toilet?

He trundles out of the bathroom as I lie in bed, breath smelling like a chemistry lab, and drops his underpants to the floor where they will remain for the night. Some mornings he might pick them up on his way back into the bathroom, but most times he'll nudge them under the bed with his foot as if they have nothing to do with him.

I look up from my romance novel as he stands beside our bed and paste on as welcoming a face as I can manage, as I've done for decades of bedtimes. He doesn't acknowledge me or say a word, which is what I expect. Perhaps he's still obsessing about the Novikov conjecture. He's told me he does some of his best thinking in the bathroom.

The Novikov conjecture, he lectures me repeatedly, is one of the more important unsolved problems in high-dimensional manifold topology, which I don't begin to understand and couldn't care about less. He's certain he'll solve it, but he won't. Mathematics is a young person's game, and he's well past fifty. He's been out of the running for a Fields Medal, the "Nobel Prize" in math, for a couple of decades.

Not that he ever had a shot. So he plods along, your worst nightmare of a math professor, an uninspired hack who alternately terrorizes his students or puts them to sleep with pedantic non sequiturs, following the Novikov conjecture down countless rabbit holes.

I turn back the sheet, patting the bed, inviting him in. He unsticks his penis from his scrotum and tugs it once or twice, looking down as if to reassure himself it's his and is properly attached. It's an almost universal tic among men I've seen countless times when they undress in my clinic, but his attempt to rearrange his dysfunctional genitals annoys me.

He reaches behind his back with both hands and scratches his butt, yawns epically, and slides in beside me.

He doesn't read or attempt conversation. Without so much as a perfunctory "good night," he'll put on his CPAP mask and turn off his lamp, a signal I should stop whatever I'm doing and switch mine off as well.

It would be impossible for him to be less attractive at bedtime if he tried.

Unless he wants sex.

That makes bedtime more complex. Sex requires him to inject "stiffy juice," as he calls it, into his penis. The little blue pills no longer work. Neither does "Dr. Seltzer's Hard-On Helper," although his herbalist swears by it.

Sex means preparation, if not foreplay. He must add some sterile water to a vial containing CAVERJECT powder and shoot up. Sounds awful, but it hurts less than a flu shot. If it were painful, he'd run the other way because like most bullies, he's a candy-ass.

He'll get a serviceable erection within a few minutes, lasting the better part of an hour—six times longer than he needs to wrap things up on his end.

I'll bookmark my novel when I hear him announce, "Houston, we have liftoff." Really. He's said that on sex night for at least ten years.

He'll swagger out of the bathroom to my side of the bed, fondling himself, and declare he is "horny," leering like a demented baboon. I'll get a scant three minutes of his version of foreplay, running his unwashed hands over my body and pinching my nipples before he declares his need for my "hot pussy."

Then he'll crawl on top of me, latch onto a breast, and reach down to fiddle with my vulva. He'll crow about how "fucking wet" he has made me, call me a "cunt," and implore me to beg for his "hot cock," which I will do to honor my part of the bargain, the pretense that our coupling is erotic, and to move things along.

The ritual seldom varies. When I complained to my shit-for-brains analyst that sex with my husband was terrible, he told me I should be more assertive, ask for what I want. So I asked my husband to kiss me.

He scowled as if I were some irksome insect and told me kissing didn't turn him on. That was the end of it.

Foreplay over, he'll enter and grind away until he finishes, then roll over onto his side of the bed, grunt his satiation, and fall asleep almost before he can strap himself into his CPAP.

Sex with him is as formulaic as a quadratic equation, though a quadratic equation has two roots and he only solves for his. Not that I mind all that much. Orgasms are easy for me, and I have other ways to get them when I wish. At least my shit-for-brains analyst helped me with that.

* * *

Early in our marriage, my husband and I agreed we would do this little dance once a week. He prefers Wednesdays. Today is Tuesday so there's nothing to delay our sleep tonight.

They say it's the little things that finally push us over the edge. Surely I could continue to endure his unappetizing bedtime proclivities. They're little more than annoyances. But DeShawn Livingston's suicide is not a little thing. My husband destroyed that young man, and I won't let him get away with it.

I've considered divorcing him, but divorce can be a messy, drawn-out public process, and it wouldn't protect anyone else from him. He would remain free to wreak havoc on others as long as he lives. Divorce would bring no vengeance for DeShawn. No retribution for the abuse he's heaped upon me.

I don't think of my husband's death as a big deal. It's the right solution to my problem. As a physician my job is to save lives, but I rub shoulders with death every day.

Of course I could wait it out. I will almost certainly outlive him since I'm in far better health than he is. But if I can shuffle him along toward his ultimate reward, what's the point of hanging around waiting for nature to take its course?

I won't take pleasure in killing him. I doubt I'll feel much of anything except relief once he's out of my life. Overseeing his demise is a mildly distasteful chore I can no longer put off, like cleaning the litter box.

The consequences of his death will all be positive. We're well off. Both of us brought money into the marriage, and our investments are substantial. He has a few patents to his credit that produce a steady trickle of royalties, dependable as those rusty old West Texas pumpjacks.

We have no debts, not even a mortgage, and I make good money as head of the emergency department in nearby Chilton. His salary at the university is larger than he deserves, and our pensions will be generous. There's a couple million dollars in life insurance on him, plus sizable amounts stashed away in retirement accounts.

When he dies, I'll have all that money sooner rather than later. I wouldn't get it if I just divorced him. While I wouldn't do him in simply for the money, I'll happily take the free cherry that comes with the sundae.

So tomorrow at bedtime, on sex night, I'll kill him.

I know exactly how to do it and get away with it. When I come home from work tomorrow, I'll replace the vial of sterile water he uses to prepare his CAVERJECT with a vial of a clear, liquid drug we use to paralyze muscles during surgery.

It will be a simple matter. His CAVERJECT doses are samples, courtesy of the drug rep who haunts the corridors of our hospital. She also reps the drug I'm going to substitute for his sterile water.

Because they're samples, I don't have to involve the hospital pharmacy or pay much attention to documenting where the drugs end up. In the privacy of my office, it won't be difficult to replace the sterile water in the CAVERJECT package with the other drug. They look the same. No one will be the wiser.

Houston will not announce liftoff tomorrow night because the drug will rush into his bloodstream, paralyzing him within seconds. Since his muscles won't work, he won't stagger out of the bathroom. He'll just drop in his tracks. He won't be able to breathe, so it will be impossible to call out. After a minute of not breathing, he will lose consciousness. He'll be brain dead shortly after.

He's in for an unpleasant few minutes, and I regret that, but it won't be any worse than the inevitable heart attack he would eventually have had.

The last I'll hear from him will be a thud as he hits the floor. He'll be dead by the time I put down my book and go check on him. I'll give him five or ten more minutes. No reason to rush.

Of course I'll make certain he's no longer alive before I do anything else. I'll check but find no heartbeat. No respiration. His pupils will be fixed and dilated.

Once I confirm he's dead, I'll tidy up. Take all the time I need to attend to details so as not to make mistakes.

Using gloves from my medical bag, I'll wipe down the floor and the vanity with toilet paper and flush it. I'll collect the contaminated vials, the syringe, the alcohol wipes, and the packaging he's discarded. Everything that might have traces of the paralyzing drug, along with the gloves, will go into the small red sharps container in my medical bag to drop into the biohazard waste bin at the hospital, destined for incineration.

I'll put on another pair of gloves and prepare a second batch of CAVERJECT in the ordinary way, with sterile water, making sure he "touches" those vials and the syringe with his dead fingers so his prints are on them.

I'll squirt a drop or two of ordinary CAVERJECT on him where the needle stick will be visible and discard the rest of the dose into his sink. Then I'll arrange all the props. The nearly empty vials, wipes, and packaging will go on the vanity where he would have left them for me to clean up. The syringe will go on the floor where he would have dropped it before he collapsed.

I'll look over everything for a second and third time. No hurry. His body temperature won't drop more than a degree the first hour in our well-heated bathroom, and rigor mortis won't set in for a couple more.

7

All that bait and switch is overkill if you'll pardon the expression. Nobody will ever check. He's already had one heart attack and is on a bunch of cardiac and blood pressure meds. No wonder he can't get it up. He has a family history of heart disease. His father died of a heart attack when he was fifty. What else could it be except his heart?

Even if someone were to suspect foul play, an autopsy would reveal no trace of the drug I've chosen. That's the great thing about it. It metabolizes rapidly into molecules naturally found in the body, leaving nothing to tip off your average medical examiner. Of course, the FBI with their expensive voodoo might find something if they were to go looking, but there will be no reason to alert the Feds for an ordinary, garden variety heart attack in a man who's a textbook collection of risk factors.

The stage set, all the props in place, it will be curtain-up for Act II. Kneeling over him, my phone on the floor in front of me, I'll call 911 on speaker. They'll overhear my fruitless attempts to resuscitate him and my pleas for help. It'll all be a sham since he'll be irretrievably dead, but they won't know. When they arrive, the paramedics will find me in my nightgown, kneeling on the bathroom floor, working feverishly over my husband's corpse.

When they can't bring him back to life, they'll bundle him off to the hospital morgue. I'll throw on a robe and ride along in the ambulance, pretending to be devastated, too much in shock to cry or talk to anyone.

After a few days playing the grieving widow and holding court for well-wishers, I'll meet with our attorney, Jerry Finsterwald, who'll wrap up the last details, notifying everyone who needs to know, including the Neptune Society. I'll raise a glass to the memory of DeShawn Livingston and all the people my husband will never harm again.

He will be dead, disposed of, and soon forgotten. I'll have a crack at a new life, and nobody will ever suspect I killed him. ∎

2

Murder

When I woke up Wednesday morning, the but-terflies in my stomach were warming up for an airshow. Thank god for the calming routine of the emergency department. An ED may look chaotic, but the chaos is carefully choreographed.

Most of us who work in emergency departments aren't adrenaline junkies. Who needs an excitable doc with shaky hands working on them? Steady, efficient, no drama gets the job done without killing more patients than necessary.

Overall, today is just another day at the peanut stand with the usual broken bones, asthma attacks, and automobile accidents. The only thing even slightly out of the ordinary, other than the colorful paper hearts hanging from the lights over the nursing station, is a patient from the jail who tried to kill herself. We patch her up, under the watchful eye of a deputy sheriff, and wait for a bed on the psych ward.

Later in the afternoon, half an hour before my shift ends, an ambu-lance rolls up with a cardiac arrest from the Leisure Ridge nursing home, dead on arrival, wheeled straight into the cold room. I sign the paperwork. No need to take him off the gurney in my shop. No doubt he'll still be

9

there when my husband rolls up in the same condition later tonight. The funeral home won't come until tomorrow morning, so they'll get a two-fer. No sense wasting a trip.

There's ample time over lunch to substitute the paralyzing drug for the sterile water and pop it into my medical bag along with the CAVERJECT sample. It'll please my husband to learn that sex night can proceed as scheduled.

When it's time to leave the hospital at the end of my shift, the butterflies are back, doing loop-the-loops and barrel rolls. Half a Valium and a few deep breaths in the parking structure help calm me for the easy half-hour drive home. The gentle curves of the tree-lined parkway seem engineered for relaxing driving.

As usual I get home before my husband and nose the Mercedes into the garage, retrieving my backpack and medical bag from the trunk. The cat comes to greet me as I open the door. I reach down and scratch his ears. He rolls over, presenting his fat belly, begging for more, but I disappoint him. Maybe later.

The mail is on the floor in the foyer where it has fallen through the slot in the door. I put it on the console table by the staircase, climb the stairs, and drop my things on the desk in my small study across from our bedroom. The CAVERJECT and the poisonous drug from my medical bag go into my husband's medicine cabinet.

I strip off my scrubs and step into the shower. The soothing water cascades down my body, splashing musically into the shower pan, making pleasant gurgling noises in the drain.

The memory of this morning's conversation with my husband intrudes into my solitude.

"It's Wednesday," he groused. "I'm all out of my stiffy juice."

"I'll bring some home tonight," I said.

He's "all out" because I disposed of his remaining supply yesterday so as not to risk a mix-up with the poisoned CAVERJECT he will use tonight. If he noticed his missing stash, he said nothing. Apparently he only checks on Wednesday mornings.

If he asks tonight why I've brought home only a couple of doses, I'll tell him that's all the drug rep had, and she'll bring more tomorrow. Of course, he won't have a tomorrow.

I'm getting out of the shower when I hear him downstairs.

"Jessamyn?" he hollers.

"Up here. Be down in a minute." As usual there's no response. He skulks into his downstairs study, and I hear him close the door.

I towel off and pull on some underwear, a pair of jeans, and a casual top. We have nothing special planned for the evening unless you count sex. If he bought me flowers or chocolates, even a Valentine's Day card, much less arranged to take me out to dinner this evening, it would be the first time in decades. I'm certain we'll be eating at home.

We'll get takeout from the Lotus Garden to eat in front of the TV. I won't ask what his fortune cookie says. Pretty sure I know what his future holds.

I give the bathroom the once over, make my way downstairs, and rap on his study door.

"On the phone," he grouches.

I open the door a crack.

"No, Friday will not be okay," he says with the disdain he reserves for bullying students. "The work's due in class tomorrow." He enjoys I am overhearing his conversation. It adds to his sadistic pleasure.

"Well, yes, that's unfortunate. I understand that you have been ill, and the timing is inconvenient. Nevertheless, it's due tomorrow. Friday will not do." A brief pause. "Still no. Tomorrow or don't bother."

Brutal. Can that be the beginning of a smile on his face?

He hangs up. "Fucking entitled, brain-dead students," he says, opening the door fully. His demeanor is smug, pleased with himself for smashing an annoying, but harmless, pest.

"How was your day?" I ask with perhaps too much enthusiasm.

"Same shit, different toilet," he says, fussing with the papers on his desk. "Same imbecile students, same lame-ass excuses. How was yours?"

We are nothing if not polite to each other.

"Good. Chinese for dinner?"

"Uh-huh."

"Pick up some eggplant with tofu for me and maybe some hot and sour soup," I say.

"Rice?"

"Of course, rice, silly."

"Call it in. I'll go get it," he grunts, picking up his keys.

"Do you want broccoli beef?" I call after him, speed dialing the Lotus Garden. He grunts his assent. He never orders anything else.

We watch CNN as we eat. He's arguing with the television as he bolts his food. The anchor, he avers, should hang for the crime of being a moron. He switches channels to a BBC rerun of David Attenborough discoursing about coconut crabs.

He gets down to business, grading papers, decrying the caliber of his students. Neither of us is paying much attention to Attenborough or each other as we finish dinner. A typical Wednesday evening.

"I'm going to go up and read in bed for a bit," I announce when I finish cleaning up the kitchen. "Take your time."

He looks up from his papers, giving me that "You-know-what-night-tonight-is" leer, and I smile, pretending to be amused.

Upstairs, I wash my face, brush my teeth, and prop myself up in bed. I grab my current romance novel, *Till Death Do Us Part*, from the drawer in my nightstand. What is it about romance novels? Clandestine attractions, fever dreams, betrayal, love conquering all, torrid yet not terribly explicit sex?

Yes, all that and more. How many thousands of these trashy novels are out there? I've read hundreds and plan to read hundreds more. Perhaps one day I'll write one. Who knows?

An hour later, the TV falls silent, and my husband comes lumbering up the stairs. He arrives in our bedroom and goes into the bathroom to prepare. Same routine as every other Wednesday night, including the part where he opens his medicine cabinet to retrieve the CAVERJECT. I hear him tear open the packaging and clear his throat. I catch a whiff of isopropyl alcohol from the wipes.

Then my life changes forever.

The expected thud as his rag-doll body meets the unyielding bathroom floor. Then silence.

My heart is pounding, my breathing shallow. After a minute or two, I call out. "Everything okay?" Of course, it's not. I don't expect a reply, and none comes. I spend a couple more minutes calming down, bookmark my place, and get out of bed to check on him. Ten minutes are up.

Everything is as expected. He is unequivocally dead. Face up, naked, with the instrument of his demise on the floor beside him. My composure returns as if I were managing an accident in the ED. I step around his body and go about my plan, setting the stage for the first responders.

When everything is ready, I kneel beside his corpse. Switching my phone to speaker, I place it on the floor beside me and call for help.

"911. What is your emergency?"

"My husband's not breathing! I think he had a heart attack. I'm doing CPR."

"Just keep doing that, ma'am. What's your address?"

"It's 1237 Maple Court in Westbury. I can't find a pulse."

"Got it, 1237 Maple Court, Westbury. We have your location on screen."

"Hurry! Doing chest compression now," I pant. It's physical work under any circumstances.

"Just keep doing CPR, ma'am. You're breathing for him too?"

"Yes."

"Is the door access code still 61717?"

"That's right."

"Stay with me, ma'am. I've dispatched fire and rescue. The paramedics will be there within five to seven minutes. Where are you in the house?"

"Upstairs. In the master bathroom."

"What's your name, ma'am?"

"Jessamyn Quilter. I'm a doctor. I don't think he's going to make it."

"We've got the ambulance patched in now. They'll take over and help you until the paramedics arrive. Go ahead, NorthStar."

"This is Miguel with NorthStar Unit 3. Dr. Quilter, can you hear me?"

"There's no pulse. I can't get his heart started."

"Hang in there, Doctor. We're almost there. Just keep breathing and compressing for him."

"Please hurry. I hear sirens."

"That will be fire and rescue. We're right behind them."

The front door flies open. Someone is racing up the stairs.

"Fire and rescue," a woman shouts. "We're coming up, Doctor."

"Let us take over, Dr. Quilter," she says, kneeling beside the body to relieve me. I recognize her. She's been in my emergency department before. Her partner applies an oxygen mask and fires up the portable defibrillator.

I pick up my phone and get out of their way. After a few more moments of broadcasting our little drama for the benefit of the 911 dispatcher, I disconnect the call.

"Drugs?" the young woman asks, taking in my carefully staged scene. "CAVERJECT," I say. She nods as if it suddenly makes perfect sense he's lying there naked next to the bottle and an empty syringe.

"He's asystolic," her partner paramedic announces. "Defib's not gonna help."

The NorthStar Unit 3 team races upstairs to join the party.

"Let's get a line in and give him some epi," someone says.

I've seen it all, and been in the middle of it, countless times. Epinephrine won't help him now. Nothing they are doing will help. He flatlined long before I began my charade with 911, and he's not coming back.

The ambulance ride to the hospital won't be lights and sirens. Just courtesy transportation to the cold room. After another fifteen minutes of hard work, the first responders know that as well.

The NorthStar crew rolls my dead husband onto a gurney and covers him with a sheet. I fill everyone in on what I want them to know, including his medical history. They nod their heads in understanding—another heart attack. Couldn't be anything else.

Sometime during all this, the police show up and take a cursory look around. "Remember to lock up, Doctor, and take your keys with you," one officer says. They leave. Nothing to see here. Everybody moves on.

The ambulance ride is oddly calming. The rent-a-doc who covers when I'm not on duty meets us at the emergency entrance. He formally pronounces my husband dead on arrival and offers his condolences. Asks if he can write me a prescription, but I decline. There are plenty of samples in my office desk drawer, thanks to the drug reps. That's where I'm headed.

The charge nurse, Patty Landner, rustles up some tea, which hits the spot with half a Valium, and she calls an Uber. She promises to let hospital admin know what has happened and to check on me in the morning. The driver is mercifully silent on the way home.

The cat comes out of hiding to meet me as I open the front door. He rubs up against me and purrs, wanting to be picked up, but I disappoint him again. "Tough titty, Miss Kitty," my late husband would have said. He never liked the cat, and the feeling was mutual. Why he called him Miss Kitty, when he's a tomcat, I don't know. His warped sense of humor, I guess. The house feels strangely empty but not unpleasantly so.

The Valium I swallowed with my tea earlier this evening has worn off. I take another half before I go to bed and drift off to sleep.

* * *

The phone wakes me about eight. It's the hospital administrator calling to offer her condolences. Someone from HR will be in touch about a leave of absence, but for now she's placing me on paid bereavement leave.

Breakfast is coffee and a frozen toaster waffle. After my second cup, I call Jerry Finsterwald.

Jerry's not the warmest roll in the basket, but he's a competent and reliable attorney. After telling him as much of the story as I want him to hear, he says he'll notify the college and arrange for the Neptune people to pick up the body from the morgue.

I get through the next couple of weeks of obligatory, grieving widowhood without incident. People are nice to me. Casseroles, sympathy cards, and flowers arrive. Nobody says I'm better off without him, but it's not hard to read between the lines. Nobody has a good word to say about my deceased husband.

The college fields a memorial service with tributes by the usual bobbleheads, including the president, the dean of faculty, and a coven of mathematicians looking like impotent wizards stripped of their magic chalk and enchanted blackboards.

They speak, with little emotion, of my late husband's devotion to pedagogy and his thirst for knowledge. They pay homage to his fizzled efforts to crack the Novikov conjecture, which nobody tries to explain, and which now languishes unsolved, waiting for the next unwitting soul to pick up the torch and stumble forth into the darkness.

The president of the student body, an otherwise unremarkable woman headed for a career in one of those majors like fashion design or criminal justice that have become safe havens for directionless young people overwhelmed by academic rigor, unveils a plaque to be displayed somewhere in the hallowed halls. I'm amazed they've had time to gin one up.

A driver sees me home, accompanied by the institution's thoughts and prayers and a framed proclamation. The college will probably wait a decent interval before someone from the development office comes calling.

Jerry Finsterwald will be ready for them. I absolutely want to help make up for all the abuse my deceased husband heaped on his students over the years. Perhaps a scholarship in memory of DeShawn Livingston. And a large bequest to the university's Gender and Sexualities Alliance. Splendid ideas that would chap my late husband's butt if he were still alive. I enjoy the thought of him turning in his grave.

I kick off my shoes, pour a slug of Tanqueray from the bottle in the freezer, and take my drink to the couch. I decide to take the bottle as well. The cat jumps into my lap, purring insistently, and rolls over to claim his raincheck belly rub. By the second glass of gin, I'm thinking about what my life will be like from now on.

There's no good reason to continue working in the emergency department. I'll ask Jerry to let HR know and close things down. Beyond that, I have no plans.

That's not like me. I typically plan my life to a fare-thee-well. All that's changed now. No more Wednesday sex nights. Perhaps no sex nights at all. That's fine. I'll take it as it comes.

By the third Tanqueray, with the help of Netflix, a crazy possibility materializes in my mind. *Captain Phillips.* An ocean voyage to transition into the next chapter of my life. Not that I have any desire to be captured by Somali pirates, but a long voyage aboard a slow freighter might be just what the doctor ordered.

The cat follows me upstairs to the king-size bed, wonderfully empty now. I claim the middle and the cat buries himself under the comforter at the foot. Neither of us misses my late husband in the slightest. ■

3

No Regrets

WESTBURY, Massachusetts   April 4

T hings are settling into a new routine. In the weeks following my husband's death, I've been thinking about what the future holds. We have scattered his ashes at sea. Jerry Finsterwald and his merry elves have tidied up the loose financial and legal ends of our defunct marriage. I have gone through my late husband's things, donating what might be useful to charity, throwing the rest of it, including photos of us, into the trash. There's no need for such reminders of the past. They hold no key to the future.

We've never had a lot of possessions, but between us we accumulated a considerable library. My deceased husband's reading tastes were not wide-ranging. He had some interest in science fiction, left over from his nerdy boyhood, so there are some classics on the shelves by the likes of Robert Heinlein, Ray Bradbury, and Isaac Asimov. There are also a few books on chess and game theory, but his biggest contribution to our library was books on mathematics.

There are also far too many outdated chemistry and biology texts, journals, and mind-choking treatises on the arcana of medical practice. Some of these I donated to the university along with the math books. Let them worry about disposing of them. They dare not refuse them because my late husband was one of their own, and the development office is still sniffing around hoping for more lucrative gifts.

I kept nothing that was his. Other books and journals I no longer need went straight into the dumpster. Recycling books is more difficult than one would think.

Except my trashy novels. It's my habit to dispose of my beloved romance novels, once read, by dropping them off at hospital patient services. The volunteer coordinator jokes good-naturedly about my literary tastes, calling me "Dr. Bodice Ripper," but she reports that my trashy novels are the first to fly off the rolling book cart.

The remaining books in our library reflect more catholic tastes. There are choice pickings, including books beloved of the college literature and philosophy professors I studied with, many I was too young to appreciate. I vowed to reread them.

I majored in humanities as an undergraduate, taking only the bare minimum of science and math courses needed to make the cut for medical school. I remember my advisor opining I could do worse than read the famous Harvard Classics, Dr. Eliot's five-foot shelf of books.

All fine if you want to limit your intellectual exposure to long-dead white men. I later bought a used set online for our library. Mostly they have just gathered cobwebs.

I blow the dust off Volume 33, "Voyages and Travels," and thumb through it. Maybe I'll draw some inspiration from "The Famous Voyage of SIR FRANCIS DRAKE into the South Sea, and therehence about the whole Globe of the Earth, begun in the year of our Lord 1577." I can't say it grabs me, though the word *"therehence"* amuses me. I put the volume back with its dusty brethren.

Still, I have an opportunity to get serious about my writing. I've always thought I would write a novel or some short stories, but something always gets in the way. Nothing's stopping me now.

Perhaps I should get out of Westbury. Take a lengthy trip. If a cross-country jaunt or even a voyage around the world could provide time and inspiration to write, why not?

I considered renting an RV, taking it cross-country, perhaps even into Canada or Mexico. But a slow-moving ship, like Captain Phillips' *MV Maersk Alabama,* where someone else is driving, is much more appealing. Not that I want to write a seafaring tale, like *Moby Dick* or *Two Years Before the Mast.* But the solace of a freighter might midwife a short story or two, perhaps a novella, if not a weightier tome.

Too much around here reminds me of the past. Without my work and my deceased husband, I've become irrelevant to everyone except the cat. So I have decided to rent out the house, put my books and other possessions into storage, find a welcoming home for the cat (I'm looking at you, Nurse Patty Landner), and hit the road. Or, rather, go "sailing over the bounding main."

The time spent in our library has triggered other memories. I was born smack in the middle of the Gen X baby bust, too late to experience the bohemian life of the beat generation or the swinging sixties. By the time I got to college, the summer of love had come full circle to the winter of our discontent. There was still a bit of raving, but it was going stale, as was my boyfriend, Pyotr.

He was brilliant. And gorgeous. It was easy to get lost in his crystalline, ice-blue eyes. He said he loved me. I'm not sure whether I loved him, but I went along for the ride. What did I know of love?

Pyotr and I were pre-med. We lived together off campus during the second half of my junior year, contemplating the mysteries of the universe and our place in it, listening to Alice In Chains, Nirvana, and Stone Temple Pilots.

Sex was wondrous at first, but in the end, undependable. He would parachute Molly and want to cuddle and hug. Or shoot smack when he should have been studying. I wasn't into drugs, although doing an occasional line with him was fun. Cuddling was fine, but I also wanted to fuck. I wanted the intensity of love. He just wanted more drugs.

Speedballing inexorably destroyed his plans to become a physician, and he followed the ass-end of raver culture to Seattle where he OD'd like Kurt Cobain, Layne Staley, and far too many young, talented dreamers who blew out their opiate receptors.

Pyotr's decision to drop out of school, and his death, left an enormous hole in my heart. I missed the sex, and the brilliance of our conversation in the early part of our relationship. Even when things went south there was comfort in knowing he was still mine.

I understand the power of drugs, but I never thought they would take him away from me. If I was in love with him it didn't make any difference now. I was overtaken by the "sweetish sickness" Sartre talks about in *Nausea*. Angry. Betrayed. Revolted by my own meaningless existence and the carelessness with which Pyotr threw himself—and us—away. I had never let myself get that close to anyone before. I resolved never to let anyone get that close to me again.

Nobody ever did. My late husband was never in the running.

All that's in the past. It's time to start living in the present, even the future.

I don't regret the past. Perhaps I should, but no. Maybe a little disappointed with myself, yes. Angry for not paying attention, for mistaking my marriage and career for a life, for allowing my soul to be sucked dry by my abusive vampire of a husband.

Do I regret killing him? No. Not sorry. Did I love him? No, you will say, since I killed him. Love isn't the issue.

Everything ends in death. My life will too. I've done my part as a physician, keeping many people from slipping into the beyond before their time. But regret for scooting my husband along toward his own private eternity? Not a smidgeon. Happy to help.

I looked at myself in the mirror last night and thought for an instant I saw the face of a killer looking back at me. Nope, I decided. Just me. No saint but no sinner either. Just a beat-up physician who's had enough of abuse.

No more, no longer. No heaven, no hell. I figured out a long time ago that Jesus doesn't want me for a sunbeam. ■

4

Hell, Yes!

I t's exhilarating, planning the next chapters of my life. The effluvium of YouTube has surfaced some useful nuggets about travel on cargo ships. The internet is enlightening me further about sea lanes, ports of call, and the logistics of modern-day freighter travel.

Gone, apparently, are the days where one might work passage aboard a tramp steamer. Modern cargo ships sometimes have room for a few paying guests, never more than a dozen and typically not more than half that.

It's even possible to find oneself the sole passenger on a cargo ship, but I hope that's not the case. I secretly hope to meet some adventuresome souls who've chosen a freighter over a Disney Cruise.

I'm compiling a list of things I might need on an extended sea voyage. It's short. Since I'll end up lugging everything myself, the shorter the list, the better.

Toiletries, some clothing I can wash out on board, identity documents, and a bit of cash. I won't need money on board, but it'll come in handy for port calls.

I never travel without my medical bag, though I don't think I'll need it beyond seasick remedies and first aid supplies. No doubt it's more security blanket than anything else, but given a choice between the purse most women can't be without and my medical bag, the bag wins hands down.

Of course I'll take my laptop and cell phone, a journal, and my Mont Blanc fountain pen. Every writer needs a journal and a Mont Blanc.

The laptop holds all the e-books and reference materials I'll need for my writing, my favorite music, and a few movies, but only a few. A writer needs to write, not binge-watch movies.

My plan is to back up my work to the cloud when we're in ports with decent Wi-Fi. If the kraken drags us into the abyss and I sink with my writing to the bottom of some watery canyon, what's the loss? I'll decompose in endless solitude as the scavengers pick my bones. I plan to stay high and dry though, living and writing, not sleeping with the fishes.

Jerry Finsterwald thinks I'm crazy, but he's much too patrician to say so. He's agreed to anchor my affairs ashore and arrange for documentation and other formalities, transfer funds en route, and do his best to bail me out of any trouble I might get into along the way.

The one hitch in this grand plan is my dislike of the sea. I hate beaches and bodies of open water where I can't see the opposite shore. I'm only partly kidding about the kraken and Davy Jones' Locker.

As a young woman I had dreams of being sucked out to sea in a riptide, watching my broken body wash ashore, dashed upon the rocks, waking up soaked in sweat, gasping for air, convinced for a long moment I was no longer alive. Occasionally I still have them.

I have confessed all of this to my shit-for-brains analyst who thinks my fear of the sea is a fear of my sexuality, a fear of being swept away and drowning in a metaphorical sea of pleasure. The French, he pontificated, call an orgasm *la petite mort*, "the little death."

I can lose myself in sex with the right person. Never with my late husband, of course, but I recall a few times with Pyotr, both of us drenched in passion, orgasm after orgasm, when we washed up on the shore, exhausted, punch drunk, sated. The French know what they're talking about. It does feel like a little death, a deliciously louche, buzzy suspension of life.

I want more of that. I'm not on the prowl, but now that my deceased husband's ashes lie in the mud off the coast of Massachusetts, and Pyotr's (I like to think) are forever thrashing in Puget Sound, I wouldn't say no to any fireworks that might come my way.

No, Dr. Freud, I'm not afraid of either *la petite mort* or *la grande mort*. Only open water. But it's time to get past that. Fear of the ocean isn't going to stop me from living the vagabond life of a shipboard writer, peeling the world like a big fat orange, sucking the sweet sticky juice, feasting on the pulp.

All of that settled, the details of getting aboard a ship remain. Where will I go? It doesn't matter. I'll start out somewhere and end up somewhere else. If a destination port catches my fancy, I might disembark and spend a few days or weeks, then catch another ship and continue my journey.

The nearest seaport to Westbury is Conley Terminal in South Boston. Or I could fly across the globe and ride the ships back home. A long voyage from Japan to the Netherlands via the Suez Canal sounds just right, two months afloat, give or take, with some time to knock around Europe if the mood strikes me.

Perhaps another long voyage after that. Maybe across the Atlantic to South America. It's heady stuff.

A few weeks ago my life was stagnant, tethered to an abusive husband, plodding through a comfortable but humdrum life. And now, this.

A future.

Hell, yes! ■

5

Tokyo

Patty Landner can be a fussbudget. "You sure you're going to be okay? You don't understand a word of Japanese," she says, emerging from the Callahan Tunnel on our way to Logan International. Patty, my favorite emergency department nurse, is my self-appointed caretaker these days since I've quit my job.

We merge with a stomach-churning lurch onto Route 1A North toward the airport. They don't call her "lead-foot Landner" for nothing. I don't see how anyone can drive in Boston, but of course, nurses can do anything.

Everyone except me seems concerned about me traveling on my own. I've stuck close to home for years except for the occasional short junket to a medical conference.

"Language won't be much of a barrier," I say. "The passenger service agent for the shipping line has paved the way as much as possible. Jerry Finsterwald has arranged for someone who is fluent in both English and Japanese to meet me at the airport and shepherd me through customs."

"Do you know what you'll be doing once you land?"

"I'm just spending a few days in Tokyo before setting sail. I'm sure everything will go well. Besides, my friends at the embassy will take good care of me," I lie.

Only Jerry knows my trip will not be a short one. I told everyone else I'd be visiting friends stationed at the American embassy in Tokyo before going to a resort in Thailand for a couple of weeks. Perhaps going on an extended cruise after that.

In fact, I have no friends at the embassy or anywhere else in Japan. And if I ever set foot in Thailand, it will only be on shore leave at some run-down port of call.

"Well, you know you can always call me if you get into trouble or need anything," Patty says. She moonlights as a nurse for a travel insurance company. She's told me about some of her white-knuckle experiences, medevacking mangled tourists and business executives from far-flung locales.

"I'll be fine, Patty, but I appreciate the lifeline." We drive up to the passenger drop-off, hug, and say our goodbyes. I make my way through security on the third floor of International Terminal E to my JAL departure gate. I feel almost giddy.

My plane is delayed several hours for one of the usual reasons, something about needing to replace a malfunctioning warning light on the thingamajig, but things get sorted and it's time to board. I roll my carry-on down the jetway, find my window seat in the first cabin, and settle in for the long flight to Narita Airport.

The flight attendants make an irritating trip more bearable by unlimited Suntory Toki whiskey. So does the Valium I swallowed an hour before liftoff. At least I nap.

Sleep has become dicey of late, unusual for me. I usually sleep the sleep of the just. I chalk up my insomnia to the many changes in my life over the past few weeks. Waking up each day, alone except for the cat, has been disorienting. I'm not lonely, but the aloneness is odd.

Speaking of cats. A few days ago I had a technicolor dream. I was standing in a clearing in a rainforest. A large cat of some sort, by the looks of it a jaguar, padded out from the undergrowth and approached me, staring into my eyes, its breath unpleasant on my face. I woke to discover, of course, that my fat tomcat had taken up residence on my chest, inches from my nose.

I shooed him off and went back to sleep. But the next morning, the image of this powerful dreamcat lingered. Unusual for me. I don't often remember dreams other than those recurrent nightmares of drowning, which don't bother me much anymore.

And last night, this same jungle cat reappeared. This time when I awoke, there was no cat lounging on me. My tomcat had already taken up residence with Patty Landner.

These dreams of cats are not nightmares. The cats are not menacing, and I'm not frightened, but I'm surprised to be having dreams at all. There is something otherworldly, something I can't put my finger on, about these dreamcats. They're unsettling.

There are no more visits from dreamcats *en route*. The Suntory/Valium cocktail has done its job well. The flight seems much shorter than the scheduled fourteen hours. Touchdown in Tokyo is smooth, customs is smooth, and the guide Jerry Finsterwald hired is smooth. Perhaps a little too smooth, but nothing I can't handle.

Part of what I told Patty was true. I booked a brief stay in Tokyo to relax before setting sail, figuring that would be long enough to make certain I wanted to get on the ship. I don't plan to chicken out, but there's always that possibility, faced with the reality of trusting my life to a hunk of metal surrounded by eternal reaches of water.

The guide deposits me at the Andaz Tokyo Toranomon Hills for a few nights of luxury and sightseeing before meeting my ship, the *MV Andaman Pearl,* and embarking on a pokey two-month journey to Rotterdam.

Tokyo isn't for me. It's too crowded, too frenetic. My tour guide doesn't understand. Why would I come all the way from America to the Ginza and not want to shop? Or why would I want to take in the scene in Shinjuku and Kabuki Cho since I'm not interested in bars, karaoke, or pretty boys?

After three nights, I abandon Tokyo and take a cab half an hour south to Yokohama where the pleasures of the city are more to my liking. Yokohama Bay sparkles a brilliant azure, festooned with working boats, luxury yachts, passenger liners, and of course, cargo ships.

I wander into Itoya on Motomachi Shopping Street, intending to buy yet another journal for the voyage. There's an astonishing collection of opulent fountain pens, luscious inks, and elegant stationery. I select a jade-green journal with a red silk ribbon and an image of a *maneki-neko*, the cheerful Asian good luck cat, debossed on the cover.

I've never journaled religiously, only when I couldn't outrun the muse. There's a folder on my laptop labeled "Scrapbook," containing infrequent notes to myself and snippets of this and that found on the web. The computer will probably be just fine for writing. My bet is the journal will remain pristine.

For all Yokohama's appeal, I'm impatient to begin my adventure at sea. For one last night on land, I luxuriate at the Yokohama Royal Park Hotel, spending the evening savoring an eighteen-year-old Yamazaki single malt, soaking in a jet tub with a view through a porthole over-looking the spectacular bay.

The bubbling water and the whiskey conspire to make me heavy lidded. This time the dreamcat doesn't wait for me to fall asleep. He just stares into my eyes as if there were something important he needs to tell me, but when I surface from my boozy haze and blink my eyes, he has evaporated like the Cheshire Cat. And then my dead husband's leering face pops into my thoughts. I don't see it as much as feel it, like pinpricks running down my back. I can't explain, but it brings to mind what some of my patients have told me about the aura they experience before a migraine.

I get out of the tub shivering, wrap myself in an impossibly soft bath sheet, pad over to my turned-down bed, and burrow in. Whatever all that was with the dreamcat and my late husband, it's gone by the time I reach the bed.

I hadn't noticed the smiling porcelain *maneki-neko* on a side table in the south-east corner of my room, his left paw beckoning rhythmically. It's identical to the one near the cash register at the Lotus Garden in Westbury, right down to the color and design—white with brown spots, its collar and the insides of its ears painted red, a golden oval koban coin around its neck.

I reflect upon this fortunate omen, the long-suffering proprietress of the Lotus Garden who apologized to me once when I caught her flipping off my deceased husband, and when she learned of his demise, sent an elaborate box of Chinese flaky pastry and egg tarts to my home with her condolences. I reflect on the smallness of the world.

At some point I must have closed my eyes because when I open them again the night has vanished and my room is awash in light. I'm starving, and I have a rendezvous to keep. I check out of the hotel after breakfast and hail a taxi to the docks and my adventure aboard the container ship *MV Andaman Pearl.* ■

6

MV Andaman Pearl

The *MV Andaman Pearl* gleams in the early morning sunlight, her white hull with gold lettering reflected in the rippling aqua of Yokohama Bay. I approach the ship, luggage in tow, as I was instructed. There's no need for a ticket. I'm expected.

The passenger agent for Andaman World Marine said all I needed to do was show up dockside and ask around. I was told that delays are possible, even likely. And that's the case today. Some containers destined for the ship have not yet arrived at the dock, but the small feeder ship carrying them is *en route*. The ship won't sail until sometime tomorrow afternoon.

Ships like the *Andaman Pearl* sail when their cargo is aboard, when the tide is right, or whenever the captain decides it's time to leave. If I'm not on board when the ship is ready to sail, she will leave without me. When should I be on board? Nobody knows for sure, but I shouldn't worry. Just show up again tomorrow about the same time.

I'm not unhappy about spending another day in Yokohama, wandering around the Cosmo World Amusement Park, an easy walk from my hotel. Theme parks have never appealed to me, but something about the Cosmo Clock 21, the world's largest clock-style Ferris wheel, draws me in.

The air is pristine and from the top of the ride, with all of Yokohama at my feet and Mt. Fuji in the background, I feel truly at peace. I'm filled with the sense I'm doing exactly what I'm meant to be doing. That I have made all the right choices.

I admit to some nagging feelings of...what? Remorse? Guilt? Not those, exactly, but a vague sense that perhaps I didn't need to go as far as I did, that I might have found a less momentous way to extract myself from the tar pit of his abuse. It's not like me though, to second guess myself. Second-guessing has never served me well.

I browse the shops in the amusement park and am seduced by a window display of hundreds of porcelain lucky cats. I select a smallish one, maybe six inches high, brown and white calico with a red collar and ears. There's something soothing about all those smiling, waving cats. Good fortune seems assured.

The following morning a taxi returns me to the quay where the *Andaman Pearl* is loading cargo. I walk toward the ship, pulling a rolling case with my clothing and toiletries. My physician's black bag, where I have stashed the *maneki-neko* for safekeeping, is strapped on top with my camera bag containing my Canon EOS 7D Mark II and laptop. I'm wearing a fanny pack with my phone, a small amount of currency, a couple of bank cards, my passport, and travel documents.

A trim, Filipino man dressed in a modest khaki uniform spots me. I'm sure I look out of place. He breaks away from the loading operation and approaches me. He appears to already know who I am, and if he has any doubts, my black bag has likely sealed the deal.

"Welcome to the *Andaman Pearl*, Dr. Quilter. Masaya Bayani, captain of the ship, at your service," he says, extending his hand. His smile radiates warmth and fits perfectly with his neatly trimmed beard.

"Jessamyn Quilter," I say, taking his hand. "So nice to meet you."

"We're still loading her so you're a bit early, but those containers we've been waiting for are all here now. We'll sail this afternoon."

He turns toward the ship and whistles through his fingers. "Eric," he yells. A slim, lightly muscled young Asian man dressed in khaki jogs over.

"Dr. Quilter, may I present the ship's second officer, Eric Reyes," the captain says, introducing us. "Eric will get your belongings to your cabin and show you the ropes on board. Don't worry, it's perfectly safe to leave your bags with him."

Captain Bayani checks his clipboard. "Owner's cabin, Eric. Sorry we don't have time to get better acquainted, but if you'll come back around noon, Eric will get you settled before we push off. We'll call your cell if we need you sooner. Now, if you'll excuse me, I'll leave you in the second officer's capable hands."

The captain trots back toward the ship, whistling and shouting something in a language I don't understand to someone whose work seems not to be meeting his standards.

Eric is handsome, and vaguely erotic feelings buzz around in my mind, looking for a place to settle in my body. I hadn't expected anything like this.

Stop it, Jessamyn. This isn't one of your sleazy romance novels.

"We should be ready to go about three o'clock this afternoon, Dr. Quilter," he says. "Once you come aboard, make sure you don't leave because we could sail without further notice, and we want to make sure not to leave you behind."

I nod my understanding.

"We have five guests for the first part of our voyage. Two couples plus you. The captain's daughter, Lovely, will join us when we make port in Manila. You'll have time to meet everyone at the mandatory safety briefing and orientation after we leave port."

Six of us altogether. I hope there's a firecracker or two in the bunch.

"I can't tell you how happy we are to have you with us, Dr. Quilter," the second officer says. "I'm the ship's PICOMC—person in charge of medical care. We seldom have a proper doctor on board, but I'm glad when we do."

"Very nice to meet you, Mr. Reyes. I'm sure you're more than up to handling anything that comes your way, but I'll be happy to assist if you need me."

"Please call me Eric if you like. I appreciate your offer and can't wait to show you our ship's cozy little one-bed hospital," he says with a broad grin.

He waves his arms to attract the attention of a squat, solidly built, middle-aged Filipino man who runs over to join us.

"Don't worry about your bags, Dr. Quilter. Lagac will get them safely to your cabin."

Lagac has a high-voltage smile and sparkling dark eyes. Already I like him. More than like. Those unexpected erotic feelings have anchored themselves in my pelvis. I'm disappointed when he breaks eye contact and hustles my luggage toward the ship, but I make a note to look for him on board.

"You might want to get lunch at the Crab Pot while you wait, Dr. Quilter," the second officer says, gesturing to a nondescript shack on the pier. "We'll feed you later this evening once we're underway."

"Better get back to work." He double checks my cell number and jogs off.

***

The seafood soup at the Crab Pot is magnificent, laden with squid, tuna, scallops, mushrooms, and bean sprouts. They tempted me to try the flying fish, but I thought better of it.

I was told during my initial video conference with the Andaman World Marine passenger service agent that meals won't be up to cruise-ship standards, but food will be plentiful and sometimes quite good, depending upon the talent and inclinations of the cook. And since the *Andaman Pearl* flies the flag of the Philippines, and has a Filipino crew, I could expect lots of rice. I hope the infirmary has a scale.

I finish my lunch at the Crab Pot, keeping the back of what I now think of as "*my* ship" in sight. Even though she's officially a medium-sized ship, I didn't appreciate how large she is. The booking agent said she was "middling," about 900 feet long and 60 feet wide, handily able to traverse the Suez Canal linking the Red Sea with the Mediterranean. She can carry 3,000 standard shipping containers, each as large as an eighteen-wheeler, stacked in the holds and on her main deck.

The full gantry cranes quayside tower over the ship, flying containers from dock to deck like some gigantic robot child, playing with multicolored toy building bricks.

My cell rings.

"Dr. Quilter? Eric Reyes here."

My heart skips a beat.

"We're ready for you. I'll meet you alongside the ship."

The second officer is waiting at the gangway with four other people as I approach.

"Ah," he says. "Here's Dr. Quilter now. Allow me to make introductions. Dr. Quilter, may I present Mr. and Mrs. Agarwal, Miss Lewes-Haley, and Mr. Yongzheng?" We shake hands all around.

"Jessamyn Quilter," I say. "Pleased to meet all of you."

"Balwinder and Chana Agarwal," Mr. Agarwal says stiffly. Mrs. Agarwal says nothing. Neither of them meets my eyes. "A pleasure to make your acquaintance."

I'm sure he doesn't mean it.

"Hello, Dr. Quilter. Shantrelle Lewes-Haley. Nice to meet you." She's a gorgeous young black woman, American by her accent, radiating warmth.

"Yongzheng Shun," her companion says, offering his hand. "Please call me Shun." Malay Chinese, I guess, slender and carefully groomed. He reminds me of a crack neurosurgeon back home. I wouldn't call him handsome, but he seems quite pleasant. His hand rests lightly at Shantrelle's waist.

No mistaking it—Shun and Shantrelle are in love. Newlyweds? I'll have to find out more later. But I'm happy they're along for the ride, something I can't say about the Agarwals. No firecrackers, they.

"Now, if you will head up the gangway, we'll be on our way shortly," the second officer says.

The Agarwals lead the parade. We gather on deck under a bright orange lifeboat suspended above us.

"In an emergency, we will all meet here. The crew will lower the rescue craft to this deck and help you board. There's food, water, a medical kit, and other emergency supplies on board and a transponder that will tell anyone looking for us where we are. It's fully enclosed, big enough for all of us, and will keep us all safe until help arrives. There's another one on the other side of the ship if for some reason this one won't launch."

I can't imagine being stuck in one of those things in the ocean's vastness. I hope I never have to.

"Flotation devices," the second officer says, handing a fluorescent vest to each of us. "Try them on now. I'll help you make any needed adjustments. It's impossible to put them on the wrong way," he says and smiles.

"Notice there's a whistle attached and a light that will activate if the jacket gets wet. You will probably never need them, and there's no need to wear them around the ship unless the captain tells us to. There's a hook just inside the door in your cabins specifically designated for your flotation device, so it will be close at hand if needed. There are extras on the rescue craft if you can't get to your personal life jacket."

"How likely are we to need any of this lifeboat stuff?" Mr. Agarwal asks, the irritation in his voice unmistakable. Mrs. Agarwal stands meekly beside him, about a foot behind.

"Not likely at all," the second officer says.

Mrs. Agarwal struggles to fasten the flotation device over the layers of clothing she wears. When Eric attempts to assist her, Mr. Agarwal rebuffs him.

"I am her husband. I will see to it," he says.

He's arrogant, possessive, and rude—qualities I dislike most in people.

"In all my many years at sea we've never needed the rescue craft or the flotation devices," the second officer continues. "Still, we must be prepared. We'll drill launching and retrieving the rescue crafts once or twice while we're at sea to make certain everything works properly."

"Do we get to ride along?" Shantrelle asks.

The second officer laughs. "Nope. The drill is only for the crew."

"Too bad," she says. "It sounds like fun."

A firecracker that one. *She* sounds like fun.

A loud clank causes us to flinch.

"Just the gangway being stowed," the second officer says with a reassuring smile. "Nothing to worry about. You'll get used to the ship's noises. It will still be another quarter of an hour before we get underway, so let's go up to F deck and get you comfortable in your cabins."

F deck is up five flights of stairs in the ship's "accommodation," the structure near the back of the ship rising from the deck like a small office building. There's an elevator, but it would have been a tight squeeze for all of us. Everyone manages the stairs without difficulty. We follow the second officer through a door from the stairwell onto F deck.

"We're in what you might call the hallway of F deck," the second officer says. "We call it the 'alley.' What you call 'walls,' we call 'bulkheads.' And our bathrooms are 'heads.' We have many more terms to confuse you but it won't offend us if you call them halls, walls, and bathrooms.

"F deck is also called the owners deck because the original owners of the ship and their friends or business associates would occupy these cabins when they joined the crew for the journey. All your cabins are on this deck. It's fancier than the rest of the ship where the officers and crew work and live," he says.

"There are three decks above you—G deck, where the captain, the chief engineer and I live, above that, the bridge deck where we operate the ship, and above that, the topmost deck called Monkey Island, housing the exposed parts of our instruments, like the radar array, our communications antennae, and the mast leading up to our 'Christmas tree,' or navigation lights.

"One deck down from us is E deck where the rest of the officers live. Able sailors and cadets live on D and C decks, and many of the ship's important functional spaces, like the galley, recreation rooms, library, and the messes are on B Deck. The infirmary, storage, and some machinery rooms are on A Deck.

I'm not sure I can remember all of this.

Eric anticipates my uncertainty. "Don't worry," he says. "There are signs on the bulkhead at every deck level and in the elevator to orient you. You'll soon feel right at home.

"Dr. Quilter," he says, "this cabin facing the bow or front of the ship is yours. Mr. Yongzheng and Miss Lewes-Haley, your cabin faces the stern, or back of the ship, across the alley from Dr. Quilter. Mr. and Mrs. Agarwal, you also face the stern, in the next cabin down across from the saloon. There's an empty cabin next to yours, and at the end of the alley is another set of stairs, which we call 'ladders,' by the way, identical to the ones we came up on so you can get to your cabins from either side of the ship.

"We have a saloon on board?" Shun asks. He's soft-spoken, relaxed, a little difficult to read.

"Just an old-timey word for an entertaining or lounging area," the second officer says. "You can think of it as a place where the original owners entertained their business guests or held meetings. The saloon has a small bar, tables, and comfortable seating. It also has a concert grand piano, something most cargo ships don't have, so if you play, you're in luck. The captain's daughter is an accomplished pianist. It wouldn't surprise me to hear her practicing all the way from Manila to Le Havre where she will leave us.

"Settle in and make yourselves comfortable. You're welcome to wander anywhere on the ship, including the bridge. Think of yourselves as the temporary owners of the *Andaman Pearl*. We won't tell corporate in Manila, although if you would like to buy the ship, I'm sure they would love to talk with you," he joked.

He opens the doors to each of our cabins and hands us keys. I peek through the door to my cabin and it takes my breath away. It's beyond fancy.

"If you want to poke around up top on Monkey Island or go below-decks to the engine room we'll have someone show you around to keep you safe," he says as we head to our cabins. "The officers and crew will do their best to be helpful to you, keeping in mind our first job is to move those big boxes piled all around us from one part of the ocean to another.

"Let's meet in the saloon in half an hour and get better acquainted. Until then, I'll leave you on your own while I see if the captain has need for me on the bridge."

I'm astonished at the lavish quarters I've been assigned. I'd heard from some nurses at the hospital who'd been on cruise ships that they barely had room to turn around in their cabins. My cabin is larger than the suite I occupied at the Yokohama Royal Park Hotel and every bit as posh. The original owners clearly required luxury, even aboard a working vessel, and had the wherewithal to afford it.

The cabin has the ambience of a private club, finished throughout with cherry paneling, gilded sconces, and chandeliers. The floor is pink marble. Handmade carpets accent the sitting, sleeping, and working areas.

The kitchenette is well equipped with a refrigerator, microwave, and other appliances. There's even a dishwasher, cabinets, and drawers aplenty, holding pots and pans, tableware, and linens. A breakfast nook wrapped in a banquette against an adjacent wall invites informal dining. Portholes provide light and a feeling of spaciousness.

A sizeable coffee table with facing black leather couches on either side defines the middle of the cabin. It's the ideal place to read and relax. A door to one side of the sitting area leads to a private deck with bamboo flooring, lounge furniture, and an unobstructed view of the ocean beyond a painted white railing. Everything is discretely screened from the bridge wing above, a perfect place for nude sunbathing, something I've never done in my life. Now I have no excuse.

I'm delighted to find a spacious workspace on the other side of the sitting area, a perfect place for my laptop. There's an ebony corner bookcase and matching desk with an integrated reading lamp, a concealed pop-up flat-screen monitor, and a pullout laser printer. A plush high-backed computer chair completes an efficient space for writing.

The sleeping area, against the wall next to the alley, as the second officer called it, boasts a California king-sized bed, end tables with lamps, and leather massage chair. The bathroom is spacious, with a bidet, toilet, double wash basin and a tiled shower larger than I would have expected. A walk-in closet next to the bathroom provides much more space than I need to store my clothes and other belongings.

I unpack, grab a bottle of water from the fridge, and go outside to my private deck. Tugs are nosing us into the bay. Gradually, as I watch the waterfront recede, the ship moves under her own power. I see it rather than feel it. It's magical.

There are no butterflies in my stomach now. I can't imagine why I was so frightened of being on the ship, on open water. I take a couple of deep breaths of fresh sea air, return to my cabin, and prepare to go next door to the saloon to get better acquainted with the other passengers and hear what else the second officer might have to say.

I have liberated the *maneki-neko* from its temporary home in my camera bag and placed it on one of the end tables beside my bed. It's waving arm beckons me toward my new life. My future. ∎

7

Mrs. Agarwal

The America I left behind is celebrating its independence today. It's been four and a half months since I declared my own independence, beginning a new life unencumbered by a husband.

We passengers are getting our bearings. It's been uneventful, almost boring, so far except for the frisson that comes as I remember I'm on the dream adventure I planned for myself back in Massachusetts.

I've spoken with the other passengers now and again in the officers' dining room or mess where all of us eat, although not at the same time, or on the decks. We're on our own internal clocks. The Agarwals keep to themselves, which is fine with me. Yongzheng Shun and Shantrelle Lewes-Haley are more sociable, if besotted with each other. I don't feel ignored. It's wonderful to see young people so much in love.

Shun is an international businessman based in Singapore and Shantrelle's a young woman who until recently worked for his company in Los Angeles. They are to be married soon. I'm looking forward to getting to know them better.

Captain Bayani is cordial when I see him, which has not been often because of his duties. He's invited me to tour the bridge any time. Eric, the second officer, has conducted his promised tour of the infirmary, which seems adequate for most of the medical situations that might pop up on trips like this one. We've talked in my cabin a couple of times. He's intelligent and engaging, even sweet, but also busy, like all the crew, with shipboard duties.

I see more of Ninoy, the messman, than anyone else in the crew. He's a young sailor tasked with helping the cook, tidying cabins, and generally looking after the passengers. Eric says if we need anything, Ninoy is our go-to, though he'll often be busy in the galley.

There are several other officers, able-bodied sailors, and a couple of cadets I haven't met yet. And then there's Lagac, the chief engineer who took my bags aboard in Yokohama.

Lagac's dominion is the engine room. I've seen him on the main deck and sometimes in the officer's mess, though our schedules don't always match. He has an infectious energy. And yes, erotic. He's been flirting with me, I think, although I'm not good at that sort of thing. But I'm open to learning now that there's no obstacle to furthering my education.

The ship's cook produced an American-style barbecue earlier today that, unfortunately, I missed because of the tragic events of this morning. Since Shantrelle and I are the only two Americans on board, that's a shame, but I know he will forgive me when he learns why. I expect he will know soon enough. News travels fast aboard ship.

We've been at sea for five days since leaving Yokohama, sailing in the South China Sea toward Manila. It's been smooth, if somewhat routine.

The second officer says the Chinese consider all the water in these parts a "Chinese ocean," which means the Americans, the Europeans, and everybody else with navies are attempting to prove them wrong, stepping up training drills, insisting on their historical right to unhindered passage on the open seas.

We've been told Chinese "fishing boats" with armed militia are swarming Whitsun Reef and other locations off the southern Philippine island of Palawan. No question they're trespassing in the Philippines' exclusive economic zone, so the government is making a diplomatic fuss.

So far the Chinese have left us alone. Their mischief-making is far enough south of us we think we can safely ignore them for now. When we leave Manila, we'll cross the South China Sea to our next port, Haiphong. We'll breathe easier when we're hugging the Vietnamese coastline.

Of course at some point we'll find ourselves in the Arabian Sea on our way to the Suez Canal with the attendant dangers of Somali pirates. We'll drink a toast to Captain Phillips and hope they don't cause any trouble. Eric says not to worry about it. I didn't fully consider until now the geopolitical storms menacing a ship like the *Andaman Pearl* as she goes about the mundane task of moving stuff from one place to the next.

When we reach Manila tomorrow, we'll be taking on a few containers and leaving a few behind. The happier reason we're stopping is so Captain Bayani and his family can celebrate his daughter's graduation from the College of Music at the University of the Philippines, Diliman. She'll be sailing with us as far as Le Havre to embark on the next phase of her musical training in Paris.

"The sun, the moon, and all the planets dance to the music of Lovely Bayani, at least in the captain's eyes," Second Officer Reyes says. "You will like her. All of us do."

Less happily, Manila will mark the end of the line for the Agarwals. I'm afraid I'm unexpectedly involved in that.

* * *

Last night, a noisy fight coming from the Agarwals' cabin awakened me. When I saw Chana Agarwal on deck earlier this morning, she was wearing even more clothes than usual. Despite her *hijab*, obvious black eyes gave it all away. She tried to avoid me, but in her attempt to escape, she fainted and slumped to the deck. I rushed over to help, and when the shawl she'd been clutching around her upper body fell away, I saw the cut lip and bruises on her neck and shoulders.

"What happened, Mrs. Agarwal?" I asked. As if I didn't know.

"I have been defiant to my husband, and he has corrected me," she whispered, struggling to sit up.

47

Cases of spousal battery like this were commonplace in my emergency department. I would have known exactly what to do there—treat the injuries and report the matter to the police. The social work department would have helped. But we're at sea, miles from law enforcement or social services of any kind.

The chief engineer, Lagac, and an able sailor I don't know saw what was going on from the deck above us and scurried down the ladder.

"One of you please fetch the medical officer," I said, "and we'll need a stretcher." The sailor rushed off to find Eric. Lagac remained behind with Mrs. Agarwal and me. I'm grateful he did.

A belligerent Balwinder Agarwal strode toward us, but Lagac blocked his approach. The engineer seems almost as wide as he is tall. Every inch of his stocky frame is packed with muscle.

"She is my wife," Mr. Agarwal bellowed. "I told her not to come out here. Leave her to me."

"Don't come any closer," I warned him.

"You do this to her?" Lagac growled, balling the fingers of his massive hands into fists.

"Get out of my way, you ugly sea-monkey," Mr. Agarwal hissed, attempting without success to get past Lagac. "This is none of your business. My wife, my business."

The second officer joined us just then, scanning Mrs. Agarwal's injuries. "I'll repeat Engineer Lagac's question. "Did you beat your wife?"

"She is disobedient, so I may beat her, so says the *Quran*. I forbid you to interfere with my wife."

"The Prophet, peace be upon him, never beat his wives," the second officer said, his voice lowered in quiet rage. "Thus says the scholar *al-Tabari*. What you have done is *haram* and a crime. I am placing you under detention, confined until we reach Manila where we will hand you over to the authorities.

"Lagac, escort Mr. Agarwal to the brig. I will interview him later, but first I must help his wife."

48

Two able sailors maneuvered Mrs. Agarwal onto the stretcher. Lagac and another sailor frog-marched a sputtering Balwinder Agarwal away.

"Don't let them see me uncovered," Mrs. Agarwal implored me. "Before God, only my husband can see me uncovered."

The second officer stiffened. "Dr. Quilter, you are welcome to accompany us, and if you wish, to treat Mrs. Agarwal," the second officer said as we made our way to the sick bay. "To be clear though, Mrs. Agarwal is not correct. Islam considers it *halal*, or permissible, even though it can place a man's soul in peril, for a male medical officer to examine and treat a woman if there is no woman qualified to do so.

"Clearly you are better qualified than I to treat Mrs. Agarwal, but you are not the medical officer on this ship, and I can't demand you serve in that capacity. The choice is yours, Dr. Quilter, not Mrs. Agarwal's."

I considered his words for a moment. The second officer is right. He handles medical care aboard the *Andaman Pearl*. He's competent to manage Mrs. Agarwal's injuries and will holler if he requires my help. There's no need to get wrapped up in something that could turn messy once we reach port. I'm not on this journey to practice medicine.

"Mrs. Agarwal, listen to me carefully. Mr. Reyes is the medical officer on this ship, and he is skilled at taking care of injured people. He has explained to both of us it's perfectly permissible, according to the teachings of the religion the two of you share, for him to take care of you. It's necessary for him to examine you carefully because your husband may have broken some of your bones and caused life-threatening internal injuries. So please put aside your fears and allow him to help you.

"Mr. Reyes, if everyone agrees, I will chaperone your examination and treatment of Mrs. Agarwal. Perhaps that will make her more comfortable."

In the end, it made little difference. Mrs. Agarwal lost consciousness before we reached sick bay. She was still breathing, but her pulse was weak and thready.

The second officer swiftly started her on oxygen, placed an IV, and hooked up monitors. Her readings did not look good.

"Thanks for your wisdom, Dr. Quilter. I don't want you to feel you must go to work because of Mrs. Agarwal's religious sensibilities. Many people misinterpret Islam. But jump in anytime with my blessings and my gratitude."

"You've got this, Eric." I helped him cut Mrs. Agarwal's clothes off.

Eric shook his head incredulously when he saw the extent of her injuries. "My god, he did a job on her. Almost certainly something nasty going on inside, likely a ruptured spleen or a brain bleed. This isn't the first time he's beaten her badly.

"We're not equipped for this sort of thing. We're going to have to do everything the old-fashioned way, and she can't even help us by telling us where it hurts." He drew back her eyelid, squinting through his ophthalmoscope.

The monitor started beeping. "Shit," he said. "We're losing her."

She never regained consciousness.

"What's next, Eric?"

"I could use your help packing her with ice. If we were farther away from landfall, we could bury her at sea. As it is, she'll be here until we can transfer her to the authorities in Manila. We'll hope nobody else needs this gurney in the meantime."

We said very little as we dressed Mrs. Agarwal's body in ice and covered her with an insulating blanket. It had been much easier in Chilton when we lost a patient. We just rolled them into the cool room.

An image of my deceased husband on his own gurney in the hospital cool room back home flashed through my mind. *Too bad Mrs. Agarwal didn't kill her husband before he killed her.*

"You should go back to your cabin and rest, Jessamyn. I'll pay Mr. Agarwal a visit and stop by your cabin a little later after I have checked in with the captain. He's going to be furious. He doesn't like people being killed on his ship."

"You did well, Eric. In our line of work, you save some, you lose some. If you ever decide to stop bobbing up and down in the ocean and go to medical school, count on me for a glowing reference."

He smiled and hurried on his way. I'm not sure I've ever seen Eric when he isn't hurrying.

* * *

In my cabin I reflect on the terror the mortally wounded Mrs. Agarwal felt thinking about Eric seeing her unclothed. We all have bodies that sometimes need the care of others. Why do we choose to live our lives in ways that cause us so much unnecessary pain?

Eric's soul is certainly in no danger from Mrs. Agarwal, nor was Mrs. Agarwal's soul imperiled by the relentless demons of heterosexual lust. Eric is gay.

He hasn't told me so, and I'm not aware of any ship's gossip to that effect, but on a couple of occasions I've seen him in kissing distance to a handsome junior deck officer. And yesterday as I walked a circuit around the container deck, trying to burn off some of those rice calories, I stumbled across Eric and the young officer in a recess among the shipping containers.

Eric's pants were around his ankles. The junior deck officer was on his knees in front of him, and Eric was holding his head, guiding his face into his crotch. The junior officer's hands were gripping Eric's buttocks, and both were in such an advanced state of arousal I doubt they would have noticed me had I waved and shouted hello.

Of course I did no such thing. I short-circuited my walk, went back to my cabin, and pondered the vagaries of love and sex, life and death, over a cup of Lady Grey tea.

Shall I tell the second officer I saw him, however briefly, in the throes of sexual pleasure with another man? What would be the point? He didn't see me. When a tree falls in the forest and nobody hears it, does it make a sound?

Still, I feel twinges of...what? Uneasiness? Disappointment? Jealousy? Eric is a good-looking man. For whatever reason, erotic feelings have ambushed me from time to time since I freed myself of my late husband. Eric sparked one of those ambushes when I first saw him on the docks at Yokohama.

I know I have no right to make assumptions about Eric's sexuality based upon what I saw. Men have surely looked for release wherever they might find it ever since they've gone to sea.

Maybe he has a girlfriend, or a wife at home like the captain, and was just taking his pleasure where he found it. Maybe he's bisexual. Who knows? But more to the point, why am I even thinking about it?

My nascent erotic interest in the second officer has evaporated, but I remain interested in other ways. Perhaps it's how Eric comported himself with Mrs. Agarwal and her thuggish husband. He struggled so valiantly to save her.

Eric is invaluable on the *Andaman Pearl*. Surely his career would meet a swift end if his foolish behavior among the containers were to surface. I'm not sure why I feel so protective of him, but I've changed my mind about ignoring what I saw. Both of us will get past the embarrassment, and he needs to be more careful. He can't afford to get caught doing something so reckless.

I need to get focused on my writing. So much has already happened since I left Westbury. It's clear much of it will get lost, just float away out of reach, unless I write things down. Since I lugged a laptop along for this ride, I might as well make use of it while the sea and time pass by six stories below me. I promise I'll get on it tomorrow.

For now, for his own safety, I need to confront Eric when I have the opportunity. ∎

8

Here There Be *Jinn*

MANILA, Philippines   July 6

ood on board is upbeat as tugs guide us into our berth at the International Container Terminal in Manila's North Harbor. Manila is home for many of the sailors and the captain has declared a twenty-four-hour shore leave for passengers and crew alike. The second officer will remain with the ship, supervising cargo operations and monitoring the weather. There's a typhoon brewing in the Philippine Sea, which could pass north of Manila over the Luzon Strait and the sparsely populated Babuyan Islands.

"They won't notice much difference in Babuyan," the second officer jokes. "The wind blows there all the time."

Our captain wants to make for Haiphong and be well clear of Manila before the winds become a problem in a day or two. The typhoon may not do much damage to the Philippines, but it's tracking toward China and may pass over Taiwan before bearing down on Macao and Hong Kong.

Typhoon aside, there's the other unpleasant business Eric must transact—dealing with the port police in the matter of the Agarwals.

Shun draws me aside at the gangway and asks about the death of Mrs. Agarwal, which is now common knowledge aboard the *Andaman Pearl* despite the captain's edict. Shun and Shantrelle were sleeping in when they woke to the commotion from the Agarwals' cabin next door to theirs. Shun says he was poised to intervene, but the noise stopped when Mrs. Agarwal left the cabin.

I tell him as much as I think appropriate under the circumstances. No need to charge headlong into a minefield. Shun thanks me and says he and Shantrelle will pray for them.

I tell Eric I'll make myself available to the authorities if he thinks it might help. I made some encrypted notes in my laptop about my role in the incident, although I told no one about them. Just a matter of habit, I suppose. Physicians are compulsive documenters.

Eric doubts he'll need me. In fact, he says it might be better if I were not readily accessible to the port police. An attorney from Andaman World Marine will accompany him to advise and keep the authorities from veering off course.

We passengers have been told not to venture too far away from the ship as we lark about Manila and to keep our cell phones at the ready. Conditions could change rapidly, and the captain doesn't want to get trapped in port. If we get a call from the ship, we're to scare up the nearest jeepney and make a beeline back.

I'm planning a brief tour of the Quiapo district at Eric's suggestion, if for no other reason than to get my feet back on land. I'll not say dry land because it's the monsoon season and everything is soaked. But we have a window of sunshine and blue sky this morning before the expected afternoon downpour returns.

Yongzheng Shun and Shantrelle Lewes-Haley plan to spend their day living like native Filipinos, haunting the SM Mall of Asia. They invited me to tag along, but I'm afraid I'd feel like a fifth wheel. Shantrelle loves to shop, and Shun seems to be made of money. He dotes on her. The feeling seems mutual, but who can be sure of anything in love?

My itinerary begins at the Quinta Market and Fishport and includes Quiapo Church, the Intramuros, and whatever catches my fancy around the Old Town. Wherever I walk, a tangle of overhead electrical wires traces intricate patterns against the sea-blue sky.

Eric recommended a visit to the predominately Muslim quarter of Quiapo and the Masjid Al-Dahab or Golden Mosque where he prays when he's home in Manila. He gave me instruction about how to dress modestly for the mosque (loose-fitting clothing that covers the arms and legs to the wrists and ankles and a headscarf completely covering my hair).

I get into the spirit of the thing and find an open-air boutique in a narrow passageway with gorgeous clothes hanging from rolling racks clogging the sidewalks and spilling into the street. The smell of sandalwood incense mixed with fish fills the air. The shopkeeper fusses over me and recommends a luminous lilac *hijab* she helps me put on properly.

She also tells me about another shop where I can buy a gift for Eric when I've finished visiting the mosque. I want to cheer him up. The Agarwal affair has shaken him.

I'm hungry and aromas from the June-Naireh Restaurant seduce me. I opt for turmeric soup and *piaparan a manoc*, a traditional dish of wild fowl, coconut, and more turmeric served with a fiery condiment called *palapa* made from still more turmeric, chiles, garlic, and shredded coconut. If turmeric lives up to its billing as a panacea, I'll live forever, thanks to this one meal. The *piaparan* is astonishingly good, a dish tailor made for an icy Coca-Cola.

For dessert, unnecessary but irresistible, I savor a *palitaw*, a flat cake made from glutinous rice and *ube,* the intensely purple Philippine sweet potato, coated with grated coconut. The cook on the *Andaman Pearl* is no slouch, but he would simmer with jealousy over this meal.

Lunch finished, I visit the Golden Mosque, an imposing but approachable building spacious enough for over 20,000 worshippers. I reflect on Eric's ability to calm Mrs. Agarwal's terror as he struggled to save her life. In the serenity of the Golden Mosque, I close my eyes and breathe my version of a prayer for Mrs. Agarwal and Eric. I'm not a religious person, but that surely won't matter. I can't bring myself to follow Shun's example and include Mr. Agarwal's soul in the package.

The day is wearing on, and I want to shop for Eric while the weather is still good. I locate the gift shop the clothing shopkeeper recommended. It smells of sandalwood, mint, and rosewater—a delectable combination. The store's proprietor is eager to help me find the perfect gift.

"I'd like something for the medical officer on my ship," I tell him. "He couldn't come ashore, but he prays at the Masjid Al-Dahab when he's in Manila."

"May I propose a perfect *sunnah* box filled with useful objects a medical officer will require when at sea?" he asks. He hands me a stunning, burnished black box with a hinged cover and meticulously dovetailed joinery. And suggests things to fill it.

"He will need Ajwa dates from Madina to keep him safe on his voyages," the proprietor says, placing them in the box. "The Prophet, peace be upon him, said, 'If somebody takes seven Ajwa dates in the morning, neither magic nor poison will hurt him that day.'

"He must have black seed oil—a cure for every disease—tooth powder, a comb, and oil scented with *oud* for his beard, for the Messenger of Allah, peace be upon him, frequently applied lotion and combed his beard."

The *oud* smells wonderful. Very masculine—woody and slightly sweet with a smoky finish. Look out, junior deck officer.

"Since the medical officer must surely be required to counter the evil eye, *jinn* possession, or black magic, he will require Ruqyah potions—powdered *Sidr* leaf, to weaken *jinn* and cleanse the residue of evil eye and black magic from the body, and Costus tincture to purify the blood and exorcise recalcitrant *jinn*. For the Prophet, peace be upon him, said, 'Allah, the bearer of greatness and majesty, has created for each illness its remedy. So cure yourself.'

"I will make the medical officer a gift of this book of plans and instructions from the *Quran* and *sunnah* for treating these maladies. And you may add these prayer beads and this crimson travel prayer mat in a pouch with its own compass to find *qiblah* toward the sacred Kaaba in Mecca, if you wish."

The proprietor has charmed me. I buy everything he recommends and am impressed he can fit it all into the elegant box. Eric will be pleased, perhaps amused, especially when I tell him how the proprietor has helped me select items he believes a Muslim medical officer requires in the middle of the ocean.

As the proprietor wraps the box carefully with brown paper and jute twine, my curiosity gets the better of me.

"I haven't heard the medical officer speak of *jinn*. What can you tell me about them?"

He becomes silent, then after a moment says, "Come. I am pleased to offer you tea."

He turns the sign in the window around, closing his business, and beckons me into a room, drawing aside a saffron curtain that separates his living space from the shop. A stunning arabesque table, black wood inlaid with mother-of-pearl, rests on the medallion of a large Mashad carpet in the center of the room. He removes his shoes before entering, and I follow suit.

He speaks some phrase as he enters, unintelligible to me, so soft as to be almost inaudible. A young woman, barefoot, dressed in a magenta malong with a deep red growing fern pattern, enters the room from the opposite end, carrying a silver tray with two silver filigree-covered glasses of steaming mint tea.

"My wife, Suyen, welcomes you to our home," the proprietor says. "I am Hamza Baraquilla."

"Jessamyn Quilter," I say. "I'm honored you have invited me here."

"Please sit," Hamza says, gesturing toward one of the two cushions at the table. He takes the cushion opposite me, and Suyen places the tea before us.

Hamza holds his tea in both hands and blows on the scalding liquid before taking a sip and replacing the glass on the table.

"I will tell you about the *jinn*," he says as Suyen leaves the room.

"Allah, the merciful, the compassionate, created the angels, the *jinn*, and men for no other purpose than to worship him. Angels, He created from light. *Jinn*, He created from the smokeless flame of fire, and men from dried clay of black smooth mud.

"There are three kinds of *jinn*. *Elifret,* the jinn used by sorcerers and witches, can move things, even from one country to another. *Alkhabal* terrorize people by stealing their possessions in front of their very eyes and cause illness like seizures and epilepsy. *Ghilan* are *jinn* that take the form of other animals like donkeys or cats.

"Cats are most vexatious. If they are not *jinn*, cats are *halal* and may enter the Masjid al-Haram in Mecca. They are beloved of the Prophet, peace be upon him, who kept a cat named Muezza, of whom he was fond. It is said that one day he discovered the cat sleeping on the sleeve of his prayer robe. Rather than disturb the sleeping cat, he took scissors and cut the sleeve from his garment.

"Some cats though are not cats at all but *jinn*. If you are afraid when you see a cat or try to scare it and it does not run, it is most assuredly a *jinni* and not a cat. If you are not ill, and your ears whistle or you smell fire when you see a cat, a *jinni* and not a cat stands before you."

I nod my understanding as Hamza continues to school me on the dangers posed by *jinn* and the importance of exorcising them.

"Reciting certain *surahs* of the *Quran* will cause *jinn* to flee, but it is also important to take precautions not to attract them," he says.

"When you undress or change your clothes, you must say the *Bismillah,* 'In the name of Allah, the merciful the compassionate,' so a *jinni* doesn't see your nakedness. Do not stand in front of a mirror naked since a *jinni* might fall in love with you and become part of you.

"There is more, but in all cases, reciting the *ayahs* or *surahs* from the Holy Book will keep the *jinn* from harming you. *Jinn* will be answerable before Allah as will all men.

"Do you have other questions?" Hamza asks as my cell phone chirps in my pocket.

"Ah." Hamza smiles, hearing the sound. "The demon we invite to dwell among us and to whom we are perpetually in thrall."

"Forgive me," I say. "It's the second officer."

"I'm afraid we need you, Jessamyn," Eric says. "The authorities insist upon interviewing you before they will complete their business with us."

"I apologize for the intrusion, Mr. Baraquilla. Unfortunately I must return to the ship. Thank you for your guidance in making selections for the second officer's gift. He will be pleased. My thanks to you and your wife for your hospitality and enlightenment."

"The pleasure has been mine, Jessamyn Quilter. *Allah hafiz.*"

I step into my shoes as I leave Mr. Baraquilla's hospitality, corral a jeepney and text OMW. Eric waits for me at the gangway when I arrive.

"Sorry to cut your shore leave short, Jessamyn. Let me fill you in." We talk as we take the elevator to the conference room on G deck.

"Officers from the port police and an attorney from Andaman World Marine are waiting for us. I have told them my story and they wish to hear yours, although I assured them that as person in charge of medical care, I bear complete responsibility for the care of the unfortunate Mrs. Agarwal."

"And what do they want from me?"

"I'm not clear so I'll let them speak for themselves."

When we enter the room, two men are seated at the conference table. Eric pulls out a chair for me next to his.

"Jessamyn Quilter, gentlemen," I say. "How may I be of service to you?"

"Hello, Dr. Quilter. My name is Florencio Goles. I'm the attorney representing the ship and Andaman World Marine in this matter. Thank you for agreeing to meet with us."

"And I am Officer Hector Santiago of the Philippine Ports Authority Port Police."

"Let me summarize for you what we understand about this situation and why we are here," Mr. Goles says. "The body of Chana Agarwal, deceased wife of Balwinder Agarwal, rests in the ship's sick bay awaiting final disposition.

"Mr. Agarwal is detained belowdecks in the brig because he battered Mrs. Agarwal on the high seas en route to Manila from Yokohama. He is not under arrest because a ship's officers do not have the power of arrest, but they may legally detain anyone who presents a threat.

"Second Officer Eric Reyes, as person in charge of medical care for the *Andaman Pearl*, treated Mrs. Agarwal for injuries Mr. Agarwal acknowledges he inflicted. Mrs. Agarwal died while the ship was in international waters, and we contend that Mr. Agarwal caused her death, whether intentionally or unintentionally. Are we all agreed about these facts and circumstances?"

Everyone nods agreement.

"Andaman World Marine will not permit Mr. Agarwal further passage on the *MV Andaman Pearl,*" Mr. Goles continues. "We propose that the port police take Mr. Agarwal into custody and remove him from our ship."

"Dr. Quilter. Were you also responsible for providing medical care to Mrs. Agarwal?" Officer Santiago asks.

"I was not. As a woman, I offered to chaperone Second Officer Reyes to make Mrs. Agarwal more comfortable. Since Mrs. Agarwal was a Muslim woman, she had concerns about a male medical officer examining her. Second Officer Reyes, himself a Muslim, assured Mrs. Agarwal that Islam permits men to treat women if they are the best qualified person available."

"Why did you not provide care yourself as a physician with more extensive medical knowledge than Mr. Reyes?"

"While I am indeed a physician, I am only a passenger on this ship, like the Agarwals. Eric Reyes is the *Andaman Pearl's* medical officer. I have complete confidence in his ability."

"Do you think Mr. Agarwal caused the death of his wife?"

"I do."

"Why is that?"

"When I encountered Mrs. Agarwal during my morning walk on deck and saw that she fainted, I went to assist her. I immediately noticed she had injuries to her face and eyes. When I asked her what happened, she told me her husband had 'corrected' her. When Mr. Agarwal observed the second officer's efforts to treat his wife, he sought to interfere but crew prevented him. He became belligerent and told us that Mrs. Agarwal had been disobedient. He said he beat her and asserted his right to do so."

"And do you think this beating caused his wife's death?"

"I agree with the determination of the second officer, although as a passenger, it's not my prerogative to agree or disagree with the person in charge of medical care. In my experience as a physician, the next step is typically an autopsy to determine the cause of death."

"Do you have evidence that Mr. Agarwal intended to kill Mrs. Agarwal?"

"I do not."

"Do you believe you might have saved Mrs. Agarwal's life, something Second Officer Reyes could not do?"

"Most assuredly not. Second Officer Reyes did everything anyone might have done on Mrs. Agarwal's behalf. I believe her husband inflicted so much damage nobody could have saved her life."

"Thank you for your observations and cooperation, Dr. Quilter," Officer Santiago says.

"Are we satisfied the next step is now to transfer Mrs. Agarwal's body to a medical facility for autopsy, if appropriate?" Attorney Goles asks.

"I am satisfied," Officer Santiago says. "We have transport standing by, and we will work with Second Officer Reyes to complete the required documentation. As for Mr. Agarwal, we will remove him from the ship and prepare charges for referral to the prosecutor."

Eric and the attorney for Andaman World Marine escort me back to my cabin. Nobody asks about the package I carry.

"What do you think will happen to Mr. Agarwal?" I ask Mr. Goles.

"It is difficult to say, but I imagine the ports authority will question him and deny him entry into the country. I find it hard to believe that anyone will want to try him in the Philippines for an alleged wrongful death that occurred on the high seas. It will be much less complicated for the government of the Philippines simply to deny him entry into the country and deport him.

"What might happen with Mrs. Agarwal's body, I can't guess. It is possible the government will repatriate it in the custody of Mr. Agarwal, depending upon the findings at autopsy. If there is to be an autopsy, which I doubt."

I'm furious. "Why would there not be an autopsy?"

"Nobody familiar with this case alleges any crime was committed in the Philippines, although Mr. Agarwal confessed he beat his wife aboard this Philippines-flagged vessel. Since there are significant questions concerning jurisdiction, it is possible the prosecutor will decline on procedural grounds to act upon the charges proposed by the port police.

"It depends upon who wants to make what point. There might be delays, but it is possible Mr. and Mrs. Agarwal will both be back in India before the *Andaman Pearl* resumes her journey."

"Do you mean Mr. Agarwal can kill his spouse and escape without consequences?" Eric asks.

"Yes," Mr. Goles says.

Eric shakes his head. "How would it be possible to live with yourself, knowing you have taken a life. Something not yours to take."

I feel a chill march down my spine. ∎

9

Embarrassment

The day is catching up to me. The interview with the port police and my sojourn in Old Town Manila has worn me out. I remove my shoes and prop myself up in bed. I try to escape into *The Scurrilous Heiress*, a paperback I found in the ship's small library, but I soon doze off.

ABOARD MV ANDAMAN PEARL   July 7

A short time later, the sounds of a piano being tuned wake me. I know there's a piano in the saloon next to my cabin. The second officer told us about it, and I noticed it when we first gathered there for our initial orientation to the ship. I didn't see the instrument itself since a fitted cover emblazoned with the Bösendorfer logo hid it, but I remember thinking money must have been no object if the owners outfitted the saloon with a piano of that stature.

I know a little something about Bösendorfers. My aunt Gwendolyn, a concert pianist on the faculty of the old Boston Conservatory, had a matching pair nested nose-to-tail like an enormous Yin and Yang in her drawing room where she gave private lessons.

Each was nine and a half feet long and cost Uncle George more than half a million dollars. Instead of the usual eighty-eight keys, Aunty G's Bösendorfer Imperials had ninety-seven. When she played the lowest note, I could feel the individual vibrations as I watched the string dance.

I resolve to inspect the piano next door once it's been tuned. But why, I wonder, are they tuning this piano now? The answer should have been obvious—the captain's daughter will need to practice.

Someone slid an envelope under my door while I dozed, containing an engraved invitation from Captain Bayani.

The Master of the MV Andaman Pearl

Requests Your Presence at a Recital

Presented by His Daughter

Miss Lovely Diwata Aquinas y Bayani

4:00 p.m., July 8

In the Saloon, Owners Deck

Reception to Follow

I take a quick shower and find some clean clothes. I smile as I realize I've done nothing to discourage any lurking *jinn* since I'm standing nude in front of a full-length mirror. As I dress, I look at the still-wrapped gift I bought for Eric on the coffee table. I'm wondering when a good time might be to give it to him as Eric taps on my door.

"Eric. Come in. How are you holding up?"

He produces a bottle of Screw Kappa Napa from behind his back. I wonder how he's found SKN so far away from the Sonoma County wine country and what a devout Muslim like Eric is doing with a bottle of wine.

"Glad to be free of the business of the afternoon," he says. "I thought you might appreciate a glass of merlot."

"Fantastic. Sorry about the mess." I wave at the rumpled bed. "Make yourself comfortable. I'll get some glasses."

We sit on the couch and toast each other. "The package is for you. Go ahead, open it."

64

He's nonplussed. "I don't know what to say. It is beautiful and most unexpected."

As the first glass of wine is followed by a second, I tell him about the shopkeeper who helped me select gifts especially useful for a Muslim medical officer beset by supernatural perils at sea. I recount how he closed his shop and served me tea as he explained the intricacies of *jinn*, the evil eye, and black magic.

Eric avoids eye contact and his posture stiffens. "We face many dangers, both at sea and in port," he says. "Some menace our bodies and some our souls."

Have I been too blithe in my descriptions?

"Eric," I say after a few moments. "I hope I've not offended you with my gift or my stories."

"No, no," he says, looking into my eyes. "I am just wondering what you must think about the tales of *jinn* and the supernatural you heard from Mr. Baraquilla. You are a woman of science, a physician. Many Muslims in my country believe in sorcery. Many non-Muslims as well believe in witchcraft and the battle for men's souls by supernatural beings."

In for a penny, in for a pound, I think, swallowing a sip of wine.

"Yes. Many people all over the world believe these things. I do not, but I don't judge them, and I don't think I am better than they are.

"But how about you? When I think of orthodox Muslims, you would not be the first person who comes to mind. Here you are, enjoying a glass of wine with me. Some of my Muslim acquaintances in the hospital drank alcohol occasionally, although some felt they shouldn't.

Eric didn't flinch.

"I have nothing but respect for you, Eric. You assured poor Mrs. Agarwal that her soul would be safe in your caring hands. Your respect for her beliefs was an integral part of taking care of her."

"I'm afraid my family would not consider me to be a good Muslim," Eric says, "although my career impresses them. They would have thought

I wonder if I did not do so out of arrogance?"

"No, Eric. Your confidence in yourself isn't misplaced. I told that to the port police, and I will tell you again. As many times as you need to hear it."

"Still, I must be blunt. Do you think you could have saved her life if I had gotten out of the way?"

"No. If I had thought so I would have *pushed* you out of the way and dealt with the consequences later."

Here goes, I think, inviting Eric to fill our glasses again.

"Now that we're being blunt and bearing our souls to each other, there's something important I must tell you. And you must promise not to run away from me, or I shall have to dog the door so you can't escape."

He smiles weakly.

"Eric, you are so important to this ship, and the ships that will come after her, that I can't allow you to place yourself in unnecessary danger. That's why I'm telling you I saw you among the containers with the junior deck officer."

Eric blanches but doesn't move. I place my hand on his and wait for a moment.

He says nothing.

"Before we go any further, we both know it's none of my business who you have sex with. The deck officer seems like a fine choice. Nor was I embarrassed or offended by what I happened upon. But I'm terrified that if anyone sees you, your career will be over in a blinding flash. That would be a tragic loss."

Eric remains silent. I continue to touch his hand as he summons the courage to speak.

"He is a man," he says. "It is *haram*. My family would disown me."

"I don't know enough about your religion or any other to weigh in on whether it's morally wrong for men to have sex with men. I do know a bit about science, however. If you are aroused by men, that's simply a part of who you are. Right or wrong has nothing to do with it. We both know it's neurobiology and nothing will change it. What you do about it is another matter."

"It seems abhorrent," he says.

Oh, Eric. I wish I could tell you the last straw, the thing that made me decide unequivocally to kill my abusive husband rather than divorce him was that he destroyed a wonderful young man simply because he was gay. DeShawn Livingston trusted my husband. My husband murdered DeShawn's soul and DeShawn took care of the rest. That's my definition of abhorrent.

"For what it's worth, I disagree it's abhorrent, but you'll have to decide that for yourself. I *know,* however, it's wrong to put yourself, and the junior officer, at such risk. Why didn't you just go to your cabin or his?"

"That would have been impossible," Eric says. "People gossip. There's no privacy on a ship, only discretion. I can't count on the discretion of everyone on board. There are very few private places on a ship, as you have learned, much to my embarrassment."

"I'm sorry to have embarrassed you, and I contemplated not telling you because of the pain it might cause you. It would have been much worse though to have said nothing and learn someone else saw you."

"Understood, Jessamyn. In time, I'm sure I will be grateful. Right now I am just drowning in shame."

"Right. But if you decide you want to talk further, I'm here for you. And if you decide to snog with that handsome young man, my cabin is at your disposal. I can always find somewhere else to be, and I'll gladly do so knowing you'll be safe."

I propose a toast, and we drink to the soul of Mrs. Agarwal. And I drink in memory of the soul of DeShawn Livingston. We sit in silence, finishing our wine.

"Perhaps I was overcome by black magic or an ill-meaning *jinni*," Eric says at last, forcing a smile.

"It hadn't occurred to me your handsome young deck officer might be a *jinni*," I say, returning his smile and squeezing his forearm. "I know how to sort *jinn* from cats, but Hamza Baraquilla didn't teach me about deck officers. Happily you now have all the materials you need in your *sunnah* box to deal with evil from whatever quarter."

"I think," he says, growing pensive again, "evil is more complicated than that."

I nod in agreement. The captain speaks over the PA. "Second officer to the bridge. Second officer to the bridge."

I let go of Eric's arm.

"It looks like we are ready to sail," he says. "The captain is at the helm."

"How long before we reach our next port?" I ask.

"Ordinarily we would plan two long days to Haiphong. But we're sailing well to the south of our usual heading rather than straight across the West Philippine Sea, which the Chinese arrogantly call the South China Sea, to stay out of the way of the typhoon. It may take an additional day or so."

"Isn't it dangerous to sail with the threat of a storm that size?" I ask. "Why not just stay in port until things blow over?"

"The consequences of staying in port when we could be sailing are onerous. Not only does Andaman World Marine lose money, but the people expecting these containers lose money and storage charges build up for containers in other ports waiting to be picked up.

"They build ships our size to navigate heavy seas. We wouldn't ever challenge a typhoon like Kaala head-on, but we can stay out of her way. Our voyage might get a little rough but don't worry, I'm sure the captain wants smooth seas for the recital tomorrow afternoon and will pick a cautious path."

"I'm confident you and the captain will get us there in one piece. Take care of yourself, Eric. We need you safe to take care of us."

I fumble in my nightstand drawer on my way to the door to see Eric out.

"Here. Have a couple of these ginger lozenges. They're great for exorcising merlot breath." ∎

10

The Captain's Daughter

J ust after sundown yesterday, we left Manila harbor. The ocean was smooth outside my porthole, no sign of any trouble brewing. Still, I slept fitfully last night, the wretched business with the Agarwals and the difficult conversation with Eric still very much on my mind.

ABOARD MV ANDAMAN PEARL   July 8

I awoke around two in the morning and wrote in my laptop journal, in part to exorcise my own demons, and in part just to update my notes about what had happened. When I went back to bed an hour later, I slept deeply, without dreams.

I wake again to leaden skies. Yesterday's sunlight no longer bounces off the surface of the slate-blue sea. I shower, dress, and go to the officers' mess to get some breakfast to bring back to my room.

After reading in bed for a bit, I fall asleep and am awakened a couple of hours later by voices and the sounds of furniture being rearranged in the saloon next door. I get up and dress as appropriately as I can for a recital and reception. Certainly nobody will dress formally, and I couldn't if I wanted to, given the travel wardrobe limitations I have imposed on myself. What kind of dress would "container ship formal" be, after all?

The messman raps on my door about one o'clock. He says the captain asked him to check on me and let me know the second officer will be pleased to escort me to the recital this afternoon.

I smile inwardly, thinking the second officer would probably prefer to escort the handsome junior deck officer. I had a notion to tease him, to help him relax and lighten up, but he's dealing with existential issues. Not to respect the depth of his struggle would be cruel. Still, he made that joke about the *jinn*. A good sign.

At quarter to four, Eric calls for me, resplendent in dress whites, and we walk next door to the saloon. The crew has arranged chairs in semi-circles in front of the burnished ebony Bösendorfer. Next to the piano, cradled in a gleaming silver stand, is a cello enrobed in a rich patina an alchemist might have conjured in the secret recesses of a medieval laboratory, lacquered with burnt umber and melted butter, shot through with candlelight.

Programs, printed on heavy cream paper, rest on the chairs.

Everyone who can be spared from shipboard duties is front and center in the saloon. Shun and Shantrelle take seats next to Eric and me. They have abandoned their usual shorts and t-shirts in favor of more suitable attire. We chat amicably for a few moments waiting for the recital to begin.

At precisely four o'clock, the captain enters the saloon in his dress whites and positions himself in the Bösendorfer's bentside. The audience settles, chatter evaporating into expectation.

"Welcome, everyone," Captain Bayani says. "This afternoon I am the happiest of men, delighted to present my beautiful and talented daughter in recital. This voyage marks an important milestone in her career as a concert musician. It also marks an important passage for me. My only child, my beloved daughter, is leaving the warmth and security of my home for the vagaries of a less indulgent world. This afternoon I am merely her driver, conveying her to a more glamorous life."

We all laugh.

"But before I surrender her, I require of her one more recital to make up for the many I missed when I have not been in port. Last week marked two other important milestones, her twenty-first birthday and graduation with top honors from university. She assures me she has surpassed the knowledge of all her teachers there," he says to polite laughter. "I am not at all surprised.

"She will sail with us as far as Le Havre where she will disembark to study at the Conservatoire National Supérior de Musique et de Danse de Paris. Fortunately for her father, she will be on a full scholarship, but if she were not, I would gladly pawn everything dear to me, except my wife or my cello, to pay her tuition.

"Ladies and gentlemen, the worst part of any concert for the performer is waiting in the wings. So, without further dalliance, I am happy to present my daughter, Miss Lovely Diwata Aquinas y Bayani."

The captain's daughter enters the room to enthusiastic applause in six-and-a-half-inch Christian Louboutin platform heels, looking for all the world like a younger Yuja Wang. She wears a floor-length dusty orchid gown with a cascade of sequins, a sweetheart neckline, slit skirt, and three-quarter length sleeves. A large triangular gold talisman on a choker graces her throat, reminding me of the *agimat* for sale outside the Minor Basilica of the Black Nazarene in Quiapo. Many believe such amulets to be a source of power and protection. Small wonder she appears so confident.

She acknowledges the applause with a practiced bow and seats herself at the piano, adjusting the height of her artist bench by millimeters. If she feels anything other than total mastery of the moment, it's undetectable.

She opens with two Scarlatti sonatas, followed by some finger-breaking Chopin. Her technique is impeccable, the music transcendent.

The program hasn't fully prepared us for the next piece, listing only its title. It is to be a duet. Captain Bayani removes the cello from its stand and seats himself downstage from his daughter, cradling the instrument between his knees, perfecting the intonation.

The captain and his daughter enchant us with Fauré for eight minutes. I wish it could last forever.

They bow to enthusiastic applause, and Lovely places her hand on her father's shoulder and kisses his cheek. "Let's see if you can do anything with this old pile of lumber," he says, handing her the cello.

"Ladies and gentlemen, what my father is too modest to tell you is that he gave me my first music lessons on this precious instrument. I had to stand on a kitchen chair, and he had to steady the instrument for me. You have just seen how accomplished he is."

There's more applause for the captain.

Lovely's Bach suite is entrancing. As the applause dies down, she adjusts the lower strings to the special tuning required for her final piece and takes a deep breath, steeling herself as if anticipating a grueling wizarding match with her instrument. She powers through the speed bumps and potholes of a technically murderous Kodály sonata with determination unlike anything I've ever witnessed before. It's perfectly glorious.

The fireworks are over by 5:30. When Lovely finishes, the captain takes his place by her side. "Now you understand, ladies and gentlemen, why I have all but given up playing the cello. Lovely has tried her best to teach me how to do that, but, alas, I am hopeless."

I'm astonished by how polished this captain is, how improbable this concert has been. I would not have expected to encounter a renaissance man at the helm of a lumbering container ship in the South China Sea. This is the same man I saw for the first time whistling through his fingers, bossing around stevedores on the docks of Yokohama.

"I hope our guests and those of you whose duty schedule permits will enjoy some refreshment," the captain says. Many of you already know Lovely, and I invite the rest of you to get acquainted. But don't say anything that will go to her head." He grins.

"Dad!" she says. "Don't you have work to do?"

"Alas, yes. I need to get back to the bridge. You all know there is a nasty storm brewing to our northeast. We will avoid the worst of it by swinging farther southwest than normal for our crossing to Haiphong, so don't worry. Enjoy."

A sailor rearranges the chairs around the bulkheads while the cook and messman uncover a splendid champagne buffet. Lagac guides Lovely to the table and coaxes a glass into her hand. He's beaming, and she gives him a peck on the cheek. His demeanor places the assembled sailors on notice: "Mess with Lovely Bayani and you deal with me." A more effective protector than Lagac would be hard to imagine.

An hour passes quickly. The crew is smitten. Lovely has come of age in the company of some of these men. They cluster about her, reminiscing about memorable times with a small, never shy, bundle of mischievous energy. They toast a glorious future. They adore her.

Lovely exchanges countless affectionate hugs and kisses with her admirers. She and I have made fleeting eye contact several times during the afternoon. At first I wonder if I'm imagining things, but it's clear after the second or third time that a connection is blossoming between us.

I watch as she fingers the talisman at her neck, receiving her admirers. Her eyes meet mine again and say, "Rescue me."

I insinuate myself into the gathering and offer my hand. "Jessamyn Quilter," I say. "I'm still trying to convince myself your recital was not a mirage. Your playing, your gown, everything about you is incomparably beautiful."

"Dr. Quilter. I'm so pleased to meet you. My father has spoken of no one else since I came aboard. 'You must meet Dr. Quilter. You will adore Dr. Quilter,'" she says, laughing. "Lagac says so too and he is always right."

He grins and rolls his eyes.

"Well," she says, "you are!"

Is he blushing? How delightful. I catch his eye and smile, making a mental note to work on my flirting skills.

73

"Adoration is my privilege," I say, steering Lovely away from the others. "I have experienced few events so exhilarating as your recital."

Lagac smiles and hands me a glass of champagne. Our eyes lock and hold a titillating conversation before he nods to the others, intimating it's time for them to get back to work. The sky is darkening. They disperse but not before filling their plates and glasses again.

By seven o'clock, Lovely and I are alone in the saloon. Lagac has closed the door softly behind him.

"I seldom find myself at a loss for words, and I hope that won't be my fate now," I say, "but I feel like a mindless groupie. I think you might be as much a devotee of Yuja Wang as I am? How do you, and she, manage the pedals in those heels?"

She giggles. "I met her once. She says everyone asks her the same question. She's just the greatest pianist who ever lived. Well, maybe, besides Khatia Buniatishvili, who's divine but so serious. Yuja Wang is perfectly glamorous. She could pedal wearing stilts. I think I channel her when I'm playing. Did you notice? I toss my head and throw my arms out, like her, after a particular *bravura* like the Chopin," Lovely says, demonstrating. "I can't seem to stop myself."

"I hope you don't try. For all your musical brilliance, the total package just says, 'Worship me, for I am far greater than you can ever imagine.'"

We laugh together like a couple of schoolgirls. "My dad says I was always a show-off, and he hopes one day I will grow into it. Do you play, Dr. Quilter?"

I tell her about my visits with Aunty G and how she and I would concertize for Uncle George on the million-dollar Bösendorfer twins. No sooner have I told her about "Heart and Soul" than she takes my hand and drags me to the piano. We sit jammed next to each other, each with one buttock off a bench designed for a single bottom.

"I love 'Heart and Soul,'" she says.

I resist only a little. After all, how can I pass up the opportunity to play with this captivating young woman who I know will one day be as famous as Yuja Wang.

I'm in for a surprise. It doesn't satisfy her just to play the chords. She turns "Heart and Soul" into a master class on theme and variation. A scene from the movie *Amadeus* flashes through my mind, the one where Mozart humiliates Salieri in front of the Emperor, transforming a plodding, workmanlike, birthday march into a sparking gem.

"You left me in the dust," I say.

"No," she insists. "You are the all-important foundation. Nothing sounds good without a rock-solid foundation, right?

"You know this racist composition?" she asks, playing the two-finger version of "Chopsticks." "We'll call it 'Flatware' instead of 'Chopsticks.' More PC. Here. I'll stand behind you because I need more room at the table. You be the knife and spoon playing the theme with two fingers.

"I'll be the forks. We'll have ten of them on the table today. Ready, Go."

We are stupendous. When she runs out of space for her hands in the bass octaves, she reaches around me and plays in the treble octaves. She only leaves me the real estate around middle C. Aunty G would have been both jealous and proud of me.

"You're not bad at this," I joke. "Maybe we had more forks on the table than we needed, but the knife and spoon were quintessential implements."

"The knife and spoon were brilliant, and you can never have too many forks. Come to my cabin with me, Dr. Quilter," she says, leading me by the hand again. "I need to get out of this gown and these stripper shoes."

I'm surprised how much I enjoy being bossed around by this child. "Okay. But only if you agree to call me Jessamyn. I'll be happy to be your lady-in-waiting."

The sun has set. It's going on eight o'clock when we walk across the alley from the saloon to her cabin, the one the Agarwals occupied. "Dad says he planned to put me in one of the spare officers' cabins, but this one became available after some passengers left the ship in Manila. I'm sure this cabin is much nicer."

This isn't the time to tell her about the Agarwals, but I'm certain the news will soon escape the moratorium the captain has placed on it. I don't know what I'll tell her when it does. But if anyone can exorcise any lingering evil or sorrow in this room, it's Lovely Diwata Aquinas y Bayani.

She kicks off her shoes and turns her back. "Help me with the zipper?"

She wears no bra and steps out of her dress and peels down her lilac thong with no hint of self-consciousness. I am no stranger to unclothed bodies, but my gaze is not in the least clinical as she hangs up her gown and puts her shoes in the closet. She has a fascinating tattoo at the base of her spine. I've seen nothing like it, but I don't indulge myself and ask.

"I need a shower," she says, looking over her shoulder. "Will you excuse me for a couple of minutes?"

"Of course. I should get back to my cabin and let you relax. Performing like that is exhausting."

"Oh, no. I don't mean that," she says, turning around to face me. She looks disappointed I would even suggest leaving. "Can you stick around? I'll only be a couple of minutes."

"Of course. Neither of us is going anywhere without the other anyhow, unless you can walk on water, which somehow, I don't doubt."

She smiles and disappears into the head, pausing to put her thong in the hamper. I hear her turn on the shower as I wait in a chair beside her bed.

It's impossible to take my mind off the fact we're in the same cabin where Mr. Agarwal beat his wife nearly to death. I've not been here before. It's unnerving. I still can't fathom how Mrs. Agarwal could believe her husband's lethal blows were for her own good, that he was "correcting" her. Or how he could believe that either. But abusers are like that, somehow making you feel you deserve being abused.

True to her word, Lovely stays in the shower only a few minutes. She emerges dripping, toweling her hair, her eyes smiling. Facing me, she bends down to dry her feet. Her breasts don't descend a millimeter. They are about the same size as mine, from the looks of things, neither large nor small, although mine are heading inexorably south. Was my body ever that full of promise, that lush and youthful?

She puts one foot on the bed to better dry herself. There's no hair on her vulva or anywhere else on her body so far as I can see, and I can see pretty much everything. She catches me looking and pats her pubis. "Brazilian wax." She laughs. "Do you like it?"

I do.

"Hurts like hell but worth every second. When I was a little girl, I couldn't wait for my pubes to come in. When they did, I couldn't wait to get rid of them." Her giggling is infectious. She sounds like a ten-year-old and has about as many boundaries. She seems completely comfortable standing here nude, finishing her shower as if we were sisters or old friends.

"I think you are braver than I am," I say. It's all I can think to say. How do you carry on a conversation about pubic grooming with a naked young woman you just met?

Her lithe body is as powerful as it is beautiful. The workout she gives the keyboard every day has been returned in spades to her arms and shoulders. They are solid muscle.

She pulls on a long, loose-fitting pink t-shirt from her closet that comes to mid-thigh. A red lip print on the front, accompanied a slogan in white script reads, "*Halikan mo ako. Pilipina ako.*"

"Kiss me. I'm Filipina," I guess.

"You get an A+ in Tagalog and performing piano duos." She smiles. She props herself up on the bed against her pillows.

I ask her if she's hungry, but the buffet has satisfied us both. No need to make a trip to the mess this evening.

Throughout it all she has not removed the *agimat*. What makes it so special? I promise myself to ask about it when we get to know each other a little better.

I'm also dying to ask about that tattoo across her lower back. I've seen tattoos in that location on some of my patients. The nurses call them "tramp stamps." Patty Landner has one, albeit not as prominent.

It clearly didn't come from one of the slick tattoo parlors in Manila. The black line drawing, a little crude, like a gang or prison tattoo, looks like a stick figure of a bird about to take flight.

Lovely grows quiet. Her eyelids droop and she jerks herself awake, apologizing. "I'm sorry, Dr. Quil...uh, Jessamyn. I guess I didn't realize how tired I am. It's been so much fun being with you. The entire afternoon was wonderful. I'll wake up. I want to talk more. I don't want today to end."

"You're beyond tired, Lovely. It's nearly nine. Here, let's get you under the covers. We've got a lot more ocean to cross before you get off in Le Havre. Plenty of time to talk. You were astonishing this afternoon."

She's asleep almost before I finish tucking her in, so childlike lying there, this powerful, gifted young woman who has the world by the throat and will force it to do her bidding if necessary. I bend down, kiss her forehead, and turn out the lights.

Back in my cabin, I step out on my deck. The freedom of my life right now feels intoxicating as I breathe in the warm, humid air. The moon is up, doing its best to light up the water, but insistent clouds remind that the typhoon is out there.

It seems like too much effort to read or write this evening. Instead I'll savor memories of this incredible day and the indomitable Lovely Bayani. I dog the door, peel off my clothes, wash my face, and tumble into bed. I doubt the dreamcats will come tonight. There's just no room in my head for them.

I doze off, not worrying too much about Typhoon Kaala, or anything else. I'm right. The dreamcats apparently have business elsewhere. The *maneki-neko* beckons, keeping watch over my dreamless slumber. ■

11

Typhoon

ABOARD MV ANDAMAN PEARL   *July 9*

I haven't seen Lovely this morning, following her *tour de force* yesterday. No doubt I'll run into her sometime later in the day. About noon, I hear her practicing in the saloon. Who would have guessed this jaunt would include world-class live music?

And who would have thought that musicians of Lovely's caliber still practice scales religiously? She makes them sound easy, even musical. It secretly delights me when she clips a note and starts swearing. My delight turns to laughter when she slaps the top of the piano and yells something unintelligible in frustration.

I had hoped to run into Lagac today, but he's undoubtedly busy in the engine room. I admit it. My horny tank is full. Lovely Bayani and Lagac on the same ship? How did that happen? My fantasy life is boiling over.

I try to chase the thought from my mind that neither of them will be interested in a middle-aged woman. Not that I'm unhappy about the way I look. I don't obsess about the wrinkles encroaching on my eyes, the extra couple of pounds on my tummy, or the increasing downhill slope of my breasts.

Still, I'm certain a *jinni* won't fall in love with me when I stand naked in front of a mirror unless he's a very old *jinni*. As for Lovely or Lagac, who knows. The voyage is still young.

The captain sent word via the messman earlier this afternoon that the ship's weather radar shows dicey conditions ahead. Ninoy's at my door again now. It will be better, he says, if passengers don't go anywhere on the ship they don't have to since the winds are picking up.

He checks the "dog" on the door to my outside deck, locking it, sealing the cabin against the sea. He cautions me against opening the door or going outside the accommodation at all until the captain gives the "all clear."

"Guests will need to fend for themselves as much as possible for the next day or two since the storm will keep the crew busy," he says. "Nothing to worry about. Just fair warning. If you get into trouble, call up to the bridge and someone will help."

I feel the butterflies return. The typhoon seems more real now, more threatening.

"Come on down to the mess while it's still relatively smooth and pick up some food to tide you over while we're riding this out," he says. "The messes will stay open because everyone needs to eat, and the crew is used to getting around in foul weather. If you must leave your cabin, be extra careful in the alleys and on the ladders.

"Don't forget to secure everything in the head and anything you have on the counters in your galley. We don't want things flying around your cabin. Until we're on the other side of the storm, just put everything in your drawers and cabinets. The latches are designed to hold in rough seas."

He's serious. This is not going to be the walk in the park I thought when the captain downplayed the seriousness of the storm at the end of Lovely's recital.

"Oh, and don't worry about anything," he says, reading my mind. "The captain is the best officer I've ever sailed with. He has everything under control."

I thank him and pop across the alley to check on Lovely.

"Jessamyn. Come in," she says with a big smile.

80

"Just wondering if you need anything. Did the messman give you the 'batten down the hatches' drill?"

"Yes. He's so sweet. Lagac stopped by too. And so did Shun. He and Shantrelle seem like such nice people. They said I can stay with them in their cabin if I get lonely being by myself."

"Good. You're welcome in my cabin any time too. Want to go to the mess and pick up some of those goodies the messman thinks we might need while we're being knocked about our cabins?"

"Sure. I was going to fetch the cello to keep it safe in my cabin, but my dad was way ahead of me.

"No practicing until we reach smoother water," he said. "He's locked the cello up in his cabin, padded the piano, and bolted it down."

"Your father thinks of everything. We're fortunate to be sailing with him."

The cook and the messman are ready for us when we get to the officers' mess. They have packed plastic hampers with sandwiches, cheese, fruit, and of course, *palitaw*—sweet, sticky coconut, sesame seed, sugar-coated rice flour treats.

"Come back for refills any time it's safe to be in the alleys," the messman says. "Eat the *palitaw* right now. *Palitaw* makes it a party." He laughs. "Nobody can resist *palitaw*, they're so yummy. Here. Take a couple more. No sense trying to save *palitaw* for later. And don't worry. We'll all be fine."

Lovely and I return to our cabins laden with enough food to last a week. She's taking the messman at his word, eating *palitaw* as we go. I wipe some stray sugar from her chin as I walk her to her cabin. I have a quick look around to assure myself she's secured everything and tell her to let me know if she needs anything. I go to my cabin and settle in for a nap.

When I wake up late afternoon, the world outside my portholes has changed dramatically. It's much too dark for this time of day.

The West Philippine Sea, or South China Sea, whatever you want to call it, seems pissed off at us and the wind is talking smack. The ocean is treating us like a mosquito crawling on its skin to be slapped at and blown away. It's throwing twenty-foot waves at the *Andaman Pearl*, crashing over the tops of containers stacked four high on her bow. Ships lose containers, and perhaps lives, in conditions like these.

I watched the crew going over the container stacks before we left Manila, making sure the lashings were tight. I have faith they understood what they might be up against, making certain the typhoon would pitch none of our containers into the sea.

Captain Bayani had been cautious but did not appear to be worried earlier today. "'A smooth sea never made a skillful sailor.' That's what your great President Franklin Delano Roosevelt said, and we've been through rougher weather than this on the *Andaman Pearl*."

The second officer rings me up to check in. He says the weather is much worse elsewhere. To our north, as Typhoon Kaala picks up fury and threatens to turn Hong Kong into an underwater theme park, sustained winds exceed 100 miles per hour. She's expected to turn even uglier, perhaps with winds over 140 miles per hour, which would qualify her as a Super Typhoon, the worst of the worst.

"Just sit tight in your cabin for a few hours and don't go outside until things are smoother," he says. "Call me if you're in trouble."

He needn't worry. I'm not going anywhere. I think about insisting Lovely join me in my cabin until we're free of the storm, but I decide against it. She's a big girl who can take care of herself. Besides, her daddy's driving the ship and he'll certainly look after her.

My cabin has a few engineering instruments on the wall. I guess the original owners were control freaks who wanted to monitor as much of the ship as possible for themselves. The clinometer confirms what I'm seeing outside. We're rolling a full forty degrees from flat under the onslaught of these waves. Back and forth. Back and forth again.

I'm stretched out on one of the couches, wedging myself in with pillows. Outside my portholes, the sea slams into the side of the ship. When we roll to starboard, I see torrents flooding the decks and containers. When we roll to port, all I can see is rain and dark sky. For a brief interval in the middle, we're flat enough to see black, furious water relentlessly attempting to swallow us. It's raining too heavily now to make out the ship's bow. The containers sway but seem secure as water sloshes over and around them.

It's beyond me how the cook and messman manage in these conditions. Preparing food is a heroic undertaking with the ship determined to flip over. Frying and boiling are out of the question since it's impossible to keep liquids from sloshing out of the pots. Still, there's plenty to eat if, like the men trying to keep the ship upright in the water during the storm, you're hungry. The thought of having food in my stomach as we roll merrily along is ludicrous. I can't imagine eating any of the wonderful things the cook and the messman packed for my cabin. Not even my ration of *palitaw*.

For the most part, I feel okay. Rationally, I know I'm not going to die. But there are intrusive flashes of panic accompanied by the realization of how insignificant I am on this floating metal toy. Alone, savaged by wind and water, we're unwelcome intruders in Neptune's realm.

The helplessness I felt in the dreams I once told my shit-for-brains analyst about seems completely rational now. Nothing symbolic here. No *petite mort*. Just wet, crushing, suffocating, bone-snapping, life-sucking annihilation.

To make things worse, we've lost the light. Darkness almost always makes things worse. The panics come more frequently.

Get a grip, Jessamyn. Stop scaring yourself like a child at summer camp. As the captain said, he's sailed through worse on this ship.

I abandon the couch, take off my clothes, and lurch into the head to get ready for bed. Brushing my teeth with one hand and holding onto the safety bar with the other is manageable, and I get the toothbrush and toothpaste back into a latched drawer when I've finished. Peeing is an unwelcome adventure, but there are no serious mishaps.

One benefit of the Owner's cabin is the California king bed. Plenty of room to roll around without getting thrown out.

I down a Dramamine but decide against a Valium. If the worst happens, I want to be awake. I check the door and assure myself my life jacket is on its assigned hook. I leave a light on in the head and literally fall into bed.

The Dramamine makes me drowsy, and I hold on to the hope that by morning the typhoon will be farther north and we'll be in smoother water to the south, perhaps a day or so from dry land.

***

I don't know how long I've been dozing when an insistent pounding on my door wakes me up.

"Dr. Quilter, Jessamyn! Are you in there? It's Lovely Bayani. Dr. Quilter? Please, if you are there, I need to talk with you."

The pounding continues. My brain fog lifts and I pull on my nightgown. "Lovely? Just a minute, dear. I'm coming."

Lovely, wearing her "Kiss me" t-shirt, is struggling to maintain her balance in the alley, tears in her eyes, shaking uncontrollably. I grab her hand, pull her into my cabin, and hold on to her while I dog the door. A sudden shift of the ship reminds me we're still in very rough seas. Lovely slams into me, and both of us nearly fall to the floor.

"Oh. Dr. Quilter. I'm sorry. I'm sorry. I'm so scared."

"Lovely, what's wrong? Come. Let's get into bed." At least we won't be rolling around on the floor.

"I'm so scared." She sobs and clutches her talisman with both hands. "We're going to die, I know it. My mother told me not to come on this ship. Her friend dreamed I would die and go to hell if I came on this trip."

"We're just in a patch of rough water, Lovely. Your father's a superb captain who's sailed this ship through worse."

She's nestled into my shoulder, her hands and feet icy against my body. She's shaking violently.

"Sh-sh, deep breaths. Sh-sh-sh. Calm down now." I pull her more tightly into me and stroke her head. "Nobody is going to die or go to hell tonight. We'll all be just fine."

The floodgates open, and she drenches my neck with tears. I hold her against me, trying to soothe her as she sobs.

"Here," I say, offering her a sip from a bottle of water I have stashed in the drawer of my nightstand. The boat pitches hard to starboard and half the bottle drenches her t-shirt.

"I can't go back to my cabin. I'm afraid to be alone," she says, sobbing. "There are ghosts in there."

Can she feel the violence of the Agarwals? I'll have to tell her as soon as the captain allows it, tomorrow when the weather settles down.

"No problem. You can stay with me. Let's just call up to the bridge so your father knows you're here. If he calls or sends someone down to your cabin to check on you, he'll be sick with worry."

She nods.

"Let's take this wet thing off and get you warmed up." I pull the soaked t-shirt over her head and toss it onto the nightstand.

Before I can tuck her in, she bolts for the head. "I feel sick," she says, falling to her knees, hugging the toilet. I follow and steady her between my knees, holding her head with one hand, hanging on to a grab bar by the toilet with the other as she retches.

When she finishes, I wash her face, grab one of my t-shirts for her, and give her a ginger lozenge to help with the nausea. I encourage her to swallow a Dramamine I hope will help her sleep, and get her back into bed, propped up against the bulkhead under the covers. I pick up the phone, which thankfully has been secured to one of the nightstands, crawl in beside her, and call the bridge.

"She's okay," I tell the captain. "I just wanted you to know she's with me, so you won't worry about her.

"No. No bother at all. Yes. I'm fine. We're both fine. Don't worry. We'll see you in the morning, Captain."

Lovely backs into me. She's clammy and her teeth are chattering. I feel her heart pounding as I pull her into my body.

I wonder briefly about Shun and Shantrelle, how they're holding up against this onslaught. I'm sure they're fine, having gotten the same warnings and gone through the same preparations I did. I picture them hanging onto each other, rolling around together in their bed.

The ship continues to lurch. While I'm less frightened than Lovely, I admit having her next to me is reassuring. I look over at the nightstand, at the *maneki-neko*, calmly smiling, beckoning. I forgot to move it into a drawer for safekeeping, but it's unperturbed. Trust a cat to keep its balance when the world's going bonkers.

I close my eyes and strive to match the rhythm of Lovely's breathing, her warming body spooning into mine like my deceased husband's never did. I can't resist the urge to kiss her temple as I smooth the hair from her face.

Bodies together in bed should be just like this. Treasured, tightly held. Lovely's already asleep and I'm close.

Blow, winds, and crack your cheeks, rage, blow.

Crack nature's moulds, an germens spill at once.

Shakespeare notwithstanding, the chaos outside can't get in here. Not into my bed. ∎

12

Agimat

MABOARD MV ANDAMAN PEARL *July 10*

orning brings smooth seas and sunlight streaming through the portholes. I untangle myself from Lovely, who doesn't budge, splash cool water on my face and brush my teeth. I throw a robe over my nightgown and look around the cabin. Miraculously, nothing seems out of place save for a couple of sofa cushions.

I make a pot of Lady Grey tea, leave it on the counter to steep, and return to the bed, sitting in the lounger at the foot. I look at my overnight guest, the previously unflappable young woman who has sought sanctuary in my cabin.

Lovely has kicked off the covers and is lying flat on her stomach, her left knee drawn up slightly, her hands clutching the pillow in which she has buried her face. The t-shirt I gave her last night has ridden up and covers little.

I'm of two minds about the propriety of watching her lying there, but ultimately, I can't look away. I allow myself to study the tattoo on her lower back. It's coal black, as if someone used ink made from a raven's feathers. What I take to be a pair of abstract wings lines the crest of her pelvis, a bold semicircle sprouting six pairs of short, stylized feathers. At the center of the line, a squatty downward-pointing arrow anchors the tattoo over her tailbone, dipping into the crease between her buttocks.

Between the wings, across her spine, three closely spaced black dots march in a horizontal row. It appears the tattoo artist has attempted to place them symmetrically, but they're slightly off-kilter, imprecise, surging with primitive energy. I could speculate, but in the end, I'll simply have to ask her about the tattoo.

I fetch a cup of tea and return to the chair. Lovely has rolled over on her back, still sleeping. Her body is a symphony of form and color. Both her shape and coloring put me in mind of Captain Bayani's exquisite cello.

She is breathtaking. I have seen many bodies in my career, but I have never looked at any of them as I am now looking at Lovely. I'm not perving, but it would be inaccurate to say I feel nothing.

To physicians, bodies are a collection of parts, regions, and problem spots. My husband's body was never interesting to me. Even Pyotr's classically sculpted body, or the bodies of other people I have slept with, have not called to me as Lovely's does. "Drink your fill," it seems to say.

My better angel says, "Look away." The one whispering into my other ear has hijacked my eyes.

The more I look, the more aroused I become. I'm conflicted. Am I even allowed to have such feelings for her? Whatever the answer to that question, I want this moment to go on forever.

Alas, it ends all too soon. Lovely stirs, opens her eyes, and stretches, propping up on a pillow.

"Good morning," I say.

"Jessamyn. Hi. Good morning," she says, smiling and rubbing her eyes. "My god, we're still alive, just like you said."

"Your father is a terrific sailor. I didn't really doubt he'd pull us through," I say, taking another sip of tea. The alternative is too scary to contemplate. "Are you hungry? Would you like some tea? Toast?"

"That would be wonderful," she says.

Lovely uses the head as I fetch a second cup of tea for myself, another cup and a bite of breakfast for her. She makes herself at home in the bed again, not bothering to cover herself with the sheet. The scrunched up t-shirt I gave her last night covers her breasts but nothing else. There's a profound innocence about her, coupled with a sense she is deliberately being provocative. Can these two things go together?

"Would you like a gown or your own t-shirt?" I offer. "I think it's probably dry by now."

"Do you mind if I don't put my clothes on just yet?" she asks.

Of course, I don't.

"I have this thing about clothes," she says, pulling the t-shirt off and tossing it on the bed. "I love to get all pimped out for my recitals or to go clubbing, but the rest of the time, I'm happier not wearing anything unless they would throw me in jail if I didn't."

"You're violating no penal code here. How do you feel after all that bouncing around last night?"

"I'm groggy, thanks to your sorcery, but so relieved we're not dead. The tea will clear my head.

"We can call up to the bridge if you like. Your father might like to hear from you if he's awake. I imagine they had a rough night while we lazed about here in bed."

Her amusement at my comment is genuine. "Any idea where we are?"

"I'm sure we're somewhere between the Philippines and Vietnam. We'll be in Haiphong in a day or two. That's the beauty about being on a ship. Without having to lift a finger, we just arrive at exotic places, all in good time."

She catches me staring at the amulet at her throat. "You like the *agimat*?" she asks, fingering it.

"I've been curious about it since the recital. I saw something like it at a vendor's stand in Quiapo but nothing that exquisite. And speaking of curious, what's the story with your tattoo. I hope you'll forgive me for staring at you. I'm just a nosey old woman."

"I forgive you, nosey old woman. I like that you want to look at me. Your eyes are filled with love. It's easy for me to see love. Now you'll have to forgive me. I fall in love all the time, but you mustn't think I fall in love with just anyone I spend the night in bed with."

Electricity races up my spine. I don't know what to make of her declaration.

"I forgive you, although I don't have the slightest idea for what," I say. "It just feels like the right thing to do."

She takes another sip of her tea. "This is a little scary for me," she says, becoming serious. "I have many secrets."

I doubt your secrets would hold a candle to mine, child.

"If you really want to know about the *agimat* and the tattoo, you must understand I am as much a part of them as they are of me." She pauses. "I think both have been speaking to you. And to me since I met you."

"Lovely, we have all the time in the world, and I'm very interested, but really, I don't want to pry."

"You're not 'prying.' You wouldn't even have been able to ask if the *agimat* and the tattoo hadn't wanted you to know. They're magical. Still, it is risky. I am forbidden to talk about them, bound by an oath to my ancestors, except to someone they call a 'thirsty soul,' a 'quester.' They told me I would know such a soul if it came into my presence. It has never happened before. You are the first. I'm certain I am supposed to share my secrets with you."

"No really, Lovely. It's none of my business."

"I think it is your business, but if it isn't, I'll know in the telling and I will stop. And you will tell me if you do not want to hear more. We will not think each other rude if that happens, okay? If we become afraid to continue?" she asks.

I expected none of this. I nod and allow Lovely to take the lead.

"My family tree is full of witches, headhunters, and cannibals," Lovely begins matter-of-factly.

I'm surprised by this revelation but resolve to keep my reactions in check.

"The headhunting branch, my father's ancestors, are from the mountain valleys of the cordillera, the Kalinga province of northern Luzon Island. Officially, headhunting disappeared in the Philippines by 1970."

"Officially, 1970?"

"Yes, that recently. Officially. But of course, it hasn't disappeared at all. In the Philippines, officials know very little of what goes on outside the big cities. They don't want to know either. Young warriors of some of the more remote mountain tribes still take heads.

"My father's side of the family has its share of witches and sorcerers, as well as headhunters and cannibals, but most of the witches in the family come from my mother's family. She's a witch herself, you know."

Of course, I don't know. I have learned, though, that whenever I'm slack jawed, it's best to shut up rather than babble. This seems like a good time to follow my own excellent advice.

"The witches of my mother's ancestry are Visayan from Siquijor, one of the small islands of the central archipelago. Even today, they call Siquijor 'Witch Island.' Tourists go there looking for advice, healing, and sometimes, vengeance.

"When I was an infant, seven days after I was born, my mother took me to Siquijor to see my great-grandmother and her people. Great-grandmother Pilar was a powerful *mananambal,* a sorceress who could heal spiritual or physical illnesses and counter the spells of black witchcraft.

"She took me to the summit of Mt. Bandila-an on the night of the full moon and held me aloft, a naked squalling infant, to announce my presence to the cosmos, charging the ancestral spirits to protect me from harm and evil."

All this stuff about witches and cannibals strikes me as a little nutty, but Lovely seems as sincere as Hamza Baraquilla had been when he told me about the *jinn.*

"Mother says that's why I want to run around naked all the time. 'The ancestral spirits clothed you with protection and must have decided

91

that was clothing enough,' she said. She could never keep clothes on me as a little girl and soon gave up trying. My father just laughed as I ran around bare butt and called me a pill. He was away most of the time, so it really didn't matter with just mother and me."

Lovely turned somber.

"There are also *mangkukulam* in my mother's family tree, witches who use black magic to harm or even kill someone. Mother says my great-aunt Carmelota was *mangkukulam*. She had a rice bag with the skull of one of her enemies stuffed with photographs and scraps of paper bearing the names of people she cursed. My grandmother Concepción swears she saw it when she was a little girl."

Lovely paused as if summoning forth courage to continue her story.

"I got my first period on my eleventh birthday while my father was at sea. Mother summoned Great-grandmother Pilar and Grandmother Concepción to Manila, and the four of us traveled to the village of Buscalan, in the northern Kalinga province, to consult with Great-grandmother Ilyang, herself a powerful sorceress. Her husband, Great-grandfather Banoy, took heads, like his father and grandfather before him. He's dead now, but the heads he took lived in niches over the entrance to Great-grandmother Ilyang's hut."

The way Lovely tells the story, it's almost possible to picture the hut with its grinning skulls.

"We spent the next few weeks in Kalinga. The women schooled me in the ancient ways. We gathered herbs together, and I learned about ceremonies, spirits, and spells. Then my second period arrived.

"The women took me to an old *mambabatok,* one of the few remaining women who practiced the art of tattooing by tapping a wicked-looking pomelo thorn dipped in ink into my skin."

Lovely gets out of bed and stands with her back to me.

"The tattoo is the sacred 'serpent eagle.' My mother says the *mambabatok* took an entire morning to complete her work, dipping the thorn into ink made from pine soot and water, tapping it into my skin with a stick, chanting all the while. I do not remember the process, although I am told I cried out every time the thorn pierced me."

I want to trace the tattoo with my fingers as Lovely stands with her back to me, but I hold back.

"Great-grandmother Ilyang cast a spell so I would hallucinate the serpent eagle as the tattooist worked. I saw the eagle in my mind as it took shape, flapping his wings and piercing me with his talons, screaming as the *mambabatok* went about her work. My cries were not cries of pain, but the screams of eagles."

All this talk of thorns and talons piercing Lovely's tender flesh sets my teeth on edge. How could they do that to a child?

"The serpent eagle signifies heavenly guidance and protection, as well as courage. I don't know for sure, but I think the *mambabatok* was the National Living Treasure Apo Whang-Od. She signs her work with three dots like the one on my tattoo. She's over a hundred years old now.

"Go ahead," Lovely says, looking over one shoulder with an impish grin. "You can touch it."

I can't resist tracing the outstretched wings along the crest of her pelvis from one side to the other and then tracing the arrow until it dips into the cleft of her bottom. The simple act of touching a fingertip to another's skin has never felt so electric.

"It makes your fingers tingle, right?" Lovely says. "I can feel it when you touch it too. When I touch it in the shower, my fingers get zapped like the shocks you get shuffling across a carpet. If I touch it in the dark, and my mind is open, I can see them—red and gold flickers like a sparkler, but if I look too hard, they're not there anymore. Sometimes it's so intense I lose myself."

I want to pull my fingers back but I can't. I'm not imagining the little jolts I'm feeling.

"It's a good thing they placed the tattoo low enough that it doesn't interfere with those backless concert gowns I rock," Lovely says, turning around to face me with a grin. She stands there for a moment, her pubis scant inches from my face. She sweeps a stray lock of my hair from my forehead as I look up into her eyes. I breathe a little easier when she moves back to the bed to continue her story.

"I know I should tell you the complete story," she says, hanging her head a little. "I'm leaving out one or two things I'll tell you about later."

Is she embarrassed about what she feels, touching the tattoo in the shower? I can guess, of course, what else she is touching, and while I wouldn't be shocked to hear about it, her childlike reticence is delightful. If you can imagine using the words "reticence" and "Lovely" in the same sentence.

"When other people ask, I tell them it's a tribal tattoo, and I was only a child when I got it so I don't know if it means anything or not. I tell them I don't remember ever not having it. But of course, I do. A few other people have touched it, but I don't let them feel the sparks, like I let you."

"You can control that?"

"Yes. Mother says I shouldn't let anyone touch it, especially boys, because it's private," she says, the grin returning to her face.

"What does your father think of all that business with your relatives?" I ask.

"Mother said I didn't have to show the tattoo to my father or explain anything about the visit to Kalinga, but I don't like keeping secrets from him. I don't know how I could hide it anyhow unless I started wearing more clothes. He was happy the women had taken me into their circle and thanked me for telling him."

"'They are wise and powerful women,' he said. 'They love you immensely, perhaps even as much as I do.' He promised he would always be in my corner, and he always has been, even when I've been a little brat. Nobody loves me more than my father loves me."

Lovely pauses again, as if contemplating whether she has told me enough. Or perhaps too much. She decides on the former. She hasn't finished her story yet.

"Before we left Kalinga, while the tattoo was healing, Great-grandmother Ilyang told me the story of Father Ignacio de Jesús and the *agimat*. Father Ignacio was the last Catholic priest in the northern provinces before the Spanish were driven from the islands in 1898.

"The Spanish never subdued the northern tribes as they did in the south. There, the Catholic church persecuted the *mananambal* and forced little boys to poop on the remains of indigenous religious symbols the priests destroyed. The tribes in the north didn't trust the priests, but they tolerated them if they behaved themselves. Father Ignacio couldn't manage that."

Oh no, I think. Not another priest abuse story.

"He was drunk most of the time and preyed upon the tribal children and adolescents. He raped and murdered a young girl named Diwata, promised in marriage to Datu, the strongest warrior in the tribe.

"Father Ignacio fled for his life, but Datu hunted him down and dragged him back to the village, hobbled hand and foot, a rope around his neck. Then he cut off his head, raised it on a pike in the center of the village, and left his body to the women."

Lovely leaves no detail unspoken.

"They gutted him, made a stew of his innards for everyone in the tribe to eat, and hacked his body to pieces to feed to the pigs. But first they cut off his pizzle and gave it to Diwata's mother. She smoked it over a fire and hung it over the doorway of their hut to dry in the sun until it shriveled to the size of a hyacinth bean pod.

"Datu asked Diwata's mother, a *mananambal,* and her husband, an accomplished metalsmith, to make an *agimat* for his next intended wife, also named Diwata.

I stare at the triangular *agimat* hanging at Lovely's breasts as she fingers it, continuing her story.

"Diwata's mother knocked the teeth from the priest's skull and smashed them to bits. Her husband took the fillings, added them to the metal from the priest's pectoral cross, and made this *agimat*.

95

"It's hollow. Before they sealed it up, she put shards of broken teeth, some sacred herbs, and pieces of the priest's dried up pizzle inside.

"Her mother placed the *agimat* around Diwata's neck, warning her it must only be removed at her death by another *mananambal* who would choose a worthy successor who must also be named Diwata. The *mananambal* who removed the *agimat* when Diwata died was Great-grandmother Ilyang. She passed it on to the next Diwata, me."

An extraordinary story, I think. I wonder how much of it's true.

"I've never taken it off, nor have I given my father the details. I would tell him if he asked, but I think it would only upset him, good Catholic that he is."

Lovely lifts the *agimat* and gives it a shake. "See? It rattles. Priest's teeth and pizzle pieces." She grins.

She crawls across bed toward me on all fours.

"Here. Have a closer look. Great-grandmother Ilyang warned that anyone who touches it will die instantly if they are not a thirsty soul. Since you are a thirsty soul, you can touch it, no worries."

I don't know what to make of all this. Of course I don't believe in all the witchcraft and hocus-pocus Lovely is regaling me with, but I think she does, at least the essence of it.

While I want to touch the *agimat*, scrutinize it more closely, the vision of Lovely approaching me on her hands and knees like some exotic cat with a bell around her neck, begging to be petted, is unnerving. She settles on the bed, facing me, her legs hanging off the end, and takes my hand, guiding it to the *agimat*.

"I've never believed it was all that powerful." She laughs. "Some of my friends have touched it, and nobody has died. But I've never told anyone except you the whole story about the tattoo and the *agimat*."

I let go of the charm. Letting go of Lovely is proving to be more difficult. But I make the effort.

"I'm starving," I say. "Let's go down to the mess and show our faces so everyone knows we're alive and kicking."

I fetch Lovely's now dry t-shirt and hand it to her. "Why don't you scoot across to your cabin and get dressed. I'll pick you up there in, say, fifteen minutes? Call your father and check in."

Lovely screws her face into an exaggerated pout, piling out of the bed. "Well, if you're enforcing a dress code, I guess I'll have to be a good girl and behave myself. But I warn you, Dr. Jessamyn Quilter, I'm not through with you. Not by a long shot."

Then, standing on tiptoe, she surprises me with a kiss full on the mouth. I must have flinched.

"Did I just do a bad thing?" she asks, pulling back, her eyes moistening.

"No," I say. "It was a Lovely thing. Come here." I draw her close, kissing her forehead. She lifts her face and looks into my eyes, and I'm powerless to resist the urge to kiss her mouth.

"Black magic?" I ask.

"Black magic doesn't work on *innocent* people." She smirks.

I turn her around, march her toward the door, and give her a playful swat on the bottom. "Scoot. See you in fifteen."

"Okay. Deal," she says, giggling as she runs out the door, across the alley to her own cabin. ■

13

War Wounds

I stand on the deck outside my cabin around noon as we berth in Haiphong Harbor. Captain Bayani has declared a twelve-hour shore leave for passengers and off-duty sailors.

I watch Lovely, Shun, and Shantrelle from my deck as they wait for the gangway to be lowered. Lovely has become close with Shun and Shantrelle the past couple of days. She speaks about them enthusiastically but has not told them her full story. She says perhaps in time, but she also wants to get to know them better before she reveals too much about herself. I don't know Shun and Shantrelle well either, but they seem like nice people. We're just getting started on our voyage. There's plenty of time to get to know each other better.

Lovely cups her hands to her mouth, shouting up to me. "Jessamyn. Come with?"

I wave and shake my head no. She'd invited me earlier, but I declined. The young people should go have fun. Their innocence will protect them from the hellscape we visited on the Vietnamese. I'm still raw after all these years from the apocalypse that swallowed up my half-brother and countless innocent souls in countries far removed from this port.

Lagac, who's not on duty now, joins me on my deck, tempting me into going ashore to get a good meal. I'll bet Lovely has put him up to this, and it's not working.

99

"Too bad," he says. "Haiphong is my favorite city for eating cat."

Cat? Had I heard him correctly? I had.

"Haiphong has many cat restaurants," he says. "If you change your mind, just look for the ones that say *'thit mèo,'* and have pictures of kittens on their awnings or windows." He seems barely able to contain his mirth.

"My favorite is the Yellow Cat Restaurant. I love to get a platter of their cat ribs, curry, and chopped cat barbecue with sesame. You wrap the juicy meat in greens and dip it in peanut sauce. So many good ways to enjoy cat. I'd ask Lovely to bring some back, but cat carryout isn't nearly as good as the fresh stuff."

Lagac is teasing me mercilessly, openly laughing at my discomfort. He seems unable to stop himself, and he's just warming up.

I play along. Lagac is not without a certain ability to charm me.

"And where do they find these cats, roaming the streets of Haiphong?"

"Oh no. Well, I mean, Fluffy could go missing I suppose, but they raise cats in the countryside for the restaurants. Even better, for a special treat more delicious than cat, come back in the fall. Then you can enjoy rats. They catch them during September and October, after they have fattened themselves all summer in the paddies. Serves them right, stealing all that rice.

I shudder.

"'Three squeaks' is a myth though, according to Snopes.com," he continues without missing a beat.

"Snopes.com? I'm impressed but I know I really shouldn't ask," I say. He adopts a *faux*-serious demeanor although he can't hide the twinkle in his eyes.

"*San Zhi Er.* Chinese for 'three squeaks.' Newborn mouse pups jostling about on your plate in a bed of fragrant leaves. When you pick one up with chopsticks, it's the first squeak. The second, when you dip the poor little thing in soy sauce. The third is when you chomp it down. Three squeaks." He chortles.

"Seriously, Lagac, do you actually enjoy eating cats and rats?"

"Me? No. I like pig." He laughs. "I think the cook plans to have a pig roast soon. It's one of my favorite things about sailing on this rusty tub."

He's still giggling as he hustles away. I have heard rumors about an impending pig roast on the main deck and I'm looking forward to it. If Lagac were to offer to accompany me ashore in Haiphong, I'm certain I would agree. And I would probably try the local delicacies if he dared me to, although I'm happy to hear "three squeaks" wouldn't be on the menu.

The queasiness I feel about venturing forth in Vietnam has nothing to do with local cuisine. The war still provokes feelings of rage and impotence in me. A much older half-brother I was too young to know well died in combat here.

I have never forgiven the wretched liars who insisted he serve his country in this meat grinder for their own political gain. Even now, from the safe distance of my private deck and decades of history, I feel like an unwitting witness to thirty years of rape and carnage.

I was grateful when the war was over. The slaughter had been appalling. Body counts. Civilian massacres. A naked nine-year-old Phan Thi Kim Phuc, running down the road, screaming in excruciating pain as her skin melted beneath sticky napalm. A little girl just like me. "Hey, hey, LBJ. How many kids did you kill today?"

No. Vietnam holds no appeal for me. The ghosts of the apocalypse menace as I look shoreward. I turn my back on Haiphong Harbor and retreat to my cabin.

I spent a good portion of yesterday thinking about my feelings for Lovely and the extraordinary circumstances that threw us together in a terror-filled ordeal two nights ago. I don't know what to make of her stories of sorceress and cannibal forebears. She has a presence that makes me want to believe she has supernatural powers, which of course is nonsense. I felt the sparks she described when I traced her tattoo with my fingers, faint tingling, but I probably just fell victim to her storytelling. Her body has been sending tingles down my spine for the past couple of days.

I'm still trying to sort out my feelings about her. I don't deny a growing bond with the captain's daughter. Trying to write about all of this has been fruitless. I sketched her tattoo and her *agimat* as best I could remember in my fancy journal. I also sketched what I imagine Great-aunt Carmelota's grisly skull looked like stuffed with photos and slips of paper. Maybe I'll show them to Lovely sometime.

* * *

I'm confused by my sexual feelings for Lovely, although I have long known some women arouse me. While she's technically an adult, she feels more like a child when I'm around her. I'll probably deny my impulses for that reason.

I wouldn't label myself bisexual, certainly not the "bull dyke" my disgusting late husband taunted me with, even though I fooled around with a couple of women in my undergraduate years. The first time, with a woman in my college cell biology study group, scared both of us into declaring our mutual straightness and drove us apart, though we had done little more than kiss and grope over our clothes. Not a button or zipper disturbed.

The second time didn't feel as weird. Elsa Hinterleitner, a beautiful Austrian exchange student, hit on me at a lesbian bar. We had been daring each other to have a drink at the "Alice B." for a few weeks, assuring ourselves we were righteous heterosexuals. We both had boyfriends we were sleeping with, gossiping about their shortcomings. We averred we had nothing against gay people but acknowledged being curious about what went on inside a lesbian bar.

What went on, we found, was women laughing, dancing, and occasionally kissing and cuddling. Nothing that scandalized or titillated either of us. Well past our third or fourth strawberry margaritas, sitting on adjacent barstools, Elsa reached behind me and rubbed my back.

It felt good, in no way threatening, so I returned the favor. She let her hand wander to my butt. I was too shy to reciprocate, but I didn't stop her. That, too, felt good. She leaned forward and whispered in my ear, "I think you're sexy, Ms. Straight Woman. Do you want to dance with me?"

Her smile could have eclipsed the sun and half a dozen of the lesser stars. We fast danced, really cut a rug, as Uncle George used to say, laughing as others laughed with us and egged us on. Then we slow danced, including some furtive kissing, testing the waters. Not kisses of unsullied innocence but of growing ardor.

"Let's go to your place, or to mine, if you'd rather," Elsa said. We ended up at hers. More kissing and fumbling. Eventually she said, "To hell with this. Let's get naked." She threw off her clothes and helped me follow suit.

It was wonderful. For the first time, I touched a woman's breasts other than my own or my mother's. My fingers explored the delicious wetness of her vulva, and hers found mine. She questioned my vagina with soft, increasingly insistent fingers. It thrilled me to follow her lead, answer her probing, since I didn't have a clue what I should be doing. She was obviously more experienced and planned the seduction well.

It felt different, so much better than when I touched myself. She clung to me as if nothing else in the world mattered.

"Do you like that" she asked? I nodded my head. "Do me," she said. Our passion built until we were both exhausted, awash with orgasmic energy.

"Do you love me?" she joked after we recovered. "Just asking for a friend."

I hesitated. We'd only known each other for a couple of months. I found her interesting, and she was pretty, but I'd never imagined having sex with her or any other woman. I was living with Pyotr, having sex with him, and it was confusing to realize sex with her could be incandescent as it occasionally was with him.

But love her? I wasn't *in* love with her. No question what we had just been doing together moved us beyond the platonic. I was about ready to tell her I did love her so as not to disappoint her, but she let me off the hook.

"That's okay," she said. "Not a fair question. Now, where were we?" We found our place and explored each other's bodies with our eyes and lips, our hands, and our skin. If there were any other way we could have touched we would have. Eventually we fell asleep in each other's arms, sated as milk-drunk infants. I felt debauched and innocent at the same time. I don't think I have ever come as close to bliss as I did that night.

The morning after was awkward. I felt embarrassed. I knew I wasn't gay. After all, I was having sex with Pyotr. Sex with him was usually pretty good. Different from sex with Elsa, and not as good if I were honest, but still fine. Didn't that make me straight?

I later understood I couldn't love Pyotr to the extent of committing my life to him. His addictions made that impossible. But I knew I wasn't "in love" with Elsa, and later I told her I didn't love her "in that way."

She shrugged it off.

"Too much thinking," she said. "I'm straight too, complete with a hot sex god for a boyfriend. But it's one hell of a ride you and I are on, and I think I love you. Not 'let's rent a U-Haul, move-in-together-settle-down-and-adopt kids' love you, but more than just buzz my joy button love you."

We both laughed, got dressed, and went about our days.

We had sex a few more times over the next week, never as intense as the first time, but still great. I no longer believed I was a four-square, full gospel heterosexual woman. Perhaps I am bi, but bi didn't exist in those days. Elsa was right. Too much thinking.

"Who cares?" she said, when I brought it up a couple of days later. "We're having a great time, and nobody's getting hurt, right? We *are* having a great time, aren't we?"

"Yes," I assured her. "We are."

"Good," she said. "Let's go back to my place. I have something else up my sleeve."

As usual our clothes came off in a flash, preparation for whatever Elsa had planned. We kissed deeply, something that always inflames me.

I tried to guide her hands between my legs, but she resisted, continuing to kiss me as she pushed me down on her bed.

"Lie there and close your eyes," she purred as she sat between my legs. "Let me recite some poetry I learned just for you."

Never before or since has anyone plied me with poetry. This was what was up her sleeve? Poetry?

"Ode to Anactoria," Elsa began. "By Sappho, poetess of ancient Lesbos."

> *Echoes ring in my ears; a trembling seizes*
> *All my body bathed in soft perspiration;*
> *Pale as grass I grow in my passion's madness*
> *Like one insensate.*

"Touch yourself," Elsa purred, moving closer. "I want to watch you do it."

The embarrassment was almost a deal-breaker, but my arousal overcame my reticence. Pyotr asked me to do this once, but I refused. He was easily distracted. So long as I jerked him off, everything was fine.

Elsa was different. She had prime viewing, seated between my outstretched legs, her hands resting lightly on my knees as I lay back on the pillows, eyes closed, and pleasured myself. When I peeked, she was watching me like a hungry hawk watches a rabbit.

"Open your eyes," she said. "Look at me." She began masturbating as she watched me touch myself.

"Is this wrong," I asked her, "for a couple of straight chicks to be lying around diddling themselves like this?"

"Shush," she said. "Just look into my eyes and stay out of your head."

I willingly obeyed, became more focused on my own pleasure. She could tell my climax wasn't far off. She stopped touching herself, watching me intently.

Here recline the nymphs at the hour of twilight
Back in the shadows dim of the cave, their golden
Sea-green eyes half lidded, up to their supple
Waists in water.
Deftly then they girdled their loins with garlands
Linked with leaves luxurious limb and shoulder;
On their breasts they bruised the red blood of roses
Fresh from the garden.
How they laughed, relating at length their ease in
Evading the Satyr.

My breathing became ragged, and I reached for her.

"No," she said, nudging my hand away. She straightened out on the bed, flat on her stomach between my legs, her hands on my thighs, pushing them farther apart. I felt her warm breath.

"Uh," I said, "I don't know." But the voice she was listening to was not mine. She moved her hands beneath me and lifted my legs, pulling me toward her, her tongue alternating between long, wet licks and rapid flicks, her hands freely exploring my body, kneading my breasts, tantalizing my nipples.

She brought me crashing, crashing, crashing, ever swelling over the edge until, in Sappho's words, I was "Like one insensate."

"Next time, you can do me if you like," she said in a throaty purr as she curled up behind me and gently rocked me to sleep.

Next time, I did. The next time and a few times after that. My inhibitions evaporated. The contrast between my lovemaking with Pyotr and Elsa was striking. I was losing Pyotr to drugs, a force more powerful than sex, and it caused me enormous pain. I grieved for him. I grieved for us both.

I was not interested in replacing him with Elsa, but the sexual drunkenness I felt, the enraptured oblivion I felt with her, was like nothing I had experienced or even imagined. And it was mine, now, for the taking.

She helped me let go of Pyotr and my grief that he was slipping away. She submerged me, drowned me in passion. I didn't want to come up for air. I didn't need air. I felt safe with her.

Inevitably, I ended up in a threesome with Elsa and her sex god boyfriend, Amos. She and I had talked about it. He didn't care or even seem interested. I fucked Amos, but it was more to please Elsa than Amos or me. Just not my type.

After that, Elsa engineered a foursome with Amos and Liam, her ex-boyfriend-with-benefits. Watching the guys go at each other, and the two of them double-teaming Elsa, was hot although I passed on a threesome with the boys. I think she was trying to hook me up with Liam since my relationship with Pyotr was on the skids, but he was more interested in Amos than me.

It was as close as I have come to an orgy, and I have no desire to get closer. The more bodies, the less intimacy. I gave Amos a blowjob because he asked, and just to be polite I fondled Liam briefly, but I don't think it did anything more for him than it did me. I could connect emotionally with Elsa, but the other two seemed like misplaced baggage.

Within a short time, the fires burning between Elsa and me damped down and burned out. We remained friends and occasionally had sex, but neither of us wanted our couplings to be a forever experience.

I don't know if I was still in love with Pyotr, if I was ever truly in love with him, when Elsa came into my life. It was hard seeing him sucked into the whirlwind. When he finally left to rendezvous with his destiny in Seattle, my grief was crushing. I coped with it as only I could, by paving it over with a brutal study regimen of textbooks and laboratories. They became my barricade against personal annihilation.

My sex life burrowed underground and didn't resurface until I met my deceased husband. But sex with him was never like sex with Elsa, or even Pyotr. It was never hot. On a good day, early in our marriage, I could expect lukewarm, although I always had to finish by myself if I thought it was worth the effort. During the last decade, on sex night Wednesdays, I would just close my eyes, lie back, and think of England.

Or murder.

But things are changing now.

I don't know what it is about the sea, this ship, this voyage, this time in my life, but my lust is rising. I know that's a healthy, if unsettling, thing.

While Lovely is a total sexual gift basket, I'm reluctant sample the goodies. I'm old enough to be her mother, and I feel protective of her. I'm not sure the maternal feelings are at all compatible with the sexual feelings so I'm taking it slow—for now.

Lagac is another matter. My fantasies about him come faster and more furious with each passing day, and I've gotten off by myself more than once imagining us together. I would never have thought I would have such powerful erotic urges at this time in my life.

Lagac's fair game. He's old enough to take care of himself, and I imagine what happens on the high seas stays on the high seas. At the end of the voyage, we'll probably go our separate ways. Or perhaps not, but I refuse to pour water on smoldering erotic embers. I have no outsized expectations, but everything's changing. I know there's more. And I want it. ∎

14

Zero

The next time Lovely Bayani gets naked in my cabin, or perhaps before that, under the right circumstances, I'll not be responsible for my actions. Do not fault me if I overcome my protective inclinations. Motherly feelings be damned.

In the next breath, I remind myself I talk a good game.

Lovely knocks on the door to my cabin around eight this morning. When I answer, she's standing in the alley wearing nothing but her *agimat.* My mother hen persona emerges immediately as I hustle her inside. "Lovely, where are your clothes?"

I head to my closet for an emergency t-shirt and hand it to her.

She just laughs.

"There's nobody up here but us girls," she says, slipping it on. "Well, Lagac comes up here sometimes, but he doesn't count.

"Shun and Shantrelle don't count either. The three of us were partying in their cabin after we got back to the ship last night, and nobody was wearing any clothes. They're still in bed, snuggled up like two kitties in a basket—purr, purr, purr. Tell you more about it later, but I thought about you when I woke up a few minutes ago and wanted to say, 'Hello.'"

Lovely hugs me and kisses my cheek.

"Lagac doesn't count? Since when?"

"He's an old family friend. Did you know he's my godfather? He used to babysit when he and Dad were in port and my parents wanted a night on the town. Since, as you already know, I didn't wear many clothes at home most of the time, Lagac's seen everything I have."

"I gathered from watching you at the recital that you've known Lagac for a while."

"When he babysat, he'd cook my favorite foods, read me stories, and completely spoil me. He'd put extra bubbles in my bath and we'd sing 'Drunken Sailor' while I splashed around. You know that song? 'Shave his belly with a rusty razor... Put him in a longboat 'till he's sober... Throw him into bed with the captain's daughter!' That one always cracked us both up, but Lagac had dozens of ideas for what to do with a drunken sailor. New ones every time.

"We'd sing until we were both hoarse, and he would finally coax me out of the tub. I'd drip dry running around the house, and he'd tuck me into bed. I'd fall asleep as he spun stories and sang to me."

"But you were just a little girl then. Wouldn't it be awkward if he ran into you now, dressed in...nothing?"

"You sound like my mom. She used to fuss at me. 'You'll embarrass him,' she said, but I knew it wouldn't. He and Dad would laugh when she fussed in front of them. Then she'd get mad at them, and they would laugh some more. I was a lost cause."

I imagine getting Lovely to do anything she didn't want to do would be a lost cause. Remind me never to try.

"Mom would tease me and tell me Lagac was going to get married some day and have his own children who would wear clothes like good boys and girls, and he wouldn't have time for me. I'd stomp my feet and tell them I wouldn't allow it.

"Lagac wouldn't have it either. He said *I* was his little girl, and if my parents didn't watch out, he'd scoop me up and we'd run away to sea together. We'd find pirate treasure and have tea with mermaids. He swore he knew a golden mermaid that ran a unicorn ranch on an island in the middle of the sea, right next to the buried treasure.

"Even as a small child I knew it was just one of his stories, but I wanted to believe it. Sometimes now I close my eyes and for a second I do believe it. Anything's possible with Lagac. He's such a love. I think he'd kill anyone who tried to mess with me."

I could certainly imagine Lagac as Lovely's godfather, and I was equally certain if anyone tried to harm Lovely he *would* kill them.

"Does Lagac have a wife and children?"

"Nope. He's still playing the field, but..." she says, her eyes sparkling with mischief, "he really likes you. I can tell by the way he looks at you. You're going to like him too. Let me know if you want me to put in a good word for you," she says, giggling and peeling off the t-shirt, tossing it on my bed. "See ya later, Jessamyn."

Another quick kiss and she leaves as she came, in a flash, scooting bare butt across the alley to her cabin.

* * *

Scratch what I said about sex with Lovely. The more I talk with her the more I'm sure it would be a bad idea. My motherly feelings toward her are undeniable.

I fell asleep around ten o'clock last night and was vaguely aware of some inebriated giggling and banter in the alley outside my cabin as Lovely, Shantrelle, and Shun returned from Haiphong shortly after midnight and fumbled at the locks, shushing each other. If the idea was to avoid awakening me, they fell short of the mark. But I went right back to sleep.

I had the most vivid dream last night. The rainforest cats, two of them, were back in full fur. A female jaguar emerged from the shadows of the trees. She wasn't the same jaguar that had previously visited my dreams—she was much smaller, less powerful, agitated as if she were in heat, paying no attention to me.

111

A second, much larger jaguar followed her. This was the cat I'd seen before—a powerful, muscular male. No question it was him. He fixed me with his gaze for what seemed like an eternity before he jumped in front of the female and tussled with her. She turned around and crouched, her lovely tail swishing from side to side, inviting, and he mounted her, holding her by the scruff of her neck with his teeth.

Their copulation took only a few seconds before she hissed at him, swatting him away. He dismounted and circled her once or twice as she lay there on the ground. Was she inviting him to try again? He mounted her a second time, thrusting for a few seconds before she snarled at him, and he broke off. He circled her as she prepared for him to mount her again. Instead he looked directly at me and growled, "Jessamyn Quilter, you must become accountable."

The female stood, and the two jaguars melted into the jungle.

I woke up in a cold sweat. The first thing I saw as I opened my eyes was the *maneki-neko* beckoning me. It took several minutes to equilibrate as I lay in bed, replaying in my mind what I had dreamed, trying to make sense of it until I fell asleep again.

When I woke up this morning around six, we were already under sail. I brewed a pot of Lady Grey tea to enjoy on my deck, savoring the warm ocean breeze before dressing and heading to the officers' mess for something more substantial.

The second officer told me yesterday we'd leave Haiphong for Phnom Penh about three o'clock in the morning. This leg of our journey will take three and a half days, give or take, and there'll be no shore leave in Cambodia. Our port time will be only a couple of hours to take on additional cargo. Fine with me. The Cambodian campaign disturbs me only slightly less than the debacle in Vietnam. God only knows what Lagac might suggest I dine on there.

Back in my cabin, the imagery of last night's dream is still with me, albeit fading as dreams will. Lovely is very much on my mind. And Lagac.

112

Are they related? Lovely? Copulating cats? Lagac? Accountability? Too much thinking as Elsa would have said.

I don't know what to do about these strong sexual feelings for Lagac. Lovely's right. He likes me. He's been flirting with me and his squat, muscular body is playing songs to which I know all the lyrics.

Eric says Lagac has someone in the Philippines, but that's his concern, not mine. Less chance of getting tangled up. And Lovely confirms he's not married.

Perhaps because of my burgeoning lust, and the utter erotic poverty of my former married life, I'm thinking more of my pathetic excuse for a husband than I have since he died. I almost said, "since I killed him," but that phrase still jars me, although I don't deny it.

I'm not deluding myself. It's a simple fact that he is dead by my intention, but I can't draw a straight line from that fact to some politico-religious imperative for suffering, penance, or even justice. If what I did was monstrously wrong, and I sometimes think it must be, I carefully arranged things so society couldn't hold me accountable. Why should I binge on self-flagellation, destroy myself with shame or fear of retribution? I don't think this is part of the universe's grand plan.

The universe's grand plan is to balance its books. Physically, not morally. It lends us matter and energy for a brief spell, at a time of its choosing, and expects repayment at another time of its choosing. The universe doesn't care what happens in the interim so long as it gets its property back. It doesn't even charge interest unless you count the joys and sorrows of living. If there's some moral arc to this grand plan, it's not evident to me.

You'll say I didn't have to kill him. Perhaps there was some other way, a way more palatable to the powdered judicial wigs, the clerical miters, the mortarboard and gown clerisy, the asshat bourgeoisie, the propeller-beanies of the cud-chewing classes, the various ideological bands of farting cherubs and hell-bent-for-leather blessings of prancing unicorns.

He hurt me, I hurt him back and fixed it so he could never hurt me again. He killed whatever joy I might have had in my life. I killed whatever dubious joy he might have found in causing further misery, torturing me and others. If there's a moral duty to atone, I delivered him from his. Who will deliver me from mine, since no one knows what I did except me? Where is the rainbow bridge to redemption? How would destroying myself in some public orgy of vengeance and retribution set things to rights? I refuse to adhere blindly to the notion I must be punished, atone, or seek forgiveness.

The jaguar in my dream snarled I must become accountable. Maybe I'll need to sort this out more fully, or maybe not. It was just a dream. For now, I know my husband needed to die for me to live, and I wasn't willing to wait helplessly for that to happen. So, you're wrong. I had to kill him.

While I can tell others he died, and even respond to some level of social curiosity about his death, I'm not so foolish as to reveal my pivotal role. We all have secrets.

* * *

It occurs to me that while I have cataloged my deceased husband's sexual inadequacy and sadistic character with abandon, if not alacrity, I have not revealed his name, although I don't consider that important except that I'm tiring of referring to him as "dead," or "late," or "deceased."

His name was Roderick. Roderick with no middle name, only the middle initial "O."

He told me he once asked his mother what the "O" stood for. She said she didn't know. Somehow a clerk mistakenly typed the "O" on his birth certificate, and nobody noticed before everything was signed and sealed.

I joked once that perhaps it was not an "O" but a zero, and someone forgot the "1." My attempt at binary humor wasn't entirely lost on him, but he didn't find it amusing. Little amused him except bullying others.

Perhaps my jest hit closer to home than I intended. In fact, he told me his boyhood chums used to call him "Zero." As is often the case in the growing-up years, it was a cruel joke at his expense. He was the last one in his urchin pack to grow pubic hair. Zero hair, zero status, zero, zero, zero.

I remember little about our first date, so that also sums to zero. We met in college at Princeton, paired by height at one of those awful mixers for incoming freshmen.

It was painful to attempt a rudimentary social conversation with him. He had no sense of rhythm, so dancing with him was like teaching a broomstick to box. I don't think either of us had fond memories of that "date."

The whole time we were in college, we rarely spoke more than a few words to each other in passing. Outside a few shared basic science classes as freshman and sophomores our paths simply didn't cross.

Pre-med is too demanding for much of a social life, though I did manage to get laid now and again, mostly with Pyotr or Elsa, but typically I fantasized about innominate cock during dates with "Bob," my "Battery Operated Boyfriend." When I needed sex, plastic was less of a bother than a pecker.

It surprised me when Roderick asked me to the senior prom. I hadn't gone out with him since that freshman mixer. I considered turning him down but couldn't come up with a good reason.

His dancing and conversational skills hadn't improved in four years. We got drunk. We had sex. He confided it was his first time, something I had already surmised. He seemed pleased with himself. I was happy I was drunk and didn't have to think about it too much.

I remember sometimes becoming aroused thinking about Pyotr or Elsa while Roderick did me. My orgasm never came cleanly, like river water building speed, spilling over a waterfall. It was messy, like spaghetti sauce sputtering in an overheated pot, spitting onto the stove and the wallpaper. Sex never got better with Roderick. Too much trouble dealing with the emotional splatter.

Sex wasn't easy for him. Erections were unreliable, turning floppy at inconvenient times. We had underwhelming sex perhaps two or three more times, and during one of them his condom broke and I got pregnant.

In our infinite wisdom, we compounded the problem by getting married. I was leery of getting an abortion, and Roderick thought we might as well have a baby. Marriage was the perfect sidestep.

We were headed to the same university, him as a graduate student in mathematics and me as a medical student. I don't know to this day why I thought marrying him was even a marginally good idea.

Nevertheless we got married the day after we graduated. A rent-a-reverend from the campus ministry performed a brief ceremony, witnessed by Elsa and Amos. And thus began our life as "man and wife." Not much of a man, and to be fair, not much of a wife either.

My pregnancy was difficult and ended with a miscarriage. I felt relieved after I got over the initial shock of the loss of the baby. When I told Roderick, he simply shrugged his shoulders and told me it was my fault. Next time, he said, I should take better care of myself.

There would not be a next time. I got my tubes tied and never told him. I told him I was on birth control. He just grunted.

I wonder now why I didn't simply divorce him after the miscarriage and chalk it all up to a failed experiment. I don't believe I ever even thought of it as a possibility. The inertia of convenience and the pressures of academics caused us to stay the course and get on with our respective careers.

When we both finished graduate studies four years later at Dartmouth, we began our post-doc and residency, respectively, at U. Mass and Harvard. That out of the way, we moved to Baltimore and a teaching position for Roderick at the University of Maryland and a fellowship for me at Johns Hopkins.

By the time our tenth wedding anniversary rolled around, we were comfortably, if not happily, ensconced in our home and careers in Westbury. Our twentieth wedding anniversary found us in the same rut. Doubtless, nothing would have changed by our thirtieth had I not helped Roderick move along.

What about the fact that you engineered his death, you ask? What about the fact you killed him? You committed murder. Surely he did nothing to deserve that.

There are moments I wish I hadn't killed him, although I can't say exactly why. On balance, I'm happier now he's dead, and that outweighs any regrets I have about killing him. Some might agree with me although many would still not forgive me.

Perhaps my view is colored by my profession. Physicians don't look at death the same way other humans do, and those who claim otherwise are simply lying. Sure, we dedicate ourselves to keeping people alive in most circumstances, even if they don't want it and we both think they would be better off dead.

Physicians know better than most that people die all the time. Accidents, wars, drug deals gone sour, hizzoner deciding some wretch's candle deserves to be snuffed out. Roderick's in good company among the dead. I don't think he held any overvalued ideas about the sanctity of life. One can't hold such an opinion and live with a physician for whom death is an everyday occurrence.

Before physicians can heal they must traffick in death. From the laboratory animals we kill in our undergraduate studies or postgraduate research to the cadavers and dying patients of our medical school years, death is not a horror. It's an ever-present mentor.

Dying can create a path to greater good. *Exitus acta probat,* as Ovid wrote. Outcomes justify actions. The end can justify the means. At least some ethicists would agree, not that I care much.

We help our patients along their path to the best of our abilities, whether it's maneuvering them along a birth canal or removing them from a ventilator. Birth and death are appetizer and dessert on the physician's menu.

Death completes the process of living, snuffing out the illusion that we can beat the house, that a life is a chance to flip off the cosmos. We fervently hope we can come out on top but know in our marrow the house always wins.

Do I see Roderick's demise as an example of *exitus acta probat?*

Perhaps. And perhaps it doesn't even matter.

It's amusing, if not always instructive, to watch ethicists tie themselves in knots over such things. It makes as much sense to me as debating how many angels can dance on the head of a pin. Since there are no angels, who gives a damn about the pin?

"Ethics" are legalistic underwear for naked beliefs. "Values" are the ruffles and ribbons on the knickers.

I killed Roderick. His death is undeniably a good thing. I'm better off, his students are better off, the whole world is better off. Nobody misses him, let alone mourns him. The universe continues to hum unperturbed by his death.

If someone were to convince me Roderick's death was a loss to anyone, it would devastate me. I would admit the end did not justify the means and attempt to make amends as best I could. Perhaps I would take my own life, or short of that, hand myself over to the authorities for punishment.

As Elsa would have said, "Too much thinking." All this thinking has made me tired, and I'm not even convinced it matters. ■

15

About Last Night

ABOARD MV ANDAMAN PEARL   July 12

Around noon, with the *Andaman Pearl* making for Phnom Penh, Lovely returns to my cabin to report on her lark in Haiphong last night with Shun and Shantrelle. They found Haiphong boring. No one ate cat, much less rat. They ate pho containing what the server assured them was chicken.

The clubs and karaoke bars rolled up their sidewalks before midnight, so there was nothing to do but come back to the ship. Still, they had plenty of time to drink too much. When they got back to the ship they were, to use a seafaring term, three sheets to the wind.

Lovely ended up in Shun and Shantrelle's cabin for a nightcap. Clothing no longer seemed useful, and the three of them wound up naked in bed.

"Shantrelle and I undressed each other, teasing Shun, calling him a pussy because he wouldn't take his clothes off. We ganged up on him and stripped him anyway," she says. "He was so shy and cute but he loved every minute."

"Why ever would you do that?" I ask, feigning horror.

"Just for shits and giggles." She laughs. "Shantrelle says he enjoys being dominated and humiliated. He was groping both of us earlier on the dance floor. Neither of us minded, but she scolded him for being naughty and said we would have to punish him when we got back to the ship.

"She blindfolded him with her bra and pushed him face down to the bed. We took turns berating him for his filthy behavior and spanked his bottom. Then we turned him over, took off the blindfold, tied him up, and 'made' him watch while she and I fooled around with each other.

"I'm not really into Shun, but Shantrelle is hot, hot, hot! She kept him tied up and fucked him without letting him touch her, but only after he begged her and promised once again to marry her and give her all his money. I fucked him too because Shantrelle made him beg me, and I didn't want to disappoint her. She likes to top me, so I play along. Shantrelle bossed Shun around for a little longer, untied one hand and made him jerk off while we laughed at him, then we all settled down in bed, cuddled, and went to sleep.

"They're getting married in a few days, you know"

"Oh?"

"They've asked my dad to marry them on the ship the day before we dock in Singapore. They're getting off there and getting married again on dry land, so there's no question about Shantrelle being his legal wife and heir. He's totally rich. Oil, gas, that sort of thing besides shipping. He's so madly in love with her he'd give it all to her, even if she didn't have sex with him. And she's head over heels in love with him."

"Do you think the three of you will indulge in more of these she-nanigans between here and Singapore? I confess I'm trying to unsee the images you just planted in my mind."

Lovely is unimpressed by my poker face. "Probably. Are you jealous? You want to join us?" She giggles but rapidly turns serious. "Sorry. I don't mean to be disrespectful. It was only a bit of drunken fun. They're sweet people, but I don't have any horndog feelings for either of them. Well, maybe Shantrelle a little. But I won't do it if you don't want me to."

I took her head in my hands and kissed her. She melted into me.

"Why ever would you think I wouldn't want you to have your drunken fun? Or sober fun, for that matter? I want you to do whatever you want. If you and Shantrelle want to 'force' Shun to suck your toes, wash out your undies by hand, or any other perverted thing that comes into your sweet little heads, why not? It's been a long time since I waded into a clusterfuck. I wouldn't know what to do anymore, and I lost the instruction booklet some time ago."

Lovely gasps and covers her mouth with her hands, her eyes widening to twice their normal size. She throws herself face down onto my bed, overcome with giggles,

"You don't think I was young and reckless once? I wasn't always a staid old-lady doctor, you know." Neither of us can stop laughing.

At last she sits up. "You really got it on like that when you were younger?"

"I did, although I insist it be a secret between the two of us, and I refuse to give you the details until you're at least as old as me, by which time you'll be like me, completely unshockable and I'll be dead, so it won't make any difference."

"No fair," she says, putting on her pouty face.

"I promise to keep your secrets as well, especially the ones about your cannibal past and that priest's pizzle around your neck. For the record though, I knew you couldn't play piano and cello like that just because you are talented and have worked your ass off practicing. It has to be the witches and the *agimat*."

"You joke, Jessamyn, but sometimes I think it *is* the witches. Sometimes I see things and hear things others can't. Like with Shun and Shantrelle. They're just one person, really. I've never been around anybody like that. They're two halves of the same soul who somehow found each other. How do they even do that? Wasn't there like some philosopher who talked about that? I could never stay awake in Sister Aloysius' class."

"Plato," I say, remembering back to my encounters with Elsa. She had explained it, between reading Sappho to me and reducing me to a warm, runny mess.

"Zeus made the original humans as a perfect pair of soulmates with four arms, four legs, one head, and two faces. They became arrogant and because he feared their power, he punished them by splitting them, forcing them to search forever for their missing halves."

"That's it. They've found each other. I just love them. It's so perfect."

The phone rang.

"Jessamyn Quilter here."

"Hello, Dr. Quilter. Captain Bayani."

"Hello, Captain."

"Just wondering if perhaps my daughter is with you. I ran into Mr. Yongzheng and Ms. Lewis-Haley in the officers' mess. They thought perhaps you might have seen her."

"She's here. Let me put her on."

"Hi, Dad.

"I'd love that. When do you think, about one thirty?

"Love you too. See you then. Bye," she says.

"Dad has some free time and wants to get together and make some music."

"Mind if I eavesdrop from next door?" I ask.

"You want to sit with us in the saloon while we play?"

"No, No. I don't want to intrude on your father's time with you. It's too precious. I'll just enjoy myself knowing you're enjoying yourself. Want to get some lunch?"

"I'm starving. Let's go."

I'm not sure I can concentrate on food. Is Lovely teasing me again, trying to seduce me with all that talk about their threesome. When we get to the mess, Lagac is talking with the cook. He looks at the two of us and laughs as we join him.

"Cook has made *rat*atouille, Filipino style," he says, emphasizing the first syllable, "but without rat because rat's not in season." Lagac loves to laugh at his own attempts at humor. He favors us with the list of ingredients—charred Japanese eggplant, onion and garlic, cucumber, peppers, and tomato. Then the secret ingredients, fish sauce, oyster sauce, and *bagoóng*—fermented fish and shrimp paste.

"Yumm," Lovely says, helping herself to the ratatouille and steamed rice. "One of my favorites."

I grab a bowl, spoon in some rice, and ladle some aromatic vegetable stew on top.

"Easy, Dr Quilter," Lagac says with a straight face. "It's a powerful aphrodisiac. Fine for us Filipinos because we're used to it, but it can drive non-Asians crazy."

I pull my poker face, hesitating only briefly. Lovely cracks up and Lagac joins in.

"Lagac," Lovely says. "You're terrible."

"I'm sure I'll be fine," I say, ladling more broth over the rice. "If I become unmanageable, I'm sure one of you will come to my aid. But Lagac, you'd better have seconds. Since your immunity is so high, you might need a testosterone boost."

It's cook's turn to crack up, slapping Lagac on the back.

I pile more vegetables into my bowl. And then more. By now, we're all howling at our collective wit.

The ratatouille truly is excellent. ■

16

Ladies of the Harbor

W

KOH SICHANG, Thailand July 16

e'll dock only briefly at Khlong Toei port in Bangkok to offload a few containers. There will also be a crew replacement here. Ninoy, our messman, will leave us to board another container ship whose route is opposite ours, heading back to the Philippines.

Eric says it's not a common practice, but crew changes along a voyage do happen. "Ships go where the cargo goes, and crew goes where they are needed, he says.

The *Andaman Pearl* is being assigned a replacement messman, a young Thai man named Narong. Eric has sailed with him before. "He's a little shy but he'll fit right in," he says. If Eric recommends him I'm sure we'll all get along fine.

We offload our containers and resume our journey, all in less than half a day. I'm surprised to learn the captain won't make straight for Singapore. Three hours after leaving port, we anchor opposite the harbor of Koh Sichang Island and Si Racha on the mainland.

"A good place for a lifeboat drill," Captain Bayani says.

I watch from my deck as the crew launches the lifeboats and retrieves them without incident.

The real reason for lying at anchor here, however, is not a routine lifeboat drill, Eric says. Koh Sichang is an open secret among seafarers,

125

a nautical Shangri-La, a legendary haven for ladies of the harbor. He says we're certain to be boarded by some of these ladies as well as a few men hawking souvenirs, electronics, jewelry, and other merchandise at deep discount.

The merchandise on offer by many of the ladies is themselves, Eric says. Captain Bayani is no stranger to the ways of men at sea, he says and the captain is prepared to turn a mostly blind eye if the party doesn't get out of control. Captain Bayani doesn't play around but he sees no harm in permitting his crew a little diversion.

"A party on the ship is better than giving everyone shore leave in Thailand," Eric says. "This way we know where the crew is and don't have to worry about someone not making it back to the ship safely."

And board they do, these lovely ladies, bringing with them cases of Leo beer, woks, and fresh ingredients to prepare mouthwatering local dishes on board. Other pleasures can wait until everyone is well fed. With the captain's permission, the crew of the *Andaman Pearl* sets up a restaurant and karaoke bar near the gangway. Things are hopping by dusk.

I walk by Lagac, lying on a mat in his tighty whities, being pounded, stretched, and twisted by two determined women with fervor that would make a chiropractor wince.

"Thai massage." Lagac smirks. "No happy endings."

Two other sailors are availing themselves of the same experience nearby. Unlike a chiropractor's treatments though, Thai massages come with smooches, given and received, and much merriment.

Clusters of sailors, each with two or three women in tow, gather in semi-secluded locations around the main deck, engaging in beer-animated chatter. Lovely, Shantrelle, and Shun are dancing with a few local men and women, one of whom has brought a boom box.

Later I spot Lagac in the restaurant, back in his coveralls, eating a plate of seafood that smells heavenly. I sit on the bench beside him at a table covered with a festive oilcloth decorated with tropical fruits.

He gestures to a Thai woman passing by us, and an icy Leo magically appears in front of me.

"Have some," he says, gesturing to his plate.

I can't resist a scallop and a shrimp or two. "What do you make of all this, Lagac?"

"Oh, you want to know about the 'prayer meetings' and the 'bible study groups' this evening?" He laughs. The runup to these "prayer meetings" looks like it might lead a few sinners into temptation rather than away from it. I make a note to check in with the second officer about the adequacy of his antibiotic supply.

"Some sailors want to have sex with the women but most of them are like me," Lagac says. "They just want to have a party and dance with the locals. We all miss our families, our wives, and girlfriends. We don't have much opportunity to talk and relax with women while we are at sea."

"What do their wives and girlfriends think about all that?" I ask.

"A few of the men will lie about Koh Sichang. They must think their wives and girlfriends are stupid. The only reason to lie is that you feel guilty or ashamed. Not me."

He takes his cellphone from his coveralls and scrolls through the messages, showing me a short video of the aftermath of his nearly nude massage. The women who had been jovially pummeling him are pulling up their tops and smashing their breasts on either side of his face, grinning like schoolgirls, albeit schoolgirls in their late thirties.

"That looks like a happy ending to me," I say, smiling. "You look very happy."

"You think?" He takes a swig of beer. "I just sent this video to my girlfriend," he says and translates the Tagalog for me. "Having a wonderful time, wish you were here!" He chortles, clearly amused at himself.

"And how did she take that?"

He scrolls to her reply. "She says, 'That the best you can do? You can have more fun back home. I know I am!'" She has attached her own flasher selfies.

His girlfriend is, as Lovely would say, hot, hot, hot. For a moment there's a knot in my stomach. How could an old lady like me compete with that gorgeous young body?

"Women," he says. "I love 'em. You going into Pattaya later? Soak up all the trashy action on Walking Street?"

Lovely, Shun, and Shantrelle had tried to sell me on a night out in Pattaya. "Come with us," Lovely said. "We'll catch a tender to the mainland, have dinner in Si Racha, and close the place down in Pattaya."

"Walking Street's a half-a-mile stretch of wall-to-wall restaurants, luxury cabarets, and go-go bars," Shun said. "There are street performers, prostitutes of every conceivable gender, and souvenir shops. The entire world meets on Walking Street."

Shantrelle chimed in. "Shun owns a high-priced building on Walking Street with a classy go-go bar called Chains on the bottom floor. He's going to give it to me as soon as we're married, and if Lovely's Paris gig doesn't work out, she and I can work there as pole dancers."

Shantrelle's cute when she giggles.

"I plead the ravages of old age and a horror of karaoke," I said. "Although if you and Shantrelle end up pole dancing at Chains, I'll certainly come all the way back to Thailand to cheer you on and buy you endless lady drinks. I hope you all have fun."

I smiled inwardly as I thought about what the trio might get up to in Shun and Shantrelle's cabin when they came back to the ship. Shun *would* own a titty bar called Chains, I snickered to myself. I'm sure Lovely will tell me all about it, and Walking Street, tomorrow.

Lagac is waiting for my reply. "I'm just going to hang out here," I say. "Are you going to Pattaya?"

"Me? No. Somebody needs to look after the ship. I'll go back to the engine room in a few minutes to make sure everything's ready to sail tomorrow."

I can't believe the next words out of my mouth. "Would this be a good night to show me around the engine room? If not, just say no."

128

Lagac's smirk vanishes. "It would be an excellent night," he says. "We'll have the place to ourselves. How about if I meet you here at the gangway in half an hour and take you below deck so you don't lose your way?"

"Sounds like fun."

"It's hot down there. I suggest you wear something cool, Dr. Quilter."

"I will. And I suggest you call me Jessamyn. See you in half an hour?"

"See you in a few, Jessamyn."

I change into a lightweight, not quite transparent shift I bought in Manila. I see no reason for underwear. After all, Lagac warned me it would be hot.

I grab two Leos from the bar and meet him by the gangway. "We might need these to help us beat the heat," I say.

He takes one, toasting my health. "Can't hurt a bit."

The engine deck is a two-story pit painted institutional marine-green with a catwalk running around three of the four bulkheads. The walkway overlooks generators and other heavy equipment I don't recognize.

I expected an oily, smelly mess but everything is immaculate. Tools march along the wall in military order. Fresh paint looks like a fussy interior decorator applied it last week. Not a candy wrapper, used coffee cup, or dust bunny in sight. Lagac maintains the place as if it were his private luxury condo.

"That's the propeller shaft housing," Lagac says, pointing to what looks like a huge pipe below us, mostly buried in the deck. Control panels, breaker boxes, tool cabinets, and emergency equipment lockers line the bulkheads.

Lagac guides me into an air-conditioned control room off one corner of the catwalk. It's quieter inside, but the vibration from the equipment penetrates the room.

"It gets pretty loud out on the catwalk and it's worse on the deck below us," he says. "The noise and the vibration aren't bad right now. We're running the engines just enough to keep us powered up without going anywhere."

He points to a plenum overhead that ends in a vent overhanging a large whiteboard on the deck below.

"That's the coolest part of the engine room," he says. "We bring in sea air from the outside to keep things more comfortable. We'll stand under the vent, but it's Thailand and the outside air isn't that cool to begin with. It's still going to be over a hundred degrees, even warmer on the catwalk since hot air rises. No air conditioning so if you need to come back to the office to cool off, feel free."

He hands me some ear plugs. "These'll filter out some of the noise. We can write on the whiteboard if we need to communicate and can't make ourselves heard. When things are kicking down here you would need goggles and a hard hat, but we won't need them tonight. Ready?"

The catwalk has steel ladders with handrails and yellow rubber treads on the stairs leading down to the engine deck. It isn't difficult to negotiate, but the realization we're now three decks below the main deck of the ship, completely under water, makes me queasy.

Lagac notices and touches my arm. "Okay?"

I nod and give him a thumbs up. We make our way to the whiteboard under the cooling vent. He isn't kidding about the heat. It's better at the bottom of the ladder, but I don't know how he manages when he must work down here.

"You'll get used to it in a few minutes," he writes on the whiteboard. He sketches out a floor plan, labeling the major pieces of equipment and points them out—generators, engines, and the long, half-round propeller shaft housing, about six feet in diameter, partly buried in the ship's belly. The scale of everything is much larger than I expected.

Lagac begins the grand tour. He's right. I *am* getting used to the heat. He takes my hand when we reach the propeller shaft housing and places it on top. It's warm, like every other surface down here, but not hot. The thrum, thrum, thrum of the slowly turning shaft and the vibration of the housing are unexpectedly pleasant.

So is Lagac's next move. He puts his arm around my waist and leans his body into the housing, pressing his pelvis against it, gently guiding me into the same position beside him. His hand moves to the small of my back, inviting me to relax.

It's an electrifying and unmistakably sexual move and while it's brazen, I remind myself this is Lagac. I'm in no danger. He's gentle, a genuinely nice guy without a malicious bone in his body. But this Lagac is no longer the playful, teasing trickster from the restaurant/karaoke bar. This Lagac is the supremely confident, gentlemanly seducer—solid, skillful, and desirable.

The hand on my back belongs to the take-charge, protective Lagac, the one who watches over Lovely, the Lagac who body-blocked an enraged Balwinder Agarwal and marched him to the brig. This Lagac is Charon, ferrying me into his underworld, sharing his secrets. Does Hades await? I don't care. I love everything happening right now.

The thrumming against my genitals is warm, erotic. I wonder if Lagac's getting an erection. His eyes are closed. I decide not to overthink things and just let him lead. I feel completely safe, if a little outrageous, as we enjoy this masturbatory dance together, arousing ourselves with one of the world's largest vibrators.

I close my eyes and lean my hips and belly fully against the housing, resting against its gentle curve. Lagac moves behind me, coaxing me forward, molding his powerful body to mine, his hands at my waist sliding up to my shoulders, never groping or grinding, matching his pressure against me as I move more intently into the vibration. I no longer need to wonder if he has an erection.

It seems like we've been molded together like this forever. My legs grow weak, but he buoys me up. I give myself up to the unmistakable surges, the urgently building waves of pleasure until I'm swept away. Lagac reads my body, each crescendo of passion, like a sailor reads the swells of the sea.

He turns me around when my orgasm has subsided and kisses me. I throw my arms around his neck and kiss him back with a passion that frightens me. I rest my face on his shoulder, tasting the pleasant saltiness, inhaling his odor. Clean, laced with spice. Somehow he shed his coveralls before he pressed against me. He's wearing only underpants, like he was earlier, during his Thai massage.

His eyes meet mine, and I kiss him again, fervently, signaling my enthusiasm. Am I nodding my head yes? I don't know. He turns me around, guiding my body against the propeller shaft housing once again, lifting my shift to my waist, molding his body to mine. His underpants are gone.

For a moment I freak out. But his powerful hands on my bottom, shielding me from his hardness, reassures me. He moves his hands slowly up my back and sweeps my dress over my head. Again he guides me into position to feel the delicious vibrations as he explores my genitals with his fingers, at last allowing his erection to rest in the cleft between my buttocks as we both bend forward.

My lust is raw. I can't wait any longer and move my hips backward. I doubt he can hear my words, whatever I'm saying, but that makes no difference. He understands the message from my body and obliges me, matching his thrusts to my movements.

The choreography is perfect. I explode before he reaches his climax, and he backs off, kissing my neck, gently massaging my back and bottom.

He turns me around once more and kisses me, caresses my face and breasts, slick with sweat. His eyes ask "Again?" I don't need to answer. He gently lifts me up and lays me along the housing as if I'm no heavier than sea spray. I'm astonished at the strength in his arms. He leaps on top of the housing at my feet with sinewy feline grace and kisses his way up from my toes to the top of my head, balancing perfectly, missing nothing, then back to my hungry mouth for what seems an eternity.

He turns me over and presses my body full against the vibrating housing, kissing his way down my neck to my bottom, at last entering me from behind. This time, he matches his climax to mine. We erupt

132

together. Fireworks exploding everywhere, showering my body with crackling, incandescent sparks. It is exactly like that.

In the afterglow, he carries me back to a chair underneath the cool air plenum. I am overwhelmed. Not aware of time passing. He retrieves my shift and holds it over my head, open, as if helping a child dress. I raise my arms and let it drift down over my body. He's still naked. I could look at his body forever. No, that's not right. I could never keep my hands off it for that long.

His smile is soft, not the rascally smirk I often see on his face, but a smile that says, "Wasn't that the most incredible feast ever? We'll talk about it later if you like, but for now, let's just luxuriate in each other." He says all of that with a simple smile, never moving his lips to form words that would dissolve in the engine room noise anyhow.

* * *

I don't know how I got back to my cabin. Perhaps Lagac carried me all the way. Perhaps he just walked me back to the elevator. I don't remember him getting dressed. I'm sure we said nothing to each other as we basked in the warmth of our shared delight. I'm sure we didn't talk about condoms or STIs, and I tell my buzzkill brain to shut up and remind me to think about such mundane things later.

There are about a million things I want to talk with Lagac about the next time I see him, and safe sex isn't even in the top one hundred. Perhaps my adult brain will make an appearance tomorrow, but tonight I'm in no hurry for it to come roaring back. I just let the magic rock me to sleep. ∎

17

Passion

Lovely knocks on my door. She wants to talk about her trip to Walking Street and a riotous performance by Shantrelle and her, fully clothed, pole dancing in a private room at Chains.

"Shantrelle has pole danced before," Lovely says, "and she was teaching me some of her moves."

I don't ask for further details, but I can visualize Shantrelle's dancing by the way she walks. She's sultry, graceful, and carries herself with uncommon elegance.

"I am a total noob but it was so fun," Lovely says. "Shun was laughing at us."

I can picture that too. Lovely goes all in, whatever she's doing. I'm sure Shun's laughter was the laughter of joy, not derision.

Lots of lady drinks were dispatched. Proposals from a gathering crowd of men to take things further were politely declined. Shantrelle and Lovely had a more exciting game in mind.

Back on the *Andaman Pearl*, the party reconvened in Lovely's cabin. The girls stripped Shun once again and disparaged his manhood, comparing it unfavorably to that of every man in the world, dead or alive, and to an outrageously large black rubber phallus Shantrelle acquired on Walking Street.

"She made him buy it for us at the sex shop next to the club," Lovely says. "We told him we were going to need something to get us through the night since he wasn't any good in that department." Lovely laughs at her own outrageous behavior and I laugh with her.

"Shantrelle bought a studded leather slave collar and a leash for him too. Of course we were only teasing him about his size. Shun's not all that small. He's sort of 'boyfriend dick.'"

"I don't know what that means, and I'm not sure I should ask," I say.

"'Boyfriend dick?' That's one you'd feel comfortable having around the house for sex several times a week or just to look at in passing. Medium, or maybe just a smidgeon more. Nice looking but nothing too big or flashy," Lovely says.

I shake my head and add a little eye roll for effect. The thought that Lovely could discourse on penises with such authority is amusing, given what is likely limited experience at her tender age. I could teach her a thing or two in that department, but what would be the point? Part of the joy of youth is learning for oneself.

"Then we put his collar on and blindfolded him."

"Don't tell me. With Shantrelle's bra."

"Yeah," she snickers, "and she led him on the leash into the alley, carrying the rubber pee-pee in his mouth like a bone. We told him what a bad dog he had been and left him in the alley, begging, scratching at the door to be let in. We were going to play fetch with him but were afraid we would make too much noise and might wake you."

"Good Lord," I say. "You mean you and Shantrelle are running around the ship with poor Shun on a leash? Naked? Aren't you afraid someone will come down the alley and see you?"

Lovely can't control her giggles. "Not really. We listen for the elevator and there's never anyone but us and you on the owner's deck. But it makes Shun's heart race when we treat him like that."

I worried at first that Captain Bayani would be shocked at the raunchy frolics on the owner's deck if he found out, particularly since his precious daughter is one of the ringleaders. Perhaps he just doesn't know.

But I doubt there's anything happening on the *Andaman Pearl* the captain doesn't know about. A mouse couldn't sneak a crumb of *palitaw* from the galley without Captain Bayani knowing.

Lovely continues her play-by-play.

"When we finally dragged Shun into the room, we flogged him and made him jerk off while Shantrelle and I played with the dildo."

"Nobody got hurt, I trust?"

"No. Didn't leave any marks. We were using the kid glove floggers Shantrelle made him buy for us on Walking Street. Shantrelle had already painted a vivid picture for him of what we were going to do with our new toys when we got back to the ship. We threatened to use the dildo, but it looked like we might be scaring him, so we backed off.

"Shantrelle offered to flog me, but I was getting tired and besides, I'm not really into that. I don't think Shantrelle is either, except with Shun."

Lovely leaves nothing to the imagination as she describes their escapades. She leaves nothing to the imagination in anything she does. She approaches her sex games with Shun and Shantrelle the same way she approaches the Bösendorfer—all in, intending to squeeze every delight from it. That's part of what I love about her. Still, there's such a thing as decorum.

"Aren't you concerned, spilling the beans about all these private sexual experiences?" I ask.

"No," she says. "I'm only telling you, nobody else. I know you won't tell anyone. Shun and Shantrelle know I will tell you everything about us. They trust you because I trust you. I enjoy telling you. I enjoy sharing my adventures with you. Should I stop doing that?"

"I'm just concerned it's none of my business. I don't know Shun and Shantrelle all that well, and I don't want to intrude on their privacy."

"You're not intruding. After all, you're a doctor. People must trust you with lots of private things about their lives, and you see naked people all the time. We're not upsetting you, are we? We love you, and we'd never want to do that."

"No. Call me shockproof. You don't want a detailed description of what *I've* seen or heard. I'm not at all surprised or offended that young people have sex, even with all those toys, even on the high seas in the alleys of the *Andaman Pearl*. I just want you to be safe. There are lots of horny sailors around here."

"Sounds like you know something juicy. Wanna 'spill the beans' as you say?"

"No, I do not." It's my turn to laugh.

"Pooh. In that case, I'll go next door and get on with my practicing. I promised Shun and Shantrelle I'd provide a little wedding music when my dad hitches them in a couple of days," she says, kissing my cheek, bounding off.

I reflect on Lovely's evening on Walking Street as her masterful scales once again drift into my cabin. How completely different her evening was from mine with Lagac.

Is Lagac "boyfriend dick?" Shaking my head I laugh at the term and myself. I can't honestly say I remember much about that part of him except how wonderful it felt when our bodies meshed. I wouldn't mind seeing him naked around my house or having sex with him a few times a week, if that's the definition. It wouldn't be a question of "minding," however. It would be perfection, so maybe he's beyond "boyfriend dick." I doubt young people have a name for it.

Lovely regales me with her sexual romps joyfully, like a clumsy puppy without shame, in the same way she tells me about other private aspects of her life, like her witchy cannibal forebears and her *agimat*.

She enjoys frolicking with Shun and Shantrelle, being included in their relationship. They all have fun. But Lovely never talks about passion. Perhaps Shun and Shantrelle reserve that for themselves. Perhaps passion is something Lovely still must discover about sex as she has discovered it about music. As Nietzsche said, "In music the passions enjoy themselves."

I take the ladder down to the main deck and make my way to the bow of the ship. It's a great place to be when the weather is good, as it is now. A place where you can only look forward. A good place to think and daydream as the ocean parts around the keel and welcomes our advance.

Look out world. I'm not sure I'd characterize my evening with Lagac as "fun," but it was a barnburner. It's been so long since I felt the fire.

> *Passion, Passion, burning bright,*
> *In the oceans of the night;*

Elsa would be pleased with me. Rewriting Blake to my liking. Ruminating on Sappho. I had wondered, with Roderick out of the picture, if I'd ever want sex again. The answer is obvious. I absolutely do.

The problem with Roderick wasn't sex. It was passion. Passion was never on offer with him. I went along with the sex for his sake. It wasn't awful—it was mostly manageable—but never passionate.

I think I've missed out on all fronts. Passion and love aside, unlike my lighthearted fellow passengers, I've never experienced sex as an opportunity to have fun. To play joyfully. Sex with Elsa, and the parties with her boy toys, Amos and Liam, were a little too uncomfortable to be called fun. Nobody was laughing. Perhaps I was too guarded, but it didn't feel comfortable to let my guard down, especially with the guys.

Sex with Lagac is like nothing I've experienced. *Lagac* is like nothing I've experienced. He's a singularity—a place where the laws of physics don't apply. A place where the curvature of spacetime becomes infinite and the concepts of both space and time break down. I'm almost afraid to think about how wonderful it is with Lagac for fear of jinxing things.

Listen to me rattle on. I don't believe in jinxes or anything of the sort. I envy the "Lovely ShunTrelles," as I've come to think of my three fellow passengers, their inventive games, their ease and childlike trust, their prelapsarian innocence. I feel very protective of them.

In this moment, I am gloriously alone in the world, pressed against the railing that wraps the forecastle of the ship, all the containers we're hauling at my back as I lean into the currents of air and spray from the bow. Smooth turquoise water surrounds us, farther than it's possible to see.

Alone except for the porpoises and flying fish during the day. Alone except for the bioluminescent plankton pulsing neon in the bow wave generated by the keel at night. I wonder if this isn't the most beautiful place in the world, this ship, this magnificent gulf of Thailand peppered with exotic islands.

Why would I not sing if I had a singing voice and knew any songs? "Southern Cross?" So it's the wrong hemisphere. I don't care. My brain buzzes with fragments about running from truth, spirits using me, and the promise of tomorrow.

Something is changing within me. As uncertain as I am about what's happening, I never want to go back to the way things were—dependable, safe, and manageable. It's exhilarating and more than a little frightening to think about how my life has changed. It's only just begun. I can't imagine what lies ahead, but bring it on. ■

18

Shun

WABOARD MV ANDAMAN PEARL *July 18*

e are once again in the South China Sea, the calm of the Gulf of Thailand replaced with wind and a little more chop. Nothing that upsets the calm in my cabin. Still, it's more pleasant inside now than on the bow where the wind stings.

Lovely's reports about her shore leave with Shun and Shantrelle have piqued my curiosity about them. I want to get to know them better in the short time that remains before they disembark in Singapore, their home base.

I want to talk with each of them alone rather than as a couple. I've invited Shun to join me for lunch so the two of us can talk without interruption from the others. And I'm looking forward to getting to know Shantrelle better at a little get-together Lovely has arranged for just us girls.

I admit Shun's submissive sexual behavior, as gleefully reported by Lovely whenever she gets the chance, has sharpened my curiosity about him. Not that I have any erotic interest in Shun or his fetish. While I've known several people who enjoy BDSM in their relationships, I'm not wired that way.

When I see Shun and Shantrelle together nothing leads me to suspect he's the sort of man who enjoys being dominated by a couple of women, allowing them to flog him and lead him around naked on a leash. Quite the opposite. He always seems so sure of himself, a bit staid, so much in control of every situation. But then that's the way it is. A fascinating part of the rich tapestry of human passion.

Shun's agreed to meet me for lunch in the officers' mess today and has already selected a table, away from the others, before I arrive. He stands, smiles graciously, and pulls out my chair as I approach.

I didn't expect he would dress up for the occasion, but he's wearing *baju melayu,* as he was for Lovely's recital. He's chosen a loosely tailored grape-colored silk tunic with long sleeves and matching trousers and a full-length muted lilac and gold checkerboard *sampin* falling from his waist almost to the tops of his black square-toed shoes. A black felt s*ongkok* sits on his head, the perfect match for the nearly round, black-framed glasses he wears.

I've never thought of Shun as especially handsome before, but I've changed my opinion. He is beautiful in a distinctive way, a slender young man, almost slight, perhaps five feet five inches tall, with a kind, open countenance.

His cropped, glossy jet-black hair, thinning almost imperceptibly at the temples, is stylishly cut, framing a high forehead. His eyes sparkle behind his glasses, and full black eyebrows peek above the rims. Just the hint of a shadow is visible where he has carefully shaved above his thin upper lip.

His skin is saddle tan with rosy undertones. His hands are small and the nails on his delicate fingers are carefully manicured. Lunch in the officers' mess is not a table for two at Le Tour d'Argent in Paris, but Shun would not have been out of place there.

"Thank you for inviting me, Dr. Quilter. I am very happy we have some time to talk at length."

"I've been looking forward to getting better acquainted. Please call me Jessamyn."

"Jessamyn, then. My pleasure. What a wonderfully melodious name," he says.

"Not as melodious as 'Lovely,' I think, and speaking of her, she seems to have become completely enchanted by you and Shantrelle."

"I think it's you who enchants her. Every other phrase from her lips begins with 'Jessamyn.' 'Jessamyn this, Jessamyn that'." Shun smiles.

"And when she's with me it's 'Shun and Shantrelle, Shantrelle and Shun.'"

"Lovely's an extraordinary young woman. She possesses the qualities I admire most in people—intelligence, forthrightness, confidence, integrity, and a playful sense of humor. Shantrelle too possesses these qualities. I trust them both, and I am not an especially trusting person. Both assure me I should trust you completely. And so, I do."

"I am honored," I say. "How did the two of you meet?"

"I met Shantrelle last January in Los Angeles. She was a marketing trainee at my company. I noticed her sitting along the wall in the boardroom behind her manager who was seated at the table. She was taking notes as his second while he fumbled his way through one of those awful death-by-PowerPoint presentations nobody wants to give and nobody wants to hear. For all her poise, Shantrelle's face could not conceal the fact she knew her boss was dissimulating. It was clear she did not approve."

As I suspected, Shun doesn't miss much.

"At the company-wide cocktail party that evening, I asked her manager to introduce us, as I typically do with all the managers. I have found it pays handsome dividends for them to observe that I am interested in hearing directly from their subordinates. It allows me to identify promising new talent and puts the old timers on notice they need to earn their keep."

"You didn't fire the manager who lied to you?" I ask, reflexively raising my eyebrows.

"Heavens no. If I fired everyone who lied to me, there would be nobody left in the company. Usually when someone lies about something there is a good reason, and one can divine much useful information, and sometimes the truth, by paying attention."

I'm surprised. Shun, who can scarcely be thirty, has rapidly disabused me of any lingering impressions I may have had that he's a callow, wealthy layabout.

"I take it you were impressed with her," I say.

"Absolutely. I extended my stay in LA and asked Shantrelle if she would join me for lunch the following day, which was a Saturday. She insisted on paying for her own tab."

It appears Shantrelle also has a lot on the ball. I can't wait to hear what she has to say about all of this.

"She told me later she fell head over heels for me at that lunch. I had done the same. She agreed to have brunch with me at my hotel the next day and allowed me to pick up the tab because, she told me frankly, the price was well beyond her means.

"Again, we talked for hours until she asked, perhaps noticing that the waitstaff were checking their watches, if I would like to invite her to my room to continue our conversations.

Aha. I've seen this movie before.

"We continued to talk in the elevator. When we reached my floor, the concierge opened the door to my penthouse suite. I'm afraid I'm quite spoiled, Jessamyn. The rooms I take while on business travel are usually elegant and quite comfortable. If the luxury of my accommodations impressed Shantrelle, she didn't betray it.

"We talked—and talked some more. We laughed together, most unusual for me, and she touched my arm casually. Forgive me for running on so. Perhaps you have already heard enough?"

"No. I'd love to hear more."

"Shantrelle excused herself. I heard the shower running and a short time later she returned, running her fingers through still wet hair, wearing a terrycloth robe the hotel supplies for guests. Then she told me it was my turn.

"It seemed a little strange, but when I finished showering, I dressed in a traditional silk gown I travel with and returned with another one for Shantrelle.

"I thought she might return to the bathroom to change or decline the gown. She hesitated only a moment before untying the bathrobe, handing it to me, and slipping into the dressing gown I offered without breaking eye contact and without a trace of coquetry or embarrassment. She was breathtaking, and I was drowning in her eyes."

He's too good to be true. She's gorgeous, and he didn't make a move on her?

"We talked on the terrace until the concierge knocked with dinner. Shortly before midnight, she yawned and said perhaps she should go home. Then she came up with another possibility. Since there were several bedrooms in the suite, she offered to stay over.

Shantrelle's the one running the show, and she's a master at this game. She's been here before and clearly knows her way around.

"I told her I would love for her to stay, thinking we could talk some more in the morning. I showed her a bedroom next to my own, leaving my door ajar as I typically do, and a couple of hours later I woke to find her standing in my doorway.

"I turned back the covers and patted the bed. She took off the gown and got in, spooning into me.

Okay. This is where this tale should be going.

"She told me she didn't think she was ready to have sex with me yet."

What? This girl sure knows how to play her cards.

"I told her that was fine. It was wonderful just to feel her body against mine. We slept curled up next to each other for the rest of the night.

"She woke up alarmed, saying she needed to call into work, to let them know she would be late. I suggested instead that she call in and resign. I planned to fly to Lima for a meeting, and I suggested she join me and learn more about my business.

"She was cautious. I promised if she felt she had made a mistake and wanted to come back to LA, I would make that happen. She had other questions.

"She wanted to know if I had women hanging all over me, if I had slept with other women like we had slept last night, if I was married or divorced.

"It was easy to tell her the truth. It was my first naked sleepover. I am not married or divorced nor do I have a stable of women at my beck and call. There is no one else."

Shun's story was catching me up in a fairy tale whirlwind. Prince Charming knows what he wants and how to get it. Cinderella's no slouch either.

"Shantrelle also asked me about my wealth. I told her my family left me a fortune, which I have turned into an even greater fortune the internet says is a couple hundred billion dollars.

"She was stunned and embarrassed. She apologized for asking, telling me she couldn't believe she had been so ill-mannered. I told her I thought it perfectly reasonable to ask, and I wanted her to ask me anything she wished."

He really does seem like an open book. He must have knocked her socks off.

"She came with me to the Port of Callao, north of the city where I had a meeting with my Peruvian freight forwarder. She was fascinated with the docks, the ships, and massive cranes, the highly organized chaos.

"That night as we cuddled in my apartment, she told me how happy she was. It was the beginning of our lovemaking, of which I'm sure you know something since Lovely says she has shared every detail with you," Shun says, his eyes dancing.

"She has. I asked Lovely if she were not concerned about invading your privacy, but she said that was not an issue for any of you. Just so you know, I would never gossip about your sex life. Or your net worth."

"It all seems harmless to me. The two of them are such honorable people, and I'm certainly not ashamed of our little games, which is all Lovely knows about our love life, but I would never wish to have you see or hear anything that would make you uncomfortable."

Lovely knows more about your love life than you may think. She's convinced you are so much in love you're not two different people but halves of the same wandering soul who have at last found each other.

"Perhaps later you will tell me something of your own life, Jessamyn, which I'm certain has been amazing."

The idea sends shivers down my spine. I would love to trust Shun with my secrets. I think he would understand, and selfishly, it would be good for me, but I would have to be insane to consider it.

"I'd love to hear more about your wedding, Shun," I say, deflecting his inquiry. "I hear you are to be married on the ship."

"That's what Shantrelle wants. And we will be married more formally in Singapore as soon as we arrive. That's what my attorneys want, and I agree because I couldn't bear the thought of someone making trouble for Shantrelle simply because we were not married on dry land."

"How did the two of you end up on the *Andaman Pearl*?"

"That was Shantrelle's doing. On our trip to Callao, she asked if my companies own ships. They do not, but I had once or twice considered leasing or even buying vessels. My people ran the numbers and identified some potential scenarios.

"Shantrelle proposed taking a voyage on a container ship. I told her if she wanted a long cruise, we could take a luxury liner or even my yacht. But she had caught the container ship bug in Callao. She persuaded me we could use the time away from my hectic business travel, moving at a slower pace, to see if owning ships would be a good fit with my other business interests.

We flew to Tokyo to have a look at the *Andaman Pearl*, one possible acquisition my people had identified."

"You're going to buy the *Andaman Pearl*?"

"No. It doesn't currently make business sense. But it has been a marvelous journey except for that horrific episode with the Agarwals. We were both captivated by Lovely Bayani at her recital, and we think the world of her. Shantrelle has found a playmate as rascally as she. And it seems I am to be the mouse to their kittens."

"So it would seem as Lovely tells the tales."

"It amuses them no end to seduce me into these games. It surprises me I also enjoy their attempts to berate me so much. They're not very good at it, which I think is part of the fun, and sometimes I must stifle a laugh, which makes them dream up something more outrageous. I think we're all learning a great deal about who we are.

"We will miss Lovely very much when we leave the ship. She is a world-class talent, and some day she will sell out concert venues around the world. We've been busy making plans that include her."

"Oh?"

"You will forgive me if I disclose nothing further right now. But we wish her to have all the good fortune we enjoy, and we will do anything possible to make that happen."

Shun smiles and then turns serious. "There is something more that I would like to confide in you concerning that terrible business with Mrs. Agarwal," Shun says.

"The outcome of the inquiry in Manila was completely unsatisfactory," I say, my mood darkening.

"I confess to you I have changed all that," Shun says softly.

"What do you mean?"

"It was as you feared. My contacts in Manila informed me that the Philippine government was eager to deport Mr. Agarwal to India rather than bring charges and involve themselves in a messy international situation. I was loathe to see him get away with murdering his wife, however unintended it might have been, without accountability because of the craven indifference of a government that cares very little about justice."

148

Shun's choice of the words "murder" and "accountability" bring me up short. The jaguar in my dreams has demanded accountability. And I murdered my spouse as surely as Mr. Agarwal murdered his.

"One of my executives in India located Mr. Agarwal and confronted him with his actions. He was shaken but still belligerent and unrepentant, even when presented with the opportunity to atone for his sin, so I arranged for him to spend some time in Puzhal Central Prison near Chennai in Tamil Nadu. If, at some point, he accepts accountability for Mrs. Agarwal's suffering and death, I can also arrange for him to leave prison and work toward his redemption in one of my businesses. If he does not, he can reside in Puzhal prison indefinitely."

"My god. Does your wealth afford you that much reach?"

"Yes. I can right only a few of the world's wrongs, but when I have the opportunity, I try to do what is honorable and just in the service of Allah."

"Remind me not to get on your bad side." I smile uneasily.

"I'm sure you have made mistakes, perhaps even done something egregious. All of us have. But I believe it is important to accept accountability, repent, and work toward redemption. Do you not agree?"

I nod, all the while uneasy that murdering Roderick puts me beyond the pale for redemption. The jaguar in my dreams speaks of accountability and Shun is providing me with a real-world account of what can happen to murderers even when civil authority looks the other way.

Punishment by the authorities is not the end of it though as Shun and my dreamcat are telling me. Lady Justice will not be denied. She demands I pay attention. Be accountable. Atone. I have not the foggiest idea how to do any of that without destroying myself, which I will not do.

"Are you familiar with the Muslim concept of *Tawba?*" Shun asks.

"I am not."

"It is repentance to Allah for sins and misdeeds. Allah expects we will sin, but He requires us to repent and promise not to repeat our evil. Allah is merciful and will forgive everything, but forgiveness is not automatic. We must seek forgiveness in sincere devotion to His teachings. We must repent and atone to earn His mercy. And we must make restitution.

"When someone kills another human being, it is not possible to make restitution to the victim. One must instead recompense the family. The law of *qisas* or retaliation gave Mrs. Agarwal's family the right to one of three paths. They could have demanded Mr. Agarwal's life in which case the state would have been compelled to execute him. Alternatively, they could have forgiven him outright as an act of charity, and Allah would have blessed them for that. Or they could have demanded *diya*, monetary restitution."

"They chose money instead of having him killed? I'm not sure I would have made the same choice in their shoes."

"That is the option they chose. I have paid Mr. Agarwal's *diya* since he could not do so himself, and he has no relatives willing to pay it for him. Now he must repay me, honoring the terms I impose on him. I am interested in his redemption, not his money.

"He can be accountable for Mrs. Agarwal's death and earn Allah's mercy, or he can harden his heart until he meets his death and damnation. I arranged for his incarceration to sharpen his focus on these choices. I will do everything in my power to encourage him to return to the loving embrace of Allah so when he is weighed in the balance on *yawm ad-din,* the day of judgment, Allah will welcome him."

* * *

I learned something else about Shun from Shantrelle, something that chills me to the marrow. He has a spy among the crew of the *Andaman Pearl*. There is literally nothing that happens aboard this ship he doesn't know.

Shun justifies the spy, one of the able-bodied sailors on board, in the name of intelligence gathering. He's the ever-careful entrepreneur, and he has tasked his spy with gathering information germane to his decision about buying the *Andaman Pearl*. Although he's not going to buy the ship his spy is still on board and will sail with her until she docks in Rotterdam, even though he and Shantrelle will disembark in Singapore.

Does Shun then also know about Eric and the junior deck officer? About my sexual reawakening with Lagac? Did one of his "spies" look into my life before I boarded the *Andaman Pearl?* Did his thoroughness extend to looking into the lives of everyone aboard ship before he and Shantrelle boarded in Yokohama?

What might he know about Roderick's death? What was it he said? "I'm sure you have made mistakes, perhaps even done something egregious, Jessamyn."

At some point, I may ask him. I'm as certain he'll tell me as I'm certain he'll tell nobody else. For the moment though, I'll simply keep my counsel and try to tame the fear in my belly.■

19

Shantrelle

ABOARD MV ANDAMAN PEARL   July 19

I t was Lovely's idea to have a bridal party for Shantrelle. Just the three of us gathering in my cabin, lounging on my private deck, and swimming in the ship's small pool. Moonlight and warm tropical air will bring magic to the occasion.

Lovely has arranged with her father to have the pool drained, refilled with fresh sea water, and placed off limits to the rest of the ship for the evening. "We can all go skinny dipping," she chirps. "No men allowed."

The prospect of hanging out with these young women is appealing, even though it'll surely involve skinny dipping with them. I'll politely decline to take part in anything else, if that's what they have in mind, and I've told Lovely so.

"Party pooper." She pouts, but she isn't serious. She doesn't try to convince me. She's sure we'll all have a great time just gabbing and getting drunk. Shantrelle is bringing champagne. Lovely will flirt with the messman and get the cook to make something special for us to eat.

Our party will allow me to get better acquainted with Shantrelle and perhaps Lovely as well. I look forward to our little *soirée*.

About three o'clock, they arrive at my door, a bottle of champagne in each fist. The messman is right behind them with a delightful array of Filipino nibbles. If we need more, he says, let him know. Lovely grabs

153

a *palitaw* before he can set the tray down and puts the champagne in the fridge.

Shantrelle and Lovely wear colorful wraps that remind me of sarongs or *pareus*. "Here," Lovely says, thrusting a beautiful rectangular piece of batiked fabric into my hands. "This one is for you."

There's nothing to do but to strip out of my clothes and allow them to drape me. "No undies allowed," Lovely says, so my bra and panties join the pile of discarded clothing accumulating on the chair by the bed.

"Isn't she beautiful," Lovely says, taking hold of my shoulders and turning me around for Shantrelle to admire before they dress me.

I'm blushing. I didn't think I could do that.

"She is," Shantrelle says. "I mean it, Jessamyn, you are. Exquisite."

I wait for the qualifier, "for an old fart" or something similar, but it doesn't come. How easy to get caught up in the energy of these two as they wrap me and fiddle with my hair. I missed such luxuries growing up, girls hanging around and playing dress up. It would not have surprised me, had I gone ashore with Shantrelle and Lovely in Pattaya, to have thrown caution to the wind and pole danced with them at Chains. They are just that irresistible.

All of us are hungry. We tear into cook's *lumpia* and Shantrelle pops the first cork.

"To good friends," she says. "Here's to drinking Shun's champagne supply dry." No need for glasses. She lets Lovely have the first swig from the bottle, and we pass it among us.

"Maybe we should ask him to bring a couple more bottles over." Lovely giggles, taking a sip. "Insist he deliver them in his buttless chaps." She's so amused with herself champagne sprays out of her nose.

"You ladies are incorrigible," I say. "I think that's part of what I like about you. Shun and I had a wonderful lunch yesterday. He's a treasure."

"I've never met anyone like him," Shantrelle says. "And to think I get to keep him all to myself. Of course, I'll share with you two."

"Shun told me a lot about your first meeting and your courtship. How did you come to work at his company in the first place?"

"I grew up in South Central LA living with an aunty who took me in when my mom and dad went to prison. I was nine. They got mixed up in some crazy drug sting. They were nice people and no question they loved me, but they neglected me. As Aunty said, they didn't have a lick of sense.

"She dragged me to her neighborhood storefront church several times a week. Saturday choir practice and Singspiration broadcast over the radio, Sunday services morning, noon, and night, prayer meeting on Wednesdays, visiting the sick and afflicted whenever we could, and the old folks in the nursing home Friday mornings. She kept me on a short leash. When the reverend wasn't preaching at me, she took up the slack."

"Doesn't sound like much fun," Lovely says.

"I was lucky. What she and her church lady friends said and did made sense to me, except for some of the sex stuff.

"Aunty kept me out of harm's way there too. She taught me the facts of life, kept the bad boys away from me, even got me on birth control when I was eleven."

"Why would she do that?" Lovely asks.

"She was taking no chances. She would look at me over her granny glasses and say, 'Child, I know what you're feeling. Been there myself. Satan's got a pile of snares for the unwary. Caught your poor momma and daddy and tied them up with a bow. Nothin' like that gonna happen to you cause I ain't gonna allow it.'

"She let me know the reverend was a scalawag and a hypocrite, preaching damnation and hellfire while trying to get as much sex on the side as he could.

"'You gotta watch out for them as preaches one thing and performs another,' she said. 'Don't you never be all by yourself with that man. Can't keep his paws off the women, and you look more like a woman every day.'"

"Gross," Lovely chimes in. "Sounds like someone should have put his pizzle in an *agimat.*"

Shantrelle laughs. "Aunty was just the one to do it if he had messed with me. She kept me 'to the path,' as she called it. She was a stickler for schoolwork. She'd had some training as a bookkeeper and would always check my arithmetic.

"I liked school. I had outstanding teachers who pushed me and praised me, whichever was necessary, and I got a full scholarship to UCLA. Marketing and business caught my attention once I figured out I'd never make a living as a writer or artist. Unlike our girl Lovely, I don't have any genuine talent."

"Who cares about talent," Lovely says. "You landed Shun. I'll probably end up with some nerdy bassoon player and need to borrow money from you to buy a decent pair of shoes."

"I seriously doubt that," I say. "But go on with your story, Shantrelle."

"I got an internship as an office assistant for Shun's company in my junior year. They hired me into the marketing department right out of college.

"All that time with Aunty had instilled a deep sense of right and wrong in me and a certain amount of caution. At first I was shocked when I saw all the fibbing and fudging the managers in Shun's company did. I didn't know how to react. Shun explained to me later how he found peoples' lies to be almost as important as their truth telling."

"He told me that too," I say. "He's a very wise man."

"I understood the managers were under a lot of pressure. I didn't understand why some of them didn't just buckle down and get to work. They were bright, talented, and fortunate as hell to have jobs with Shun.

"We all made good money. I was making more money than I ever thought possible, sending some of it to Aunty who just sent it back, telling me to put it in the bank.

"I only knew Shun by reputation. When he came to LA to check on our operation, I was awestruck. He was kind and unassuming. He knew which managers were pulling their weight, and who was phoning it in. And it didn't seem to bother him. He treated them all with dignity and respect. When he asked my boss to introduce me to him, I thought I would melt into the floor. His eyes never left mine. He looked at me as a person he was honored to meet. I believed him."

"He has remarkable eyes," I say. "Very kind and sparkly."

"I know, right?" Lovely says. "As gorgeous as he is rich."

Shantrelle smiles. "He was easy to talk to. He was looking at the real me with those eyes, not just undressing me with them. I'm not easily impressed by slick talking men. Shun was almost courtly, polished but not slick, and I hadn't appreciated the difference before then.

"When he invited me to lunch on a Saturday, I sensed potential danger and staked out my boundaries immediately. But there was nothing to be afraid of. He knew exactly what he wanted but never pressed his advantage. He respected me and treated me like a lady as he relentlessly pursued."

Lovely took a pull at the champagne bottle and passed it to me.

"I tested him. When I got naked in front of him for the first time, to put on an exquisite gown he offered me, he passed the test. He looked into my eyes and didn't get handsy.

"He answered every question I put to him, however impertinent, and went out of the way to make me feel it was okay to ask him anything. He made it seem like it was just a normal part of getting to know each other, even when I asked him questions about his companies, and OMG, how much money he was worth."

"You what?" Lovely interrupts. "You asked him how much money he had? You could have just Googled that. I'm surprised he didn't peg you for a gold digger and run like hell."

"He just answered me as if I had asked him his astrological sign or what time of day it was. He shared details of his business operations, far beyond my ability to comprehend. Never any hesitation. He made me feel like I was perfectly entitled to ask him anything.

"In my caution, I instinctively set traps for him, with my questions and my body. I needed to make sure he was really the man I believed he was and not some loser, inflating his net worth and penis size to match his overblown opinion of himself. But he passed every test I put in front of him."

The champagne has made its way back to Lovely. She takes a gulp from the bottle and passes it my way.

"I thought I was in control," Shantrelle says. "And in one sense I was. But in another, I didn't stand a chance. When Shun decides about something, he'll never take no for an answer. I fell in love with him before I realized he had already fallen in love with me. We fit together like two puzzle pieces, and we didn't need to look at the picture on the box to figure out how the rest of it fit."

"You understood perfectly, didn't you Lovely? Two halves of one soul, you said. That's exactly right."

"I did," Lovely says, beaming. "And, you know, I think this whole thing about him wanting you to dominate him is all about him giving up some responsibility to someone he trusts absolutely. Someone he can explore intense feelings with. Right, Jessamyn? I mean, you're the doctor."

"It's true. People who enjoy those domination/submission games talk about "exchanging power" and are big on trust and communication," I say.

"Right, Jessamyn," Lovely says, grabbing the bottle from Shantrelle. "It says on YouTube that the bottom runs the fuck. Maybe we should ask Shun about that."

"Or maybe we shouldn't." Shantrelle laughs. "Although I'm sure he would tell us. I wouldn't want to spoil things for him by getting too far into his head right now. Stop hogging the bottle, Lovely."

Lovely upends the bottle, draining it. "All gone," she says, turning it upside down.

"You'd better uncork another one, girlfriend," Shantrelle says.

Lovely fetches more champagne from the fridge and opens it. "Only two left after this puppy," she says. "We might have to call Shun after all."

She's giggling at the prospect as she hands the champagne to Shantrelle and gets back into bed.

"Shun taught me everything I know about sex. He says he never had sex with anyone before he met me. Sure, he had gone to titty bars, even live sex shows in connection with his business and entertaining his clients, but they never meant to him what they meant to most people."

Lovely isn't buying it, and she's had enough champagne to destroy any boundaries she might have. She grabs the bottle from Shantrelle, takes a pull, and passes it to me.

"Come on. I mean, he owns Chains with all the pussy floating around there, and he never had sex with anyone until you guys did it the first time? No strippers, no pole dancers, not even a hand job from some hooker? No way. He's the second or third richest man in the world. I Googled it. Oops, sorry. Maybe I shouldn't have done that."

Shantrelle giggles.

I give the bottle to her but not before having another little nip, given the direction this party is going. In case of snake bite.

"No sex. Nothing except mother palmer and her five children," Shantrelle says.

"He's so good at that. It's double hot to watch when we make him do it," Lovely chimes in.

Shantrelle rolls her eyes.

"Sex aboard the *Andaman Pearl* has been hot for Shun, and I want him to have that. He deserves hot. I trust him to let us know his limits, and I trust us to honor those limits."

"Well, you can trust me to push the limits." Lovely giggles. "That's just a witchy cannibally thing I do. Of course I'd never do anything you two think isn't right. Or you, Jessamyn. I'm not sure how Shun figures that out, but he seems so sure. And this little nautical clusterfuck doesn't disturb his sense of right and wrong."

"He thinks it's all good," Shantrelle says. "Shun asks himself if anyone is unhappy or being hurt. His moral compass is calibrated in those terms. And what we're all doing makes everyone feel happy and hurts nobody. Shun would be the first one to know if it's wrong and would call a halt. In the meantime, I'm having great fun having sex with Shun and Lovely. You're a great lay, Lovely, as if you didn't already know that."

Lovely has the champagne now. "Why, thank you kindly ma'am," she says, raising the bottle to toast Shantrelle. "Right back at ya. Jessamyn, you're too quiet. Have some champagne."

The bottle comes my way. "Well, this little nautical clusterfuck, as you describe it, will end soon. Shantrelle and Shun will disembark from the *Andaman Pearl* in a couple of days, leaving poor Lovely and me to our own devices, at least until Lovely leaves the ship in France and hooks up with someone else."

"I'm really going to miss Lovely, and you too Jessamyn. If I know Shun, he'll find a way for us all to stay in touch. Until we figure that out, I guess we can dirty Zoom."

"Speaking of dirty, we haven't heard the sordid details of Jessamyn's sex life. But let's go skinny dipping first. Soften her up," Lovely says."

We decide to leave the champagne bottle inside on the nightstand. The tiny outdoor pool, filled with fresh sea water is cold. My guess is we won't last fifteen minutes until we flee the pool for the warmth of my cabin. I have that much time to prepare for my inquisition.

Back inside, with hot cocoa instead of champagne, we all dry off and get back into my bed. I'm the filling in a cozy Shantrelle/Lovely sandwich. It's comfortable, not even a little awkward. Nobody is unhappy or getting hurt. Shun would approve.

"Okay, Jessamyn," Lovely says. "Spill the beans."

I tell them about my awkward romantic youth. About Elsa, Pyotr, and the lesser lights of my sex life. I don't tell them about Lagac. I wouldn't want to betray his confidence. Talking about Roderick is tougher. But I decide to tell them the truth, or as much as I can tell anyone.

They feel me tense, and they rub my shoulders as I describe "sex night" and the unfulfilling trajectory of my life with Roderick. Since they ask, I tell them I'm not grieving about Roderick's "heart attack," that I'm happy now to find a different course for my life.

Of course I can't tell them about how I poisoned his stiffy juice. I'm surprised to find how much I regret having to lie to them by omission when they have been so transparent with me. The twin curses of old age and experience, I tell myself.

Roderick's murder keeps popping up in unexpected ways. He's living in my head far too often and it makes me angry. Afraid.

"What next?" They are genuinely curious but I don't know. Shantrelle says she thinks the second officer has eyes for me. Lovely quickly provides the information that he's gay. I have told nobody about the scene I inadvertently witnessed among the containers. Is the rumor mill in overdrive?

"How do you know he's gay?" Shantrelle asks. "Maybe he's bi, and he and Jessamyn could still get it on."

"Jessamyn's not interested," I say.

Shantrelle laughs.

"My *gaydar* is never wrong," Lovely says.

"Well, Lovely, you can use your witchy powers to hex one of the hunky sailors and turn him into a mindless sex zombie for you and Jessamyn to party with."

"Again, so not interested," I say to much teasing and laughter.

Lovely stifles a yawn with the back of one hand. "I'm getting hella sleepy," she says. "I think I'd better get back to my cabin and call it a night. It's been so fun."

"Yes, it has been fun," I say. "You're both very special. I'm so happy I'm with you on this voyage."

Lovely climbs out of bed and wraps her sarong around her. "Nighty night," she says, giving me a peck on the cheek. "See you guys tomorrow. Big day. Shantrelle and Shun are tying the knot."

"'Night, Lovely," I say. "See you in the morning."

"Yeah, good night," Shantrelle says. "Get plenty of rest. If you louse up the wedding march tomorrow, I'll have to flog you."

Lovely flips her the bird as she leaves my cabin.

"I should get going too," Shantrelle says, retrieving her sarong. "It's been great to be with you, Jessamyn. Lovely and Shun think you're an angel, how you stepped in and protected Mrs. Agarwal before anyone came to your aid. Me too.

"Eric says you're an amazing doctor, and Lagac can't keep his eyes off you. You've probably been up to other things we don't know about, making everyone care so much for you. Now I've become your biggest fan too. I'm so glad we had this time together."

"I'm happy for you and Shun," I say, getting out of bed to see her to the door. "Your story is a fairytale, magical almost. And I know it's going to have a 'happy ever after' ending for both of you."

"May I give you a kiss, Jessamyn?"

"Of course you may, my dear. How wonderful."

We hug, and Shantrelle kisses my cheek and rubs my back as she pulls me closer. I'm suddenly aware I'm naked. My sarong is still on the couch.

"You seem troubled, Jessamyn," she says, her eyes reflecting her concern. "Shun and Lovely are concerned something's worrying you."

"I have some things on my mind. To make things worse, I'm thinking how much I'll miss you and Shun when you leave the ship."

"I'm sure Shun will make sure we stay in touch. The world is his backyard, and he doesn't let go of people he treasures. He's a rock star to have on your side. If you're worried about something, Jessamyn, I'm sure Shun can help. All you need to do is talk with him."

"Shun's a prince. He's completely changed my prejudice against rich people. Then again, he's not just any rich person. His wealth is breathtaking but not as breathtaking as he is.

"He shared with me what he's doing to coax Mr. Agarwal back into the human race. I'd have tied him to an anchor, tossed him overboard, but Shun's way is better."

"Shun doesn't believe people do bad things without a reason, Mr. Agarwal included, and he thinks that by doing good things, we can make up for the bad ones. I still know little about Islam, or Shun's take on Islam, but I absolutely trust him."

"I know little about it either," I say. "Eric explained some things to me, and I had the most interesting conversation with a shopkeeper named Hamza Baraquilla in Manila, who enlightened me about the evil eye and how to deal with *jinn*. Especially how to tell them apart from cats." I laugh, recalling the conversation.

"I'm not sure I believe in *jinn*," Shantrelle says. "Shun hasn't talked about them. I'll have to ask him what he thinks. Have you seen any suspicious cats lately?" It was her turn to laugh.

"Not while I've been awake, but I keep having these dreams about jungle cats. Mr. Baraquilla warned me that *jinn* can assume the form of cats, but I don't think the dreamcats I have run into are *jinn*.

"I'm a physician, an ultra-rational person by temperament and training. But there are so many things I don't understand. Lovely with her witches, her *agimat*, her cannibal relatives, and all. Did she tell you she let me touch the *agimat*, and it didn't strike me dead? Still, I'm secretly hoping that special rattle it makes really does come from that evil priest's teeth and shriveled up dick."

Shantrelle laughs. "Lovely insisted I touch it as well, and I came away from the experience none the worse for wear. Maybe we're all special in some way. Immune from witches' curses."

"You and Lovely certainly are special and so is Shun. And for all the teasing about the second officer and Engineer Lagac, they're also very special people to me. I've never met as many special people in one place as I have on the *Andaman Pearl*."

Shantrelle puts her hands lightly on my arms and locks eyes with me. They sparkle like a meteor shower. Standing there before her I have never felt so naked in my life.

"You're special too, Jessamyn, and more vulnerable than you imagine. We all see it. We're all looking after you." She kisses me softly on the lips, and I kiss her back.

"Good night, Jessamyn. Sleep well," she says.

I stand there immobile for what seems like forever after she closes the door to my cabin. I walk out onto my private deck and look at the sky and the full moon. Tears fall silently down my face, running down my body. I don't know why or for whom I shed them. I return to my cabin and burrow into the safety of my bed, feeling excruciatingly alone. The *maneki-neko* beckons, friendly and reassuring as ever.

I must have fallen asleep almost instantly. When I open my eyes, the sun shines brightly through the portholes. There were no dreamcats but the *maneki-neko* stands guard.

The sea is like a mirror. Lady Grey tea sounds like a marvelous idea. ■

20

Lechon

C

ABOARD MV ANDAMAN PEARL   July 20

ook has decided today is the right day. There's only one suckling pig aboard the *Andaman Pearl*. It's been traveling with us in the ship's freezer since we left Tokyo. There could have been more, and it's possible to buy a pig at almost any of our ports of call, but more than one pig would spoil the fun, the anticipation of a special occasion.

Today is just the right day to bring the honored guest from the galley to the main deck, coddle it for hours over glowing coals, and savor the aroma and flavor of every succulent morsel of roast suckling pig.

Pig roast day coincides with the day Shun and Shantrelle have chosen for Captain Bayani to marry them. The ceremony took place a couple of hours ago in the saloon, the Bösendorfer under the command of Lovely Bayani who ditched her peek-a-boo gown and hooker shoes for the occasion. The bride and groom wore casual clothes, as did the rest of us, including the pianist, the captain, and the second officer.

Theirs is not a legal marriage. Shipboard nuptials are the stuff of legend, like the wedding of Bogart and Hepburn aboard the *African Queen*, but mostly they happen only in the movies or as part of the slick marketing campaigns for a handful of Bermuda-flagged cruise ships.

The captain of a Philippines-flagged ship can only marry people if one of the people getting married is dying and won't make it off the ship

165

to walk down the aisle elsewhere, Lovely told me. Shun and Shantrelle clearly don't qualify.

The captain gamely agreed to officiate a commitment ceremony instead, using a script written by Shun and Shantrelle. As Shantrelle said, "Our hearts are getting married on the *Andaman Pearl*. The rest of us will get married in Singapore."

The ceremony went off without a flaw. If Shantrelle wants to flog Lovely tonight, she'll need a pretext other than her playing, which was perfect.

The pig had been roasting for hours before Shun and Shantrelle's ceremony took place. Narong, the messman who joined the ship at Khlong Toei, handles much of the spit-turning under the watchful eye of the cook. The pig weighs about thirty pounds and will take eight to ten hours to roast to perfection. Narong's spelled in his duties by an able-bodied sailor and a cadet, all of them off-duty and fortified by a stash of Leo beer left over from Koh Sichang.

Tomorrow, when we make port in Singapore and the roast pig is a fading memory, Shun and Shantrelle will solemnize their civil marriage. They have asked Lovely and me to witness papers their lawyers and financial people will have waiting. Then we'll spend the rest of the day celebrating.

Lovely and I will stay overnight in Shun's penthouse condo in the exclusive Wallich Residence before bidding farewell and returning to the ship to resume our journey. Shun has said we'll also have the pleasure of a special guest in Singapore, but he won't tell us who. He says Lovely knows her by name, but they have never met. Lovely hasn't a clue who it might be, and it irritates her. Mysteries will unfold when they unfold, Shantrelle says with her Mona Lisa smile.

The unusual nature of this marriage is not lost on me. This mega billionaire and his beloved, who could have a wedding envied by royalty, have married their hearts on a container ship in the South China Sea. There's no pomp and circumstance aboard the *Andaman Pearl,* nor will there be any in Singapore. No additional friends, family, or important business associates, according to Shantrelle. Just us rag-tag passengers of the *Andaman* Pearl and a government functionary or two.

The pig roast seems unusual too, although I'm informed it's a time-tested ritual aboard passenger-carrying container ships. Unusual in the sense that the *Andaman Pearl* has several Muslim officers and crew like Eric and passengers like Shun. Most of the sailors are Catholic, Eric says, and the Muslim sailors have learned to accommodate the heathen pig-eaters.

Some Muslims eat pork, Shun explains, although it's ritually unclean and forbidden, trusting that Allah will be merciful, the same way some Catholics don't observe Ash Wednesday and Good Friday as obligatory days of fasting and abstinence, trusting in the mercy of God. Most of the Muslims on board, Shun among them, will give the pig a pass, but there will be plenty of delicious food, drink, and merriment without pork for those who choose not to eat it. For the rest of us, a thirty-pound porker invites premeditated gluttony.

The pig turns hypnotically on the spit in an atmosphere of great anticipation. The captain stops by to offer his two cents' worth. Everyone, including Lagac, has found time away from shipboard duties to cast an eye on the pig and make certain everything is copacetic.

"Cook does pretty good, considering what he has to work with," Lagac says. "Too bad this poor little piggy will not be *lechon,* cooked over a hand built *lechonan* like the pit at my father's house in Cebu. Poor little piggy will not be privileged to be rolled across the *lechonan* on a green bamboo pole by a world class *lechonero* like myself," Lagac chortles. "In all modesty."

The Lagac show has begun, and I'm enjoying my front-row seat. Modest is not a descriptor that comes immediately to mind for Lagac.

"Do you realize that King Humabon and Queen Juana of Cebu fed *lechon* to Magellan in 1521? Next thing you know, Magellan converted the king, the queen, and 400 servants to Catholicism. The power of *lechon.*"

Lagac warms to his sermon, like a tent preacher dispensing the gospel to hungry sinners. Like all good preachers, he holds everyone spellbound, promising some transcendent revelation.

"Here's how to make authentic *lechon*," Lagac says. "Gut the pig, wash out the cavity, and pour boiling water over the skin so you can scrape off the hair. Rub the inside with salt, pepper, and spices like star anise. I can't reveal all my secrets or a *mangkukulam* would put a spell on my manhood. Even *lechon's* not worth that.

"Next, you stuff the cavity with lemongrass, green onions, garlic, tamarind leaves, and saba bananas and stitch the piggy up with twine around a green bamboo pole so the *lechonero* can roll it slowly back and forth, back and forth across the *lechonan* for hours."

I can just see him strutting about on a TV cooking show, like Anthony Bourdain's, chivvying the host about rolling the pig too fast.

"The skin's the most important part. To make it crackly and golden, you must mop the pig with Dr. Pepper. Or Coca-Cola but not Pepsi. No self-respecting *lechonero* would ever drink Pepsi. Or you can use condensed milk and fresh coconut water.

"As soon as it's done, before anybody can beat you to it, steal some skin from the back, right behind the shoulders, and some of the meat underneath. Wash it down with real Filipino beer like San Miguel. That's the best part of being the *lechonero*.

"Cook's pig and his Leo beer will be pretty good though. You'll find me at the head of the line, fighting for the skin."

Lagac is all in. Lovely describes him as "amazeballs." She has no idea. Mother Nature must have been dreaming about Lagac when she brewed up testosterone. He is to lust as Ferrari is to cars. When I catch a glimpse of him, my body revs like it's revving now as I listen to his sermonizing. Preach it, brother. Can I get an "Amen?"

We've had sex twice since the first time in Lagac's engine room. Each time more intense than the last. When he kisses me, I dissolve. One of these days, I'll trap him into talking about it. Talking about us. Our sexual connection just keeps getting better. My emotional connection to him is deepening as well, and I want to get Lagac's side of the story.

I'm surprised at the intensity of my feelings for him. After I killed Roderick, I made no promises to myself about sex and relationships, but I hadn't expected this. With Roderick's foul thumb off my heart, my sex drive has blossomed.

I'm fantasizing more these days about how a life with Lagac might look. That's insane of course. He's a sailor with a girlfriend, maybe more than one when he's in the Philippines. They sext, for goodness sake.

I can't see myself living in the Philippines, and I can't see Lagac giving up his career even if it turns out we have a connection greater than sex. There's a lot of voyage left, and I'm hopeful some of these "love" things will sort themselves out.

But I'm in no hurry. I don't want the talking to impede the doing. If I had a Ferrari parked in my driveway, would I sit on the porch reading the owner's manual? Not with the white-hot concupiscence I feel for the first time in decades. I've got a full tank of racing fuel.

When it's ready, the suckling pig is amazeballs, as Lovely says. Even Lagac, who has stolen a piece of skin and some meat from the choice spot right behind the shoulder and is alternating feeding morsels to me and consuming them himself, says so. He knows about the choice spots, no doubt about it.

While Lagac waxes eloquent about *lechon*, my body wonders how we can get together today for a feast of a different sort. Even just a quick snack. I touch his shoulder and whisper in his ear. His eyes sparkle. He'll find a way, he says. He feeds me another morsel of delectable pig. Then another.

Gentlemen, start your engines. ■

21

Fireflies

SINGAPORE   July 21

There's something magical about fireflies, even to physicians who don't traffic in magic. Thousands of fireflies signaling in synchrony can stand in for magic in a world all too impoverished of its touch. Shun has decreed that we women will share one of his magical childhood memories, the fireflies twinkling in the mangrove swamp of Pasir Ris Park, a short drive from the press of downtown Singapore.

But first the formalities of the marriage. Shun's driver is waiting for us when we debark. He ferries all of us to Shun's Wallich Residence penthouse in Singapore's Tanjong Pagar area.

A butler helps Lovely and me settle into our rooms while Shun and Shantrelle meet with attorneys, accountants, and assorted wizards, gnomes, and financial conjurers in his corporate offices a few floors below in the Guoco Tower.

Shun has given orders to the assembled suits to guarantee Shantrelle is as rich as he is. That his wealth is her wealth. He is determined to coronate Shantrelle, Queen of the World. *Ratu Dunia. Ratu Shantrelle.*

The stunning sixty-fourth floor condo has three bedrooms besides the master suite, all of which have sweeping views of the Singapore Strait. Lovely and I are ushered into our respective bedrooms. The door to the other bedroom is closed. Our mystery guest?

171

Shun says we should explore the shopping areas on the first six floors of the tower and the other amenities of the building, including the infinity pool on the thirty-ninth floor.

He promises us a whirlwind tour of the city this afternoon. We expect the *Andaman Pearl* to leave Singapore tomorrow morning, so we have little time here. Shun has us booked solid until then.

Shun and Shantrelle dispatch their business in short order. The lawyers have asked Lovely and me to sign only a single document swearing we know them to be honorable people, acting of their own accord, in possession of all their marbles. They'll need to wait a couple of weeks for the government bureaucracy before filing a Notice of Marriage and engaging a Licensed Solemnizer.

They are waiting for us in a private dining room in the Guoco Tower. A radiant young woman about Lovely's age stands next to them. She smiles at Lovely, who, for a moment, seems puzzled. Then it hits her.

"Èlia," she says, running over and hugging her. "Oh my god, Èlia! What are you doing here?" From the edge of the room, Shun and Shantrelle smile like the proverbial cats who've gotten into the cream.

Èlia doesn't have time to answer before Lovely drags her by the hand to meet me. "Jessamyn, this is Èlia. She's going to be my roommate and study-buddy in Paris."

Èlia extends her hand. "Èlia Palacios Lozano," she says with a lilt. Very pleased to meet you."

"Jessamyn Quilter, the pleasure is mine."

"You rats," Lovely says, punching Shun's arm. "You said I knew her but never met her. That's not true. We've met, just not in person. We've already Zoomed tons of times and made elaborate plans. Oh my god! Èlia. I can't believe you're here, and I totally don't understand. I thought you would fly to Paris next month.

She looks at Shun for an explanation with a mixture of puzzlement and accusation. Shantrelle rescues him. "Mysteries will unfold when they unfold," she says.

"Let's celebrate this moment," Shun says.

A server passes a tray of drinks. "Pisco sours, in honor of our friend, Èlia, who comes to us from the Peruvian Amazon by way of Lima where she and her family have recently settled.

"We thought Èlia might appreciate a little taste of home. *¡Salud!* Cheers!"

We clink glasses all around.

"*Tagay!*" Lovely says, taking a large sip, nearly losing it. "OMG, that's strong. But so good," she says, taking another sip.

It's my turn to offer a toast. "To Shun and Shantrelle, remarkable people and consummate hosts, and to Lovely and Èlia."

"To Lovely," Èlia says, "and to all of you. I can't quite believe I'm here and all this is happening."

We would learn later that afternoon that Shun sent one of his "little jets" to Lima, where Èlia works for his company, to fly her to Singapore. No wonder she looks a little nonplussed.

Èlia is striking. She's an inch or two taller than Lovely with a shapely, stocky build. Her straight jet-black hair, hanging to the middle of her back, is cut low, straight across her forehead, shoulder length around her face. Her burnished brown skin, tinged with red, looks like some exotic jungle hardwood.

Her clothes are elegant. She wears a gold sateen blouse with a parrot-green yoke edged with embroidered borders in browns and buffs and a magenta wrap skirt embroidered with complex geometric patterns in bright reds, pinks, indigos, and azures.

Except for her intense brown, almost black, eyes and full lips, Èlia's face is covered with tattoos from her forehead to her neck, continuing under her chin, even across the bridge of her nose in patterns that remind me of a Keith Haring painting, except there are no figures There's only geometry like the designs in her skirt. A closer look reveals they're not tattoos but meticulously applied brownish-black ink. I try not to stare but it's impossible.

Èlia bears all this scrutiny with grace and dignity. There's so much I want to ask her, but I'm leery of moving too fast. Still, we haven't much time together before Lovely and I must go back to the ship. I genuinely hope I'll have time to get to know this young woman better before we leave.

"Èlia's story is one that may take some time unfolding," Shun says, anticipating my concern. "Fortunately you have time. She will join the two you on the *Andaman Pearl* as you make your way to Paris."

I look at Lovely, who shrugs her shoulders as if to say, "I had no idea," and look back at Shun. "You never cease to amaze me, sir," I say, raising my nearly depleted Pisco Sour. "I couldn't be happier I won't be trapped alone with Lovely for the rest of the trip."

"You're a rat too, Jessamyn," Lovely says. She sticks her tongue out at me for good measure.

"Let's see what the chef has prepared for lunch," Shun says.

Waitstaff pull out our chairs. Shun sidles in between Shantrelle and me, Lovely sits next to me on the other side and Èlia is seated between Lovely and Shantrelle. Mocha, mahogany, and ebony. I have never felt whiter, with all that presupposes, in my life. And yet all of them wrap me in the warmth of their color.

The chef has assembled a cold seafood buffet atop an enormous Chinese revolving platter lined with julienned sea vegetable, rice balls, lobster, prawns, smoked octopus, crab salad, mackerel, salmon, scallops with roe, and oysters on the half shell accompanied by a variety of dressings including a stinging wasabi *crème fraîche*.

Sea creatures I have never seen before are nestled beside the more familiar, and I vow not to let any of them go unsampled. Sea slugs, for example. Their salty, smoky flavor is intense, the texture akin to chewing on a pencil eraser. My favorite is the creamy uni, sea urchin roe in black spiny shells.

A yummy Bordeaux rosé of cabernet franc and crisp New Zealand chardonnay are also on offer, perfect matches to the seafood.

After lunch we climb into a waiting limousine for the city tour Shun promised. Our itinerary takes us north through the tangle of Chinatown. Our first stop is the Buddha Tooth Relic Temple, a late twentieth century monastery and temple built in Tang Dynasty style. Legend has it the tooth in question, which we do not see because it's only shown to tourists on Buddha's birthday and Chinese New Year, was discovered by a monk in Myanmar. Shun doesn't believe the story. He doubts the provenance of the tooth, telling us it's probably cow or water buffalo.

When we leave the temple, we walk to the Sri Mariamman Temple, the oldest Hindu temple in Singapore.

"The Hindu priests welcome everyone, believer or not," Shun says. "It's a daily reminder of how diverse we Singaporeans are, both politically and spiritually."

He guides us through the Tamil traditions we need to observe when visiting the temple. We remove our shoes and leave them at the entrance with hundreds of others. We purify ourselves, washing our hands and sprinkling water on our heads.

"Once inside," Shun coaches us, "we must show the priests respect and not enter any of the shrines. We mustn't sit with our feet pointing at the deities or other people."

The paneled double entrance doors to the temple's main prayer hall, four times as tall as a person's height, are hung with rows of bells and garlands of fresh bananas, mangoes, and neem leaves.

"The doors remind us of how insignificant we are compared with the divine," Shun explains. "Ring one of the bells to alert the deities of your presence. You can make a wish if you like."

I don't know about the others, but I wish for the safety and well-being of all of us, those sailing tomorrow on the *Andaman Pearl* and those we'll too soon be leaving behind in this city-state.

As impressed as I am by the opulence and ritual, I can't help thinking it has ever been thus with religions. Don't disrespect the priests or get too close to their private playpens.

And I reflect that all the sculptures in places of worship around the world look like the people who make them. These Hindu gods have Tamil faces, at least the one that doesn't look like an elephant. Buddhist deities have Asian faces. The plaster Jesus and all the saints in Catholic churches look like Spaniards. Only the Muslims and the Jews seem to have gotten it right by banning such frippery outright.

Our driver whisks us to Fort Canning Park and the nearby National Museum of Singapore and then on to Bugis Street, a feast for the senses and the palate. We poke through boutiques and street stalls. Shun dares Lovely to try some Dragon's Breath, fruity colorful cereal balls treated with liquid nitrogen that release smoke through her nostrils when she bites into them. She coughs, then roars and contracts her fingers into dragon claws, feigning an attack on Shun. Èlia laughs and demands some Dragon's Breath too. I smile as I picture these two young women running amok in Paris.

The Kampong Glam Muslim quarter is next on our tour with its golden domed Sultan Mosque, but daylight is fading and Shun is eager to get to Pasir Ris park before sundown. At Pasir Ris, we become a small flotilla of one person kayaks, our gentle-spirited guide shepherding us through the darkening tangle of mangroves.

Swarms of fireflies, thousands flashing in synchronous display reward us. Nothing much leaves me speechless, but chills run through my body when Shun sings a wedding song to Shantrelle, a phrase at a time, and she sings back to him, their call and response reprising the pulsing of the fireflies. I wonder if the child Shun, enchanted by the pale fire of this place had any inkling he'd return as a young man with his beloved, the luminance of their devotion surpassing the magic of the fireflies, at least to my eyes.

The ride back to the condo wraps us all in the warmth of Shun and Shantrelle's happiness. Shun insists we stop at the Raffles long bar and experience authentic Singapore slings. One sling leads to another. We have no sooner piled back into the waiting limousine, pleasantly tipsy, when Lovely and I receive texts from the second officer. We must return right away. The *Andaman Pearl* will sail as soon as we can get back.

We promise Eric we'll be at the docks within the hour. Shun calls ahead to the Wallach Residence to instruct the concierge to pack up our things and meet us at the portico in ten minutes. Then, with Shun and Shantrelle still in tow, we speed back to the *Andaman Pearl* and climb the gangway, waving and shouting tearful goodbyes from the deck of the ship as the crew makes ready to cast off.

My heart overflows with memories and love for these special people I met only a couple of months ago in Yokohama. I've shared so much life with them already. I remember Shantrelle's promise—Shun will find a way for us all to be connected, he doesn't let go of people he treasures.

The next leg of our journey takes us to Sri Lanka. It'll be a week before we make landfall in Colombo, our jumping off point for the far reaches of the Arabian Sea, the Suez Canal, and our transit from the storied reaches of the far east to the more familiar precincts of the Mediterranean Sea.

I chide myself that I've written no more than a few disjointed thoughts in my journal. I lecture myself that I need to buckle down, but I have no more idea what I'll write about than I did when it first crossed my mind that a long ocean voyage would be the perfect venue for writing.

And now Èlia becomes part of the journey. There's something unsettling about her. She may be Lovely's age, but she has little of Lovely's youthful fizz. She carries herself with preternatural dignity, an aura of the ancients. I feel no judgment from her, but I'm sure she can see right through me.

While it's unsettling, it's not off-putting. Indeed, it's intriguing. What does she see? As Shantrelle said, "Mysteries will unfold when they unfold." ■

177

22

Unsettled

ABOARD MV ANDAMAN PEARL   July 23

Our departure from Singapore was too abrupt. I under-stand schedules are driven by the ocean's whim, and the captain's, but I've not experienced the disconnect-edness of a departure from port so acutely before.

We'll be hugging the coast of Sumatra through the Straits of Malacca on a long journey to Colombo, so it's an excellent opportunity to learn more about the ship. The second officer has been explaining some of the finer points of container handling.

Deck officers load, unload, and secure the containers, a weighty responsibility, although they call on help from able-bodied sailors when things get hectic, as they often do in an insanely busy port like Singapore.

"The captain gets a manifest specifying the exact position of each container on board, how much it weighs, where it's to be loaded or offloaded, and what it contains," Eric says.

"Or rather," he says, using air quotes, "what it is '*said* to contain.' They hold the captain responsible for the contents, legal or not, but most of the time, he doesn't really know what's inside."

"Doesn't customs make sure of all that?" I ask.

"Customs is supposed to inspect and seal the containers, but there's so much graft on the docks, the captain can't be sure. Sometimes the captain or crew of a vessel are in on the scam. Of course Captain Bayani would never take part in anything like that.

"A few weeks ago, off the Coast of Cartagena, Columbia, the captain of an Ecuadorean-flagged ship and several members of his crew were jailed when police got wind of a scheme to traffic middle eastern nationals into servitude in Eastern Europe."

"On a tip, they searched a container 'said to contain' tires and automotive parts but found instead fifteen undocumented women. Despite their high value as chattel, many likely would not have survived the journey under those conditions."

"People? Human beings just stuffed into a container?"

"Yep. A regular old container. Sometimes we ship live animals, like horses or zoo animals, in special climate-controlled containers with proper facilities for feeding and watering them, but those women didn't have those luxuries. Some people don't care about other people, especially if there's money involved."

Beyond staying alert for contraband, Eric explains, the deck officer makes sure containers are loaded and offloaded in the correct order so the ship doesn't list. And he reiterates that there can be personnel changes at major ports.

"I think you know we took on an additional deck officer while docked in Singapore," Eric says. "A Tamil named Nasir Rajaratman."

"I've seen him but not met him." Unlike everyone else on board, Rajaratman has been standoffish, curt, and thoroughly unpleasant to the rest of the crew. When I share my opinion of him with Lagac, he laughs and reminds me not everyone in the world is as charming as he is.

"One of Rajaratman's duties will be to recruit and direct the squad of mercenaries we'll pick up in Sri Lanka," Eric says.

That's a surprise. "What do we need with mercenaries?" The one-word answer sends chills down my spine.

"Pirates."

"Pirates? Really? These mercenaries are armed?"

"Yes, they're armed. Pirates are a fact of life for any ship transiting the Suez Canal, especially around the Somali coastline," Eric says. "Although they don't cause as much trouble as they used to."

"So, not like *Captain Phillips* anymore?"

"Not anymore. Pirates are not much interested in hostages these days. They stopped hijacking Philippines-flagged ships a long time ago because the government is too stingy to pay ransoms.

"Usually they try to board using grappling hooks, steal stuff from a few containers, and speed off in 'go-fast' boats. It's better to keep them from boarding in the first place, so we pick up mercenaries in Sri Lanka or India to keep them off the ship.

"We hire them in Colombo and drop them at Port Said on the Mediterranean side of the canal. Some other ship will pick them up and hire them for the trip back to the Indian Ocean. It's all routine."

I seek out Lagac for a second expert opinion on the matter of the pirate menace. "Have you ever been attacked by pirates?" I ask him, reprising the second officer's explanation of the situation.

"Me? No. I'm a lover, not a fighter." He laughs. "If pirates attack the ship, I know lots of hidey holes. I'll come get you, and we'll think of some way to pass the time until they get tired and go home," he says, still laughing.

Lagac has already shown me a few of his "hidey holes" in which we've indulged ourselves. It's almost certain I've seen more of the *Andaman Pearl* in this way than most of the passengers she's carried. At least if Lagac is telling the truth when he says he doesn't pick up a new lover on every voyage.

"Most of the passengers are too old, too young, too married, too male, or just plain too ugly for me." He snickers. I'm sure he says things like that to get a rise out of me, but it doesn't matter. On this voyage, at least, I'm his prize and he's mine. I'm content to leave it at that.

Every ship in the world seems to be in the Strait of Malacca, heading toward Singapore or away from it. Traffic thins out as we exit the Strait into the body of water that gave our vessel its name, the Andaman Sea. Once we clear the northernmost tip of Sumatra, we'll navigate more westerly toward the Nicobar Islands to our north and then the lengthy stretch to Colombo.

The ocean is unsettled and so am I. Eric says we're in for chop like this for a few days, and we'll just plow through it. Nothing like Typhoon Kaala, but my chats with Eric and Lagac about pirates haven't calmed my spirits, and the weather isn't helping.

Something else is bothering me, and I'm not sure what it is.

Perhaps it's the lingering memory of a dream when I awoke this morning to the leaden skies and rough seas outside my porthole. The jaguar was back, the one who threatened me in an earlier dream, but he wasn't menacing last night. He seemed protective.

"Jessamyn," he chuffed. "There is danger around you. Be very careful." And then he vanished. He is a cat of few words, coming and going as he pleases as cats will. Why would I even pay attention to a dreamcat, a cartoon character created by my imagination? Why am I beginning to regard him as real?

Over the past few days, I've wondered if I can force him to show up more often. I have questions for him, which is silly, I know, but he's appeared far too often for me to think he'll suddenly go away. I don't know why he's taken up residence in my head, and I'm resigned to his annoying habit of appearing only when he chooses, but that doesn't prevent me from being pissed off that I have no control over him.

***

Shun and Shantrelle's departure left a surprising hole. Surprising because I didn't know them long, but once we connected our relationship was intense.

The new passenger situation is not yet comfortable. Lovely seems completely absorbed with Èlia, and I am...what? Jealous? I listen to them laughing together in the saloon as they work on their music. Lovely plays piano or cello, and Èlia sings as they compose music I've never heard before. From time to time, the music sounds reedy, something like a flute or an oboe. I wonder if Èlia plays an instrument as well as composes, though I'm sure she could get into the prestigious Paris Conservatoire with her composition and vocal skills alone.

Lovely and Èlia are together constantly. While they're friendly and engaging with me, my position in Lovely's world has shifted. I remind myself they are young people. Video friends with glorious destinies in Paris to be shared for a few years at least. Then there will be careers and accolades. My future is less certain. I don't know what I'll do when I reach the end of my journey on this ship.

I've thought about getting off in Paris, rather than sailing all the way to Rotterdam. But that doesn't seem like a good choice. What do they need with a fifty-something "groupie?"

I spend a little time with Lovely this morning at breakfast before Èlia wakes up and joins us.

"Èlia is amazing, Jessamyn. Of course, you're amazing too, it's just in a different way." She hugs me as if she senses my schoolgirl worries about being replaced as a bestie.

Èlia is warm, all smiles for both of us when she joins us, but something in those enchanting eyes of hers transfixes me. For no fathomable reason, I'm fearful of her. Ridiculous. There's absolutely nothing off-putting or threatening about her. Like Lovely, she's truly a gem.

"Lovely keeps going on about you," Èlia tells me. "I'm looking forward to getting to know you much better. She says you are wise, kind, amazing in every way, and I'm sure she is right."

I can't hold Èlia's eyes, kind and understanding as they are. I don't know why.

"If I can ever pry the two of you away from your music, I'd love to spend some time with you," I tell Èlia. "What I hear coming through the bulkhead between the saloon and my cabin is mysterious and magnificent." I smile, but my words feel patronizing and unconvincing, although I mean every syllable.

"That might not be possible," Lovely teases. "We're completely addicted to Èlia's music."

Èlia smiles and touches my arm. "There's nothing stopping us from sharing *our* music with you," she says.

"Jessamyn, you'll be blown away when we show you Èlia's music. I still don't believe it," Lovely says. "I mean, I'm the luckiest roommate ever."

"Well, my dears, I'm all ears."

"All ears won't do, will it Èlia? Like I said, we'll have to show it to you. I can't really explain," Lovely says.

"Well, ears, eyes, whatever else you think I'll need, I will happily provide. It sounds 'amazeballs.'"

They laugh at my attempt to mimic Lovely's slang.

"Can we stop by your cabin tomorrow evening?" Èlia asks. "After we have worked some things out and practiced more?"

"I'd love that. I'll be waiting with wine and snacks whenever you like."

They both hug me, and Lovely kisses me as we get up from the breakfast table. "Sorry we've been neglecting you, Jessamyn," she says and kisses me again.

I feel a little better. As much as I'm reluctant to admit it, what I need now is Lagac's company. I go looking for him and find him, stripped to the waist with a ginormous wrench in his hand, swearing at some piece of machinery on the forecastle.

His face lights up as I approach. "Don't come any closer," he warns. "I'm greasy, sweaty, and I smell like an octopus that's been lying in the sun for a week." He laughs in that way that makes me want to do exactly the opposite of what he says.

I come closer and we bend toward each other, lips pursed, managing a quick A-frame kiss. He doesn't smell all that bad. He's busy, but he picks up on my mood.

"You okay?" he asks, putting the wrench down, wiping his hands on a rag. If I ever had any concerns I wasn't more than just a sexual diversion for Lagac, the way he searches my eyes when he asks if I'm okay chases them away.

"Mostly," I say. "I just wanted to see your greasy, sweaty face."

He mops his forehead. "I'm off in a couple of hours. How about I get cleaned up and stop by your cabin then?"

That jolt of erotic energy starts in my toes and shoots upward but fizzles out. That's not what I need. I just need to be with him for a little, have him hold me, hear him laugh. If he wants sex, why not? But what I really want is just him.

"That would be lovely," I say. "No hurry. Take your time." We lean forward for another kiss.

"See you soon then," he says, crouching on his hands and knees to retrieve something that's fallen underneath whatever he's been working on.

There's something wild about Lagac, and the instant that thought enters my mind the fabric of reality rips. He transforms into my dream-cat, muscles rippling on his back, his shoulders, and his powerful limbs. Mottled light dances on his glistening skin, forming rosettes. He raises his head to look at me and speaks in a throaty rumble.

"Jessamyn, there is danger around you. Be very careful."

Blood drains from my face.

"Jessamyn? Everything still okay?" He is clearly worried.

I blink away the mirage, smile unconvincingly, and shake my head. "All okay," I say. "See you soon."

He smiles and gets back to work. I walk to my cabin, wondering what just happened.

Yes. I'll be very careful. But what endangers me? I'm scared. My dreams are becoming a waking reality and that can't be good. I don't know what's happening and haven't a clue what to do about it. ∎

23

Shipibo Music

Last night's sleep was peaceful. Lagac stopped by my cabin as he promised, bringing a couple of cold beers. *In vino veritas, in cervesio felicitas.* In wine there is truth, in beer, joy. The joy is most welcome.

Lagac has showered, shaved, and splashed his face with his trademark aftershave. It's a rum and spice scent I now identify with him, and it's enough to send pleasant little tingles through me. He laughs and tells me it contains secret pheromones that drive women crazy. It works perfectly with his body chemistry. And mine.

Lagac homes in on my loneliness, my sadness about leaving friends behind in Singapore. I make some tentative sexual overtures in case he wants to go that route, but he parries them gracefully. We talk and cuddle and he snuggles his body against mine.

I don't remember falling asleep or Lagac leaving, and I don't recall my dreams. When I awoke this morning, the only cat around was the relentlessly cheerful *maneki-neko* beckoning engagingly, as is his custom.

The sting of Shun and Shantrelle's departure will fade, I tell myself. I'm consoled by the knowledge things are going well between Lovely and Èlia, as they are between Lagac and me. If the magic aboard the *Andaman Pearl* has changed, at least it hasn't disappeared.

I'm surprised how needy I've become. Lovely spends more time with Èlia than she does with me, and I miss her buzzy energy. I have few distractions. It's the perfect environment for writing, but my muse is in hiding.

The sea and the sky are the same choppy gray they've been since we left Singapore. I'm serenaded intermittently by Lovely and Èlia, working next door in the saloon. Èlia apparently has a flute or a panpipe. Such a transparent, breathy sound. I'll have to ask her. It sounds wonderful mixed with the laughter that filters through the bulkhead.

I'm turning over in my mind what Lovely said about wanting to "show me" Èlia's music as if the music were visual. Perhaps she's referring to musical scores, but if that's the case, I'll be lost. My ability to decode musical notation is almost nonexistent.

The evening has rolled around sooner than I expected. In anticipation of tonight's "show and tell," I went to the mess, assembled an assortment of munchies, and made sure there was white wine chilling in the refrigerator. I am prepared. Or so I think.

Èlia taps on my door around six o'clock. She's wearing embroidered indigenous clothing and a gold nose ornament. As in Singapore, her face and neck, as well as her forearms and hands, are adorned with labyrinthine patterns, inked in red, deep blue, and black.

"Lovely not with you?" I ask, peering into the alley toward her room.

"She'll be along in half an hour or so, but I hope we can have a few minutes with just the two of us. We haven't spent any time alone since we first met," she says softly. "I want to introduce myself to you formally, as is the custom of the Shipibo, my people, and to thank you for your warm welcome."

Inexplicable anxiety washes over me even as her smile melts my heart. The same feeling I had earlier when she looked at me with those eyes in which I feared I might drown but didn't care. It feels absurd to be afraid of her. There's no conceivable reason to fear this beautiful young woman. I invite her in and close the door behind us.

She reads my thoughts and goes straight to my heart. "You are afraid, Jessamyn, and you think you are afraid of me," she says, taking both my hands gently.

We move toward my sofa and sit side by side.

"It is not me you fear. You are afraid because something is not well within you. I hope my music will help," she says, sitting down beside me, her shoulders touching mine.

"I feel very foolish right now, and I don't know why," I say, making my confession as if she were an omniscient priestess. I rage at myself.

Look at yourself, Jessamyn. You're on the verge of tears. The strong, competent physician who stares death in the teeth and does not flinch, who never cries, simply cannot look this serene young woman full in the face.

From somewhere deep in her chest, she sings a simple nasal melody in the alto register. Is this the reed instrument I've been hearing? I instantly feel calmer. She continues to sing, more elaborately now, and I muster the courage to look at her for the first time since I met her, pulled into the intricate tracings on her face.

She's been looking at me as she sings. When she pauses, I speak, not having any idea what gibberish I'm producing, and she begins anew, her melody rendering me mute, her eyes holding mine.

The tracings on her face flash iridescent, like the contrail of a hummingbird flying through a rainbow in some plunging waterfall. Not only do I look at her—I can no longer look away.

When she finishes her song, she places her hand over my heart and says, "I have sung you an *ikaro* against fear, a magical song entrusted to me by the teacher plant *piri-piri*, a reed that grows in the marshy backwaters of the rainforest. Your fear called me to sing it to you. *Piri-piri* gives its medicines freely, but the plant teaches its sacred *ikaro* only to those who can hear it."

"How do you know these things?"

"I have learned them from the teacher plants and my elders. On the full moon following my first menstruation, when I was eleven, the women in my village placed a drop of *piri-piri* juice in each of my eyes and one in my navel so the *kené* could reveal themselves to me. Forgive me for going on so, but for my people, all things are connected. There is no beginning or ending place.

"My people are what Europeans call synesthetes. We experience each of our senses through the other ones. We hear music, for example, but also experience it as colors and shapes."

"What are *kené?*"

"*Kené* is our word for pattern. These designs on my clothing and my body are *kené.*"

"They're so beautiful," I say.

"Yes. They are indeed beautiful, yet so much more," she says. "Watch."

She traces one of the *kené* on her arm with a forefinger and sings a simple tune as the finger follows the turns and the straightaways. Then she traces the pattern in the opposite direction, singing the same tune but in reverse.

"That's astonishing," I say.

She only smiles. "*Kené* map the energy of the rainforest and the Milky Way, the emotional and spiritual strands of the *néte,* the world, or as you say, the cosmos, with all its stars, plants, and animals. *Kené* record the healing songs and visions given to indigenous peoples during medicine ceremonies where we consume the mother plants. These visions and songs are the *kené* of our pottery, fabrics, and the colors we apply to our faces."

I sit like a deer blinded by headlights, on the edge of mysteries I'm too obtuse to comprehend. The fear is gone. Wonderment has taken its place.

"I would like to tell you more about myself, and that also is a complicated matter since there is no place to start or end. Even my name is complicated." She smiles.

"My *janekon,* or true name, is '*Tsiri Biri.*' That is the name given to me by my grandparents when I was four months old, once it was clear that I would not die in infancy.

"'*Tsiri*' is the name of a brightly colored little bird, an ally or messenger to the *chamán,* and '*Biri*' means dazzling, brilliant like lightning.

"So you have two names?" I interrupt.

"More than that," she says, smiling. "Although they are really all one name since they are all me.

"In my naming ceremony, the *chamán* blew tobacco smoke over my body to protect me from evil. He revealed my *janekon* after he and my grandparents considered the advice of the *chaikoni,* invisible men and women who counsel him on important matters like naming children.

"Before I had a true name, the midwife named me Èlia, a *nawan jane,* or a temporary mestizo 'foreign' name. Midwives give a baby a temporary name as soon as they cut the cord, long before a child's true name can be known. Without a *nawan jane,* evil spirits might name the baby and claim it as their own.

"My father's mestizo last name is 'Palacios' and my mother's is 'Lozano' so my *nawan jane* or 'foreign' name is 'Èlia Palacios Lozano.' That makes my name '*Tsiri Biri*/Èlia Palacios Lozano,' or '*Tsiri* Èlia Palacios Lozano *Biri,*' or 'Èlia Palacios Lozano/*Tsiri Biri.*'"

She pauses and smiles. "I told you it is complicated."

I smile as well. It is complicated and, as she has promised, there's no real starting or ending place.

"To confuse things further, my village gave me the *shiro jane,* or nickname, *Wano,* which means 'marry a man.' You could call me 'Èlia,' or '*Wano,*' or '*Tsiri Biri*' but not just '*Tsiri*' or '*Biri.*' That would confuse the *chaikoni.*"

"I would call you a beautiful, remarkable young woman in any language, Èlia. Or *Tsiri Biri* if you would prefer."

"Either is fine," she says.

"Èlia it is, then, so my English rendition of Shipibo doesn't confuse the *chaikoni*. I look forward to learning much more from you."

"I think we have much to learn from each other." She leans over and kisses me on the forehead.

Someone taps at the door. Èlia answers it and it's Lovely.

She stands in the alley barefoot, as if in a trance, enveloped by a full-body cape of white cotton trimmed with embroidered multicolored *kené*. Like Èlia, her face and hands are emblazoned with red, deep blue, and black labyrinthine markings.

"Are you okay, Lovely?" I ask, getting up to join them. It's not like Lovely simply not to come bounding through the door into my cabin.

Èlia answers for her. "She is pleasantly bewitched by the music we were composing earlier. It's like being a little high or enchanted. Believe me, she's having a good time right now," she says, laughing.

It looks that way. Lovely wears a Mona Lisa smile and the faraway look of paradise found, or at least paradise glimpsed, her eyes heavy lidded. Èlia takes her hand and leads her into my cabin as she would lead a child.

"Make yourself comfortable, Jessamyn," Èlia says. "The concert is about to begin." I sit on the sofa. Èlia moves the coffee table back toward the other sofa, giving Lovely and her more room.

"First the musical score," Elia says, removing Lovely's cape, laying it beside me on the couch. Lovely wears nothing beneath it except for a few bangles on her wrists and the *agimat* around her neck. *Kené* cover her entire body, the ink colors matching those on her face and neck. Èlia has provided Lovely a nose ornament to match the one she wears.

"My people do not embellish the entire body with *kené*," Èlia says, "only the face and hands. We reserve full body *kené* for figural pottery and carvings, so these *kené* on Lovely's body differ from our traditional art. We have used her body as the manuscript paper for our compositions. She is part of a performance art piece we have been experimenting with.

We want to perform some of it for you, but first allow me to tell you a little more about our work."

I sink back into the sofa, fascinated by what's unfolding before me.

"Our music has some fragments of the *ikaros* the teacher plants have taught me. Also our names," she says, pointing to matching *kené* on their foreheads.

"This one," she says, pointing to a pattern on Lovely's right cheek, "is from the master teacher plant *mapacho* or jungle tobacco, the plant the *chamán* used to protect me at my naming ceremony."

She sings a throaty, smoky fragment of a melody, thick and soft like a slowly moving cloud as she traces the *kené* with her right index finger. She switches to her left index finger and traces the *kené* again in the same direction. This time the melody sounds darker and more turbulent, like a thunderhead.

"See? It is different.

"This *kené*," she says, pointing to a pattern over Lovely's breastbone, "is *huachuma* or *San Pedro* cactus. *San Pedro* produces visions. We call it *San Pedro* because, as St. Peter holds the keys to heaven, *San Pedro* cactus holds the keys to *néte*, the cosmos.

"And this," she says, turning Lovely so her back is toward me, pointing to portions of the complex labyrinth covering her buttocks, "is an *ikaro* the master teacher plant, *ayuhausca,* learned from the skin of Anaconda Woman, the guardian of balance in *néte*. "

"I'm curious, does the serpent eagle of Lovely's tattoo contain an *ikaro*?" It did not look out of place among the kené on Lovely's back.

Èlia smiles. "I traced it several times with my fingers but could not coax a song from it. I felt only sparks of electricity and saw flashes of light before Lovely started shaking and asked me to stop. I'm sure it contains music but from teacher plants whose *ikaros* I don't yet know. Perhaps the pine or the pomelo."

I remember what Lovely told me. The wicked pomelo thorn. Ink made from pine soot.

"There are several fragments from the *ikaros* of the teacher plants in this composition," she says with a sweep of her hand over Lovely's body, turning her to face me once again, "and some quotations from the master classical European composers Fauré and Bach."

I'm curious which European classical fragments they've chosen and how they'll weave them into the performance. The whole concept astonishes me.

"This one and this one," Èlia says, pointing to designs on Lovely's stomach, "I wrote myself. I would not dare call them *ikaros* even though they contain fragments in homage to a few songs the teacher plants have sung to me.

"There are many *ikaros* the plants have not yet agreed to teach me. And there are *kené* like this one and that one," she says, gesturing toward Lovely's pubis, "of *ikaros* I have heard but am strictly forbidden by the plants to sing because they have not yet finished their teaching. You will need to hear them in your imagination."

How in the world am I supposed to do that, I wonder? Riddles within riddles.

"Lovely has written music too," Èlia continues. "I painted *kené* for themes from two of her cello compositions on her breasts, surrounding her heart, so we can sing them. Is it not astonishing how beautiful the *kené* for her music are? The teacher plants would be jealous."

I'm transfixed by Èlia's demonstration of their musical "score." I wonder what Aunty G. would've made of it. "Magic," she would probably have said.

"We would like to perform some of this music for you now," Èlia says. She whispers something into Lovely's ear, and she closes her eyes. "Forgive us if it is still unpolished and not as well rehearsed as it should be, but we are excited to share it with you."

Èlia sings the music on Lovely's right shoulder and neck, tracing the *kené* with her forefinger.

The melody is light and shimmery, flashing like the *tsiri* birds of Èlia's namesake. She continues tracing down Lovely's breastbone, into the area where she has inked the *San Pedro* fragment. Her voice drops into a lower register, slower, vibrating with such intensity the hair on my arms stands on end.

The sound resonates octaves below what she's actually singing. Deeper than the lowest note on Aunty G's Bösendorfer. I see the air vibrating around Lovely's body, oscillating like the lowest piano string, forming peaks and valleys like a pebble thrown into a pool of still water. It's impossible for any woman to sing a note that low, but I hear it clearly.

"Other *kené* are singing it in your head but not through your ears," Èlia says, perhaps noticing the puzzled look on my face.

She whispers something to Lovely, and Lovely's own finger traces a pattern inscribed on her stomach, the *kené* Èlia has taught her to sing. They sing together, Lovely's voice the color of her skin, Èlia's voice evoking the timbre of the breathy panpipe I heard through the walls of the saloon. Perhaps it wasn't an instrument at all, but how could that remarkable sound spring from Èlia's throat?

Èlia takes Lovely's hand in hers. Together they trace the *kené* centered over Lovely's navel.

Their singing knocks the wind out of me. I hear myself, far away from my body, pleading with them to stop. I'm terrified.

Lovely emerges from her trance and hugs my quaking frame. Èlia has taken my hands and kneels in front of me.

Tears pour down my face. "What just happened?" I ask when I can speak.

"You became frightened and asked us to stop," Èlia says.

"Did we scare you?" Lovely asks, her voice cracking with tension.

I can't answer her. What could the two of them have possibly done to scare me? They were only making the most beautiful music.

"Jessamyn," Èlia presses softly. "What's frightening you?"

I scream as a jaguar, crouching on the coffee table behind them, lunges at me and vanishes as rapidly as it materialized, a fraction of a second before tearing out my throat.

Lovely's body presses against mine, sobbing, wrapping me tightly in her arms. Èlia sings the *ikaro* against fear. She reaches up to wipe the tears from my face.

"Jaguar," is all I can manage.

Èlia's face beams. "You saw the jaguar," she says excitedly, pointing to the *kené* over Lovely's navel, "the mother spirit of the teacher plant *puma chacruna*. We sang a fragment of her *ikaro*. You are highly favored, Jessamyn. She shows herself to very few people. Lovely and I didn't see her. But you did."

"I thought she was going to kill me, and then she just chuffed and evaporated," I say. "She was so close I could smell blood on her breath. I've seen the jaguar before. In my dreams. But how could it be a 'mother spirit?' The jaguar I just saw was male."

Èlia shakes her head knowingly.

"I've seen both male and female jaguars in my dreams, but yesterday when I was talking with Lagac, he turned into a jaguar for a split second. He warned me I was in danger. Then he was Lagac again. The Lagac jaguar was clearly male. This mother spirit jaguar that attacked me was male, but it wasn't the Lagac jaguar. It was much smaller. I can't say I'm happy about meeting any of these jaguars while I'm wide awake."

I force myself to stop babbling. I'm afraid of revealing too much.

"The mother spirit can be female or male," Èlia begins calmly. "Sometimes both. The jaguar can be black, but it can also be white or tawny with black rosettes.

"Our traditions teach that an ancient *chamán* once saw a rainbow-colored jaguar. The mother spirit may frighten you, demand you listen to her, but she will not harm you. She is a fearsome predator, but what is she stalking? Perhaps she is trying to kill what is inside you, making you sick."

"Are you sick, Jessamyn?" Lovely asks. "What's wrong with you?" The fabric of reality splits.

I'm kneeling over Roderick's naked corpse in my bathroom back in Westbury. I have exorcised one evil, but at what cost? Another has taken root inside of me. I scream. I'm trembling uncontrollably.

"Jessamyn," I hear Lovely yell in the distance, panicked. "Shall we call Eric?"

"She's fine," Èlia says from the same distance, soothing us both. "Jessamyn is traveling with the spirits. We just need to hold her until she returns to us." She sings the *ikaro* against fear.

Eventually I return. I have stopped shaking. In time I can speak.

"I don't feel ill, Lovely, but Èlia says something is sick inside me. I don't know what's wrong, but when Èlia sang me the *ikaro* against fear, whatever it was went away. Or so I thought."

I want to tell them more, but I can't. We continue to hold each other in silence as we calm ourselves and our breathing returns to normal. Èlia hands Lovely her robe, but she's in no hurry to put it on. I insist. As much as I would like to study the remarkable *kené* on her body, I don't want to awaken any sleeping mother spirits, or worse.

"You must be very sensitive to the world of the mother spirits, Jessamyn. I did not know our music would call the jaguar. We will need to be cautious as we develop this new music in our studies."

"Do you think it might be dangerous?" Lovely asks.

"I don't think so. I think this is more about Jessamyn than about our music," Èlia says.

"The Conservatoire National Supérieur doesn't know what's about to hit it," I say. "I think your teachers will pee their pants at your doctoral recital. They'll be happy to leave your diplomas on the table as they run for the exits."

They giggle.

Lovely can't let the image go. "Èlia, do we know the *ikaro* against peeing pants?" She chortles.

I laugh as well, and Èlia rolls her eyes.

"Hush," she says. "Do not be disrespectful of the teacher plants." A flash of the terror I just experienced jolts me, then subsides. I wonder if Shun and Shantrelle have any inkling about the phenomenon named Èlia Palacios Lozano/*Tsiri Biri* for whom they have arranged passage on the *Andaman Pearl*?

I need to get a grip on my fear and ask her some important questions. I'm resolved to find the courage to do that. But for now, I'll listen quietly as Lovely and Èlia chatter excitedly about the teacher plants and music they've written.

Lovely touches the design on her navel. "Pretty dope, huh?"

"Respect," Èlia reminds her.

I hope the jaguars are sleeping and have forgotten where I am. ∎

24

G Deck

Blistering, peeling, rusting. Chipping, grinding, painting. Maintenance and repair have been ongoing since we left Yokohama, although I've paid little attention to it. Because there's not much else for the deck crew to do in the Arabian sea, pursuing rust has reached a fever pitch. Depending upon where they're working, the incessant whining, scratching, and banging are mildly grating, like a determined mosquito in your ear, or painful, like standing under a jumbo jet at takeoff. I make the mistake of kvetching about it to Lagac, so he has undertaken to give me another lesson on life at sea.

He insists I wear goggles, earplugs, and a dust mask since we'll be getting up close and personal with the big toys—pneumatic chipping hammers, jet needle guns, scrapers, disc sanders, rotary wire brushes, and a Trelawney Pneumatic Deck Scaler. Lagac calls it the "lawn mower." It's carbide teeth crunch through rust like tortilla chips so long as you can hang onto it.

Lagac points out blisters and rusty gunk everywhere, in places a passenger like me would never notice until it's too late. "They make ships of steel and not much else," Lagac says. "Take good care of it and a ship will last thirty years or more. Neglect it and it will let you down when you can least afford it."

199

He sounds like my dental hygienist, nagging about the exigencies of flossing.

"I once saw a bosun's mate knock a hole completely through a rusty hull with a pneumatic hammer. Fortunately the guy next to him had a wad of epoxy putty handy and plugged the hole. Also fortunately it held until they made it to port."

One never quite knows when Lagac is imparting accurate information or spinning a yarn, like he did with the "three squeaks."

We tour the coatings locker where I'm schooled on primers and paint. "This is just a little room," he tells me, ducking into a large closet, "where we keep enough paint for our day-to-day work. We have a big room belowdecks that holds enough for an entire run." Both, apparently, figure in Lagac's inventory of hidey-holes.

"The deck officer is like a Michelin-starred chef," Lagac says. "Too little hardener and the paint will take forever to dry. Too much hardener, or the wrong kind, and it comes out like lumpy cream of wheat."

"Speaking of the deck officer," I say, "what's the deal with Nasir Rajaratman?"

"Still checking him out," Lagac says. "One of my people who knows about these things swears Manila corporate forced the captain to bring him aboard. What I can't figure out is why him. The captain usually hires his own crew. Probably graft. Some suit's cousin needing a job or something. There's more corruption in Manila corporate than there is rust in the Philippine navy."

Later that afternoon, the captain makes his way down from the boat deck to find Lovely, Èlia, and me larking about. His face is tight, his hands behind his back. This isn't a social call.

"Ladies, I want to brief you about the men we brought aboard in Colombo," he says without small talk. "As you know, Deck Officer Rajaratman boarded in Singapore to give us a hand with operations. But we also asked him to assemble a group of men we picked up in

Colombo to provide extra security if we should need it as we approach the Suez Canal."

Èlia speaks for all of us. "I've heard rumors about Somali pirates," she says.

"Well, the pirates haven't been very active lately. Everyone's gone after them with a vengeance, patrolling the shipping lanes with frigates and providing air support. The International Task Force will probably give us an escort for at least part of our approach to the canal."

I can't say any of this is making me feel calmer.

"If some bad guys do board the ship, someone from Mr. Rajaratman's security detachment will escort you to our secure operations center on G deck. We can bypass the bridge, operate the ship from SecOps, and defeat any attempt to hijack the ship until help comes or the pirates give up.

"By 'security detachment' you're referring to the mercenaries that came aboard in Colombo?" I ask.

"That is correct. They are well-armed and are instructed to protect you and the crew as a priority, above defending the ship or its cargo.

"They will shortly begin modifying the ship to make it harder to board. That includes, I am afraid, concertina wire and gun turrets on the main deck from which the men will occasionally fire at practice targets to calibrate their weapons."

It never occurred to me the *MV Andaman Pearl* would become a gunship. And when Rajaratman's mercenaries string the evil-looking razor wire around the entire perimeter of the main deck and mount machine guns along the railings, the pirate menace seems very real.

I ask Lagac what he thinks about the pirates. Of course he knows about the secure space on G deck and assures me the engine room and other strategic areas of the ship are also hardened against intruders. He seems mildly amused at my concern.

"We can do a dry run and check out a couple of my hidey-holes." He chuckles.

I call his bluff. "Fine with me unless you'd rather go over the security arrangements in my cabin," I say.

My cabin wins out. I relax in his arms, waking him when it's time for his scheduled watch.

"The mercs will probably start their target practice in a couple of days," he says. "We're still five or six days away from any areas where there might be pirates lurking. Nothing bad's going to happen, Jessamyn."

He reminds me that in all the time he's been sailing on the *Andaman Pearl* he's never seen a pirate. Nor does he know of any other ship pirates boarded.

Hearing all of this from Lagac is more reassuring than hearing it from Captain Bayani. He's so persuasive that when Lovely and Èlia need to talk about the pirate menace, I'm comfortable reassuring them as well. They tease me.

"Well, if Lagac says so, of course we won't worry," Lovely says, rolling her eyes.

And if G deck doesn't pan out, there are always Lagac's hidey-holes. I don't tell them about that part. ∎

25

Nasir Rajaratman

I am watching a movie I downloaded to my computer before I left home, *Captain Blood* with Errol Flynn, Olivia de Havilland, and Basil Rathbone when the shooting begins. I recall Lagac telling me the mercenaries would test their weapons. It sounds like they've begun.

ABOARD MV ANDAMAN PEARL   August 1

The intermittent bursts continue. I abandon the movie, undog the door and walk out onto the deck. In the distance, several white plastic barrels dot the water. Bullets trace a path toward one and strike, causing it to leap out of the water and spin end over end before falling back into the ocean.

Rajaratman is making the rounds on the main deck, talking to his men. I hear occasional laughter. They seem to enjoy themselves.

Rajaratman waves at me, a surprise since he has scarcely seemed aware of my existence. I wave back reflexively, and he continues directing fire at the unsinkable barrels.

He surprises me again at lunch in the officers' mess when he approaches my table, holding his tray.

"Good afternoon, Dr. Quilter. I am Nasir Rajaratman, deck officer in charge of the ship's security detail. It was my honor to join the *MV Andaman Pearl* in Singapore."

"Good afternoon, Mr. Rajaratman. I've seen you pursuing your duties from time to time."

"Will you allow me to join you?"

"Of course."

"I apologize for not introducing myself earlier," he says, seating himself across from me. "I have wanted to make your acquaintance, but our schedules have not coincided."

The formality of his language and his bearing are striking, as is his impeccable grooming. He speaks English with polished "received pronunciation" that suggests he might have studied in the UK. His face with its lush eyebrows and glistening handlebar moustache is a carbon copy of one of those fierce Tamil deities I saw in Sri Mariamman Temple. He smells of lime and sandalwood.

"Captain Bayani has told us passengers who you are, Mr. Rajaratman, and something of your mission here. Thank you for providing the extra measure of security the ship might require should we come under attack."

He bobs his head sharply in acknowledgment. I imagine his heels clicking together under the table.

"I am told you are a first-rate physician, Dr. Quilter. Your reputation on the ship is stellar."

"I practiced emergency medicine before I cut myself adrift and joined the *Andaman Pearl* for this voyage," I say. "It's been my pleasure to assist the second officer occasionally when he's needed another pair of hands in sick bay."

"May I be so bold as to ask where you went to school, Dr. Quilter?"

"I went to medical school at Dartmouth and did my residency at Harvard with a fellowship at Johns Hopkins. How about you? What did you do before you became a sailor?"

"My father was in the diplomatic corps, so I bounced around as a child before settling into boarding school. I completed my A-levels at Eaton, although I started at less prestigious schools, and entered university at The London School of Economics and Political Science.

"I took a master's but had no interest in studying further. I went home to Tamil Nadu and taught secondary school pupils briefly. I soon forsook that thankless undertaking to join the Indian Merchant Navy."

Out of the corner of my eye I see Lovely and Èlia enter the officers' mess. When they have filled their trays, they take another table rather than join me at mine as they usually do. Perhaps they have no desire to break bread with Mr. Rajaratman, or perhaps they just feel awkward joining a conversation in progress.

Lagac sticks his head through the door, looks at me, and leaves with a scowl on his face. I'm amused at the thought I will certainly hear from him later.

"I am intrigued, Dr. Quilter, about your decision to sail aboard the *Andaman Pearl*. Why not pick a cruise ship instead, something with comforts more befitting your station?"

"I have found there are many comforts on the *Andaman Pearl* and opportunities to get to know a few people well, both passengers and crew. And I wanted a change from my usual hectic life, to take things slower with no real agenda or destination. It's been a wonderful experience so far. I don't miss the throngs of tourists I'm told inhabit cruise ships."

"Forgive me if I am intruding, but I am told you recently lost your husband."

Now how in the world would you know that, and what earthly business is it of yours?

"You have been correctly informed, Mr. Rajaratman."

"I am sorry for your loss."

"Thank you, but please don't trouble yourself. It wasn't an ideal marriage."

"I meant no offense."

"And I took none, Mr. Rajaratman. Do you have family?"

"No one to speak of. I have never married or desired to be married. I am happy not to be tied down."

I smile politely.

"I have enjoyed getting to know you a little better and hope I can continue to do so over the course of the voyage," he says. "Please do not hesitate to let me know if I can be of assistance to you. If you will excuse me, I must return to my duties."

"It's been a pleasure to meet you, Mr. Rajaratman. I'm sure our paths will cross again. It's a small ship."

He rises from the table, clasps his hands behind his back, and executes a pro forma bow before leaving. No sooner is he gone than Lovely and Èlia snatch up their trays and scurry over to my table.

"What was that all about?" Lovely asks.

"Nothing, really. Mr. Rajaratman got it into his head that we should become better acquainted, so I indulged him."

"We saw Lagac peek in and make his unhappy face. Maybe he thinks Rajaratman is trying to beat his time?" She snickers.

"My goodness, ladies," I say, raising my eyebrows and looking down my nose at them. "Whatever can such well-bred young women be thinking?"

They are not chastened. Far from it. They laugh and carry on, aping Rajaratman's body language. Soon every eye in the mess is on us.

"I, for one, am going back for more *señorita* bread and another coffee," I say, getting up from the table. "Can I get you ladies anything?"

"I wouldn't say no to six inches of whatever you're having," Lovely says, cracking herself up.

"Too soft for me," Èlia says. "Maybe some more of cook's plump longganisa sausage or as Lovely calls it 'Lagac-anisa.'"

They're both hooting by now.

I have a hard time maintaining my old lady doctor face, but I give it my best shot. "I'm going to pretend I didn't hear any of that since I think so highly of you, and you have clearly been at sea too long."

"We promise to behave ourselves better in the future," Lovely says, placing both hands, fingers crossed on the table. "Secret sign, Èlia. It means we're lying through our teeth."

"Cross my heart and hope to die," Èlia says, making the signs on her chest.

Their monkeyshines are too much for them, and they completely lose it when I flip them off. I smile, walking over to the coffee urn. Mr. Rajaratman would likely have had a heart attack had he witnessed such goings on among us supposed ladies of quality. Lagac, on the other hand, would have had a ball. I can't wait to hear what he has to say about Rajaratman. ■

26

Warning

Lagac is not a subtle man, despite what he thinks. He made himself scarce most of the day yesterday. It wasn't until I was getting ready for bed last night that he knocked on my door. As usual, I was glad to see him, but he was not his jocular laid-back self.

He carried himself tightly, walking on the balls of his feet like an agitated cat. The only other time I've seen him like this is when he intercepted Balwinder Agarwal, clenching and unclenching his fists, positioning himself between Mr. Agarwal and his battered wife. I noticed his right eye twitching then, as it is now, evidence of his stress.

"Lagac. Come in. Are you okay? What's the matter?"

"Jessamyn, I know this is none of my business. I just don't trust that Rajaratman. That's the ugliest band of mercs I've ever seen. I think I'd rather deal with the pirates. I saw Rajaratman had you cornered at lunch, and I was worried about you."

"Well, let me tell you what happened. I was having lunch, and he came over to my table and asked if he could join me. He didn't really corner me. He said he wanted to introduce himself."

"What else did he want?"

"Nothing, really. He asked about where I went to medical school, and I asked about how he came to become a deck officer. He asked

209

about the death of my late husband, but I cut him off. I didn't feel like sharing more personal information with him. Lovely, Èlia, and I saw you stick your head through the door and leave. It didn't look like you were very happy."

"Like I said, I don't trust that guy. I overheard him talking to someone on his satellite phone. I couldn't hear everything he said because he was speaking some language I don't understand, but I heard him mention your name.

"My name?"

"'Dr. Jessamyn Quilter,' he said. Twice. And something about 'Harvard' and 'Johns Hopkins.' Like I said, I couldn't understand everything. He shut up and put his phone away when I got closer to him."

"I can't imagine who he might have been talking with and why he would mention me," I said. I was terrified by what Lagac was telling me. Who could be interested in what I told Rajaratman? Law enforcement back home? Interpol? Is someone looking into Roderick's death? Is there some kind of bounty on my head?

It seems ridiculous. I didn't tell Rajaratman anything that isn't already common knowledge. On second thought, I as good as told him my marriage to Roderick was a bust, and I wasn't broken up over his death. If anyone is looking for a motive for murder, that will do. I resolve to be very careful about talking with Rajaratman, but I see no need to drag Lagac into my paranoia.

"Okay, Lagac. I get you don't like him. I don't think I like him either, but he seemed to try, so I just gave him the benefit of the doubt. What are you worried about?"

"I don't usually do this, but this guy is so wonky I'm checking him out with friends back home. That crew he brought with him? All Tamils. I overheard a couple of them talking about connections to the old Tamil Tigers. Do you know about them?"

"Tamil Tigers? I've heard the term, but I know nothing about them."

"Well, they're guerillas. They tried to form their own country in the north of Sri Lanka and waged a twenty-five-year war against the government. Most of the majority Sinhalese in Sri Lanka are Buddhist and the Tamils are mostly Hindu, so it boiled down to a religious thing.

"The Tigers were out of business by 2009, but they were very dangerous before that. Some say they still are. They pushed all the Muslims out of northern Sri Lanka and smuggled weapons from al-Quaeda affiliated Pakistanis to *Abu Sayyaf* Islamic terrorists in the Philippines. Assault rifles, surface-to-air missiles, stuff like that.

As Lagac continued, my doomsday scenario involving Rajaratman seemed less likely. Still, I wondered who he was talking to that might be interested in me.

"Oh. And they also invented the suicide vest. They taught the Islamic crazies how to get their women and children to commit mass murder and blow themselves up in the process. The Tamil Tigers committed more suicide bombings than all the terrorists in the world combined before they were crushed a few years back."

"Why do you say they 'are' into all those things, Lagac? You said they're no longer in business."

"I think the Tamil Tigers are just biding their time. They had feeder organizations everywhere, including North America, funneling money to them not that long ago. They're a very sophisticated international bunch of bad guys. Who's to say they're still not active, running weapons or giving advice to other loonies out there?"

There are times I wonder if there's anywhere in the world that's safe for seafaring. The South China Sea is no pleasure cruise, what with the Chinese insisting they own every drop. From what Lagac tells me, the entire Pacific coast of Central and South America, from Mexico to Tierra del Fuego, is a playground for pirates and smugglers. And I've just learned a part of the Arabian Sea is apparently so dicey shipping companies think it's a good idea to have armed mercenaries on board just in case.

I'm looking forward to the day we transit the Suez Canal into friendlier waters. It should only be a week if our luck holds.

Meanwhile the target practice continues. They're wasting a lot of ammunition on those floating barrels. I hope they save some for the pirates.

Lagac spent the night with me and was calmer this morning. Still, if Lagac is concerned about these mercenaries, I'm concerned. Who are they really?

Rajaratman was smooth, revealing little of importance about himself and his mission. He found out more about me than I did about him. It felt almost like a job interview.

I guess it doesn't make much difference. I doubt we'll cross paths often since his duties take him to places on the ship I wouldn't venture while target practice is going on.

Lagac assures me the target practice will soon be over. We're in Somali waters now, within reach of the Suez Canal. He tells me not to worry, that he'll keep his eye on Rajaratman and his crew. I'll trust him to do just that. ■

PART TWO

Unmoored

*I say unto you: one must still have chaos in oneself
to give birth to a dancing star.*

FRIEDRICH NIETZSCHE

Thus Spake Zarathustra: A Book for All and None

27

Lifeboat

I am trying to work out where I am and how I got here, but a jaguar is licking my face. My body is tethered to something, a stretcher, I think, and will not move. The cat is talking, but I can't make out what it's saying.

I know this feeling. It's ketamine. I'm coming out of sedation, and the jaguar is a hallucination that resolves to Nasir Rajaratman washing my face with a rough cloth. He's talking, but I can't make out what he's saying. The best course of action is to go back to sleep.

"Dr. Quilter? Time to wake up, please. Dr. Quilter, can you hear me?"

It's unmistakably Rajaratman, and unfortunately I can hear him all too well.

"Mr. Rajaratman?"

"Hello, Dr. Quilter. Yes. Nasir Rajaratman, here with you."

"Where is here?"

"You are on a stretcher, aboard the *Andaman Pearl's Rescue Craft #1*. The lifeboat. You are safe. Nobody is going to harm you."

Stretcher? Rescue craft. How?

217

Memories filter into my groggy brain as Rajaratman drones on. I remember he came to my cabin around midnight and knocked on the door, waking me up.

"Sorry to disturb you, Dr. Quilter," he said. "The second officer has asked me to escort you to the infirmary. There has been some sort of accident."

"Okay, give me a minute to throw on some clothes," I said through the door. I dressed quickly in jeans and a top and opened the door. "What happened?" I asked.

"I don't know. The second officer didn't say. He asked me to find you and escort you to make sure you are safe," he said.

"Okay. Let's go."

When I got to the infirmary, Eric wasn't there. Instead, there was a beefy, foul-smelling man with rotten teeth holding a syringe.

"I apologize deeply for the subterfuge, Dr. Quilter," Rajaratman said, pinning my arms against my side, backing me toward a gurney.

I called out, but the mercenary with the syringe put his hand over my mouth. I felt a needle stick in my right deltoid.

I kicked at Rajaratman's shins and tried to scream to no avail.

"Ketamine, Dr. Quilter. I'm certain you are familiar with it. Perfectly safe, but you will soon lose consciousness so it would be better if you were to lie back on the gurney now. We'll watch after you."

A wad of gauze stuffed into my mouth replaced the mercenary's hand. The two men maneuvered me onto the gurney, woozy and unable to resist. I knew the ketamine would overwhelm me completely about four minutes after they jabbed me. I hate ketamine. Great for some people, but it gives me the heebie-jeebies.

I hear Rajaratman's clipped voice before I check out. "You're safe. No harm will come to you. I will explain later, but for now, just go to sleep."

***

Rajaratman is speaking again. "How do you feel, Dr. Quilter?"

Like shit, you overripe turd.

"What the fuck have you done to me, you bastard?"

218

"Let's take it slow, Dr. Quilter. There's a lot to tell you, and I don't want you to get hurt. We gave you some ketamine to get you on the gurney, but it's wearing off and will be gone soon."

Fuck, fuck, fuckityfuckfuck, fucking ketamine. I fucking hate fucking ketamine. The worst fucking drug you could give me. Fuck. Fuck. Double fuck!

I smell the mercenary who drugged me before I see him seated at the controls of the lifeboat, grinning through his rotting teeth. I look out a porthole and see nothing. The sky is black.

"Let me begin the story," Rajaratman says. "You are traveling in the *Andaman Pearl's Rescue Craft #1*, on an extremely important mission. Your safety is paramount to us, and your well-being is guaranteed."

You have no fucking idea how pissed off I am right now, fuckface. Fucking ketamine? My head feels like a pink elephant is standing on it, and you wouldn't believe the murderous thoughts I'm having about you and that shitpile driving this lifeboat.

"My security detail has taken control of the *Andaman Pearl*. Everybody on the ship is safe, locked in their secure area on G deck, but unable to communicate or sail her since we have disabled their controls. My crew is piloting the ship toward Caluula, on the northernmost tip Somalia where they will anchor offshore briefly. That is also where Rescue Craft #1 will soon beach."

"So, you're Somali pirates?" I ask, incredulous.

"No, not really. We are Tamils, as you know, and we are arranging for a portion of the *Andaman Pearl's* cargo to be diverted to *al-Shabaab* in Somalia. I'm sure you have heard of *al-Shabaab*. I would be happy to explain more if you wish."

"Tamil Tigers?"

"More correctly, 'Liberation Tigers of Tamil Eelam,' but Tamil Tigers will suffice, though we don't advertise who we are. But we'll reach our destination in another half an hour, and there is still much to tell you."

"How did you manage to get on board the *Andaman Pearl*?"

"It is an interesting story of what you might call international terrorism. Briefly, an operative of the *Abu Sayyaf* Muslim separatist organization in the Philippines was engaged in random hacking and penetrated the Andaman World Marine network. He stumbled upon a most interesting finding. One of the company's vice-presidents has been engaging in a highly illegal activity involving child trafficking. *Abu Sayyaf* threatened to expose him unless he cooperated.

"The result is the plan we are now executing, with the vice president's full knowledge and cooperation, to load a container with small arms and other contraband onto the *Andaman Pearl* in Sri Lanka and deliver it to Somalia.

"We seized control of the ship and are diverting her to Somali waters where *al-Shabaab* soldiers will board her, load the contraband into their go-fast boats, and transport it to shore where trucks will be waiting to take it to the interior."

These fuckers are dangerous. Keep your wits about you, Jessamyn. Never mind. You currently have no wits.

"I will not bore you with all the details but suffice it to say we have disabled satellite positional data, radar, and other communications aboard the *Andaman Pearl* and this rescue craft. Nobody knows where either the ship or the lifeboat is at this moment.

"Before authorities locate them, my crew will leave the ship with the soldiers on *al-Shabaab's* go-fast boats. Captain Bayani will get his ship back and report his dilemma to Andaman World Marine, which will dissimulate and order him to continue to the Suez Canal without further interruption. The guns will be in Somalia, nobody will have gotten hurt, and my men and I will disappear."

"What does all of this have to do with me? Why didn't you just leave me on the ship? Am I a hostage?"

"Nothing to do with the merchandise we are diverting," he says. "You're not being held for ransom. With all respect, you are simply a high-value target of opportunity. We have temporary need of a well-trained physician."

"You shanghaied me because I'm a doctor?"

"In the time that remains before we land, which is not great, I will explain what I can. A high-ranking *al-Shabaab* commander languishes in a hospital a few kilometers from Caluula, a medical facility that *al-Shabaab* controls. That is your destination. The patient who awaits you is Ahmad Ali Arif. All you need to know about him is that he is gravely ill. Somalia is impoverished in uncountable ways but one of them is medical resources. There are fewer than four physicians, nurses, or midwives per 10,000 people in Somalia.

"When *al-Shabaab* learned that a passenger aboard the *Andaman Pearl* was an Ivy-league trained physician, Ahmad Ali Arif insisted I bring you for consultation. That is all anyone wishes. *Al-Shabaab* has no interest in holding you for ransom or harming you. That would be far too dangerous since it would invite the American dogs to bark at their door."

This keeps getting worse. How am I ever going to survive this?

"Like me, Ahmad Ali Arif speaks excellent English. When you have finished your consultation, he will arrange for your safe passage to Djibouti where the Americans maintain a diplomatic presence and a military base.

"You will find all the necessary visas, tickets, and travel documents among your belongings, as well as a hotel reservation in Djibouti. It will not be an easy journey, but by the end of the day, you will once again be free to consider your future and resume your travels.

"I am deeply sorry it is necessary to involve you in this plan. I will not ask forgiveness for trespassing against your liberty since what I have done is unforgivable, but I'm certain you understand that sometimes the universe makes demands upon us for reasons that do not put our personal needs foremost. Alas, we are all captives of fate."

Fate my ass, you ugly jugfucker. I know what you look like, you and your little dog driving this boat, and I will hunt you both down.

"More unpleasant news, I'm afraid, Dr. Quilter. The *Andaman Pearl* must continue its voyage without you."

"What? You're going to strand me somewhere in, where did you say, Djibouti, wherever the hell that is? Good Luck? Toodle-oo? Have a nice day?"

"My men on the *Andaman Pearl* have briefed Captain Bayani about your whereabouts, and he will be notified when you have arrived in Djibouti. Alas, he will have no option but to continue without you, but at least he will know you are safe and might still aid you.

"Your possessions will travel with you. We packed all the belongings in your cabin into the suitcases you brought with you when you left Yokohama. You will find nothing missing. We are visionaries, not thieves."

Not visionaries. Fuckwits. Thugs for life. Chill, Jessamyn. You need to calm down and keep your eye on the ball.

"When we reach the Somali coast, we must engage in more subterfuge. An ambulance will be waiting to take you to the hospital. That will deter anyone from interfering with your passage."

As the reality of my situation seeps into my brain, I wonder why I am not terrified. Drugged. Kidnapped. Headed for a country crawling with terrorists and pressed into service on behalf of an *al-Shabaab* chieftain. Of course I should be terrified. But I'm not.

I realize the ketamine is providing a false sense of safety, knocking down my anxiety about what's happening to me. What could be happening to me. I don't like it. If I'm going to be tortured, raped, or killed by these madmen, don't I have the right to be terrified? The right to the flight or fight reflexes that could help protect me? The drugs won't let me react normally. I couldn't escape if I tried. There's no choice but to go along for the ride. Still, I can object, for all the good it'll do.

"The more I hear of this plan, Mr. Rajaratman, the less I like it. How on earth do you expect me to be even remotely helpful under the circumstances you have engineered? What in god's name do you expect from me?"

"I imagine all of this is quite overwhelming, Dr. Quilter, and again I apologize for the disruption to your life made necessary by our mission. I am sure you have many more questions, but it is not prudent to indulge your curiosity further. The less you know, the safer all of us will be.

"Local authorities or the American Consulate in Djibouti will want to question you about your venture in Somalia, but there will be little you can tell them they will not already know. You may choose to give up the identity of your patient, if your medical ethics allow, but by the time you do, he will have gone off the radar, no longer a target for the MQ-9 Reaper drones at Camp Lemonnier.

"I have thoroughly enjoyed making your acquaintance, Dr. Quilter, and I genuinely wish it might have been under different circumstances. Alas, we will not meet again. Once you have reached Somalia, our paths will diverge.

"Rest now and perhaps reflect on the notion that you will be one of very few American citizens to visit Somalia safely in recent times. I wish you every success."

Intolerable prick. If I never see you again, it will be too soon. In the meantime, I will fantasize in detail about what I will do to you if I get the opportunity. That is, if I can wake up. ■

28

Ahmad Ali Arif

The sky is becoming lighter and the sun will soon devote its undivided attention to scorching the land. *Rescue Craft #1* eases its way to the shoreline where Rotten Teeth deliberately runs it aground. He opens the side entrance hatch, jumps out into the shallows. Rajaratman walks me to the hatch and Rotten Teeth lifts me into the water.

He walks me to the beach, supporting my unsteadiness, and hands me off to a no-nonsense looking woman wearing a black *abaya* and *niqab,* sporting a white armband with a large red crescent.

He returns to the rescue craft and retrieves my suitcases, setting them beside an idling ambulance, the engine coughing, spewing blue smoke from the tailpipe. Without a word he shoves the lifeboat off the bottom, pulls himself inside through the open hatch with an assist from Rajaratman, closes the hatch, and motors away.

The ambulance looks more like a repurposed hearse, its rust-marked white paint tricked out with red crescents on the doors and the roof. Age-pitted chrome-plated sirens perch on the front fenders, looking like they were pilfered from a classic Schwinn bicycle. A red bubble gum emergency flasher sits on the roof.

The make, much less the model of the vehicle, is unfamiliar to me, but it looks vintage, perhaps late sixties, early seventies. It also looks completely untrustworthy.

My welcome party includes an armed male driver who is perhaps sixteen years old, the thirtyish woman with the armband who has escorted me to the open rear door, and a rough looking twenty-something guy standing in front of the ambulance on the passenger side. He's armed to the teeth, pointing an automatic rifle skyward, wearing a bandolier filled with ammo clips, a pistol, and enough grenades hanging from his belt for a minor war.

I ask the woman if she speaks English, and she replies, "Yes. A little." Her accent is French.

I tell her I need to urinate, and she barks something to the two men who snap their gazes forward to avoid looking at me. She says I should squat down behind the ambulance. I do so without hesitation, one hand on the bumper for balance as she stands guard. My bladder has been bursting for an hour.

When I'm finished, she hands me a scrap of toilet paper from the back of the ambulance and says, "Just drop it on the ground." She gives me a hand up into the ambulance, loads my luggage, and joins me inside. The man at the front of the ambulance comes around to close the rear door and installs himself up front in the passenger seat. I have ridden in ambulances before but never one with an armed terrorist riding shotgun.

I notice the driver and his sidekick have donned red crescent armbands. The woman gestures for me to lie on the gurney. She is very gentle as she places me in loose four-point restraints. She tapes a needleless IV to the back of my right hand. *"Je suis dèsolè,"* she says. "Very sorry. We pretend you are a patient. In case of checkpoints."

When we're underway, I ask her how long it'll be until we get to the hospital. She tells me two or three hours, depending. She doesn't say depending on what, but the road is so bad it feels like we're driving on a washboard. I notice she's holding my medical bag in her lap.

I ask about the patient I'm supposed to see at the hospital, but she puts a finger to her lips and shakes her head. She asks if I would like something to eat or drink, but I decline. I'm not eager to repeat my last experience with elimination somewhere alongside the road.

She hums a tune that could be a lullaby. Her jet-black eyes shine as she looks down at me and adjusts a folded-up blanket under my head. I would guess she's smiling, although it's impossible to know since the *niqab* covers her face, except her eyes.

"Not fear," she says. "No worry. Just rest."

I must feel reassured because I fall asleep against all odds. Perhaps the ketamine hasn't completely washed out. I don't know how long I slept, but when I wake, she says "We are there soon. Ten minutes."

We pull off the road into a compound of makeshift buildings in the middle of a hot, sandy nowhere. We back up to one of the buildings, larger than the others. It doesn't look much like a hospital but there are red crosses and crescents on its double doors.

My caretaker removes the fake IV and the restraints. "We arrive," she says, helping me sit up. A heavily armed soldier, *keffiyeh* pulled across his face, obscuring everything except his eyes, opens the rear door to the ambulance. There is no mistaking his demeaner for welcoming or friendly.

A woman in a white *abaya* and matching *niqab* stands a pace behind him, her hands on a rickety wooden wheelchair with more holes than webbing in its woven rattan back.

"Now more fake," my caretaker says. "We use *le fauteuil roulant*."

The woman in white helps me into the wheelchair, places my medical bag in my lap, and rolls me into the building and parks me in a bilious green room sparsely furnished with a chipped white enamel-top exam table and two wooden side chairs. My caretaker follows and the three of us wait in silence, enduring the sharp smell of antiseptic hanging in the oppressive air.

Moments later a man, about my age, wearing a stained white lab coat, a stethoscope dangling from his neck, enters the room, and stands stiffly in front of me, hands clasped behind his back. He smells like he's bathed in sandalwood.

"Good morning, Dr. Quilter. I am Dr. Omar Mahmud Awad, the physician in charge here. Your reputation precedes you, of course."

I stand to greet him.

"Yes, of course," he says. "You do not really need the wheelchair."

Dr. Awad is not hiding his feelings well. He is tightly wound, and his mouth looks like I interrupted him sucking on a pickle. I suspect I'm here because someone who calls the shots isn't happy with him. And now, he's forced to suffer a foreign woman thrust into his dominion, to check over his work, and possibly upbraid him for his incompetence.

I attempt to sidestep his petulance. It takes every ounce of niceness I can muster to greet him with civility. "Thank you for your hospitality, Dr. Awad. How can I be of service to you?"

"I will take you to see the patient. Bring your medical bag and walk with me." We enter a short hallway.

"How shall I address him?"

"You may call him 'Leader' if you like, although he will take no offense if you simply address him by name."

"And what have you determined to be his medical status?"

"He is severely jaundiced and has ascites. He has hepatitis B and possibly hepatocellular carcinoma in addition to end stage liver disease."

"And how are you approaching his treatment?"

"We are supporting him with palliative care, but we don't have access to the newer immunotherapies. The very fact that you are here against my advice means we will have to move him elsewhere as soon as you leave. It will not be safe for him to stay, or safe to move him, yet here we are."

"What would you like from me?"

"Myself, nothing. The patient will tell you his wishes."

He opens the door to Ahmad Ali Arif's room. Three armed bodyguards in the room barely pay us any notice. Dr. Awad remains just inside the spacious room near the door as I approach the patient's bedside.

"Good morning, Leader," I say, arousing him from apathetic torpor. He looks at me blankly for a moment and quickly regains his bearings.

"Dr. Quilter," he says. "I'm so happy to see you and equally apologetic for forcing you to come all this distance. I hope you will, in time, forgive me."

"How are you feeling, Leader?"

"As you can see, I am gravely ill, though in no particular pain, thanks to the kind ministrations of Dr. Awad."

"Will you permit me to examine you, sir?"

"Yes. Of course."

He says something to his bodyguards they dislike in a language I don't understand. They have taken my bag from me and are rifling through it. He switches to English.

"Enough," he tells them, switching to English. "You may wait outside. I'm sure I'm quite safe with Dr. Quilter. And you, Dr. Awad, may join them if you please. I wish to speak with Dr. Quilter privately."

They return my black bag to a bedside tray table. I see no place to wash my hands, but I have sanitizer. It will have to do.

I retrieve my stethoscope and disinfect it. Again I approach the patient's bedside as Dr. Awad turns on his heel and brusquely leaves the room. He's clearly miffed at being excluded. I'll have to address that later, but now I need to pay attention to the terrorist chieftain who lies before me, yellow as corn on the cob.

When I lower his coverlet, I can see his navel is popped up like the plastic thermometer in a holiday turkey. His flanks are bulging and his scrotum is distended with fluid. His bloated, Pikachu-yellow body could be mistaken for a balloon in the Macy's Thanksgiving Day Parade.

I touch him gently, although I don't need my hands to confirm what my eyes tell me. I'm pondering what I might say he doesn't already know.

229

I have no further need for diagnostic instruments, so I replace his coverlet, clean off the stethoscope and replace it in my bag. I open the door and invite Dr. Awad, but not the guards, inside.

"What can you tell me, Dr. Quilter?" the leader asks.

"I can confirm what I'm certain Dr. Awad has already shared with you. It appears you have received excellent medical care at his hands. I only wish we could offer you a more optimistic prognosis. Unfortunately I have no magic bullet against the viral hepatitis and the irreversible damage it's done to your liver."

The room is silent.

"I will ask both of you, since Dr. Awad has been reticent to tell me what he thinks about my chances of survival. How long have I left to live?"

"I will allow Dr. Awad to express his own view. Mine is that your chances of surviving another half-month are fair to poor, even with Dr. Awad's care.

"I'm often wrong in such matters, since no physician is gifted enough to predict the length of a patient's life, and I hope I'm mistaken, but I think what we can best do now is summon family to your bedside and to keep you as comfortable as possible. Dr. Awad?"

"I agree completely with Dr. Quilter," he says, standing a little taller, relieved I haven't cut off his balls and handed them to him in a Dixie cup.

At length, the Leader breaks the silence.

"Both of you are excellent physicians, and I appreciate your attention and compassion more than you can imagine. *Allah,* Glory be to Him, alone knows when I will enter paradise if that be His will. I am comforted by the knowledge that I have devoted my life to His service, and I will continue to do so for as long as I draw breath.

"I fear it is not in my future to be comforted by family. I must return to jihad in service of the Islamic Caliphate. But tell me, Dr. Quilter, how is it you can come here today, abducted and compelled as you were, and treat me with such compassion, knowing that I have killed many people and will continue to do so for whatever time remains for me?

Did you not have thoughts of killing me as I lay before you a moment ago? Do you not have thoughts of ending my life so I will not return to killing others?"

It's my turn to be silent as I consider my response.

"You sought me out as a physician and I came to you, albeit under duress, as a physician. I therefore owe a duty not to harm you. What I, or others, think of you is of absolutely no importance. My oath as a physician is a binding covenant. While I regrettably cannot do you much good, at least I will avoid harming you."

"And I have promised to return you safely to your world, Dr. Quilter," he says. "Go in peace."

Ahmad Ali Arif, *al-Shabaab* terrorist, closes his eyes, perhaps contemplating the shape of his remaining life, and turns his face away. I hope he dies before he kills anyone else. But even if he does, I know there are others eager to take his place, committed to kill for the glory of their god, by whatever name, in this insane part of the world.

My eyes catch Dr. Awad's, signaling that the next move is his. He opens the door, inviting the guards to resume their station. I don't look back at the Leader or say anything further as Dr. Awad motions me to join him.

"After you, Doctor," he says. *Noblesse oblige.* He seems satisfied that my invasion of his *sanctum sanctorum* has produced no lasting harm to him or his infamous patient.

I can't wait to get out of here. ■

29

Palace Kempinski

Dr. Awad and I have little to say to each other as we walk to his office. The woman, who tended to me in the ambulance, no longer wearing her red crescent armband, is waiting. She has brought an *abaya* and *niqab* for me.

"Amlina Astur has brought local clothing for your journey to the airport," Dr. Awad says. *Nabad gelyo*, Dr. Quilter," Dr. Awad says, leaving me with her in his office. "*Allah maake.*"

I must look puzzled. "He says '*nabad gelyo*,' 'goodbye' in Somali. 'God be with you,' '*Allah maake*' in Arabic," she says. "I help you dress now. Over your own clothes. We take airplane to Mogadishu. Do not worry. About two hours. Plane very safe."

I'm very glad she said "we." Our ambulance ride to the one-runway airstrip carved out of unrelenting desert southwest of Caluula is uneventful. The airplane looks like a crop duster. There's room just for the two of us. my luggage, and the pilot, but it gets us to Aden Adde International Airport in Mogadishu without incident.

By the time we arrive, it's getting dark. Amlina Astur somehow catches the eye of an official when we land, who approaches us with a porter.

"They help you now, Dr. Quilter," she says, embracing me. "All safe now. Wear Somali clothing until you land in Djibouti. "*Nabad gelyo. Allah maake.*"

I thank her and make a stab at the Somali goodbye she has translated for me. I'm sure it's incomprehensible, but she hugs me again before telling me "*Nabad gelyo. Allah maake.*"

The official doesn't introduce himself as he asks for my documents. To my relief, I find them tucked in a side pocket of my camera case. He directs me away from the main passenger area where others are queued into a small office where he looks over my documents, then smiles and holds up a piece of official looking paper.

"Now, there is just time to make your plane. We will board you before the other passengers if you follow me. Your luggage is already on board. Have a pleasant, restful flight," he says, handing me my documents.

What a clusterfuck of a day, as Lovely would say. Drugged by Tamil Tiger mercenaries and kidnapped from the *Andaman Pearl* in the wee hours of the morning, a lifeboat trip on a gurney to the Somali coast with my captors, an "ambulance" ride to a tatterdemalion hospital somewhere in in the northernmost Horn of Africa, a quick clinical consultation with a critically ill terrorist "Leader" and his physician, a puddle jumper flight to the Mogadishu airport disguised as a Muslim woman, and now, a flight to safety in Djibouti.

So far, everything has gone according to my captors' plan, but I don't feel safe until the plane leaves Somali airspace.

No surprise the moment I set foot on the tarmac at the Djibouti-Ambouli Airport, local officials are eager to question me. Their interest is perfunctory, but the American authorities are another matter. A military SUV is waiting to take me to Camp Lemonnier, a heavily fortified U. S. navy base on one end of the airport, a brief ride away.

I'm exhausted, having been up for eighteen hours. I spend several additional hours trying to recall the details of my ordeal for my inquisitors.

They show me photos. Yes, it was Ahmad Ali Arif I examined. Where exactly did I examine him? I can't tell one small hospital on their map from another, and their reconnaissance photos don't help.

I confirm the details they have about Nasir Rajaratman and the hijacking of the *Andaman Pearl*. They tell me the ship has resumed its journey and is headed to an unscheduled port call in Muscat, Oman. The Combined Task Force intercepted the getaway boat and the Tamils are on their way to Mombasa, Kenya, for "processing." They will charge them with terrorism, piracy, kidnapping, and a host of other serious offenses. The thought fills me with joy.

Do I know where Ahmad Ali Arif was going when he left the hospital? I know nothing except that he planned to leave the hospital and to rejoin his comrades, fighting for the establishment of an Islamic state somewhere in the region.

How is his health? I doubt he will last the week. He's terminally ill. If he stayed in the hospital, perhaps he would have lived another month. Unless, of course, someone took him out with a drone strike.

Everyone I speak to is polite but uninterested in my personal welfare, disappointed as they are that I can't serve up some important *al-Shabaab* terrorist or co-conspirator. An attaché from the American embassy offers a consular physician to examine me if I wish. I do not.

She gives me a ride to the Djibouti Palace Kempinski where I finally arrive, miraculously with my luggage, well after midnight. It has been over twenty-four hours since my ordeal aboard the *Andaman Pearl* began. I take a long shower and get into bed exhausted.

I want nothing more than to sleep, but I awake early, the sun pouring through my windows overlooking the magnificent Gulf of Tadjourah with its hazy backdrop of distant mountains.

I help myself to the in-room tea service, dress as nicely as my clothing in its current state will permit and take advantage of the luxurious breakfast buffet at the hotel's Lac Assal restaurant. It's a far cry from the officers' mess on the *Andaman Pearl*. My plan, after breakfast, is to ask the hotel to assist me in booking a flight out of Djibouti. To where, I don't know. Or care. Almost anywhere seems better than the Horn of Africa.

I had the foresight to charge my cell last night, and I'm thankful I did because the phone rings as I'm finishing my third cup of coffee at Lac Assal.

It's Yongzheng Shun. I'm stunned.

"Shun. Where are you?"

"Hi, Jessamyn," he says. "I'm happy I found you. I'm in Singapore. Everyone is fine. The question is, how are you?"

I try to condense the events of the last couple of days for him, but I'm afraid I'm jabbering as the enormity of what I've just been through overwhelms me. I babble and I cry.

Shun listens patiently as I attempt to describe the hijacking of the *Andaman Pearl* and my kidnapping by the very people Captain Bayani brought on board to protect us from pirates. I'm in tears before I finish, angry about the entire ordeal, and surprised at feeling so emotionally raw as I talk to Shun.

"We all feel bad for you, Jessamyn, but everything is going to be fine. Really. The important thing is that you are safe. Lovely and Èlia are safe. I just talked to them. The captain put them ashore at Muscat so they could fly the rest of the way to Paris. The *Andaman Pearl* and all her crew are safe. Everyone was scared, but nobody was hurt."

Shun chuckles and adds, "Except Lagac," he says. "He is still pissed they had the audacity to steal you from under his nose. He's ready to swim to Mombasa, where they're holding Rajaratman, and take matters into his own hands."

I calm down a little. Shun, as usual, is way ahead of me and has everything under control. How? I remember Shantrelle telling me Shun has a spy aboard the *Andaman Pearl*.

"Mombasa? Shun, I'm almost afraid to ask whether you had anything to do with the capture of Rajaratman and his filthy band."

"I helped a little," he says. "When Rajaratman's men left the ship on their 'go-fast,' they made for *Rescue Craft #1* to pick up their boss and the lifeboat pilot. We intercepted their radio chatter and called in the coordinates to Combined Task Force-151, the multinational naval antipiracy task force.

"CTF-151 scooped them up like a shoal of mullet. They'll probably end up in Shimo la Tewa, a maximum-security prison outside Mombasa. We can keep an eye on them there."

We? Shun's global reach again? I think it better not to ask.

"Shantrelle and I are flying to Muscat to pick up Lovely and Èlia," Shun continues, "and then all of us are coming to Djibouti to rescue you."

"I don't know what to say, Shun. Everything's happening so fast, but it's so reassuring to hear your voice."

"I know Lovely and Èlia would love to hear from you. Do you have their cells?"

"Yes. I do. I'll call them."

"How about Lagac's?"

I don't.

"He'll be out of cell range anyhow on the ship. I'll get word to him that we've spoken and you are safe. Oh, I almost forgot. He told me, 'Tell Jessamyn I love her.'"

I could almost see Shun's face. Smiling.

"He loves me?"

"His words precisely and I don't doubt it."

I'm ready to cry again. "Shun, you're amazeballs."

He laughs at my characterization. "Shantrelle and I are at the hangar in Singapore. The plane is almost ready. We're bringing *Ratu Shantrelle*, the "big plane," so everyone will be more comfortable. It will take us about seven hours to reach Muscat. We'll spend the night there with Lovely and Èlia and the four of us will fly to Djibouti to pick you up tomorrow morning.

"We'll all go to Paris where everyone can breathe a little easier and make some plans. Okay?"

"More than okay, Shun. If I believed in miracles, this would be it."

"Not miracles, Jessamyn. Just technology, although miracles happen. Shantrelle, for example, is a miracle."

"Give her a hug and kiss from me. Please? I miss all of you so much."

"Enjoy the Djibouti Palace Kempinski. It's a beautiful hotel, and the Lac Assal restaurant is one of the best in the country. We'll all be together tomorrow. You're only a three-hour flight from Muscat, and I'll call you tomorrow with more specific information before we leave Oman. Don't forget to call Lovely and Èlia, okay?"

"I'll call them as soon as we hang up. Bye, Shun. See you all tomorrow."

"Tomorrow," Shun says. "Sleep tight. You're completely safe in Djibouti, and we'll get you out of Africa as soon as we can. Bye for now." ■

30

Reunion

S hun's Boeing 747-8i business jet touches down smoothly and taxies across the tarmac, pulling into the gate. The name emblazoned on the fuselage dwarfs the Yongzheng Pte. logo on the tail. What else would Shun name his "big plane" except *Ratu Shantrelle,* honoring the wife he calls "my queen"?

"I forced him to do it," Shantrelle bragged when she told us about naming the plane back on the *Andaman Pearl.* "On his hands and knees, stark naked, kissing my favorite black leather thigh-highs, begging me to let him name the 'big plane' after me."

"All true." Shun grinned.

"I looked terrific," she added, striking a pose.

"It is all true, my *ratu."* Hc laughed.

It seems like a lifetime ago.

The plane comes to a stop and shuts down its engines. The door opens and Lovely bounds down the stairs, across the tarmac to where I'm waiting outside the terminal, almost knocking over a customs officer.

Èlia and Shantrelle follow at a more measured pace while Shun waits for officials to board the plane. A few minutes later, Shun leaves the aircraft and joins the gaggle of chattering women gathered around me. There are hugs and kisses everywhere. I'm smothered in love.

The flight crew joins us and Shun makes introductions. Local cleaners board the jet to freshen up the cabin while a ground crew fuels the plane and checks it over.

"We know you're eager to leave this part of the world, Jessamyn, so we'll be wheels up as soon as the captain says the plane is ready," Shun says. "You will meet our chef, Anne-Stéphanie, when we board. She is still on the plane preparing lunch. We tried to get her to de-plane, but she says she dare not lest the béarnaise break." He laughs.

The "big plane" is truly big. Ordinarily its two levels would be configured to carry about 450 passengers. Shun says the *Ratu Shantrelle* has been configured for nineteen passengers, plus crew. The plane sleeps everyone comfortably, in spacious cabins with en suite bathrooms and showers.

There's plenty of room for socializing, working, dining and the foosball table Shun has brought along.

"I got hooked on foosball at Le Triplettes de Belleville, one of my favorite *cafés* in Paris' 20th arrondissement Shun says. "Lucien, the bartender, wouldn't sell me his, but he helped me find an identical one."

Right now, Shun's the reigning foosball champ of *Ratu Shantrelle*, trouncing both Lovely and Èlia with ease.

The captain gives us the okay to board. A cabin attendant takes my luggage and off we go.

Despite what Shun has told us, I'm overwhelmed by the interior of the big plane. It's a flying hotel, the space meticulously designed and appointed. We find seats in the lounge and settle in for takeoff. A cabin attendant takes our drink orders, and Anne-Stéphanie comes through with a tray of appetizers.

She is exactly what one would expect from a world class chef, doubling on our plane as a maître d' and sommelier. She greets us as if we had presented with reservations at her Michelin starred Lyonnaise *bouchon*, in which Shun is a silent partner. She's been taking a break, learning more about Asian food in Singapore, staying with Shun and

Shantrelle at the Wallich Residence. He's pressed her into service on
our flight and will drop her back home in Lyon once he gets the rest of
us settled in Paris.

Shun has work to do, so he slips away after lunch to his office on
the second deck. Lovely and Èlia have already set up housekeeping in
one of the larger sleeping quarters and decide a little nap is in order
before dinner.

Shantrelle and I do some catching up in the lounge. She and Shun
have been blissfully happy in Singapore, although one or both are away
frequently on business. They have often thought about us and the time
we spent together on the *Andaman Pearl*. Without wanting to intrude on
our lives, they have kept as close tabs as possible. They enlisted Lagac
to help. He was the one who alerted them to my capture by the Tamils
and the hijacking of the *Andaman Pearl*.

"Lagac was beside himself and Shun was furious," Shantrelle says.
"I have never seen him so angry. But Shun is nothing if not resourceful.
He pulled every string to keep track of you. If you had not reappeared
as quickly as you did, I think he would have single-handedly invaded
Somalia to rescue you."

I remember how floored I was when Shun called me in Djibouti. I
can't imagine how he maintains these networks over the entire world.
He doesn't miss a thing.

"Fortunately, one of the Tamils bragged about Rajaratman's plan
to Lagac while the *Andaman Pearl* was en route to the Somali coast to
offload the contraband. He assured Lagac you weren't taken for ransom
and would be released safely once you were no longer needed. When
the Combined Task Force liberated the *Andaman Pearl*, Lagac called
Shun and told him as much as he knew. Shun put the pieces together
from there.

"Shun persuaded Captain Bayani to disembark Lovely and Èlia in
Muscat so they could fly to Europe without further risk. The Tamils told
Lagac you would turn up in Djibouti in a couple of days if all went well,

and Shun contacted people he knows at Kempinski Hotels in Munich who closed the loop for us with their Djibouti property.

"The Djiboutis, using clandestine contacts with *al-Shabaab*, confirmed you were being taken to examine Ahmad Ali Arif. They got in touch with Dr. Awad and bribed him to tell them when you left the hospital for the Mogadishu airport.

"We've had eyes on you ever since. Shun has already let Lagac know you are with us now, so Captain Bayani, Eric, and the entire crew of the *Andaman Pearl* know you're safe and unharmed."

"I have no words to thank all of you for what you've done," I say, choking back tears. "It's just now hitting me what a shit storm I've been through. Something could have gone sideways at any point, from the moment they drugged me and forced me onto the lifeboat to the time my plane left the Mogadishu airport. Instead of sitting here with you, I could be dead, or worse."

"Well, not if Shun and I had anything to say about it. You know how much we all love you. Why don't you try to rest or nap? We'll have dinner later, and after that you can sleep as long as you wish. When we land, we'll probably just stay aboard the plane, then have a light breakfast before going into the city. Let me show you your cabin."

She turns back the duvet on my bed and rearranges the stack of pillows into a cozy nest.

"Take a shower if you like. There are pajamas and a robe in the closet and some extra clothes in case your own didn't make the trip in the best of shape. I'm going to tell everyone else they should come to dinner in their pajamas, so I expect you to be comfortable as well."

I had a shower earlier that morning at the hotel, so I just strip off my clothes and get into the bed. Shantrelle pulls the sheet and duvet over me, tucks me in, and shows me the panel with the lights and call button.

"I don't know what I'm going to do," I say, my voice quavering.

"Well, Shun and I have some ideas, at least for the short term while you figure out what comes next in your grand adventure." She smiles.

"We own a five-story building in the 19th arrondissement, close to the Conservatoire National Supérieur de Musique et de Danse de Paris where Lovely and Èlia will spend the next two or three years. That's where we'll go in the morning.

"Stay a few days, a few weeks, or months, while you figure out what you're going to do next. Right now though, just get some rest. Come to dinner later if you like or just sleep through."

I sleep through dinner. When I wake up, we're parked on the tarmac in Paris. Somehow, neither the noise from other airplanes nor the giggling of Lovely and Èlia, who have insinuated themselves into my bed, have awakened me.

"Wakey, wakey," Lovely whispers in my ear. "Time for breakfast."

Èlia brushes stray hair out of my eyes. I grab both and squeeze them to me as tightly as I can. I never want to let them go again. ■

31
I ❤ Paris

PARIS   *August 7*

Ah, I love Paris. No matter that it's a muggy ninety-five degrees today or, as the French would say, thirty-five degrees Celsius, which sounds cooler but isn't. The French are not believers in air conditioning. Perhaps some remnant of medieval superstitions about the dangers of drafts. They are also not believers in putting a useful amount of ice in a Diet Coke. Who knows where that comes from.

Fortunately for us, Shun and Shantrelle buck the trend and our air-conditioned Paris home is very comfortable. Still, why stay cooped up in an apartment when you can go to the beach? In Paris, anything is imaginable and anything imaginable is possible.

Anyone with the means to do so fled Paris weeks ago for *les vacances* and won't return until *la rentrée,* the first part of September. For those who can't leave, the *city* brings the beach to Paris.

Paris Plages. From the Pont des Arts to the Pont Marie, the banks of the Seine transform into a "beach" complete with red and white umbrellas, deck chairs, and potted palms.

"They used to bring in thousands of tons of sand from the Normandy beaches," Shun says, "but the company that barged it in was indirectly funding Daesh in Syria. The final straw came when they bid on America's

245

border wall. One of the city officials declared the sand was 'stained with blood' and banished it for eternity from the City of Light."

Shun says there will be plenty of time over the coming weeks and months to explore the "tourist Paris." Since he and Shantrelle must get back to their business in a few days, he wants to make sure we see more of our own neighborhood before they leave. He has in mind an outing to a unique part of *Paris Plages,* closer to where we live, le Bassin de la Villette in the 19th arrondissement.

It's the largest artificial lake in Paris, linking the Canal Saint-Martin and the Canal de l'Ourcq. Few tourists even know about Bassin de la Villette, much less visit.

We walk around in our bathing suits, eat ice cream, and become part of the press of adults and children trying to escape the sizzling heat. Some are swimming at La Baignade, in one of three pools built into the side of the lake of differing depths to accommodate everyone—the splashers and children too young for a regulation pool, older people and those with physical disabilities, and serious lap swimmers. Some people are playing paddle board polo on the lake, pedal boating, or kayaking.

"Foosball!" Shun shouts. Sure enough, we find foosball and ping-pong tables and kids jumping on trampolines or splashing in fountains. We brave a gaggle of them to stand under a man-made forest of *brumisateurs,* misting towers that bathe us in cool fog.

Back home, we dress and pay a visit to the Belleville-Ménilmontant market with its explosion of fruits and produce, cheeses, stacks of egg-crates, mannikin heads displaying fancy turbans, and to Shantrelle's delight, a bin of outrageously colorful bras in extraordinarily large sizes. She buys two of them, one Popsicle lime, the other neon orange with black tiger stripes, and dangles them in front of Shun's face. She could wrap them around her chest twice. Clearly they are not destined for her personal wardrobe.

Hemingway described Paris as a "movable feast," not because of all the bohemian hangouts, the *vin ordinaire,* or the tempting aromas of *frites, pâté* and *espresso* wafting from *cafés-terrasses*, though perhaps that was part of it, but because of the total experience called "Paris." Paris is a presence that lingers when you're not in Paris and slaps you in the face with a righteous truth—Paris and not-Paris are the only two places on earth. As if God, on the first day of creation, separated light from darkness and the light he called Paris and the darkness he called not-Paris.

It's an image, this movable feast, that pervades my senses as we walk down the Boulevard de Belleville, the hot, barely moving air tempting us with wisps of fragrant garlic, exotic Thai condiments, curries, and grilling meats.

We cross the street to Les Triplettes de Belleville restaurant for happy hour and conversation. The foosball table beckons once again, and Lovely has no trouble beating Shun whose reflexes are suffering from too much wine.

As the evening cools, we sit outdoors and eat pizza, *bavette* with fried onions, and Caesar salad, watching the world go by, people just strolling or bringing their purchases home from the market, some on foot and others on motorcycles, like the young woman riding pillion on a Harley, dressed in a multicolor *abaya* and coordinating robins-egg *hijab*, rocking oversized sunglasses.

Eventually we make our way home to Shun's building, our appetites sated and our heads swimming with images. Les Triplettes de la *Andaman Pearl,* Shantrelle, Lovely, and Èlia, haven't had enough of talk. They congregate in Lovely and Èlia's new digs. Shun and I repair to mine. He is somber.

"Jessamyn, I'm so happy and relieved you are safe. It was wonderful playing and relaxing with everyone today, but I am very concerned about you."

"I'm fine, Shun, really, I am. I don't understand why, but I feel okay."

"Still, one doesn't get doped up and shanghaied by terrorists, bullied into examining an *al-Shabaab* warlord, dumped unceremoniously in a country most people don't even know exists, and walk away unscathed."

"I know. It doesn't make much sense. And yet, here I am."

"I have taken the liberty of priming the pump, Jessamyn. I hope I'm not overstepping my bounds. A couple of years ago, we had an ugly hostage situation involving our company, and I brought the best negotiator I could find to Singapore to handle the situation. She was terrific. A psychiatrist and she's also a world-renowned expert in the management of trauma."

"Let me guess. She's here in Paris," I say, laughing.

"Not exactly. She's on holiday in the south of France. But she will be back in the office the second week in September. I reached out to her and told her a little about your situation. She would be happy to see you, but she stressed, and I am in complete agreement, the decision must be yours."

"So, you think, Dr. Shun, that I might need a few screws tightened after all I've been through?"

"I know I would," he says.

"I'll give her office a call and see what I can set up. What can it hurt? And by the way, I'm clearly the beneficiary of you overstepping your bounds, or we would not be here talking together. I shudder to think how this all might have turned out if you hadn't rescued me."

"Do you have any thoughts about what might be next for you, Jessamyn?"

"Only that I'm not ready to go back to Westbury. Try as I might, I can't think of any good reason to go back to the States. I sent Jerry Finsterwald an email just to check in and told him I'd be in touch with more details in a few days. Right now I'm tired and more than a little confused about my future."

What I don't tell Shun is that I'm experiencing increasingly frequent episodes where I lose track of time, when real-world boundaries dissolve before my eyes. The light shimmers for a few seconds, accompanied by the most strangely beautiful sounds, before everything slides back into position. Or I see things I know aren't there, like copulating jaguars who speak to me. I lose my place, and it takes a few seconds to reorient when the real world comes back. I feel completely unmoored.

The third or fourth time it happened after my rescue, I figured it must be ordinary hallucinations if there is such a thing. I put it off to the ketamine and told myself things would settle down. After all, the medical literature reports that many people have mild hallucinations a few days, sometimes weeks, after getting Special K.

But why does my hallucination involve a jaguar licking my face? And why, even before getting clobbered with ketamine, did I hallucinate a jaguar attacking me as Lovely and Èlia traced *kené* around Lovely's navel? What's with the jaguars?

That has nothing to do with ketamine. Èlia's explanation that some gender bending "mother spirit" favored me with that fright-fest seems crazy.

I doubt even an expert in trauma, like the psychiatrist Shun recommends, will make sense of what I'm experiencing. I wonder if it would be safe even to tell her.

So, while I promise Shun I'll follow through, I have my fingers crossed behind my back. I'll just have to see what things are like when his trauma expert returns to Paris.

After all, today has been a completely normal day with my *Andaman Pearl* family. No dissociative episodes. No hallucinations. Why wouldn't tomorrow be just like today?

I wish Shun a good night and look around this beautiful apartment in this crazy, exciting corner of Paris. I'll be sorry to see Shun and Shantrelle leave again. But I have the feeling they never really leave. They just go away until there's a good reason for them to return.

Meanwhile, I'll be close to Lovely and Èlia while they settle into their new life as students. I have all this glorious city at my doorstep with plenty of time to think about the next steps. Paris or not-Paris? I'd be crazy to think about not-Paris. I don't think about it, and I take that as evidence I'm not crazy. Tired, but not crazy. ∎

32

Ring Scam

PARIS   September 9

I almost reneged on my commitment to Shun to call Céline Zecrí, the psychiatrist he thinks might shrink my head. And then, two days ago, I had another one of those boundary dissolving incidents that scares the shit out of me.

I was sightseeing along the Seine, and my first stop was Musée du Quai Branley—Jacques Chirac. There, I hoped to learn more about pre-Hispanic Peruvian art, especially the art and cosmology of the Shipibo people, to better understand Èlia's world. Unfortunately the museum's displays were limited. The *kené* on the textiles and pottery on display were gorgeous, but there were too few pieces. I would have to talk with Èlia to learn more.

From the museum, I was walking along the left bank of the Seine on my way to Les Invalides and the tomb of Napoleon Bonaparte, near the American Church of Paris, when a well-dressed young woman in her mid-thirties approached me and attempted to engage me in conversation. She first tried French, then German and what I took to be Russian or a similar Slavic language, before she said, "You are American?"

"Yes," I replied.

She stooped in front of me and picked up something from the grass.

"I found your gold wedding ring," she said, offering it to me.

I didn't take it.

"I'm afraid it's not mine. In fact, it couldn't possibly be mine."

"Too bad someone lost it," she said, slipping it on her ring finger. "But as you see it's far too large for me. You should have it," she said, taking my hand and closing my fingers over it.

"No, thank you. It doesn't belong to me. Please take it back."

"Well, it's very valuable. Pure gold. Perhaps you can buy it from me for fifty euros or even forty. I need the money to feed my children," she persisted.

Clearly it wasn't pure gold. Nor were her intentions. Flaking paint revealed the base metal underneath, likely iron. Since she wouldn't take it, I placed the ring on the seat of a nearby park bench.

"Please do not ask again, *madame*," I said and walked away. She grabbed my sleeve.

I tried to speak, to say, "Take your hands off me," but what emerged from my throat was a hair-raising growl. She blanched, turned, and ran, abandoning the ring. The world around me rippled as a jaguar sat back on its haunches beside me in a clearing in some rainforest. The giant cat was tranquil. Not menacing. He simply yawned, then stretched out beside me as if to take a nap.

When Paris re-materialized, I was sitting on a bench overlooking the Seine. An old woman sitting beside me, Roma by her appearance, was humming softly, fingering the ring I had placed on the bench.

"She tried to cheat you with the 'ring scam,'" the old woman whispered, "but your power is too great for her."

Power? What power? I couldn't answer. I felt only terror.

The woman placed the ring in her pocket, gently took my hand and examined my palm.

"Something inside you is not well. You carry a great evil that will destroy you if you do not break free." She placed my hand in my lap, got up from the bench, and walked away.

I'm a rational woman. It's impossible to continue chalking these intense hallucinations up to a ketamine hangover. I need some answers.

I had stored *Mme* Zecrí's contact information in my cell, as Shun suggested, so I give her office a call.

To my surprise, she answers her own phone. She seems pleasant enough, if not warm and fuzzy, entirely fluent in English. She sets an appointment for us to meet the next day.

Mme Zecrí's office is on the Left Bank, near the Sorbonne. It's not too complicated to negotiate the *Métro* from my apartment in Shun's building, and I locate her address easily. I walk up a single flight of stairs and ring the buzzer beside the polished brass nameplate by her door.

"*Bonjour,* Dr. Quilter. Céline Zecrí. I am pleased to make your acquaintance."

"Jessamyn Quilter. Thank you for agreeing to see me on such short notice."

Mme Zecrí dresses fashionably. She ushers me politely through the waiting area into her consultation room, directing me to an elegant sofa fronted by a coffee table. She sits in one of a pair of comfortable chairs opposite me.

"I know a little about the reason for your visit after talking earlier with *Monsieur* Yongzheng Shun," she says. "Perhaps you can tell me more."

I tell her about my journey, how I met Shun and Shantrelle, and my gratitude for all they've done for me in the aftermath of my abduction from the *Andaman Pearl.*

"I understand only a little time has passed since then. How are you coping with all that now?"

"It's been just over a month," I say. "I believe I've taken everything in stride, but I've been having some perceptual alterations, which until recently I attributed to the ketamine used in my abduction."

"And you now believe ketamine is not responsible for your ongoing symptoms?"

"That's correct. The ketamine should have washed out by now."

"Can you tell me more about these 'perceptual alterations'?"

I tell her about the boundaries dissolving between this world and some other and the episodes with the dreamcats, beginning before I left for Yokohama.

"I don't understand what cats have to do with it and why they now appear to me with increasing frequency, no longer confined to my dreams, but now sitting beside me or lunging at my throat while I'm awake. Of course I realize they're not real, but they seem very real."

"I understand. It must be puzzling. I'm wondering if you have ever worked in counseling or therapy before coming to see me."

I tell her about my previous work with my shit-for-brains analyst. I soft-pedal what I think of his professional competence, but I'm certain she gets the message about my general distrust of therapy, and by extension, therapists.

Her next words catch me off-balance.

"Do you think you are controlling the comings and goings of those cats? Could you make one of these large cats appear now if you wished?"

"I don't think so."

"Would you be willing to try, realizing that I will be with you here in this room, knowing that these cats are not real and therefore cannot pose any danger to either of us?"

"How would I ever do that? And no, I wouldn't be willing. I don't trust them or trust myself."

"How does it make you feel right now, just to think about it?"

"It scares the bejesus out of me. While I understand they're not real, I worry I might not come back from one of those reality warps."

"I understand, and yet the last time the cat appeared, during the ring scam, it did not menace you but someone who was trying to take advantage of you. Then it waited quietly beside you in a peaceful clearing in the rainforest until you were ready to return to the present moment.

"Did you see the cat before it growled, or more accurately, *you* growled, as you say, 'scaring the bejesus' out of the woman harassing you? Can you tell me what was frightening about that?"

"No, I didn't see it until we were in the jungle. You're right. It wasn't the cat or that annoying woman that scared me. It was the fact I found myself suddenly in the middle of a jungle when I was certain I was standing on a green in Paris, only to discover I was no longer in the jungle or standing on a green but seated on a park bench next to a total stranger who was holding my hand and telling my fortune. A woman who told me I carry a 'great evil' inside me that will destroy me if I don't free myself from it."

"I see. And do you carry a 'great evil' inside you?"

"Others might say I do."

She waited for me to expand upon my answer. I was determined not to do so.

"And what might that be?" she persisted.

"Before we go another step, I need to ask you what you might do if I were to confess I do."

"In France, physicians are held to much higher standards of confidentiality than in the United States. A patient's confidentiality is inviolable. With great reluctance I might break that confidentiality to get you additional help if I believed you were a danger to yourself or someone else. But I sense you may not yet be ready to disclose this secret of yours."

"What would be the point of confessing such a so-called 'great evil' if I were to have one inside me," I parry. "Do you think these shifts in perception I'm experiencing result from doing something evil?"

"It is probably not as straightforward as that. In the first place, one might want to distinguish between doing something evil and holding something evil. A distinction, for example, between committing an evil deed and carrying an evil secret."

I wasn't sure where all this might be going.

"There are people who commit evil deeds and because they appear to be missing a conscience or do not believe what they do is evil, suffer no emotional ill effects from their behavior. And there are people who have done nothing wrong who suffer because they believe they bear responsibility for something that is not of their doing.

"But for people who bear the crushing shame of a painful memory, whether they did something evil, and who sequester an untellable secret, one way to get temporary relief from the emotional agony is to dissociate. You become 'not you' for a few moments to escape the pain of being 'you.' Hallucinations, dissociative episodes, alterations of perception where one 'loses time' or 'loses place' are common markers of unresolved trauma."

"So you suggest I might have some unresolved trauma that's causing me to hallucinate?"

"It is certainly one possibility. Can you identify any such trauma?"

I was not about to tell her about Roderick.

"I can't, but if I could, what would I do about it?"

"The simplest way to begin is to tell someone when you are ready. I would be happy to listen to anything you might wish to tell me. If not me, you might choose to tell someone else who you trust. It is only a beginning but an important beginning."

Who might I tell. A priest? Notre Dame was a short walk eastward toward the Seine. I could go to confession if I believed that would help, but I don't. If nothing else, it seems gauche, even fraudulent since I'm not a religious person.

I could confess anonymously to one of those internet websites like Rawconfessions or Postsecrets. Really no need to bother with a priest when I can confess with a couple clicks of a mouse.

The thought crossed my mind that perhaps writing a letter of apology to Roderick might help. I could ask one of those scriveners stationed outside Shakespeare and Company across from Notre Dame with their little stands and typewriters to write one for me. One of them has a chalkboard advertising he'll typewrite anything, from a love letter to a suicide note, for three euros. But to whom would I send this letter? Roderick's family or friends? He has none. The world at large? Myself?

Likely I'd just tear it up and toss it into the Seine, which would probably get me arrested.

I laugh at the possibilities. In the end, I discard the idea of telling anyone. I'm not sure if I will see *Mme* Zecrí again. What she said makes sense, but I don't think it will work for me. It's too dangerous.

I can't draw a straight line between killing Roderick and having these symptoms involving dreamcats. They don't seem interested in punishing me, although one insists I need to become accountable. On the contrary, they're being protective. But what are they protecting me from? As always, I end up with more questions than answers.

If there's a clear path forward for me, I can't see it. I'll just need to toughen up and let this thing work itself out. And hope I find a solution before I dissociate myself into a fruitcake factory. ■

33

Come to Jesus

Sleep just would not come last night. No matter how much I tossed and turned, I couldn't get comfortable. I gave myself a good talking to though, since I was awake anyhow. Something like this:

Okay, Jessamyn old girl. Get a grip. As improbable as it may seem, Mme Zecrí is probably right about the trauma thing. You went to her because you were frightened of losing your mind. Nobody forced you. You went seeking help, and she hit the nail on the head. You ran the other way.

Big revelation? The jaguar who's been stalking you is you. You're making these big cats appear and disappear yourself. You're just not aware of doing it.

You didn't have these cat dreams until you murdered Roderick. Let's just say it out loud. Murder. You murdered your husband in cold blood. You switched his medication with poison, and it doesn't matter that you didn't push the plunger on the syringe.

You planned his death to the nth degree. It was inevitable because you made it so. You knew he was suffering and dying on your bathroom floor while you pretended to read a book. You said you had no regrets. What kind of person does that? A killer. The kind of person you are.

But why are you being molested by these facts now? Things have changed. You escaped a situation where you faced harm, even death. Al-Shabaab is a lethal organization with no compunction about killing, and you were a pawn in a deadly game. You could have died.

I know, I know. You were tired of Roderick. He was a wretched piece of garbage. Abusive. You needed to escape. Of course you could have escaped without killing him, but you chose to kill him. Why you did it isn't even important. You did what you did.

The great big world would certainly condemn you for that. Massachusetts doesn't have the death penalty, but it's likely that if anyone found out about the murder, you would spend the rest of your life in prison. You knew that. Otherwise, why would you have planned the perfect crime? Nobody suspects anything, and if they do, they can't prove it.

And so, the night passed. Now I feel guilty about killing Roderick but still have no regrets except having to deal with the guilt. When I killed him, I also killed part of my life, the part with the abuse and trauma. To add to the trauma I must at least consider the possibility that murdering him heaped more trauma on my head, rather than getting rid of what was already there.

So now I feel guilty at times, but generally at peace with what I've done. It makes no sense at all. How am I able to deal with trauma when I feel like this? How am I able even to acknowledge the possibility that the jaguars might be part of my trauma response?

As the sun rises, I email Shun at the Proton Mail address he left with me and ask if we can set up a time to video chat on my secure Doxy.me channel, the one I used for online follow-ups with my patients. Within minutes of sending him the link, my laptop chimes, announcing Shun in my virtual waiting room. I'm still in bed, wearing my pajamas, propped up against my pillows. I connect us.

"Hi, Shun."

Hi, Jessamyn. How are you?"

"I'm very glad to see you. If this isn't a good time, it's not an emergency. We can talk later."

"Now's fine. Shantrelle says hello and sends her love. She misses you. So do I. How is Paris?"

I give him the ten-cent recap, including the ring scam, the fortune teller, and my session with Cécile Zecrí.

He listens in compassionate silence. One of Shun's greatest gifts is his ability to listen.

"*Mme* Zecrí thinks I need to discover and confess what she believes is a 'dark secret' that may be connected to trauma. She thinks that might be the first step to getting rid of these scary hallucinations and out-of-body experiences."

"And do you trust her assessment?"

How like Shun to ask this question instead of probing about my "dark secret."

"I don't know. I've only seen her once. She seems very competent."

"Do you plan to continue working with her?"

"I don't think so, but I haven't entirely decided. I've been talking with Lovely and Èlia without giving them too much detail. I trust them completely, but they're so young and school is heating up. I don't want to worry or distract them.

"We talked again late last night. Lovely says I can wear her *agimat,* but she doesn't think it's as powerful as it's cracked up to be. We had a good laugh about that."

"What does Èlia think?" Shun asks. "She's an amazingly perceptive young woman."

"She thinks I should go live with her family in Peru. She's convinced something's wrong inside me, by which she means my spirit, and whatever it is will kill me if I don't deal with it. She believes her people can help me figure out what's wrong and fix it.

"She says that's why the mother spirit of the jaguar teacher plant appeared to me. The mother spirit is leading me to Shipibo wisdom about what's happening to me. She thinks the teacher plant protected me against Rajaratman and *al-Shabaab,* and she believes those bastards couldn't have hurt me if they tried.

"'Why go to all the trouble of getting you back to safety after they had kidnapped you?' she asked me. 'Why didn't they just kill you? It would have been so much easier. The jaguar stopped them, that's why.'"

"Well," Shun says, trying to lighten the conversation, "I don't think your jaguar's a *jinni,* at least if we trust Hamza Barranquilla's teachings about how to distinguish between cats and *jinn.*"

I appreciate Shun's gentle humor and consider again confessing to him about Roderick, as I almost have many times. I trust him that much. After all, I remember how he dealt with Mr. Agarwal, offering him a path to redemption, "protecting" him in prison until he sees the benefit of atoning. But somehow this seems different, more dangerous, and I don't want to jeopardize him or Shantrelle.

"What do you think, Jessamyn?"

"I don't know what to think. Èlia lives comfortably in the world of the supernatural. *Mme* Zecrí lives in a world of science where disclosure of the unspeakable is the beginning of healing. I now live in a world where the boundaries between what's real and what isn't real become more porous every day."

"Forgive my bluntness, Jessamyn, but with respect, does *Mme* Zecrí think you are crazy? Does she think you should be in a hospital?"

"No, she doesn't. She's sure I have a firm grip on reality."

"And do you agree with her?"

"Yes...yes, but."

"But?"

"But this jaguar wherever it came from is no longer making an appearance and leaving. It's lying on the foot of my bed. Right here and right now, as you and I talk."

I turn the camera around to show him. "Please tell me you can't see him."

"I can't, but that doesn't make him any less real. Are you frightened?"

"Not really. I'm getting used to him. His company is reassuring. He was waiting for me outside *Mme* Zecrí's office when I finished my session yesterday. He startled me at first, but as I walked away, he simply followed at my side. He boarded the *Métro* with me, sat at my feet, transferred lines when I did, and got off with me at the Belleville stop near your building. He walked home with me, slept on the bed with me last night, and has been with me ever since."

"Jessamyn, you know I am a spiritual man. It feels to me you are on a spiritual quest. Many cultures believe in spirit guides, aides in such quests. Could that be the role of your jaguar?"

"Why? You know I'm not religious. What would I do on a spiritual quest?"

"Being religious and spiritual can be two different things. Perhaps you are questing because something feels deeply wrong, something that threatens to annihilate your soul, although you may not believe you have one. Others have told you of the danger you are in, and it doesn't seem wise to dismiss their observations. Maybe you have only an inkling, or maybe you can't see it at all yet, but I hope you will trust yourself not to get in your own way."

"I don't know, Shun. I know trauma can fuck people up, but this is all sounding a little airy-fairy to me. I mean, a jaguar spirit animal?

"I know you to be a deeply compassionate person. Are you in danger of losing your way? Is it possible you must re-evaluate something about your life that does not mesh with who you truly are?"

"This is so far beyond me. I have a pet jaguar who doesn't exist. I'm clearly doubting my sanity, but other than the hallucinations, which can be frightening, I'm perceiving the world as it is.

"If I were hearing about experiences like mine from a patient, I would ship her off to a shrink without hesitation. And I think the shrink would prescribe a butt full of Haldol. But I don't see myself as that crazy person and neither, apparently, does *Mme* Zecrí. It's something else. She might be right about my trauma. I also think Èlia might be right. But these two worlds don't match up. I don't think Haldol would fix anything."

"So, how can I help? What would you like to do?"

"Well, you've helped immensely already. You haven't activated Psychiatric Emergency Services or its Parisian equivalent while we've been talking. I don't see any men in white scrubs with butterfly nets in the street waiting to scoop me up."

Shun laughs. "I'm afraid your pet jaguar might eat them all if they tried to intervene. Besides, I agree with you and *Mme* Zecrí. You're not crazy. I don't think you need help from men with butterfly nets or doctors with drugs."

"I've been thinking Èlia is right. Perhaps I should go to Peru. Èlia says her parents would welcome me and help me figure things out. Besides, a jaguar seems completely out of place on the street of Paris."

"I think that's a good choice. Do you know when you might want to leave?"

"As soon as possible. Staying here is getting creepy. I don't think it's good for Lovely and Èlia either. The last thing they need is an old nutter hanging around the building."

"Tell you what. You go see the girls. Let them know you'll be leaving tomorrow. Give them our love. I'll make some calls to our Lima office and call you later today. They can help with the arrangements. Don't worry about anything. You are going to be fine, and we'll all be keeping an eye on you."

"What about *Mme* Zecrí?"

"Don't worry about her. You can leave a message on her service telling her goodbye if you like and thanking her for her help. I'll be in touch with her and add my thanks for taking such good care of you. She will completely understand your choice. Now, let me get to work on Peru, and we'll talk again in a couple of hours."

"I can't tell you how much all of this means to me, Shun. You and Shantrelle are such perfect gems."

"You are precious to us. We would do anything for you."

My jaguar stirs. It will undoubtedly follow me to Lovely and Èlia's apartment. I wonder if either of them will be able to see or sense him when I introduce them. Probably not. But I'm certain they'll believe me. So, if I'm crazy, that makes them crazy too. And Shun and Shantrelle.

That's five of us. *Les quintuples fous de Belleville.* Not such a bad thing to be crazy with other crazy people who love you. ∎

34

Ino

PARIS *September 11*

Lovely and Èlia know the bare bones of my plans to go to Peru. We're not ready for another separation, but everyone understands why I need to pack up and leave.

Èlia senses my jaguar when I enter her apartment, dipping her head in acknowledgment to the animal at my right side as if it were perfectly normal to be accompanied by an emotional support jaguar.

"The jaguar is called *ino,* in the Shipibo language," Èlia explains. "*Otorongo* in Quichua."

She sings to him. "An *ikaro* of welcome and homage to jaguars. He has not revealed his *janekon,* but if you need to address him, he will understand *ino*. It is a respectful way to address him and not overly familiar. If he prefers another name, he will let you know."

I'm astonished. Èlia simply takes this dreamcat at face value, as if I had just walked through her door with a big friendly dog she could scratch behind the ears and ask, "Who's a good boy?"

"Why can't I see the kitty?" Lovely asks. "Apparently my witchy powers are of no use at all." She pouts, fingering the *agimat* around her neck.

Èlia smiles and gives her a kiss on the forehead. "One day you may," she says. "I can't see him either, although I know he is here with us. It is up to *ino* who may see him. You are learning the old music and writing

267

the new. Spirits of the teacher plants hold you in high regard. But I can tell you, those little pieces of priest hanging around your neck don't impress *ino*."

"I know." Lovely grins. "Not a single person who has touched my *agimat* has keeled over dead. Maybe that dude's pizzle is just too old."

Lovely cracks me up.

"*Ino* might be part of your real name too, Jessamyn," Èlia says. "But only a *chamán* would know for sure. If it were, it would be the second part of your *janekon*, like the second part of my *janekon* is *Biri*. In Peru, you might find a *chamán* who can consult the *chaikoni* about your *janekon*."

Èlia has unsettling news, however. She's lost touch with her parents who have recently left Lima to return to the rainforest. Lima is becoming ever more hostile to indigenous people who settle in the city. Many of them are leaving and returning to their native lands since the guerilla danger there has diminished.

Èlia encourages me to go to Peru anyway and says she'll put me in touch with her parents when she finds out where they are. She will continue to ask around and put the word out that I am in Lima. She's certain someone from her village can help us find her family.

She sings me an *ikaro* for travel, and it's as if the magnificence of Paris, the dust of Somalia and Djibouti, and the ghosts of the *Andaman Pearl*, blow away on a refreshing breeze.

My rational self is having second thoughts about the entire plan. The craziness of setting out for Lima on the other side of the world, hoping to connect with someone who's not there, is not lost on me.

Shun calls back.

"Hi, Jessamyn. Got some news for you."

"Shun, do you know that Èlia's family is no longer in Lima?"

"Yes. I just found out, but don't worry. Everything is going to be fine. Let's just take it one step at a time. Got pen and paper?"

"Yes. What are we doing?"

"Okay. Your flight leaves from Charles de Gaulle at 2:30 tomorrow afternoon. You will need to be ready to leave about 10:30 tomorrow morning. We've arranged for a car to take you to the airport. You have a nice first-class seat so you and your jaguar can stretch out and relax on the way to Lima."

If it had been anyone other than Shun, I would have thought he was making fun of me.

"When you arrive, Ignacio Mejias, who works in our Lima office, will meet you at Jorge Chávez International and help you negotiate customs. There shouldn't be any difficulty."

"What about a visa?" I ask

"The Peruvian authorities will grant you an entrance visa with your American passport as a matter of course. We can get you a work visa after that if you want to stay longer than ninety days.

"Ignacio will take you to the apartment Shantrelle and I use when we are in Lima. We love it. It's in the Miraflores district of the city, a short walk from the cliffs overlooking the Pacific Ocean. He'll help you get settled. There are restaurants and shops close by, and the Wong supermarket is terrific. They can deliver or it's an easy few blocks walk if you wish."

"That's wonderful. I don't know why I'm so afraid. It's just not like me."

"Everything's going to be fine. You'll see. While we figure out where Èlia's family is settling, you can enjoy the many pleasures Lima offers. There are some guidebooks and maps in the apartment if you need ideas. Oh. And some leftover coca tea bags. Shantrelle loves the stuff, though I don't care for it."

"Coca? As in the drug?"

"Yes, and no. You'll find it everywhere. Mildly stimulating, but nothing like cocaine."

"Maybe I'll just stick to Lady Grey," I say.

"They'll have that at Wong too. And if you've ever wanted to sample more kinds of Pisco than you ever imagined existed, try the bar in the restaurant at the amazing ruins of Huaca Pucllana in the heart of the city. You can crawl around on the stepped adobe pyramid left by the indigenous Lima people. You might want to do the pyramid first and the Pisco shots later." He laughs.

"I've got to tell you, this whole Peru thing is a little intimidating."

"You're going to be fine, Jessamyn. Many Peruvians speak English, and it's easy to get around Lima by Uber, but Ignacio will be available to drive you or make any other arrangements you might need. He'll swap your euros for *soles* at the apartment.

"He's trying to track down Èlia's family. Ignacio knows people who know people who know people. That's his job with us, and he's very, very good at it. Okay?"

"Okay. I wish you were here though. I'd like to give you and Shantrelle a great big hug."

"You are not to worry. You have more important things to do. Your quest is what matters most now. There's nothing to be afraid of and everything to look forward to. Whatever's making you sick, we'll figure it out and find a healing path. How's your jaguar?"

"He's right here beside me and shows no signs of being angry with me."

"I'm sure he's not. He's your guardian, guide, and mentor. I wish I could meet him. How do you know it's a 'him', by the way?"

"Èlia told me. Though it's possible 'he' is a 'she' or both at the same time since *ino* is the mother spirit of a plant whose name I can't remember. Don't ask me how she knows these things, but she does.

"I still can't get over the fact that he's with me, though I know he could kill me at any moment. People around me would see nothing and just assume I'd had a heart attack."

That scenario causes my blood to run cold. That's what people thought happened to Roderick. Died of a heart attack. It's what I wanted them to think, made them think. It would serve me right to find myself on the short end of some cosmic payback.

"Jessamyn? Are you still there?"

270

I snap out of it. "Still here. Still here and terrified."

"You are going to be okay. Soon you'll be in Peru, and I'm certain you'll find the answers you need there. Meanwhile, perhaps you don't have to wait for your jaguar to talk to you. Try talking to him. Even if he doesn't respond, he will hear you, of that I am certain."

"Really, Shun? Talk to a 'haint' or whatever the hell it is nobody else can see? They'll lock me up for sure." I laugh nervously.

Shun laughs too. "Seriously, Jessamyn. But maybe just talk to him inside where nobody can hear you, not on the *Métro*. Like talking to yourself. But I'd better say goodbye now so you can finish up there and get to bed."

"What time is it where you are?"

"It's about 4:30 in the morning. Soon be time to get up and go to work." He laughs.

"My god, Shun. I'm sorry. I completely forgot about the time difference. I'm so sorry."

"Don't worry, Jessamyn, I can always go back to bed and have Shantrelle call in sick for me. It's great to be the boss."

"Good night, Shun. I love you. Tell Shantrelle I love her too, and if you need a doctor's note for missing work, we can work something out."

"Good night. Say good night to your jaguar for me. Pleasant dreams."

I send Jerry Finsterwald a quick email and let him know I'll be in touch again when I get settled in Peru. I brush my teeth, wash up, and get into bed. The jaguar bounds up to sleep at my feet.

"Good night *ino,* you magnificent creature. Shun says good night too. Thank you for protecting me, and please don't eat me in my sleep."

The jaguar is asleep before I can turn out the light, his soft abdomen gently rising and falling. Perhaps one of these days I'll work up the courage to touch his beautiful fur. I make a mental note to ask first.■

PART THREE

Metsá Ino

*The world of the quark has everything to do
with a jaguar circling in the night.*

ARTHUR SZE
"The Leaves of a Dream are the Leaves of an Onion,"
River River

35

Lima

Lima   September 14

It's been three days and no word from Shun. I don't want to call because I know he's busy, and I'm certain he's working on my problem. Still, I feel uncomfortable, stuck.

I've done the Museo Larco, the Huaca Pucllana, and the Museo de la Nación. I'm astonished how little I know about this country and its civilizations, what indigenous cultures flourished here while Christianity struggled to gain a foothold on the other side of the world, while Mohammed lived and died, while Rome declined and fell, while the Han Dynasty succumbed to barbarians, and the Byzantine empire blossomed.

I've walked down to the Parque del Amor a couple of times, with its gorgeous mosaics and enormous sculpture of two rosy-hued lovers entwined, kissing, floating above a fountain against the sky, oblivious to everything other than themselves. I've thrilled to the paragliders, soaring above the ever-present vultures, tracing the cliffs along the shining Pacific.

I watch the paragliders take off and land. I'm too old to try that but wish I weren't. It's a peaceful spot, but I feel at loose ends. I'm anxious and can't focus.

My jaguar seems anxious too. Pacing more, not content simply to walk or lie beside me. Sometimes he darts off and disappears for hours

275

at a time. I wonder if he'll return. He always has, but I wonder where he goes and why he's behaving so strangely.

I'm angry and I don't know why. The closest I can come is that I'm pissed off to be in this city, beautiful though it is, waiting for what comes next, not knowing what I'm waiting for. I like it less than most people when I can't control things.

I miss Lagac. It's been a little over a month since I was hijacked from the *Andaman Pearl*. Shun said Lagac loves me. I didn't know what to do with that when Shun told me, and I don't know what to do with it now. There's no way we can be in touch with each other. It's so complicated.

A call from Shun snaps me out of my rumination. He tells me he has a lead on Èlia's family. He thinks they might be somewhere in the Peruvian jungle along the Ucayali River. Not surprisingly, I don't even know a river called the Ucayali exists, much less where it is.

"The Ucayali is the source of the Amazon," Shun says, "and rolls along across the eastern slope of the Andes toward the rainforest city of Iquitos. Èlia has distant relatives living along the river, so we're making inquiries to see if anyone there knows where her immediate family might be. You might say we have it narrowed down to a thousand-mile stretch."

"A thousand miles? In the jungle? Shun, we'll never find them. I should think of what to do next. I don't know why, but I'm feeling more and more agitated. Angry too, and it makes no sense. I should be happy and content here. Lima is amazing. Ignacio Mejias has been a dear, checking on me and making sure I'm well taken care of."

"How's your jaguar?"

"Weird. He seems restless too, pacing back and forth like he's looking for something. And then he just disappears for hours before I see him again."

"It makes a certain amount of sense to me. Èlia told me the jaguar would likely help us. Maybe he's scouting the banks of the Ucayali when he's not with you."

"Is that supposed to be funny, Shun?"

"Sorry. Don't worry. We'll find them. I must run, but I wanted to update you. Just hang in there. I'll be in touch."

"Okay. Thanks. Love to Shantrelle. Bye."

How much weirder can it get? I have a dreamcat, perhaps prowling the Peruvian rainforest, looking for people who Èlia says will help me understand why I even have such an animal living with me. And Shun, precious Shun, has his scouts looking for those same people along a thousand mile stretch of river.

You need to chill, Jessamyn. Just relax and let Shun, and possibly the jaguar, do their thing.

Before I left Paris, Èlia suggested I drink some coca tea in Peru to help me relax. Coca tea from the supermarket is like regular tea in flow-through bags but full of drug-containing coca leaves, guaranteed to send the narcs knocking at my door if I were in the United States. Shun didn't exactly recommend it but only because it wasn't to his taste.

This is Peru, though, and not the United States, which by the way doesn't have a monopoly on good ideas. I saw more than half a dozen kinds of coca tea at the Wong supermarket, brands like Delisse, Herbi, Energy Green, and Wawasana.

Elia sang the *ikaro* of the coca plant for me in Paris.

"You can make cocaine out of coca, a marvelous medicine and a troublesome recreational drug, or you can make coca tea, which is a soothing, relaxing beverage," she says. "You can chew the leaves for an energy boost. Teacher plants offer us gifts and knowledge but don't dissuade us from our own willful foolishness."

Èlia is right. I sip my Wawasana coca tea, brewed from Shantrelle's leftover stash, in a thermal mug in the *Parque del Amor* as I watch the sun setting over the Pacific. The terracotta flesh of the enraptured lovers glows redder in the fading sunlight as if they are blushing, the privacy of their amorous embrace invaded by passersby.

I feel a hint of pressure against my thigh and look down. The jaguar is at my side. I swear he's purring. My cell rings almost at the same instant.

"We found them," Shun says.

"Yes. The jaguar just told me."

It's impossible to one-up Shun.

"I'm happy he's back with the good news. Èlia's family is living on the outskirts of Iquitos. Her father, Don Mateo, is making his way along the river to join them. He'll be working at the Pilpintuwasi Wildlife Rescue Center and Butterfly Farm near Padre Cocha, about half an hour north of Iquitos. His brother, Jose Luis, already works there. Do you want to stay in Lima a little longer or would you like to go to Iquitos?"

"I'm eager to meet Èlia's family. I'd prefer to go to Iquitos as soon as possible."

"Ignacio will arrange everything. He'll get you on a flight tomorrow morning, and we'll book you into the La Casa Morey in Iquitos. I envy you. I love La Casa Morey. I love Iquitos. You're in for an adventure you will not soon forget."

Another call comes in as I'm speaking with Shun. It's Ignacio. "Bye, Shun," I say. "Ignacio is calling."

"Bye. Talk soon."

It's all finally coming together. Ignacio confirms flight arrangements from Lima to Iquitos and asks if he can do anything else for me. I tell him I'm good. My plan for this evening is to brew some Wawasana coca tea and polish off the remaining *alfajores* I bought at Wong. I've become addicted to *alfajores*, a shortbread sandwich filled with *manjar blanco*, which is like caramel or *dulce de leche*.

My jaguar and I walk back to Shun's apartment in the fading evening light. I say hello to the concierge, and the jaguar and I take the elevator to Shun's penthouse.

"Thank you for finding Èlia's family, Ino. Tomorrow we'll go together to Iquitos and meet them."

I speak the words to myself rather than say them out loud, and then I remember Shun's suggestion I talk to my jaguar. I repeat my gratitude out loud and the jaguar looks at me knowingly. Does he actually nod?

278

He bounds out of the elevator and doesn't wait for me to unlock the apartment. Somehow he just passes through the door. Inside, I see he has taken up residence on the sofa. Perhaps I don't need that coca tea after all. Perhaps I need it more than I think. ∎

36

La Casa Morey

My LATAM airlines Airbus 320 shimmies and shakes in the turbulence over the mountains but seems likely to hold together as we make our way northeast toward Iquitos. Once we cross the Andes, the view from my window seat is unendingly green. Invitingly green from up here. "Green Hell," a fellow passenger calls it. If we fall from the sky, no one will ever find us.

IQUITOS, Peru   September 15

When the plane touches down a couple of hours later in Iquitos, the butterflies in my stomach are back. I don't know what to expect here, literally in the middle of nowhere. There are no roads in or out of Iquitos. You can fly in or take a slow boat, dodging some dangerous people along the way, but those are the only options.

It strikes me as crazy I'm here surrounded by rainforest, looking for people I don't know, for reasons I don't understand. People who may not even be here.

We disembark via steep portable stairs rolled up to the front of the plane and walk across the steaming tarmac to the terminal. The air is thick and smells like asphalt and jet fuel. Airports are never in the most picturesque part of a metropolis, but this one is in the middle of shabbyland. As first impressions go, I'm underwhelmed.

My jaguar doesn't bother with the stairs. I find him already inside the terminal sitting beside a short, stocky man wearing chinos, an off-white shirt, and a vermillion pork pie hat. He's holding a chalk board reading "Dr. J. Quilter." This, of course, is Shun's doing, or rather Ignacio Mejias'. I approach him, smiling.

"Good morning, Dr. Quilter. Welcome to Iquitos."

"Good morning, sir," I say, fanning myself with my travel documents.

"Carlos Huancahuari *a sus ordenes,* at your service. *Señor* Ignacio Mejias has asked me to drive you to your hotel and help in any way you might require during your stay."

"May I call you Carlos?"

"Everybody calls me Huanc, but Carlos is okay too," he says, flashing a gap-toothed grin.

"Huanc it is, then. Please call me Jessamyn. Is it always this muggy here?"

"It's a beautiful spring day in the jungle," he says. "Warm in the mornings, but it will cool down later, after our usual afternoon downpour. Let me collect your bags, and I'll be right back."

He returns with my rolling bag and takes my camera case and medical bag, which I kept with me during the flight. We head out of the terminal, into the overwhelming sunshine toward his shiny black Camry. A young man, perhaps fourteen, has been minding the idling car while we were in the terminal. Huanc hands him a twenty *sol* note, and he's off.

The Camry is a recent model, not new, but polished to a fare-thee-well. Best of all, the air conditioning has been running. My jaguar seems right at home and hops into the back seat beside me.

As we pull into the street fronting the airport, the first thing that strikes me is how few cars there are on the road. Three-wheeled motorcycle rickshaws covered by colorful canopies with wide passenger seats in back swarm us on all sides.

"*Motocarros,*" Huanc explains. "Very good for getting around. Not as safe as my car though." He beams. "You won't need a car in Iquitos. You can walk downtown to the Plaza de Armas and the cathedral from La

Casa Morey or along the riverfront on the Malecon Tarapaca. If you need to go somewhere farther, the desk will call me, and I'll come right over."

Our trip into town takes less than half an hour. My impression of the city improves. There's still plenty of shabby, but there are also majestic buildings and open spaces.

We arrive at La Casa Morey, which Huanc tells me was formerly home to an early twentieth century rubber baron. It's an elegant two-story mansion on the Plazuela Ramon Castilla featuring columns, cornices, ribbons, and wreaths sculpted from plaster complementing white wrought-iron balconies and window grilles. He points out the *azulejos*—blue, tan, and white porcelain tiles imported from Portugal a century and a half ago—that cover the exterior walls. It looks like we've stepped onto the set of *Fitzcarraldo*.

He carries my bags inside and exchanges pleasantries with the manager who hands me an envelope marked Jessamyn Quilter, M.D. He squires me to my suite, past an exquisite library filled with old steamer trunks and carved glass breakfront bookcases, through a central courtyard with a small pool and fountain. Scattered along the way are five-gallon dispensers of drinking water on wooden stands—essential since the tap water is not safe to drink.

The entrance is through French doors, opposite the fountain in the enclosed courtyard, leading to a small sitting area furnished with elaborately carved Victorian furniture, a chair and double settee, perhaps mahogany, upholstered in gold brocade.

Furnishings in the large main sleeping area are simpler. Twin beds flank a small nightstand along one wall. On the opposite wall, a massive, mirrored armoire attached to a shorter chest of drawers holds a modest television. A writing table and chair complete the furnishings.

There are no windows, so no views from the room, but it feels quite spacious with its high ceilings. A large chandelier hangs from a sturdy chain. Sconces are mounted high on the walls and an eclectic assemblage of paintings, historical photographs, and allegorical engravings ring the room just above eye-level.

I'm surprised how cool the room is. To make certain it stays that way, Huanc turns on the ceiling mounted air conditioner with a remote, which unlike its counterparts in Paris, blasts copious volumes of cold air. He wishes me a good day and hands me a card with his number. "Call anytime, day or night," he says. *"A sus ordenes."*

The jaguar has already chosen his bed. I lie down on the other one, kick off my shoes, and open the envelope the manager handed me.

It's a message from Ignacio, suggesting I might like to see something of the city until a meeting with Èlia's family can be arranged. He has provided a phone number for the Dawn on the Amazon Explorers Club on the Malecon Maldonado with instructions to ask at the restaurant for a guide named Felipe.

It's still very warm, but a pleasant breeze wafts off the nearby Rio Itaya, and I decide to walk down to the Dawn on the Amazon Café and introduce myself. Of course my jaguar comes along for the adventure. He rarely leaves my side now.

Felipe is a handsome young man with a slender build, perhaps five feet six inches tall, twenty-five years old with light brown skin, neatly cropped dark brown hair, and laughing dark eyes.

We enjoy lunch and agree to meet on the Malecon tomorrow morning at eight. He'll show me around the sprawling open-air Belén market, then we'll hire a small motorboat for a closer look at the village built on stilts in the floodplain of the river. Later we'll take a *moto* across town and catch a boat to Pilpintuwasi.

"We will stick to the safe parts of the market," Felipe says, "where we don't have to worry about being robbed or hassled by thugs. Belén is the poorest neighborhood in Iquitos, and there are parts of the market even I would not venture into.

The next morning, Felipe, my jaguar, and I walk down the Malecon from the café to the market. Felipe doesn't appear to sense the presence of the jaguar. We are greeted near the entrance to the market by the spectacle of a naked little boy, perhaps four years old, playing King of the Mountain on a pile of discarded produce and assorted rubbish. He's laughing and peeing happily on a hairless mongrel dog foraging around the bottom of the heap. The dog doesn't seem to mind.

"There are bathrooms in the market," Felipe says, "but most people can't afford to use them. The dog is part Chimú or 'naked dog,' a hairless dog once bred by the Inca. They're an important part of Peru's heritage."

The stalls in the market are spilling over with pineapples, a dozen kinds of bananas, cashew apples, melons, and tropical fruit I've never seen. My jaguar runs ahead, never very far, checking out the stalls. There's an unimaginable variety of fresh produce on offer—burlap bags filled with multicolored potatoes, yams, and onions. Stacks of yucca root and ears of colorful corn. Bowls of dried legumes. Gigantic blue ceramic crocks brimming with cured olives.

A pair of tables display spatchcocked hens, oviducts left in place, revealing a procession of egg yolks in various stages of development, a sort of two for the price of one meal. A girl, maybe nine or ten years old, and a younger boy are playing "chase me" around the table, oblivious to the hens. Flies are everywhere. Shopkeepers engage in desultory shooing, but it's a lost cause and nobody seems too concerned.

Vast quantities of fresh fish, cleaned and scored, ready for the grill or frying pan, are on display. "These beauties are peacock bass," Felipe says, pointing out a glistening pile of butter-yellow fish, about two feet long with multicolored "eyes" on their tails. Their iridescent skin does remind me of a peacock's feather with its stripes, spots, and extravagant red and blue colors.

"Those little round fellas with the shimmering greenish gold scales and red bellies are piraña. Delicious!" he says.

Hideously ugly too, I think. A mouthful of spiked, razor-edge teeth promises no quarter for anyone who gets in their way. For a moment, their ugly faces remind me of Rotten Teeth who I hope never gets out of prison.

A table piled high with what looks like hindquarters of some jungle animal, hooves, hairy hocks, and all, catches my eye.

"Smoked peccaries," he says. "'Bush meat,' from wild rainforest animals is officially illegal, but the authorities apparently can't see as well as you can."

Other "bush meat" is for sale. Turtles are splayed out on their backs, bottom shells removed, next to two-foot sections of *caimán* tails.

"Hungry?" Felipe asks. We are passing by braziers with a variety of meat and fowl skewers. Everything smells delicious. "Ah, my favorite," he says with a rascally grin that would do Lagac proud. He selects a skewer with half a dozen fat, white caterpillars the size of my thumb, grilled to golden perfection.

"Palm weevil grubs," he says, picking one off the skewer and popping it into his mouth. He hands me the skewer, grinning like a naughty boy daring a schoolgirl to eat a worm. "Careful. It's hot."

I accept his dare. I eat the grub headfirst, crunching its charred black head between my teeth. My taste buds explode with the buttery, toasted coconut goodness of its fat, juicy body.

"I'm not giving these back," I say, wiping my chin with the back of my hand, keeping the skewer out of his reach. I un-spike another savory grub. "If you want more, you'll have to spring for another skewer for yourself," I say, stuffing the grub into my mouth.

Felipe buys another stick of grubs. "Secrets of the jungle," he says. "Don't tell the *touristas.*"

"You owe me one of yours," I tease him, "since you ate one of mine." Felipe's a good sport. He pulls the fattest, juiciest grub from his skewer and hands it to me as we make our way along the vendors.

My jaguar tags along wherever we go. We pass tables with women wrapping stout cigarettes and braiding ropes of tobacco as thick as my wrist. "*Mapacho*," Felipe explains. "Very important in shamanic healing rituals."

At another table, a young man wearing a red and blue striped Nike polo shirt fills a pastry bag from a five-gallon bucket of pink buttercream icing and pipes elaborate garlands, roses, even swans and *caimanes*, onto a white marble slab, demonstrating his artistry. "He will decorate a cake for you, if you like," Felipe says.

I pass on the cake but buy four bracelets made of silver wire and glossy black and red *huayruro* seeds from a woman sitting cross-legged on a table nursing an infant to send to Lovely, Èlia, Shun, and Shantrelle. How I wish they all could be here with me, especially Èlia. I buy another one for myself.

Felipe guides me into the Pasaje Paquito, "medicine alley," he translates. The vendors here specialize in charms and potions. Plastic bins overflow with herbs, bark, twigs, and vines. Repurposed jugs and bottles are filled with sludgy-brown liquid, *ayahuasca*, Felipe explains, and jungle honey.

Animal skulls rest on tables next to desiccated boas and anacondas, festooned with red satin ribbon, tightly coiled and poised to strike. *Caimán* heads, eyes replaced with colored glass and semi-precious stone cabochons, regard me as I pass by.

Everything in this rainforest pharmacopeia comes with expert advice from the shop's proprietors. The bottles of cane liquor with snake heads next to emerald-green tins of cow bile will bring good luck if left in a cupboard or drawer, one shopkeeper explains.

"Rubbing some of the liquid on your skin will attract women, but only the beautiful ones," another shopkeeper tells Felipe. "It will chase the ugly and plain ones away so they no longer pester you. But I can see you have no need for more beautiful women," he says, looking in my direction.

He's charming and I'm flattered.

We walk out of the market down a muddy slope to the Belén stilt village in the Rio Itaya. I was going to ask Felipe about the source of the unpleasant smell overtaking us as we make our way to the river's edge, but there's nothing mysterious about the odor of raw sewage. We dodge puddles of slop in the road as best we can. My shoes will be goners.

Piles of burlap bags filled with charcoal rest in the muddy roadway. The sidewalks are decaying, where they exist at all. Charcoal dust mixes with the fetid mud, coloring it black. Men shouldering enormous stalks of green bananas trudge uphill from the river to the market.

As we putter along the channels of the Rio Itaya in our hired motorboat, among the tin-roofed shanties on stilts, people wave politely. Some smile but most don't, preferring to take refuge in their homes.

"They distrust tourists," Felipe explains.

I nod. It feels uncomfortable, voyeuristic to be here, and I'm glad we'll not be spending much time. "I don't think I would welcome strangers gawking at me, looking into my windows and doors," I say.

"They are very poor," he says. "There is no money to be made from tourists passing through in boats. No place to dock and buy their handicrafts.

"There are a few food stands in places where one can walk across crude bridges between the closest stilt dwellings and the market, but few tourists ever visit. Even with a guide, it's not advisable. They're in a bad part of the market that isn't safe.

A little girl about three years old in faded pink panties and a tattered sleeveless blue jumper not quite long enough to cover them, a plastic grocery sack perched jauntily on her head, waves from a doorway as we pass by. An older boy, perhaps a brother, hustles her out of view. Not before I wave back with a lump in my throat. Not before she flashes a million-dollar smile that breaks my heart.

I'm relieved when our brief tour is over. My jaguar jumps out of the boat, Felipe pays our boatman, and we slog back uphill through sewage and black mud. Felipe hails a *moto* and we pile in. I'm sure Huanc would have been happy to take us to Bellavista-Nanay port, but these muddy roads would swallow up his Camry without mercy.

"You'll love Pilpintuwasi," he says, "It's the life work of an Austrian woman who came to Peru after college and started out by selling jewelry on the streets. She's come a long way. Besides raising butterflies, she rescues rainforest animals. She has established a sanctuary for a troop of red-faced bald uakari monkeys—rare in these parts. Hot shot primatologists from all over the world nag her about taking them home to study. But she fends them off. She's also got a jaguar named *Pedro Bello* who she rescued as a kitten."

I look at my jaguar lying at our feet. He has no visible reaction to the news. I steel myself for the *moto* ride.

To avoid looking around me as traffic thickens, I divert myself with images of the Belén market fresh in my mind. And the *Andaman Pearl*.

I wonder what has happened to Lagac. Shun said it outraged him that the Tamils kidnapped me. Likely he's ashamed he failed to protect me as he promised. I think the ordeal with those mercenaries would have made anyone want to hang up their spurs.

I envision Lagac back in Cebu, at least for a while as he recovers from the trauma of our betrayal by the terrorists. I picture him fortified with unlimited iced San Miguel beer, preparing suckling pig over his father's hand-built *lechonan*, mopping the skin with Dr. Pepper until it crackles crispy mahogany brown, stealing the choicest pieces for himself, from the back, right behind the shoulders, the perquisite of a world class *lechonero*.

My body electrifies and my heart aches as I recall our pleasures in the engine room, his many hidey-holes, and my magnificent cabin on the *Andaman Pearl*. I wish we could be together again and try to steel myself against hoping for it, realizing how unlikely that is. I am, really, trying not to hope. And failing miserably. ∎

37

Pilpintuwasi

W

IQUITOS, Peru   September 15

e jolt our way to Bellavista-Nanay port and miraculously arrive in one piece. It helps to look ahead and think about something other than death and destruction as the other *motos* maneuver maniacally, rushing past us like a river flowing around a protruding rock.

At the port, a small aluminum motorboat takes us upriver on the Rio Nanay to the Pilpintuwasi Wildlife Rescue Center and Butterfly Farm. Felipe waits with the boatman as I scramble up a muddy path to the entrance, a wire-mesh tunnel separating me from the surrounding rainforest. As usual, my jaguar has gone ahead.

I feel something watching, then hear it scrambling on the mesh above me. Looking up, I find myself face-to-face with a shaggy rust-colored monkey about the size of a toy poodle, its deep brown eyes sunk in a blazing red face. It's completely bald and sports a stubby six-inch tail that looks like some errant tailor shortened it a bit too much. It's as handsome, in its own way, as it is exotic.

I immediately understand how the tables have been turned. I'm the one in the cage. The monkey, and half a dozen of its kind, roaming free in the canopy overhead, drop to the mesh and join the parade, following me like puppies as I walk toward a wooden pavilion to await a docent who'll show me around Pilpintuwasi.

A compact, muscular dark brown man who I judge to be about my age approaches. He's wearing khaki cargo pants and a short-sleeved work shirt trimmed in what I instantly recognize as Shipibo embroidery. An infant monkey perches precariously atop his head, its gangly arms gripping his neck and forehead, its chin resting in his hair, giving him the appearance of having two faces, one stacked on top of the other.

My jaguar lies at my feet, looking up at the lobster–red faces of the monkeys peering down at us. They are unperturbed by his presence. Perhaps they don't see him.

My guide extends his hand, and the baby monkey covering his head looks down into my eyes. "Welcome to Pilpintuwasi, *señora*. Jose Luis Palacios, *a sus ordenes*. It will be my pleasure to show you around today. Hang on to your hat for dear life." He grins. "Those bald-faced red uakari monkeys would like nothing better than to steal it from you."

"Jessamyn Quilter," I say. "It's a pleasure to meet you. Thank you for agreeing to show me around."

"The pleasure is all mine, Dr. Quilter. I have heard about you from my brother, Don Mateo Palacios de la Selva, who is our precious Èlia's father. Èlia—we also call her *Tsiri Biri*—is my niece. Don Mateo sends his warmest welcome and looks forward to welcoming you personally when he arrives. Their band is still making its way along the river to Padre Cocha, a couple of miles from here, but they expect to be here tomorrow or the next day."

"I look forward to meeting him. Èlia has told me so much about him. It surprised me to learn her family was no longer in Lima, but I'm happy to know they are on their way here."

"Lima has not been good to the indigenous people," Jose Luis says. "Many were forced to move there when the Maoist Shining Path insurgency drove us from our ancestral lands along the Ucayali River. Many, like Don Mateo and his family, settled in Lima's slums where they were not welcome.

"Since there is no longer a serious threat from insurgents, we have been returning to the rainforest. Some have settled on the outskirts of Iquitos where they sell tapestries, pottery, and other wares on the streets of the city. Others, like Don Mateo and myself, have found jobs to supplement what our families can earn by selling art."

I find myself wondering what would have happened to Èlia had she not been fortunate enough to work for Shun in Lima and he had not learned of her extraordinary musical abilities. Would she now be displaced from her home, wandering about in the jungle instead of preparing to set the musical world on fire in Paris?

"So here we are," Jose Luis says as we approach an airy screened pavilion where brilliant blue morphos and other brightly colored butterflies fly freely, sipping nectar from cut fruit placed about the enclosure. Dozens of green and brown chrysalises, pinned to a corkboard, ripen, waiting their turn to hatch. Exotic looking larvae feast on their host plants growing in containers.

A gray and brown butterfly with enormous yellow-ringed eyespots lands on Jose Luis' trousers. "An owl butterfly," he says, gently capturing it and handing it to me. "This one is ready to release if you would like to do the honors." The beautiful creature flutters from my hands as we step outside the pavilion.

We walk along a path passing several animal enclosures, home to rainforest rescue animals. He introduces me to a tapir who strokes my arm with its flexible snout and invites me to scratch its back. In another enclosure, a tangle of upside-down baby sloths spill halfway out of a basket wired to a tree, regarding us with soft eyes. A trio of macaws scrap in a palm tree above us, and a pair of marmosets cling to the fence of their enclosure.

"These marmosets, like many of our animals, were rescued from the illicit pet trade. You can buy them on the streets of Iquitos, although it is illegal, but you quickly learn you can't care for them," Jose Luis says.

"Marmosets can only live on one kind of tree where they feed by piercing the bark with their incisors and sucking up the sap. People try to feed them all sorts of things, and they simply die from starvation. The sloths can't tolerate the pace of human life below the treetops and they too, perish. The lucky ones end up here."

"Who in their right mind would want to buy a tapir or a sloth, or a marmoset for that matter, as a pet?"

"I don't know. Rainforest animals belong in the rainforest. Let's see if our most famous resident is receiving guests," Jose Luis says.

We approach a sturdy chain-link enclosure, the home of *Pedro Bello*, a tawny jaguar abandoned at Pilpintuwasi as an infant.

"He was only a quarter of his normal birth weight when we got him twenty years ago," Jose Luis says. He is a healthy boy now but small for a jaguar."

My jaguar abandons us, racing along the fence line of *Pedro Bello*'s enclosure that disappears into the rainforest. Jose Luis has brought an offering of fresh meat, but *Pedro Bello* does not show himself. I wonder if he and my own jaguar have more important things to do at the other end of his enclosure where the surrounding trees block them from our sight.

Suddenly my jaguar is again walking alongside me, but *Pedro Bello* declines to make an appearance. The sky has darkened. Thick drops of rain fall straight down. We hasten back to the butterfly pavilion as the first fat drops begin to soak me. Juan Luis' monkey hat squeals and clutches his head more tightly as we sprint inside to avoid the downpour. "Spider monkeys don't like rain." Jose Luis laughs, toweling the wet animal dry, comforting him.

As quickly as it appeared the downpour vanishes, leaving a brilliant blue sky and pristine clouds in its wake. The macaws are still screaming at each other. I thank Jose Luis for his services and leave enough cash behind in the tip jar to feed *Pedro Bello* for a week.

On the way back to Bellavista-Nanay, a pod of pink dolphins plays in the wake of our boat. I think again about Lagac as I prepare for bed.

My jaguar is asleep on his chosen bed. I wonder what he dreams about. I'm certain he and *Pedro Bello* conversed today. What would they have been talking about? The business of jaguars, no doubt.

I wish Lagac were here. He has family on the other side of the world, so it's patently ridiculous, but I think he would be at home here in Iquitos. He's no stranger to rainforests.

How I'd love to tease him with a skewer of palm weevil grubs, he of the cat and rat meat. I wonder what he'd make of the smoked peccary, the *caimán* tail, the piraña.

How I'd love to have his body next to mine tonight, on top of me, behind me, all over me. I stop the fantasy before it gets too far out of hand, or rather before my own hand gets too far into the fantasy. I'm exhausted from the day and sleep comes quickly. No cats crash into my dreamscape tonight. ■

38

Don Mateo de la Selva

IQUITOS, Peru   September 16

Breakfast at La Casa Morey is heaven on earth. I start with orange/passionfruit juice, the ripest imaginable chunks of papaya, nuggets of pink-fleshed Isla bananas with their sweet/tart lemony tang, buttered toast, and coffee from the buffet. I'm thinking about going back for more, supplemented by scrambled eggs and ham, when Guillermo, from the front desk, approaches me at my table.

"Good morning, *Doctora* Quilter."

"Good morning, sir."

"I am sorry to interrupt your breakfast, but there is a gentleman in the lobby inquiring about you. By his appearance, he is indigenous. He says his name is Don Mateo de la Selva. Shall I ask him to wait while you finish breakfast? I could provide him with coffee. Or perhaps you wish him to join you?"

My heart catches in my throat. "I have been anxiously awaiting him, Guillermo. It would be wonderful if he could join me."

"I'll show him back right away and ask Luz to bring a place setting for him."

He returns moments later in the company of a short, muscular man of indeterminate age with graying black hair and sparking dark eyes walking respectfully a pace behind him.

"*Doctora* Quilter, may I introduce Don Mateo de la Selva? *Señor*, la *doctora,* Jessamyn Quilter."

I would have recognized him anywhere. Èlia's eyes shine in his eyes, and his face, especially his mouth, mark him indelibly as her father. We exchange "*¡Mucho gustos!*" and I invite him to sit. Luz is at his elbow. "*¿Café, señor?*"

"If it is not too much trouble, *señora*, I would prefer chocolate," he says. She returns with a small silver tray containing a pot of hot evaporated milk fragrant with allspice, and a bowl containing chocolate tablets. She transfers one to his cup with silver tongs, fills it with steaming milk, and stirs it with a cinnamon stick before adding freshly whipped cream.

Don Mateo beams.

"Shall I bring one for you, *Doctora*?" she asks.

"I think I'll stick with coffee this morning, although tomorrow I will definitely try one of those."

"I will make it especially for you and make sure we have some panettone for dunking," she says. Really? Chocolate ecstasy with panettone in the rainforest? Quite a change from grilled palm weevil grubs and cashew apples. I can see why Shun sings the praises of La Casa Morey.

Don Matteo speaks after taking a sip. "The best chocolate I have ever had," he says. "I apologize for not giving you formal notice of my intended arrival today, *Doctora* Quilter. I am so thrilled to see you and learn more about my *Tsiri Biri*. She writes you are very special to her and require my help, and I will gladly do anything I can to help such a friend of my daughter's. We are so proud of her. How is she getting along in Paris?"

"She's doing splendidly," I say. "She's a very special person, and you have every right to be proud of her, Don Mateo. But please call me Jessamyn. Your daughter has been teaching me some of the wonderful ways of the Shipibo people," I say.

"*Tsiri Biri* has many gifts," Don Mateo says. "Has she told you of the many *ikaros* given to her by the teacher plants? Very unusual for one so young, but then the plants know better than we about who should receive their songs."

"She has sung me some of them," I say, "especially the *ikaro* against fear." I surprise myself that I would so quickly divulge something so personal.

Don Mateo nods his head sagely. His eyes drift away from mine, toward the entrance to the dining room where my jaguar sashays toward our table. I don't think Don Mateo sees him, but he seems to understand something has changed in the room.

"*Tsiri Biri* is a very insightful young woman. The ancestors have blessed her with much wisdom. Did you have need of the *ikaro* against fear?"

"I will ask you to forgive me, Don Mateo, if I burden you with matters you do not wish to consider. We have only just met, and I am reluctant to bring disquiet or turbulence to your life, but yes, I had need of the *ikaro* frequently. Èlia is the reason I'm here in Iquitos because she says I'm in danger. She insisted, therefore, that I should come here and seek out her family."

"Do you know what endangers you?"

"I do not. *Tsiri Biri* says she doesn't know either, but she says I'm ill, that some evil lives in me. I know I'm physically well, but she's speaking about an illness of the spirit. She's quite certain she's right, and I trust her judgment."

"Did she say how she knows you are not well?"

"She says messengers from the *chamán*, her namesake *tsiri* birds, came to her while she was sleeping and told her she must help me. 'Bring the healing,' they told her. Not that she should heal me because she isn't a *chamana*, but only that she 'bring the healing.' She says if I don't find out what's wrong, it will kill me."

Don Mateo listens in respectful silence.

"Added to that, in Paris, a fortune teller, a total stranger, sat beside me on a bench along the Seine and told me I carry a great evil that threatens to destroy me. I don't know what to make of all this, but it scares me. So, yes, Don Mateo, *Tsiri Biri's ikaro* against fear is something I have very much needed."

Don Mateo remains silent, thoughtful. And then he speaks. "Shall we walk along the Malecón, the three of us, and determine how I might help?"

"The three of us?"

"Something protective accompanies you. I do not know what it is, but I felt it join us here a few moments ago."

I tell him all about the dreamcats and the jaguar that has attached itself to me, how I do not believe them to be real but can't explain them away.

"Èlia, I mean *Tsiri Biri*, says the jaguar is real, though she can't see it. She calls him *ino* and sang him the *ikaro* of welcome and homage to jaguars. She thinks I should go to the rainforest and find a *chamán* who might help me understand. Perhaps, she said, *ino* is a part of my *janekon*, but only a *chamán* could tell me for sure, after consulting with the *chaikoni*, of course." I laugh nervously.

"We also call her Èlia. Everyone in the village knows her both by her *janekon* and her *nawan jane*. I see she has taught you much about our culture. Does the *ino* walk with us now?"

"Yes. He allows me to stroke his fur," I say, reaching down to touch his back. "I can feel him breathing, purring. I can't believe I'm touching a wild predator, but he tags along with me more often than before.

Don Mateo closes his eyes briefly, as if to concentrate on the essence of the jaguar, then opens them, looking in the direction of the cat's face.

"He walked with me through the Belén market, hopped into the *moto* for the ride to Bellavista–Nanay, even got in the boat and came to Pilpintuwasi, although he left me for half an hour while I was there.

"He sleeps on one of my beds at La Casa Morey. Makes himself perfectly comfortable and does whatever he wants. I was afraid of him before, but no longer. He apparently means me no harm and may even be protecting me from something."

"Did you see the jaguar, *Pedro Bello,* at Pilpintuwasi?"

"No, *Pedro Bello* apparently didn't feel like coming out of his den. Your brother, Jose Luis, says sometimes he remains hidden, even when they tempt him with food."

"Perhaps he was engaged with your jaguar. Perhaps they were conversing. I suggest you return to Pilpintuwasi with me tomorrow. It will be my first day working there, and my brother will show me around. Perhaps we can find a time for your *ino* to introduce you to *Pedro Bello.* He is an ancient and wise jaguar. I will sing an *ikaro* of welcome and homage to all of you.

"If the jaguars wish, the three of you can talk. If not, you can walk among the butterflies again, reacquaint yourself with the tapir, the infant sloths, the uakari monkeys, and the macaws. It is a beautiful place."

As we continue to walk along the Malecón, we approach the Museum of Amazon Indigenous Cultures. Don Mateo suggests we go inside. The museum is stuffed floor to ceiling with the most amazing artifacts and dioramas devoted to the rainforest peoples of Peru, Columbia, and Brazil—weapons, tools, clothing, and jewelry, ceremonial headdresses fashioned from brilliant feathers, even the occasional shrunken head. Don Mateo steers us toward a collection of Shipibo clothing and pottery.

"Those are Shipibo," an earnest young woman says as she joins us. Don Mateo smiles. "But of course, you know that. Forgive my presumption, but are you Shipibo?" she asks Don Mateo.

"I am."

"Allow me to show you something special," she says, leading us to a pair of enormous pottery jars, one shaped like a woman, the other like a man. Every surface is emblazoned with exquisite *kené.* Each jar is so large that if two people tried to encircle it with their arms, they could not touch. Nor could one see the other if a jar stood between them.

"These pieces are at least a century old," our docent says. "I am told that two women worked on the jars simultaneously, one decorating the front and another the back and yet the *kené* encircling them match up precisely. We do not know how that is possible since the two artists could not see each other."

Don Mateo smiles again. "My grandmother told me a story about women who made pots like these. She said they didn't need to see each other because they sang the *ikaros* revealed by the patterns while they worked, so they knew precisely where to place the *kené*. Their ears were their eyes for seeing what to paint."

Our docent is humbled. "Thank you for sharing that story," she says. "We have so much to learn from the peoples who are represented in the museum."

"On board the *Andaman Pearl*, I listened to *Tsiri Biri* sing the *kené* she painted on Lovely, tracing them with her fingers," I tell Don Mateo as we walk back along the Malecón toward La Casa Morey. "As she sang, a jaguar lunged at me then disappeared. *Tsiri Biri* said he was the mother spirit of the teacher plant *puma chacruna* and that the mother spirit could be male, female, or both. She thinks he might have been hunting whatever is making me ill. She said he's a powerful protector who would not harm me."

Don Mateo nods sagely.

Approaching the Dawn on the Amazon Café, we encounter a middle-aged woman and two adolescent girls selling embroidered tapestries along the Malecón. One of the girls runs over to greet Don Mateo, grasping his hand and pulling herself into his body.

"This beautiful, if impetuous, young woman is my daughter Marisol," Don Mateo says, smiling. "And this is Marisol's sister, Esmerelda, and her mother Azucena. Ladies, this is Jessamyn Quilter, Èlia's friend."

"Tell us about *Tsiri Biri*," Marisol says. "We miss her terribly."

"She's a wonderful woman," I say. "I miss her too. She sends her love to all of you."

"Where does *Tsiri Biri* live? When is she coming home?" Esmerelda chimes in.

"She's in Paris, going to school, studying music. She's living with another friend of mine, Lovely Bayani, who is also studying music.

"She already knows lots of *ikaros*," Marisol says. "Why does she need to study in Paris? Is Paris in the rainforest? Do they have teacher plants in Paris that are different from ours?"

"No, Paris is a city like Lima on the other side of the world. There's no jungle there, but there are lots of trees and plants. I'm sure they will teach *Tsiri Biri* their *ikaros*. And *Tsiri Biri* will teach the people and plants of Paris, the entire world, her music. She tried to teach me, but I'm not very smart."

The women smile and assure me that can't be true.

"I know the *ikaro* of welcome and homage for *inos*," Esmerelda says, glancing to my right. She sings it and my jaguar perks up his ears. Does Esmerelda sense his presence?

"I will sing an *ikaro* of welcome and homage to you, *Doctora* Quilter," Marisol says. And she sings one of the most beautiful songs I've heard yet.

"We welcome you, on behalf of *Tsiri Biri* and all our family, *Doctora* Quilter," Azucena says. She too sings an *ikaro*. I recognize it as the "*ikaro* against fear," and my spine tingles as she finishes.

"Ladies, we must get back to our camp," Don Mateo says. "Jessamyn, I'm sure your *ino* will keep you safe as you return to La Casa Morey." The women don't bat an eye at the mention of the jaguar. They accept the elegant predator beside me even though they can't see him.

"Farewell, *Doctora*. Until we meet again," Azucena says. She hands me an ornately embroidered shawl, white with red and black *kené*. "Even in the rainforest, the nights are sometimes chilly," she says, smiling warmly.

"Thank you, all of you. Thank you for the shawl, the beautiful *kené*, and for the *ikaros*. And thank you for sending Èlia into my life. I'm sure we will all meet again," I say.

"I will see you tomorrow morning at La Casa Morey, Jessamyn," Don Mateo says. "About eight o'clock? We can take a *moto* to Puerto Bellavista-Nanay and catch a boat to Pilpintuwasi. We'll see if *Pedro Bello* has anything to share with us."

"I'll let Guillermo and Luz know you'll join me for breakfast. Ignacio can drive us to Bellavista-Nanay if you don't mind. If we take a *moto*, I'm afraid you will have to sing me the *ikaro* against fear the entire trip. ∎

39

Pedro Bello

My jaguar, Don Mateo, and I dock the next morning at the muddy landing leading to Pilpintuwasi. We meet half a dozen indigenous women along the path, walking the other direction as we approach the rescue center. They look very different from Don Mateo's family.

"Bora people. Their village is that way," he says, pointing.

"I've heard of them."

"They're a very popular tourist attraction, especially among people who like to dance with half-naked '*Indios*.'"

"I wonder why they agree to be exploited like that."

"The Bora view it with good humor. They are not embarrassed to dance dressed only in their traditional skirts and it's easier for them to guilt the tourists into buying souvenirs they don't really want. It's an example of indigenous people learning how to exploit the colonists. It brings much needed cash into their economy.

"Their village is close by. The pavilion where they dance and entertain the tourists is not in the village itself. In the village, people dress much the same as us, like the Bora we just met on the path."

We make our way to the butterfly pavilion, and I luxuriate in its beauty while Don Mateo checks in with Jose Luis about the day's work.

Jose Luis is still wearing the spider monkey on his head. I wonder if he ever gets a break from his infant hairpiece.

We go to call on *Pedro Bello*. Before we reach his enclosure, my jaguar steps in front of Don Mateo and me, blocking our path. The message is obvious. Permission and introductions are required. My jaguar will see to them.

Pedro Bello permits Don Mateo to present his offering of breakfast meat, which he eats with gusto while Don Mateo sings the *ikaro* of welcome and homage for jaguars.

When *Pedro Bello* has finished licking his chops, my jaguar nudges me toward the enclosure.

Pedro Bello stands on his hind legs, propped against the chain-link fence that imprisons him. We are eye to eye, belly to belly as he fixes my gaze. Suddenly I am no longer outside his enclosure at Pilpintuwasi. Instead, I am seated in a clearing in the rainforest, perhaps the one I have seen in my dreams, cross-legged on the ground.

I hear Don Mateo singing the *ikaro* against fear as if from some nearby cave, his music distorted and echoing. I sing a version of the *ikaro* of welcome and homage for jaguars as best I can. My jaguar and *Pedro Bello* emerge into the clearing, tails swishing. They don't look entirely friendly as they approach, hovering only inches from my face.

Pedro Bello speaks. "Jessamyn Quilter, are you accountable?"

Despite the *ikaro* against fear echoing in my ears, *Pedro Bello's* words make my flesh crawl. "Accountable?" What does he mean, accountable? This isn't real. It can't possibly be real.

My jaguar growls. "Jessamyn Quilter. There is great danger nearby. Be very careful."

"Do not speak, Jessamyn Quilter," *Pedro Bello* says. "Only listen."

I hear a rustle of leaves behind them. They hear it too and turn to face the tree line. A snake larger than I have ever seen, a behemoth of light and shadow large enough to swallow me or the jaguars whole, has descended halfway from a tree and is slithering toward me.

"Wel*come, Ronin kené hueua,* 'Song of the Design on the Great Boa,'" my jaguar says.

"Welcome Anaconda Woman, guardian of the rainforest and the universe you brought into existence. Welcome *Ronin,* bringer of death and transfiguration, upon whose skin is inscribed all *kené* since the beginning of time. The rosettes of the fur of *ino,* the veins of the leaves of every teacher plant, the feathers of the *tsiri* and the *kana,*" *Pedro Bello* says.

The jaguars part to allow Anaconda Woman to pass.

"Listen, but do not speak, Jessamyn Quilter," *Pedro Bello* repeats. "Your voice will only give offense. *Ronin* knows your thoughts. Do not speak them."

The great snake coils around me, squeezing gently, imparting the unmistakable message she can crush the life from me on a whim and nothing in the universe is powerful enough to stop her. Her cold, dry tongue flicks across my face. She is pure evil.

"The evil you fear is not me," *Ronin* says, looking into my eyes, her voice ancient and dry as a desert riverbed. "The evil you fear is within you. Are you accountable?"

I am terrified. Please do not kill me, Ronin.

"Your terror means nothing to me, Jessamyn Quilter, nor does your plea to spare your life. I care nothing for your fear and few desire death. Yet killing you would restore balance, take your evil into me and clear it from the *néte,* the cosmos, as I have done since the beginning of time."

The only evil here is you, Ronin, I think, choking down my impulse to say it out loud as my jaguar chuffs, reminding me to be silent.

"You are wrong," *Ronin* says, squeezing more insistently. "Look again. You must be accountable for the imbalance." She releases me from her embrace and vanishes into the shadows.

I'm no longer seated in the clearing but standing inside *Pedro Bello's* enclosure, my breathing labored, my back against the chain-link fence. The old jaguar stands with his front paws over my shoulders, pressing me against the fence with his body, and licks my face, his meaty breath heavy in my nostrils, his muzzle bloody from the food Don Mateo has brought him.

I lick his muzzle in respect. The blood I taste evokes violent flashes of light behind my eyes, blinding me to everything except a familiar form, that of Roderick, with half a hard-on, his reeking body thrusting clumsily against me even in death. I scream in horror.

Roderick is gone, and so is the crushing weight. *Pedro Bello* and my jaguar sit beside me inside the enclosure. I touch their fur, hug them to me, to reassure myself their protection is real.

"We will help you look again as *Ronin* demands, *Metsá Ino*," Pedro *Bello* says, getting to his feet. He and my jaguar bound away into the rainforest as if they have further business to attend to. I slide down the fence, my legs giving way, but I'm no longer inside *Pedro Bello's* den. I'm outside, seated beside Don Mateo who continues to sing the *ikaro* against fear. He switches to the *ikaro* of welcome and homage to jaguars. "Welcome, *Metsá Ino*," he sings to me. "I welcome you and pay you homage."

My jaguar returns and stretches out beside us. He turns his head and fixes my gaze with his eyes. "Tell him," he says.

I spew out incoherent recollections and the terror I felt at my encounter with *Ronin* and the two jaguars in the clearing. Don Mateo continues singing, his demeanor tranquil. I don't mention the revolting encounter with Roderick.

"You have been traveling with the spirits," Don Mateo says. Your body has not left my side since we arrived at *Pedro Bello's* enclosure, and he accepted my offering.

"Your jaguar called you *Metsá Ino*. I did not hear this with my ears but with my spirit. *Tsiri Biri* was right. *Ino* is a part of your *janekon*. *Metsá Ino* is a Shipibo *janekon* meaning 'Beautiful Jaguar.'"

"I thought only a *chamán* could suggest a *janekon*, after consulting the *chaikoni*."

"I think no intelligent *chamán,* nor the *chaikoni,* would quarrel with a jaguar about a *janekon.*" He smiles, standing and starting up the path to the butterfly pavilion.

When I stand, my jaguar puts his paws on my shoulders and licks my face.

"Why did you not tell him about your repulsive dead mate?" he says.

"I don't know," I whisper. "I'm ashamed." My face is in the fur of his chest. If Don Mateo hears me, he doesn't comment.

"We must get you out of Iquitos, deeper into the jungle," Don Mateo says as I join him on the path back to the butterfly pavilion. "Guillermo and Luz will arrange for you to go upriver, to a less settled part of the rainforest, to the Pink Dolphin Rainforest Lodge. You can live there for a while in the company of indigenous people as you seek answers to your questions."

"Questions? What questions?" I ask.

"Perhaps that is the first question you will want to pose to yourself," he says, smiling. "I will speak with Jose Luis and Carlos Huancahuari about arrangements for leaving some of your belongings at La Casa Morey for safekeeping while you journey upriver."

My mind is ablaze, unfocussed. The terror has returned. My jaguar chuffs and the chaos resolves. I look into his eyes and thank him.

Back at the butterfly pavilion, I say goodbye to Jose Luis.

"Was *Pedro Bello* receiving guests?" he asks.

"Yes. He graced us with his presence," Don Mateo says. "I think I know why he sometimes does not appear, even to feast on the meat you offer," he says thoughtfully. "I think when he does not appear, he is not in Pilpintuwasi but attending to *ino* business elsewhere."

"How is that possible?" Jose Luis asks.

"Grandfather once told me there are not several jaguars, but only one, the same *ino* created at the beginning of *néte. Ino* goes where he wishes and is seen when she wishes to be seen. They can be in one place or many at the same time. It is not possible to confine *ino.*

309

"At first I didn't think it was possible, and I told Grandfather so."

"How could *ino* mate and have cubs if there were only one?" I asked him.

"You would have to ask *ino* that question the next time you see them," he replied. "But do not annoy him with too many questions. Like me, she is old, and may be short on patience.

"Besides, you do not need to know these things, Mateo. *Ino* does not need you to understand their ways. Welcome and homage are sufficient. Yet it may amuse them to answer, you never know."

"My beautiful jaguar," I say to my protector. "What is your name? How shall I address you?"

"You may call us *Metsá Ino*. We are *Metsá Ino* as you are *Metsá Ino*. I will no longer call you by your *nawan jane*, Jessamyn Quilter. I will call you by your *janekon*, your true name, *Metsá Ino*.

We make the trip back to Nanay-Bellavista in silence, save for Don Mateo's occasional *ikaros*. Pink dolphins follow us and break off as we near the port. Carlos Huancahuari is waiting, polishing his black Camry. *Ino* and I doze for most of the ride across town to La Casa Morey

"How was your trip to Pilpintuwasi?" Guillermo asks. "Did you see *Pedro Bello*?"

"He is nothing short of wondrous," I reply.

"I will have some food sent to your room, *Doctora* Quilter. You must rest now. We have arranged everything for your trip tomorrow up the Amazon to the Pink Dolphin Rainforest Lodge."

By the time the food arrives, both *Metsá Ino* and I have fallen asleep in our beds. I wake up long enough to eat and fall back asleep easily. My jaguar comes and goes throughout the night. It's always reassuring through the fog of sleep to hear his throaty cough when he returns and bounces onto his bed.

It's morning before I know it. I savor an early breakfast at La Casa Morey with a pot of Luz's celestial hot chocolate and panettone and walk down the Malecón to rendezvous with my boat upriver. ∎

40

Pink Dolphin Lodge

Peruvian Amazon   September 18

Rickety wooden steps descend from the Malecón to a slip where the 200-horsepower *Anaconda* will take me up the Amazon to the Pink Dolphin Rainforest Lodge. Don Mateo advised me to pack lightly. My pilot, Taurino Gallegos, is a man about my age who works at the lodge. He will both ferry me upriver and be my guide in the various activities planned during my stay.

"Good morning, Dr. Quilter," he says, taking my small carryon, my medical bag, and my camera case, stowing everything in a compartment near the front of the boat.

He has brought a cooler with bottled water, processed cheese sandwiches on white bread, peeled oranges, bananas, and chunks of sweet, aromatic papaya. "Help yourself when you're hungry," he says. "We have roughly a three- and-a-half hour trip ahead of us."

He peels a banana, slips into the captain's chair, and turns the ignition. Moments later, we ease into the Rio Itaya, heading north along the shoreline of Iquitos until we reach the confluence with the Amazon where we turn south, upriver, toward our destination.

Guillermo at La Casa Morey told me guest accommodations of varying degrees of luxury dot the Amazon and its tributaries to the north and south of Iquitos.

To the north, he said, downriver from the city, the lodges are more resort-like with air-conditioning and even catwalks in the canopy for a closer view of birds and other wildlife.

Upriver to the south, he said, toward the restricted buffer zone of the Pacaya—Samiria National Reserve and the protected Tamshiyacu—Tahuayo Regional Conservation District, things get more primitive.

The Pink Dolphin Lodge, where I am headed, is in this wilder part of the rainforest. Here, small bands of indigenous peoples live traditional lives, hunting, fishing, and gathering plants.

The lodge is a collection of modest cottages with thatched roofs built on platforms and stilts, as described on the website I consulted at La Casa Morey, to accommodate water levels that change with the season. There are no cell towers in this part of the rainforest and no Wi-Fi. The lodge has a satellite phone for emergencies, as does my pilot, but electricity at the lodge is spotty.

Guillermo said solar is making inroads in the rainforest, but power at the lodge is usually limited to what diesel generators can supply, a couple of hours each evening. He said I'll be able to top up my laptop or camera batteries once a day at a charging station in the communal pavilion and perhaps turn on a reading lamp in my cottage for an hour or two each night, but most of the juice is earmarked for keeping food and essentials like beer cold.

We're headed to a quiet black-water tributary of the Amazon, my pilot says, about 100 miles upriver from Iquitos. Whatever the lodge requires, including guests, comes up from the city once a day on boats like the *Anaconda*.

There are fewer than a dozen guests at the lodge at a time, he says. Most stay for three or four nights. The lodge employs a handful of indigenous people who live a few miles farther upriver as guides for forays into the surrounding rainforest, or as cooks and maintenance staff for the facilities.

Guillermo told me it's sometimes possible for lodge guests to spend a day and overnight with an indigenous family in their village. I'm looking forward to that.

I'm not completely clear about why I'm here, other than that Don Mateo de la Selva says I should be. "Spend a few days," he told me, "and perhaps the reason will become clearer. If not, you can return to Iquitos."

It seems incongruent, traveling by speedboat through this quietness, now and then interrupting a flock of egrets or other tropical birds skimming the river as if daring us to catch them.

About two hours into our trip, Taurino slows the boat to a crawl. We're somewhere in the middle of the Amazon river. I have no clue where. I can make out both banks in the distance, but they stretch worlds apart. Taurino points to a pod of a dozen or more dolphins approaching our boat, mottled pink and gray, the largest perhaps eight or nine feet long.

"Nobody hunts the dolphins on this part of the river, so they are not afraid of us," he says. "I think they know this boat, perhaps by the sound we make."

I marvel at these beautiful creatures, their bodies glistening in the morning light as they breach around us.

"I take guests at the Lodge to another part of the river to swim with the dolphins," Taurino says. "One must be careful of pink dolphins though because some are enchanted by evil *chamanes* and cause *daño*—pain and suffering. These dolphins are free of such curses. I have seen them often and sung to them.

"Do you swim, Dr. Quilter?"

I was going to say I'm terrified of the water. I was going to say it would be great fun to swim with them. I was going to say I would like nothing better right now in the entire world than to swim with the pink dolphins. What came out of my mouth was, "I'm afraid I didn't bring a suit."

The dolphins approach and circle the boat lazily. I put out my hand to stroke the largest one who eases alongside the boat. Beautiful, mottled pink and gray, sleek, but surprisingly rough to the touch. He's seducing me with his sleek elegance in broad daylight, wearing nothing but his pink and gray skin.

"Of course, it is up to you," Taurino says offhandedly, "but I don't think the dolphins would mind that you don't have a suit. People on the river don't wear many clothes, usually none in the water."

Come on, Jessamyn. When will you get the chance again to be with these lovely creatures in their own world?

"I've not seen the dolphins come this close before," Taurino says. "I would swim with them, but I must stay with the boat. We're in no hurry to get to the lodge, so why not linger among them?

"The river here is very safe and smooth, as you can see, and warm. Just the way the dolphins like it. I will sing them an *ikaro* honoring dolphins while we rest here with them."

We sit, seemingly motionless in the current while the dolphins circle, and Taurino sings the *ikaro*. "I will teach the *ikaro* to you," he says. "They will understand you are new to their world and won't mind if you don't get it perfect."

Taurino sings a phrase in his nasal tenor, the melody line shining, curving like the light in the water. I repeat it in my quavering alto as best I can. We sing to them for half an hour while they circle and breach, answering us with clicks and squeaks, the music enchanting. Perhaps I'm imagining it, but the ripples on the water seem to form into *kené,* disappearing and reforming almost as soon as they appear. I'm certain the dolphins become more brightly colored as we sing to them, and they to us.

Metsá Ino leaps into the water. The dolphins break from the boat to circle him cautiously once or twice as he swims toward shore, but they return to the boat as he swims away.

"The dolphins see something we don't, but they have decided all is well," Taurino says.

"I want to swim with them," I say, summoning courage from I don't know where. I strip and take the plunge. For an instant, I feel I am drowning, never to return to the boat or this life again. But the dolphins circle me as they had *Metsá Ino* and buoy me up with a net of silky bubbles that must be enchanted because it takes all my fear away. I'm lost in their beauty, aware I'm an honored guest in their world.

Taurino continues to sing the *ikaro* honoring dolphins. I hum the *ikaro* as best I can, bobbing among them, caught up in magical formations.

After what must have been a thousand years, swimming with these mystical pink beings, immersing myself in the *kené* forming and reforming on the surface of the river, *Metsá Ino* returns and nudges me away from the pod toward a small clearing on the riverbank. *Pedro Bello* is waiting for us there when we go ashore. He licks my face and I nuzzle him.

The two cats have a conversation I don't understand at the margin of the rainforest while I lie back in the warm mud on the riverbank. Taurino's boat looks like a toy, a white dot lost in the vastness of the river.

Are the jaguars talking about me? Likely, but I think it unwise to intrude. A medium-sized *caimán* slithers toward me from the margin of the trees, but a much larger anaconda snaps him up. *Metsá Ino* snarls, sending the snake scurrying for cover as fast as it can move with its lumpy body distended by its *caimán* lunch.

Pedro Bello turns away and disappears into the forest. I have no sense of passing time, or memory of reentering the water, but I find myself back at the boat, hanging onto the side. Taurino reaches out to help me aboard and offers me a towel. *Metsá Ino* jumps aboard, shakes the water out of his fur, and settles down to nap in the stern.

I dry my hair and give my body a few swipes with the towel and sit on it to dry in the warm breeze. I feel serene.

Taurino sings another *ikaro* I know as he pilots the boat upriver—the *ikaro* against fear. I try to sing it with him. He sings in short phrases so I can learn.

The insanity of sitting naked in a boat in the middle of this magnificent river, one I'm told carries twenty percent of the flowing fresh water on the planet, with a man I have only just met, doesn't escape me. Nor does it frighten me. I trust Taurino to deliver me safely to the Lodge. I trust *Metsá Ino* to protect me. I trust the universe knows what it's doing, immersing me in this wilderness filled with pink dolphins, jaguars, *caimanes*, anacondas, and magical *kené*.

When I'm dry, I dress. Taurino points out a pair of sloths in the distant treetops and some scrapping monkeys. We round a bend and the boat slows and turns toward the shore, past a small village with naked children laughing and chasing each other in the shallows. Women of all ages, from young teens to women much older than me are washing clothes in a rock-rimmed lagoon they've created on the riverbank.

Three empty dugout canoes are moored nearby. Men and adolescent boys spear fish in the lagoon. One of the boys proudly holds up a full stringer. Taurino laughs and yells something to him I don't understand, but the boy is obviously pleased.

We continue along the shore and fifteen minutes later arrive at the Pink Dolphin Jungle Lodge. Two men help Taurino berth the boat. They help me onto the dock, and Taurino hands one of them my belongings.

"Welcome to the Pink Dolphin Rainforest Lodge, Dr. Quilter," the taller one says. "I'm Gustavo, your host for the next few days. We have you in Cabin F. When you get settled, you can come back to the Commons building and we'll check you in."

My cabin rests on a platform near the tree line, close to the riverbank. I step out onto the balcony where a welcoming hammock enclosed in mosquito netting awaits. I can see Taurino squaring away the boat. He flashes a smile and waves as he makes his way to the Commons building.

When I finish checking in and join him, he's seated in a fraying rattan chair, of which there are several, eating yet more fruit. He gestures to the basket on the long community-style dining hall table.

"Try the cashew apple," he says. "It's a little sour but has an interesting taste." He explains that the short curving stem on the fruit, which looks like a cashew, is precisely that. With a single nut to each apple-sized fruit, it must take bushels to gather enough for a bag of the buttery roasted nuts.

"Let's go for a walk," Taurino says. He produces a pair of calf-high galoshes, warning me the jungle is muddy in spots, and hands me some mosquito repellant.

We set off on no path I can discern, and I heel him, minding the exposed roots and buttresses of massive trees as he taps them with his walking stick. "Don't trip," he says. I take note that *Metsá Ino* has apparently decided to be elsewhere.

The buttresses of a gigantic tree he identifies as a kapok must be fifteen feet tall before they join the trunk soaring into the canopy. As I stand between them, closer to the trunk, he warns me to be careful where I put my hands. He points out a steady stream of ants, half an inch, parading up and down the trunk.

"Those are called bullet ants," he says, "because if one of them stings you, it feels like you've been shot. You won't die unless they gang up on you, but you might wish you had. Some tribes subject adolescent boys to bullet ant stings during initiation, to prove they can handle pain like men."

I give the ants a wide berth. "Has a bullet ant ever stung you?" I ask.

"Yes." He laughs. "Some people call it 'the 24-hour ant.' It takes a whole day for the pain to go away. Everyone says they know someone the ants attacked and died, but I don't."

He points to a tree a few feet ahead and whistles softly between his teeth. A tiny fuzzy head pokes out of a hole twenty feet above us where a branch has fallen off. A diminutive monkey scrambles out and scurries around to the back of the tree, hiding from us.

"That's a marmoset," Taurino whispers. He whistles again and the monkey peeks around at us. "We call the animal *shipi* and take our name from it. Shipibo are the people of the marmoset. The animals are very rare in Peru. They eat only the sap from this tree and sometimes a few flowers.

"Are you interested in rainforest medicine, Dr. Quilter?"

"Yes. I'd like to learn more. I found the medicines available in the Belén market fascinating."

"There is still much I do not know," Taurino says. "The plants give up their secrets slowly and then only to those who are worthy. They are very choosy. The teacher plants have more time than the animals. Only the cosmos, the *néte*, has more time than the teacher plants." He points to a thick tangle of lianas growing on the trunk of a kapok sapling.

"This vine is a master plant, one of the most important teacher plants. It's used to make *ayahuasca*, a medicine that opens the portal to the spirit realm. And *chacruna*," he says, pointing to a low bush with large glossy emerald-green foliage, "is added to *ayahuasca* to usher in the visions that allow us to commune with the beings that inhabit the spirit realm."

He points out *mapacho,* or jungle tobacco, the plant I saw women shaping into cigars and ropes in the Belén market. "*Mapacho* is very important in many healing ceremonies," he says. "The smoke purifies and protects." He identifies many other teacher plants essential to the lives of indigenous people, as well as others that are simply beautiful, like orchids and other flowers.

"Do people come here to take *ayahuasca?*" I ask.

"Some are *ayahuasca* tourists, but the Pink Dolphin Lodge is not designed for them. There are more than a hundred lodges and centers much closer to Iquitos that provide *ayahuasca* experiences. Some of the *chamanes* are authentic spirit guides but many more are frauds."

"It seems dangerous."

"It is," he replies. "Taking the medicine requires the guidance of an experienced *chamán*. Preparation is very important because the teacher plants are jealous and will refuse anyone who has drugs, alcohol, or other impurities in his body. One must do a *dieta,* at least a month long, to prepare for the *ayahuasca* ceremony, and guidance during the medicine ceremony is essential.

"For example, Dr. Quilter, look around. Do you know which direction to walk if you want to return to your room?"

I don't. Nothing looks familiar, and I acknowledge I'm completely lost.

"Can you tell me for how long we have been walking? Where the kapok tree with the bullet ants is? Which tree is home to the *shipi*?"

"I think we've been walking about half an hour," I venture. "I don't know which of these trees is home to the marmoset or the ants."

"We have been walking twice that time," he says. It is easy to become disoriented in the rainforest. There are many ways to die in the rainforest, in this miraculous place so full of life.

"*Ayahuasca* is like the rainforest. In Quichua, '*aya*' means 'spirit' or 'soul.' It also means 'dead body' or 'corpse.' *Ayahuasca* has been called the 'Vine of the Dead,' and 'The Grandmother.' To take *ayahuasca* is to invite death at the hand of Grandmother *Aya*. It's easy to become lost and never return."

We're silent, standing together in the rainforest for what seems an eternity.

"Are you ready to go back?"

"Yes, please."

"This way, then."

I recognize absolutely nothing on our return until Taurino whistles softly and "our" marmoset makes an appearance. A little farther and he points to the giant kapok with the dangerous bullet ants. His lesson is obvious. I'm a complete outsider in this world. Without a trustworthy guide, I will surely perish.

Taurino has been a superb guide and mentor. Clearly I'm right to trust him, whether swimming with pink dolphins he knows to be free of curses or hiking in the rainforest discovering its secrets.

I still don't know why I've come here, interesting and enjoyable as it's been so far. What does Don Mateo have up his sleeve?

"Ah," says Taurino with a twinkle in his eye. The lodge appears as if by magic. "Let's have some lunch, and you can rest afterward if you like. Later today we'll go out in the boat and catch dinner."

Metsá Ino and *Pedro Bello* are sleeping under my hammock when I return from lunch. *Pedro Bello* jumps down from the platform and disappears into the shadows. *Metsá Ino* opens one eye, yawns, and goes back to sleep. I'm used to *Metsá Ino* hanging around, but this is the first time *Pedro Bello* has visited me on my turf. I don't know why he would want a sleepover with *Metsá Ino* in my cabin and not his own home in Pilpintuwasi. I've much to learn about jaguars. ■

41

Tingo

I wake from my post-lunch nap in the hammock to a gentle knocking at my door. Taurino invites me to meet him at the dock where I find him aboard a small motorboat decorated with the face of a snarling jaguar. My jaguar is already aboard, stretched out in the stern.

Peruvian Amazon   September 18

Taurino has brought fishing poles, bait, a nest of woven baskets, a couple of plastic buckets, and the ever-present cooler with bottled water and fresh fruit. He nudges the boat away from the dock and heads upriver, toward the opposite bank.

He turns into a lagoon choked with water hyacinths, their glossy green leaves and attractive violet-colored flowers blanketing the surface. "A very useful plant. The leaves are good to eat," he says, handing me one he has stripped from the woody vine. They taste like celery, delicious if a little tough.

We fill some of the baskets he's brought with the greens. "We weave these baskets from the stems of this plant," he says.

Taurino navigates through the floating tangle until he comes to a stretch of open water dotted with water lilies. The pink and white blossoms are the size of basketballs. I'm surprised how fragrant they are. The leaves are enormous, perhaps ten feet across, floating on the black water like gigantic platters. On a few of them, small *caimanes* laze in sun.

321

"*Victoria amazonica* lilies," he says. "The leaves won't support us, but they can easily hold a fifty or sixty-pound child. The blooms only last for a day or two."

We drift toward the tree line, a tangle of fallen branches and vines dipping into the water. Taurino stands in the boat and baits a hook with scraps of raw chicken. He casts the baited hook into the water, about four feet from the boat, and froths the water vigorously with the tip of his pole. Within seconds, he jerks the pole upward, displaying a red-bellied piraña about a foot long, dancing at the end of his line.

"Dinner." He laughs, easing the fish into a plastic bucket and carefully backing out the hook, avoiding the ugly, snapping jaws.

"Here, you catch one," he says, guiding me through the motions. I hook one, a quarter the size of his. We both have a good laugh. "This one still needs its mother," he says, unhooking it and tossing it back. On my second try, I land a keeper. We each catch several more in short order.

"Do you think we can eat more than this for dinner?" he asks, only half seriously. "No? Then we have everything we need. We'll steam the fish on a bed of water hyacinth. I'm hungry already thinking about it," he says.

He eases the boat out of the lagoon through the floating green carpet back into the river. I'm surprised we don't head back to the Pink Dolphin Jungle Lodge. Instead, Taurino takes us upstream another half hour until we come to a collection of thatched huts and small houses sporting multicolored corrugated steel sides and roofs, not unlike the village we passed on our way to the lodge. We haven't spoken a word since we hooked the piraña. Daylight is fading.

He runs the nose of the boat onto the bank and several villagers help us tie up and come ashore. It's impossible not to notice the deference with which they treat him. They are calling him "Tingo," not "Taurino."

"It is my Shipibo nickname," he says. "Unlike most *shiro jane*, mine means nothing. You may call me Tingo if you wish." I remember Èlia telling me about her *shiro jane*, her nickname *"Wano"* that means "marry a man."

Events unfold rapidly. The men of the village surround Tingo. A woman roughly his age with five children in tow joins us.

"My wife" he says, "and some of my children." I wait for further explanation, not wanting to offend anyone.

Tingo's wife takes my hand and urges me toward a large thatch-roofed building in the center of the village. The children follow, offering me bananas and pieces of smoked meat. Tingo laughs at my cluelessness. Suddenly I put it together.

"Welcome to my village, Dr. Quilter," he says, confirming my guess.

A girl on the verge of womanhood joins us as Tingo's wife and children scatter, going about their business."

"Another of my beautiful children," Tingo says. "This is my eldest daughter, Sofia. She knows some Spanish and English and will help translate for you."

Sofia walks a pace behind us.

"You said when you came to the Pink Dolphin Rainforest Lodge, you would like to overnight in an indigenous community. I thought it might be pleasant to surprise you with the opportunity this evening.

"If you are uneasy, I will happily take you back to the lodge, but I hope you will be our guest. The piraña and water hyacinth we harvested will make a welcome addition to our evening meal."

My overnight turns into several. I'm honored to be invited to live among these wonderful people. They teach me freely about their ways but never pry. I'm welcome to stay for as long as I wish, Sofia tells me on behalf of her mother.

Although Tingo has told everyone I'm a physician, nobody seeks my professional advice. I'm a welcome guest who they don't wish to inconvenience. There is a *curandera* in case of accidents or illness, but there's been no need for her services while I've been here.

Still, I feel uneasy without my medical bag, which Tingo informs me, Gustavo at the Pink Dolphin Rainforest Lodge will send back to La Casa Morey with my camera and all my other belongings. I'm here with literally nothing that belongs to me, having exchanged my own clothing for indigenous attire at Sofia's invitation.

Tingo's wife now owns my shift and looks better in it than I ever did. I don't know where my bra is and I don't miss it. My panties were last seen, to my great amusement, falling off the bottom of a small boy trying to hold them up by the waistband with one hand while being chased into the water by a gaggle of like-aged kids.

"Don't worry, Dr. Quilter," Tingo says. "If you want any of your belongings, we can get them back in a day. I kept your Japanese cat for you," he says, handing it to me. "We all have talismans important to our well-being, even if we do not know whether they serve that purpose or we think them unimportant."

* * *

I've been freeloading here for what seems like forever. I've now lived with these lovely people more than three weeks, and I'm perfectly content. The women encourage me as I try my hand at pottery making and weaving baskets from water hyacinth stalks.

Sofia teaches me how to paint the rectilinear *kené*. She praises my efforts, despite my lack of skill. I'm equally inadept at cooking but manage to be helpful gardening with the other women, scrubbing little heads of hair, and washing clothes in the lagoon.

Tingo leaves the village from time to time to work at the Pink Dolphin Rainforest Lodge, as do a couple other men from the village. *Metsá Ino* comes and goes whenever he pleases to engage in whatever jaguar business calls him.

He returns one day in the company of *Pedro Bello*. They lead me to the edge of the forest.

"It is time," *Metsá Ino* says.

"Time for what?"

"Time to confront the evil inside you. You must speak of this with the *chamán*."

They disappear and I seek out Tingo. I tell him what the jaguars have told me and he nods his head in understanding. I'm glad someone understands. I do not.

"How do I find this *chamán?*" I ask.

"We will go into the rainforest this evening," he says. "There are more marvels I want to show you, and you can tell me why you have need for a *chamán*. Do not worry. We will spend the night among the teacher plants and return to the village in the morning."

We take the boat upriver as the sun sets. Tingo motors slowly toward the opposite shore and slows in a backwater where a thousand pairs of eyes dance in the beam of his headlamp on the surface of the lagoon. He thrusts his hand into the water and brings up a pair of those eyes attached to a foot-long *caimán*. He tries to hand him to me, but I flinch.

"Do not be afraid, Dr. Quilter. The *caimán* is not distressed, and if you hold him as I am, you are in no danger of being nipped." He pronounces the name as Spanish speakers do, kah-ee-MAHN, three syllables with the accent on the last one.

Reluctantly, I take the creature from him.

"Is he not a marvelous animal?" Tingo asks.

He is beautiful indeed, covered with greenish black scales shining in the light of the rising moon. I turn him over and stroke his sleek white belly, still wet with river water. He makes a few small squeaks, whether out of pleasure or annoyance I don't know.

"*Caimán* is lord of the river, eating whatever fish he wishes. Yet herons and larger fish eat *caimán* when he is young and jaguars eat him when he is full grown, even if he is larger than they are. So do anacondas. He knows this is as it should be and does not fear dying. It is simply the way of *néte*, the universe. You will not eat him, however, so when you finish admiring him, just lay him in the water."

He swims lazily away as I release him, disappearing into the multitude of his clan, their eyes shining in the dark river as constellations of stars. I wonder if he thought about anything when he was my captive. Why did he not fear being eaten? I would have been terrified if a creature many times my size snatched me from my home. Perhaps he knew, as Tingo says, it's simply the way of the universe.

Tingo pulls us ashore on a muddy beach, ties the boat, bow and stern, to some nearby trees, and leads the way into the rainforest. There's a definite path here. Someone, perhaps Tingo, has been here before. He again reminds me not to touch the trees.

We stop two feet away from one of them, and he shines a flashlight on the trunk. The bark is peppered with spiders as large as my hand, twenty-five or thirty of them, lying motionless. Thick purplish green hair, shimmering in Tingo's light, covers their bodies. The tips of their legs flash bubblegum pink.

"Tarantulas," he tells me. "Pink-toed purple Peruvian tarantulas, prized by collectors. They will not harm you unless you frighten them. You could safely allow one to crawl along your arm, but if you startle them, they will throw stinging hairs. They're painful, and they itch like a thousand mosquito bites. They are lying in wait for foolish moths and insects to get too close. The larger ones will eat an occasional careless bat or a small bird.

"Some people capture them for the pet trade. Others roast them and eat them. I have never eaten one, but I am told they taste like shrimp."

I tell him about my experience with the palm weevil grubs in the Belén market. He shakes his head dubiously and says he has no plans to eat those either. "Why eat spiders and grubs when fish and peccary are plentiful?" he asks.

The air is whirring with the sounds of insects, birds, and other creatures of darkness. One sound catches my attention—the barking of a small dog. I wonder if we're approaching another village.

Tingo chuckles when I ask. "Not a dog," he says. "Let's see if we can find this noisy creature." His ears lead us to a marshy area where the eyes of semi-submerged creatures reflect the beam of his flashlight. More *caimanes*, I suspect.

His beam stops at the edge of a puddle, illuminating a greenish brown toad the size of a dinner plate. "There's your dog." He laughs softly. As we watch, the toad barks, but my eye is drawn to the slow movement of a snake sneaking up on it. I shudder at the sight of the serpent, much smaller than Anaconda Woman, but still a snake like the one that menaced me.

"*Ronin,*" Tingo says. "She is too small to harm us. Frogs and toads are her favorite meal." As we watch, the anaconda dispatches the toad and disappears into the darkness.

We approach a clearing surrounding a rectangular pavilion with a thatched roof, large enough to shelter a dozen or more people, and several smaller buildings. "We will rest here tonight and discuss the matters weighing on your heart," he says.

I am relieved. When Tingo said we would be staying overnight in the rainforest I pictured sleeping on the ground. I was certain I would not even close my eyes, imagining assorted creepy crawlies waiting to make a meal of me.

"Those two small buildings over there," he says, gesturing to the edge of the clearing, "are privies. Check carefully with your flashlight before you sit."

With visions of pink-toed tarantulas, bullet ants, snakes, and god knows what other demonic creatures running through my mind, I check carefully indeed, shining my flashlight on every surface, into every chink, and even the latrine pit. I don't need to be reminded that nature is red in tooth and claw. It looks safe, but I'm still uneasy about plopping my butt down. The only thing I scare up is a few flies and I escape unscathed.

But where are we? What is this place?

When I rejoin Tingo, he's started a fire and is roasting vegetables—purple sweet potatoes and onions. The aroma reminds me I'm starving. We wait in silence and watch sparks from the crackling wood ascend into the sky. I can't tell where the sparks end and the stars begin.

"I must tell you something," I begin hesitantly.

Tingo listens respectfully as I tell him about *Metsá Ino* and *Pedro Bello*. I tell him about the other jaguars and dreamcats, the fortune-teller in Paris, the incident with Èlia and Lovely aboard the *Andaman Pearl,* and the frightening encounter with Anaconda Woman.

He sits with me, looking into the fire, bearing witness to my confession, incomplete as it is. I think of *Mme* Zecrí and her advice that I should unburden my soul to someone I trust. I absolutely trust Tingo. I want to tell him about Roderick, but my tongue becomes bitter and thick in my mouth, and I can no longer speak.

"Some of this I have heard from Don Mateo," he says. "I have sensed the jaguars, although I do not see them, and my spirit perceives the turbulence of your heart."

"Why do Don Mateo, Èlia, everyone know more about this than I do? I don't have a clue about how to put all this to rights."

"That is why you have come to us, Jessamyn Quilter. It is time to seek guidance from Grandmother *Aya.* I will assist as she directs, but you must first prepare yourself. You must be willing to hear. You must reckon with a self you will loathe, and you must prepare to be destroyed, to die at the hand of Grandmother *Aya*, if that is what *néte*, the cosmos, requires."

I shiver with fear. I suddenly understand about Tingo. He is far more than a guide at The Pink Dolphin Jungle Lodge. We are not here looking for a *chamán*. The *chamán* has brought me here.

"You are the *chamán* I seek, aren't you, Tingo? Only a *chamán* knows these things about pink dolphins, sorcerers, the teacher plants, and the world to which I'm mostly blind and deaf. Èlia and Don Mateo know some of these things, but they know they are not *chamanes*. That's why they have sent me to you."

"Yes. I am the *chamán*," he replies without emotion.

"Please, Tingo, I mean no disrespect. Are you a *chamán* of great power? I believe I have need of one."

He answers me by flashing a vision into my mind that leaves no doubt. It's like witnessing the dawn of creation or the apocalypse—a vision terrifying in its power and beauty. I want to scream but do not have the voice. Instead, I sit before a blazing fire and quiver like a seal face-to-face with a polar bear on an ice floe.

At last he speaks.

"My *janekon* is *Ronin Rawa*, 'Slithering Anaconda' in the Shipibo language because the *chamán* who suggested my name to my parents had a vision in which Anaconda Woman devoured me in my mother's womb and rebirthed me as one of her children.

"I have known since we met, Jessamyn Quilter, that there is evil within you. You must now decide whether to face it. If you do, you will suffer or even die. If you do not, it will certainly destroy you, even if your body survives a little longer than your soul."

"Anaconda Woman threatened to kill me," I say, still not quite believing I'm talking about her as if she were real and has power over me. "She wrapped me in her coils and threatened to take my evil inside herself to restore the imbalance in the cosmos. She demands I be accountable for the imbalance."

"Yes," Tingo says. "Are you accountable? What will you do?"

I shudder. "The exact words Anaconda Woman spoke to me."

"And what is your answer?"

"I don't know. But I will do what is asked of me."

"You are afraid?"

"Yes." My breathing is as labored as it was when Anaconda Woman threatened to choke the life from me.

He sings me the *ikaro* against fear. Across the fire from us, *Metsá Ino* and *Pedro Bello* sit regarding us calmly.

"They are here now, your *inos*?" he asks.

"Yes," I answer.

"They will protect you, Jessamyn Quilter. Now we must rest. Tomorrow we will return to the village and prepare you for the destiny Anaconda Woman designs for you. Everything is written in the *kené* on her skin. Everything in *néte*."

"What does that mean, Tingo?"

"Enough questions for now." He produces a cigar from the folds of his clothing, lights it from the fire, and puffs several times, producing a prodigious amount of smoke before he rises to walk toward the pavilion. I have not seen him smoke before.

"Come," he says.

I follow him.

"*Mapacho*," he says. "Jungle tobacco, the gift of one of the five master plant teachers." He asks me to wait outside the pavilion while he enters, puffing and filling the room with smoke. I hear him chanting as he addresses the four corners of the pavilion.

"Come inside. *Mapacho* has purified and protected the space for us. We are welcome here and will be safe."

Tingo lights candles around the room. When my eyes adjust, I see a dozen small platforms about two feet high with thick woven mats arranged along three walls of the pavilion. Close to the other wall, there is a slightly higher platform behind a long, low table.

"*La mesa del chamán*," Tingo says. "My shaman's table. During medicine ceremonies I place objects on the *mesa* that please the spirits and help me divine what they would have me do. I will sleep on the platform behind the *mesa,* and you can choose any of the others as your bed tonight. Sleep well in this safe place, Jessamyn Quilter. We will leave for the village in the morning and return here in a month's time to learn what Anaconda Woman requires of you.

Despite my fear, I fall dead asleep in an instant, *Metsá Ino* and *Pedro Bello* sleeping on either side of my platform. In the morning, at first light, we leave for the Shipibo village downriver. I'm oddly calm, resigned to my fate. Tingo's right. This is why I came to this place. ∎

42

Dieta

As our boat nears the village, Tingo calls out to his eldest daughter. She runs to meet us.

Peruvian Amazon   October 10

"Take Jessamyn Quilter and give her food, Sofia. She may eat only plants now. She is undertaking the *dieta*, preparing for the ceremony of the 'Vine of the Dead.' Help her bathe and dress. You will be her guide as she prepares."

Sofia smiles, takes my hand, and leads me to the firepit in front of her mother's dwelling. A pot of some sort of gruel is bubbling over the coals. She dishes up a bowl and hands it to me.

"You must be starving," she says.

I am.

"Some people don't like this, but it's one of my favorites. A mush of manioc and bananas," she explains, helping herself to a bowl.

I taste it cautiously. It takes getting used to, but it's not bad. The second spoonful tastes better than the first.

"What's all this about a *dieta?*" I ask. "What does that mean?"

"It's the Spanish word for diet. To prepare for your *aya* medicine ceremony you must eat a diet of only plants for a month. It is part of a sacrifice you must make, so the teacher plants will learn to trust you. They will guide and protect you, strengthen you, and perhaps give you the ability to learn from them if they find you worthy.

"They may teach you some of their *ikaros,* but teacher plants are very jealous. They will not share their gifts if there are other medicines or poisons from forbidden foods or pleasures in your body. The *dieta* will cleanse you of them.

"You and I will live together in a special shelter, away from the village. My father and I will care for you and help you care for yourself. He will be the only man who will visit us and even then, he will not visit often. He will prescribe the foods we will eat, and I will help prepare them."

She leads me to a secluded part of the riverbank—a beautiful grotto filled with ferns, tropical flowers, trees, and bushes laden with fruit. A clear spring spills into a pool. We will live together in the nearby thatched bungalow for the next month.

We undress and she leads me to the pool where she helps me bathe and washes my hair with spring water and sap from leaves she's crushed in her hands, singing *ikaros* to the surrounding plants. The sap foams like shampoo and leaves my hair silky, smelling citrusy. She presents me with a woven headband, like she wears, to hold back my hair, and a beige gown like hers with red, blue, and black embroidered *kené.*

"Preparation for taking the medicine means sacrificing many pleasures to purify ourselves for *aya* and the other teacher plants. We must not drink alcohol, eat meat or fish, or indulge in sweet, salty, spicy, or rich foods. " We must not touch ourselves or have sex with anyone during this time.

Great. Now I have a girl young enough to be my granddaughter telling me not to masturbate for a month, not to drink alcohol, or eat anything except vegetables without salt or spice. Bananas must be okay, if they are not too sweet, since Sofia tells me we will consume the manioc/banana gruel we ate this morning as a staple.

"Why would the teacher plants care if we touch ourselves or eat forbidden foods?"

"Because they wish us to sacrifice our pleasures. Sacrifice is a gift to the Mother. Touching our sex creates feelings in our bodies that change our energy. It makes the teacher plants jealous because our energy is not given to them. Eating foods simply because we prefer them tells the plants our wishes are more important than theirs. They will not share their secrets because they will deem us unworthy.

"We must also live away from others while we are preparing for the medicine ceremony because they might unwittingly tempt us or lead us astray. Later we will gather *huito* fruit and paint *kené* on our hands, faces, and feet with the juice. The dark blue markings will let the people of the village know we are preparing for Grandmother *Aya* if they encounter us, and it will announce to the teacher plants that we are sacrificing to receive their wisdom."

"Have you done a *dieta* before, Sofia?"

"I keep the *dieta* when I am helping my father prepare for the *aya* medicine ceremony. It is necessary if I am to be useful to him and learn more of the ways of the *chamanes*.

"My father is a powerful *chamán*. And my mother says she sees much of my father in me and believes one day I will be even more powerful than he. But we must never tell him that. It would be disrespectful to him and to Grandmother *Aya*."

"Are you a *chamana*?"

"No," she demurs. "But I hope it may be my destiny. My *janekon* is *Kana Soi*, a 'nice blue and gold macaw.' Nice but nothing special." She smiles. "Only the spirits know about my destiny. The *chaikoni* can suggest a more special *janekon* later, if they wish, but it would be up to my parents to change it.

"Sometimes I feel a powerful energy coursing through me I can't explain, and the teacher plants have entrusted me with some of their secrets already. They have also taught me I have much to learn."

"Do you follow the *dieta* all the time, sacrificing pleasure for the teacher plants?"

"Oh no! I only follow it for ten days when I am helping my father with the medicine ceremony, though I will follow it for a month this time as we prepare together. At other times, I am still careful to be worthy. Mother says I may give myself pleasure sparingly when I am not following the *dieta*, but I must not allow men to give me pleasure until the teacher plants show me how to receive it without risk of bearing children.

"I think Mother knows how to do this, although she loves bearing children, but she will not tell me." She laughs. "'That is a job for the teacher plants,' Mother says. 'Young women should not be thinking so much of such things. Thinking about pleasure too much makes young women too much like young men. Women must be better, stronger, and wiser,' Mother says."

"In my culture it's like that too," I say. "Women must work twice as hard, be twice as strong and twice as smart as men to be taken seriously. And sometimes that still isn't enough."

"My girlfriends think about sex all the time," Sophia says, "and some of them take pleasure with each other, but Mother says that is not the intended way, and they risk the wrath of Anaconda Woman. It is especially hard for me to give up pleasure during the dieta. I like men very much."

I think of Lagac and smile. I also like men very much.

"I told Mother I think Anaconda Woman likes men too, or she would not have trusted them with the baby anacondas that live between their legs. Mother laughed at me and said I talk too much and too much of what I say is nonsense.

"I also like peccary, but it is easier to deny myself peccary than pleasure. Still, I will do what Mother tells me to do. She is wiser in these matters than I am."

I find this young woman utterly charming. She reminds me so much of Lovely Bayani, that untethered spirit, master of the music she makes and the world that's her oyster. Sofia is also indomitable, if humbly obedient to the father and mother she honors. She will surely become a great *chamana*, not remain just a "nice blue and gold macaw."

"How about your father? I know he eats fish and meat, and he eats more sweet fruit than anyone I know."

Sofia laughs. "He is only a man. Men are different. They must have meat and pleasure to stay healthy. The teacher plants make allowances for them and do not take offense because they understand men are weak.

"But even men must make the sacrifices at least ten days before the medicine ceremony, or Grandmother *Aya* will be furious. Mother says teacher plants reveal much more to women who seek their wisdom than they reveal to men. That is why only women can become the most powerful *curanderas* and *chamanas*."

Sophia has it all figured out. I'm glad she is my teacher in preparing for this medicine ceremony because every time she talks about it, it scares the hell out of me.

"Let's go find some *huito*," Sofia says. "After we have marked ourselves with the juice, I will introduce you to other teacher plants."

She shows me dozens of plants and sings the *ikaros* of those plants who have taught her. She crushes the berries and paints us with *kené*, using blades of grass. I do not know why, but the markings make me feel beautiful, a feeling largely unfamiliar to me.

She shows me the "Vine of the Dead" growing up a large kapok tree and the *chacruna* bush growing a few feet away that she and her father will gather at the end of our *dieta* to make the *ayahuasca*.

"Why do they call it the 'Vine of the Dead'?" I ask.

"It is also called the 'Vine of the Soul,'" she says. "These are Quichua words, not Shipibo. In Quichua, '*aya*' means 'spirit' or 'soul' and it also means 'corpse' or 'dead body.' '*Waska*' means a rope, like a woody vine. Just like that one on the tree. The vine is the spirit or soul of *ayahuasca*, the gatekeeper to the spirit world.

"*Aya* medicine contains both the 'Vine of the Soul' that opens the spirit world and *chacruna*, which brings visions. Before we became humans, the Mother made souls and taught them how to make *ayahuasca*. She also taught them to use *ayahuasca* to return home if they forgot where they came from after they entered human bodies or left those bodies when they died."

I look at this beautiful young woman, wise beyond her years, and my soul aches for Èlia and Lovely, for Shun and Shantrelle, for Eric and Lagac, friends and lovers aboard the *Andaman Pearl*.

Why is it, I wonder, I never felt close enough to my college friends, or anyone since, to miss them? Why do I not miss Elsa, the girl who awakened unknown desire with her tongue and sapphic poetry? And why do I not miss Pyotr who may have loved me but failed us both with his addictions? I remember them but do not miss them, and I don't know why.

"Do you know Èlia—*Tsiri Biri*?" I ask Sofia.

"I do not know her, but everyone has heard of her. She is the greatest of all Shipibo musicians, and her story is a legend among our people. All of us sing to her when we see the little bird of her *janekon*, messenger to the *chamanes*, flying in the rainforest. Look, there is one now, sitting on the 'Vine of Souls.' I will sing her the *ikaro* of welcome and homage for *Tsiri*."

And as she sings, I weep bitter tears of longing. I feel pain I have never felt before.

"Tears falling for those we love is warm rain sent directly from the Mother," Sofia says, putting her arm around me and holding me close. "Do not worry. *Tsiri Biri* is not lost to you. Or to us. She will come back to us when it is time." ∎

43

Rage

F
or two weeks now, Sofia has been mentoring me as I keep my *dieta*. Yesterday I heard the unmistakable voice of a teacher tree. She was making a rasping sound, like dry rushes rubbing together. I couldn't understand what she was saying, but the patterns and inflections made it clear—the tree was speaking.

Sofia heard it too. I would not have recognized the sound as an *ikaro*, but Sofia says *ikaros* take many forms. "She says you are welcome here, Jessamyn Quilter, you and your jaguars. She knows they are here with us. Jaguars cannot hide from the teacher plants."

"They sleep in our bungalow at night," I tell Sofia. "*Metsá Ino* is the one I call 'my jaguar,' a big male. *Pedro Bello* is the jaguar his keepers believe they have caged at Pilpintuwasi, but jaguars can't be caged. Like *Pedro Bello*, they play along and fool their keepers, but they go where they will as they please."

"You are fortunate the jaguars protect you. They are very powerful spirits who hide from us as they do in the rainforest," Sofia says. "Tell me more about your *ino*."

"*Pedro Bello,* who often accompanies *Metsá Ino,* is also a male but much smaller than most jaguars. His captors mistreated him when they took him from his mother, so his growth was stunted, but Pilpintuwasi rescued him. He is very wise because he has already lived twice the time jaguars are supposed to live."

I sing as much of the *ikaro* of welcome and homage for jaguars as I can remember. Sofia sings with me. The jaguars lick my face and then lick Sofia's.

"What was that?" she asks, touching her face. "Something rough and wet."

"The jaguars greeted you. They are gone now."

"I have never been kissed by a jaguar before." She touches her face again as if to convince herself the jaguars really licked her.

My mood darkens without warning as it has several times in the past few days. I don't know if it's the *dieta* or something else, but it's more than anger. At the pit of the blackness that overwhelms me is rage.

"None of this makes any sense to me, Sofia," I say. "It's all fairy-tale wonderful, but none of it makes any sense."

"That is why you must take *aya* medicine. Some evil is trying to kill you."

I am beyond irritable. I have had a belly full of this talk about some lethal evil infesting me. The fiery rage surging through my body is as great as that I felt when I watched Balwinder Agarwal try to reassert his authority over the mortally injured Chana. "This is none of your business," he said as I cradled her in my arms. "My wife, my business. I forbid you to interfere with my wife."

Who is this child to tell me about my business? Or her father, for that matter. How can they possibly understand? I rein in my anger as best I can. After all, Sofia doesn't deserve my wrath.

She's not oblivious to my rage, nor does she seem frightened by it or even think it inappropriate. She sings the *ikaro* against fear.

"Why are you doing this to me?" I ask, melting into hot tears. "Everyone here says they're trying to help me, but I hurt more than I ever have. I think I should leave this village, this rainforest, and Peru. I should pack up my stuff and move back to the civilized world."

What an extraordinarily stupid idea, Jessamyn. Back to Westbury and eat antipsychotic medications for breakfast? Minuet with your shit-for-brains analyst and tell him about the jaguars and Anaconda Woman? Or confess to Mme *Zecrí and end up in prison, or worse?*

"You are living in the civilized world, Jessamyn Quilter," Sofia says softly. "This civilization is millennia old. Much older than the civilizations you left to journey here.

"I think the teacher plants are sending you wisdom," she says. "Wisdom is sometimes not welcome. We may not want it despite what we say. Wisdom can bring rage—rage at ourselves, rage at others, rage at *néte*. Rage will move you closer to healing. Do not fight against the rage. Give it to the teacher plants."

I don't fight against the rage. How could I possibly? Rage overwhelms me like the waves and the water that so terrified me when I was younger. I run into the forest and tear at the vines with my bare hands, uproot plants, strike every tree I can reach with a dried root I find lying on the ground.

"Okay, teacher plants," I snarl. "You oh-so-wise, ancient, highly civilized fuckers. Out with it. What do you want from me? Why don't you cure me of this evil you say is within me instead of persecuting me?"

I look back at Sofia with tears in my eyes, like an out of control two-year-old throwing the mother of all tantrums. Sofia, flanked by the jaguars who have returned, is singing, watching calmly.

"Rage will move you closer," *Metsá Ino* says.

"Go ahead, Beautiful Jaguar," *Pedro Bello* purrs. "Make a gift of your rage to the teacher plants."

I kick a massive kapok tree and drop to the ground in front of it, pounding it with both fists, snot shooting from my nose as I blubber and wail and curse the gods and man with all the rich vocabulary at my command.

Who are these rainforest dreamcats to lecture me? Am I now to take advice from hallucinations as well as children?

Anaconda Woman looks down upon me from the kapok.

"Are you accountable?" she hisses. "What will you do?"

"Get away from me, bitch," I roar. "Why are you tormenting me?"

"You torment yourself, Jessamyn Quilter. It is not my charge to inflict suffering. My charge is to preserve the balance in *néte*. I could kill you, squeeze the breath from you, and take the evil you carry into me. That would restore the balance and end your sickness.

"I will not show you that mercy though, at least not yet. It is better that you rage and confront the evil within you since it is your creation. Restore the balance you destroyed."

"What balance? Accountable for what? What the fuck are you talking about, 'evil' and 'sickness'?"

"You can't be at peace when you are hiding from yourself, Jessamyn Quilter. You must stop and become accountable. I will not wait forever."

My jaguar looks up at Anaconda Woman and growls. She vanishes into the canopy.

"Your *inos* are agitated," Sofia says. "Though they do not yet allow me to see them, I know they protect you. Are you in danger?"

"Didn't you see all of that?"

"I saw your rage and helplessness. I felt the power of Anaconda Woman and your jaguar's warning to her. The *ino* could see what you saw, but much is hidden from my sight."

"I must be going crazy. Trees talking to me, jaguars no one sees chasing away snakes that aren't there. It's lunacy."

"I mean no offense, but it is the evil and your profound illness. You are ill and lost, but you are also strong. You will find the way. The jaguars will help you. My father and I will help and so will Grandmother *Aya*.

"Do not swallow your rage. You require the fire of this rage to light your path."

I'm exhausted and profoundly ashamed of myself, behaving as I have in front of this loving child, even if she has more wisdom than a woman three times her age. I am hopelessly untethered.

"There is no shame in powerful feelings," Sofia says. "Only wisdom." *Where did that come from? How can she know so much about these things?*

"Feelings tell us whether something is right or wrong. Do not deny these feelings," she says.

There's no question about it. I am ill. I'm hallucinating. I can't really be consorting with wild cats, arguing with deadly snakes in the treetops, hearing the voices of plants I know are incapable of speaking. Then there are the gaps when reality goes missing, and I end up in fantastic dreamscapes. All of this is insane, *I* am insane. By definition. But why is this happening to me?

I don't have a fever. I'm not delirious. Poisoning? Highly unlikely. Stress? The only thing stressing me is these little fits where I take leave of my sanity. That leaves trauma. Cèline Zecrí was right. But what trauma have I suffered? I have the answer if I will listen to myself.

How about the decades of grinding humiliation and sadistic belittling Roderick so easily unleashed on me? The unspeakable tragedy of his deliberate destruction of DeShawn Livingston and the desolation of that lovely young man's suicide? The horror of Chana Agarwal's suffering from her husband's beatings and the utter disdain of the authorities about her death? The crimes of Nasir Rajaratman, drugging and abducting me on the high seas, depriving me of the love and safety of Lagac and my family on the *Andaman Pearl*. And of course, the conjuring of a cold-blooded husband killer from the soul of the life-saving physician Dr. Jessamyn Quilter. I did that. I must be accountable.

Revenge? Desperation? Yes.

Trauma. Absolutely.

Here in the muggy heat of the rainforest the raspy voice of a teacher tree freezes me to the marrow. "Your soul is in mortal jeopardy. You are battered. Your spirit bleeds. You must ask Grandmother *Aya* for healing."

My jaguar stares into my eyes. "Listen carefully, *Metsá Ino*. The teacher tree offers you wisdom. You have heard her before and not understood. She offers it to only those she deems worthy. Listen."

Sofia senses danger. "The teacher tree is shivering," she says. "Give her your rage, the rage that flows from your pain. The fire from your rage will warm her. How have you become so injured? What has been done to you? What have you done to others? Give everything to the teacher tree. Everything."

I rage blindly for more than an hour. I say nothing that can be heard by others but the teacher tree knows my pain. She doesn't need my voice, my confession She only needs my rage and I give it to her unstintingly in a whirlwind of fire.

The teacher tree is silent now. The air is filled with birdsong and brightness. Did I really unload on some tree or was that just another hallucination? I pick myself up off the ground and head back to our pavilion with Sofia. She's singing an *ikaro* I have not heard before.

"It is the *ikaro* for protection of the soul in the body," Sofia says.

I don't ask any questions.

People I like and trust—Don Mateo, Tingo, Sofia, and Èlia—tell me what's happening to me is normal. Even Shun buys into the jaguars. It's real. Not some Saturday morning cartoon.

They are certain I'm normal. What I'm going through fits the definition of normal in their world. It makes sense to them I'm terminally ill with some sort of spiritual illness, but normal.

It's hard for me to swallow. What does it even mean to have a spiritual illness? As a physician, I'm grounded in the body's physicality and the realities of the physical world that bodies move through. I have little truck with the airy-fairy spirit world. I don't believe in pixies, sprites, angels, demons, or *jinn*. If there's a sky god, or a bunch of them, they're so far removed from my physical world as to be irrelevant.

No, I think spiritual illness is as bogus as Lovely's *agimat* and the dried-up pizzle it's rumored to contain. Pizzles and the men they hang from are bogus, unreliable at best, like Roderick, Pyotr, and perhaps even Lagac, and sometimes dangerous, like Mr. Agarwal.

Shun and Tingo may be the exceptions that prove the existence of the rule, but my precious Lagac has sailed away. I lost him to a whim of the universe, like I lost Pyotr. I am betrayed by their unreliability. Fuck them. Fuck them all.

Part of me knows I should pick myself up by the scruff of the neck and knock some sense into my head. Buckle down to business and get on with my life back in Massachusetts.

The other part of me knows that's impossible. My intellectual legs have deserted me. Running is unthinkable. I must sort this out here. In the rainforest. Or perish.

I must answer Anaconda Woman's questions. Urgently. Whatever is going on feels lethal, even if the feeling is irrational, and she says she will not wait forever. ■

44

Grandmother *Aya*

Peruvian Amazon   November 8

The sun rises early, bright and hot on the thirtieth day of my *dieta*. My mood has not improved. I'm ill-tempered and my anger is still on red alert. Fear chews on my stomach. The near total isolation from the main village, and the world, chafes more with each passing day.

Sofia is always wonderful. That irritates me too, but I try not to take it out on her. When I slip, she only smiles, encourages, and tries to soothe me.

Today, as every day in this period of *dieta*, we go to the spring to bathe before beginning our day with the plants.

Tingo approaches out of sight, singing the *ikaro* to protect children, giving us both his blessing and fair warning to dress. He has visited us only twice in the past month, each time singing the *ikaro* as he approaches our bungalow.

"Do you think we should just surprise him and stay naked?" I ask Sofia irritably.

She smiles and says, "I doubt he would take any notice. He is only being respectful by announcing his presence. He does not want to interrupt our work."

"I'm sure you're right," I grouse. We dress, as always, when someone visits us.

I remember how the strength of my compulsion to swim with the pink dolphins had overcome my initial embarrassment about not having a bathing suit, how Tingo had guided me without my knowing to the understanding that embarrassment wasn't protecting me from something harmful but was blocking the path to a transcendental encounter.

Tingo is not among the men I count as dicks, although I secretly wonder if he will betray me also. Why would I want to cause him distress? The thought makes me more dissatisfied with myself. We slip on our embroidered robes, smooth our hair, and wait to receive him.

"Welcome, Father," Sofia says, her face lighting up.

He hugs us both warmly. "Tonight we will conduct our first medicine ceremony," he says. "I am certain the *dieta* has prepared you both well. I have heard the plants singing, giving an excellent report of you. All is in readiness."

A nauseating fear grips me, settling low in my pelvis.

"The evil causing your fear is strong," he says, "but Grandmother *Aya* is stronger. She will show you the way."

He takes both my hands and holds them against his heart as he looks into my eyes, singing the *ikaro* against fear. Sofia and I join his singing. I think I hear the soft voices of teacher plants chorusing with us.

"Healing takes place in small steps," he says. "We will perform the medicine ceremony each night until you no longer require it. Between ceremonies, you and Sofia will rest in the medicine pavilion. Someone from the village will bring food without interrupting so you can meditate. It is important that you do not break your *dieta*.

"Sofia, fetch baskets and tools from the village for gathering the 'Vine of the Dead' and the *chacruna*."

She bolts off, returning with the items Tingo has requested almost before I realize she's gone. I lose any sense of time as Tingo continues to sing his *ikaro*s of welcome and respect to the teacher plants, communing with their spirits. A tear comes to my eye as I wonder how anyone can do something so amazing.

346

"There," Sofia says, pointing to a ropy brown vine encircling the majestic kapok we discovered in our earlier excursions to learn from the teacher plants. Tingo produces a jungle tobacco cigar from the folds of his clothing and sets fire to one end with a white disposable lighter.

I find the incongruity of flicking a Bic in the primeval rainforest amusingly incongruous, especially the red "I ❤ Iquitos" logo, and the heaviness of my mood lifts for a moment at least. I assume he picked it up from a street vendor on the Plaza de Armas during one of his trips ferrying passengers between Iquitos and the Pink Dolphin Rainforest Lodge. Every shaman needs a Bic for moments like these. He raises thick blue-gray clouds of *mapacho* and blows them toward the vine, purifying it.

He hacks off a length and chops it into smaller pieces. Sofia gathers them, filling one basket she has brought from the village. She points to a nearby *chacruna*, which Tingo blesses with the rich smoke, and Sofia selects choice parrot-green leaves from the bush, filling her second basket to the brim.

I hear a voice from a tree beyond the kapok, like the clearing of a throat or a jaguar's chuff. A perception, not quite a vision, flashes before me of earnest young interns and students in short white coats and scrubs, tagging me around the emergency department back in Chilton.

This is how young shamans learn their craft, I say to myself, looking at Sofia going about her work. Whether in the rainforest or the hospital, watching and imitating is the best path to knowledge and skill.

"And this is how old physicians learn to be new again, learning the craft of *chamanas*," a teacher tree sings gently. "You could become a great *chamana, Metsá Ino.*"

I'm shocked, both by the words and the clarity of the voice, although I don't know which plant has favored me with that opinion.

"If I don't die first, Teacher Tree," I respond, walking closer to the source of the sound.

"You will not die first, *Metsá Ino*. When you become accountable, you will find the path of the *chamana* and restore the balance to *néte*. Anaconda Woman will have no cause to threaten you."

A deathly chill courses through my body.

"I don't know how to do these things, Teacher Tree, and Anaconda Woman has warned me she will not wait forever."

"Tingo and Sofia will prepare you. The *inos* will protect you. Grandmother *Aya* will show you the way. Your time approaches, *Metsá Ino*."

"How do you know my *janekon*, Teacher Tree?"

"The *inos* have informed me."

"May I know your name?"

"I am called *Chuchuhuasi*. You heard me shivering, and you gave me your rage to warm me. When you are ready, I will teach you my *ikaro*. Until then, the root lying in the path before you will help you on your journey. It is a part of me you can take with you until I teach you my song."

I pick up the red root as Tingo and Sofia finish gathering ingredients for *ayahuasca*. I recognize it as the one I used to strike the kapok as I raged in the forest earlier. I look at it more closely and see it's shaped like the *chuchuhuasi* roots I saw in the Belén market, the ones whose roughly carved tops resembled the head of a penis.

"One could also see the shape as the glans of a clitoris, *Metsá Ino*, or perhaps simply a beautiful root. Perhaps all of these."

Yes, I see. Of course. I am almost laughing at the silly turn of conversation with the teacher tree.

"We are ready," Tingo says. "The boat is waiting."

It's still early as our boat docks near the path to the ceremonial pavilion. The astonishing encounter with the *chuchuhuasi* teacher tree still rings in my ears, and the smile evoked by the repartee about the shape of the root lingers on my face. Tingo and Sofia must think me a perfect idiot.

We unload the boat and transport our cargo to the clearing. Tingo begins preparation of the *aya* medicine for our ceremony, now and then asking Sofia for help.

He sets a large iron cauldron with an inch of spring water over a fire ignited with his trusty Bic and layers pieces of the "Vine of the Dead" in the cauldron with *chacruna* leaves, alternating layers until it's brimming with plants. He incenses the cauldron with *mapacho*, singing softly as we watch the brew come to a boil.

"It will be many hours before the medicine is ready," Tingo says. "The tea will boil and become a thick brown syrup. I will tend it and you may watch, if you wish, or you may spend time among the plants.

"Sofia can guide you in the rainforest. You do not have to say anything special to the plants. You might thank them for their wisdom. Sing to them. Or just listen.

"There is food here but eat sparingly because the vine will cause you to purge. It is necessary so the *chacruna* can bring the visions. Drink as much water as you wish. Do not allow your body to become dry. Rest in the pavilion if you become tired."

Sofia and I go inside the ceremonial pavilion, leaving Tingo to tend the bubbling *ayahuasca*. Tingo's *mesa* is transformed.

It's covered by a woven runner intricately embroidered with *kené*. Sofia describes the treasures arrayed on the *mesa*—crystals, shells, *mapacho*, a carved wooden dish painted with the image of an anaconda filled with coca leaves, a bottle of perfume, a gourd rattle with the carved face of a snarling jaguar, a tapir bone whistle, a wristlet of red and black *huayruro* seeds, and a *chakapa*, a flat bundle of dried leaves bound with palm fibers, tipped with downy red, yellow, and azure *tsiri* feathers.

"We must not touch the objects," Sofia says. "They are sacred. My father may add some objects or remove some, depending upon what the spirits reveal as he tends the *ayahuasca*."

I'm surprised to see my *maneki-neko* on the *mesa*. Tingo has positioned the cat so it will face me as I lie on my platform. There's something comforting about its arm rhythmically beckoning.

My platform holds a thick woven mat covered with embroidered cloth, pillows, and a blanket. At the foot is a green five-gallon plastic bucket and a roll of toilet paper.

"To wipe your mouth during the purge of your upper body," Sofia explains. "For the lower purge, you will use the privies outside the pavilion."

The other platforms are bare. "Where will you rest?" I ask her.

"I will serve you and my father during the medicine ceremony," she says. "I can rest in that chair at the end of the *mesa* when I am not needed, and I can also nap on my father's platform.

"When it is time to drink the *ayahuasca*, you will come to the *mesa* and I will pour for you. You may drink however much you want—half a cup, a quarter of a cup, or let the spirits decide for you. They will know what you need and guide my arm as I pour."

"Sofia, did you hear my conversation with the *chuchuhuasi* teacher tree while you were gathering the plants for *ayahuasca*?"

"No. I see you brought one of her roots with you to the pavilion."

"I'm not sure if she made any actual sounds, but I heard her as clearly as I hear you now."

"I know the tree you are describing. A little way beyond the kapok where the 'Vine of the Dead' grows. I have listened to her when she is willing for me to hear. She does not speak often. She is one of the wisest of the trees, one of the five master teacher plants. Did she teach you her *ikaro*?"

"No. When I am ready, she said, she will teach me. The teacher tree knows my *janekon*. The *inos* told her. She said Grandmother *Aya* will show me the way. She told me this root will support me on my journey."

"It will help during the medicine ceremony, especially the purges," Sofia says. "It must be very special if the teacher tree gave it to you.

Chuchuhuasi is a potent medicine. She has honored you. *Chuchuhuasi* is the staff of *chamanes*."

Darkness is deepening as the sun dips past the western tree line. Sofia and I go back to the fire to check on Tingo. He's chanting, tending the fire, watching the medicine brew. It's become thicker and gives off an earthy herbal aroma.

"It will be ready by midnight," Tingo says. "I will brew it for two more hours, then I will remove the spent plants and allow the medicine to cool. I will pour it into the bottle I have brought and present the *ayuhausca* to the *mesa*. Then it will be time.

"You should bathe in the spring now and rest in the medicine pavilion for a couple of hours," Sofia says. "I will wake you when it is time to begin the ceremony."

The spring glows from within like the phosphorescent sea in the Gulf of Thailand that entranced me from the deck of the *Andaman Pearl*. My body drips light when I emerge. I put on my embroidered robe and tell Sofia about the flashing ocean. She says the spring is different.

"The water spirits bestow this light upon us but only on nights of the medicine ceremony. Other times the spring is dark, except for the light it gives back from the moon and stars."

She offers me a gourd filled with spring water.

"Drink this and we will return to the pavilion to sleep," she says. "Take the light of the water spirits inside you. Grandmother *Aya* demands all your strength and devotion. I will watch over you from my father's platform."

The *chuchuhuasi* staff is at the foot of my platform. I'm anxious now and hyperalert. I'm sure I will not sleep, but when I'm awakened by Sofia's gentle strokes on my arm, drizzles of moonlight fall through a few gaps in the thatched roof. Dozens of lighted candles flicker throughout the pavilion, casting a warm glow on the walls.

Tingo is sitting cross-legged on his mat behind the mesa dressed in a robe and hat emblazoned with kené. He wears a nose ornament that looks like the one Èlia wears. He's in a trance, rocking almost imperceptibly, chanting, and singing. Candles on the *mesa* bathe his face in flickering light.

Sofia approaches my mat and touches my forehead. "My father is journeying with the spirits, receiving their instructions," she says. "We will watch silently until he returns."

Moments later, Tingo opens his eyes. "It is time," he says, approaching the *mesa*. "The spirits welcome us."

He purifies the *mesa* with copious volumes of *mapacho* smoke. He tips a mouthful of *Agua de Florida* from a glass bottle into his mouth, a perfume made from millions of flower blossoms, and spritzes each of the candles on the *mesa* with a mist so fine it doesn't extinguish the flames. The scent of flowers and rich tobacco smoke suffuse the pavilion. I can only imagine that heaven smells like this.

Sofia takes my hand and leads me to the *mesa*. A glass bottle of nut-brown liquid and a small hollowed-out gourd rest at the center. The spirits decide on a quarter gourd for me.

The *ayahuasca* tastes better than I expected. It's thick and loamy, almost chewy. Smoky like the earth beneath a cooking fire with tinges of chocolate, pepper, and pungent herbs.

As I drink, Tingo purifies my platform, his own, and Sofia's chair with *mapacho* and *Agua de Florida*. A sweeter place for the spirits to convene I could not imagine.

I return to my mat and lie back on the pillow. As soon as I do, I burp. The aftertaste isn't pleasant. It's sulfurous, sepulchral, burning bitter in the back of my throat and nose.

I'm not looking forward to all the puking and shitting to come, but Sofia assures me it's necessary. "Grandmother *Aya* is jealous of other spirits," she says, "and will not tolerate them in your body, so she will kill them and cast them out."

As anxious as I am, I doze off and wake a couple of hours later with an irresistible urge to defecate. I pick up the *chuchuhuasi* staff from the foot of my platform, and Sofia follows me to the latrine where my bowels explode. She helps me remove my robe and hands me a roll of toilet paper, reassuring me as I sit on the rough seat over the pit, steadying myself with my staff. When the cramping subsides, we start back to the pavilion.

I don't make it that far. Back in the privy, the process repeats. I stay longer this time, waiting for the cramping to stop.

"That will be the worst of it from the lower part of your body," Sofia says solicitously. "Do you want to wash?"

We walk the short distance to the lucent spring, but I can't appreciate the magic of the light because of the churning in my gut. A wave of nausea engulfs me, sending me to the side of the path. I drop to my knees on the muddy ground, my staff beside me. Sofia hangs my robe on a nearby branch and brushes my hair back, holding my head as I vomit and retch until nothing further comes up. My throat burns and my eyes sting.

She brings a gourd of spring water. When I sip it, the vomiting begins anew. The first time I vomit, I'm certain I turn my stomach inside out. I hug my abdomen in pain. I hope the upper purge is over. After all, I have eaten little in the past twenty-four hours. But I'm just getting started.

The second wave of vomiting empties my lungs. Impossible, I know, but I'm certain of it. I clutch at my abdomen just below my ribs as the third wave empties my liver, the fourth my pancreas, the next my kidneys. Every organ in my body is being wrung dry. Grandmother *Aya* is ruthless. There's no hiding place. Anything that offends her doesn't stand a chance.

I struggle to my feet with Sophia's help and lean on my *chuchuhuasi* staff, hanging onto it with a death grip as she steadies me from behind. The top of my head blows off. My brain splatters into the rainforest beside the path, dripping from the branches overhead, sparkling like a million stars, each turning into a wriggling, incandescent baby anaconda.

The snakes dive back into my head and infest me, dividing like malignant cells, eating voraciously, devouring everything in their path.

I can see them inside me, splitting, slithering through my body like spermatozoa, piercing every cell they encounter as if they're ova to be fertilized. But they leave only emptied husks.

The spermatocondas escape from my pores, crawl from under my fingernails and toenails, erupt from every orifice of my body, puddle at my feet in a pool, shimmering like mercury in sunlight, mirroring the tessellations of néte, becoming Anaconda Woman, her skin emblazoned with *kené* mapping the cosmos. She wraps herself around me, constricting gently but insistently.

A powerful erotic cataract inundates my body, cascading over my breasts, spilling over my navel, drenching my vulva, thighs, and lower limbs. The intensity rachets to the tipping point, building toward ecstasy but refuses to resolve. I'm tortured on this plateau of desire for what seems like hours as I tremble and my limbs spasm uncontrollably against her unforgiving coils, striving for climax, shrieking scratchy vocalizations like a cat in heat.

Lagac is behind me, thrusting passionately, kissing my neck, wrapping me in his powerful arms. I cry out his name and tell him I love him. I hear him say he loves me, and I no longer doubt it. But release will not come and he abandons me again.

Anaconda Woman relaxes her grip, and the erotic feelings dissipate. "Lagac cannot descry you," the giant snake hisses. "He languishes in torment of losing you. The disturbance in *néte* hides you from him."

I feel cheated, wronged. I scream with rage and want to run as far from this place as possible, to find Lagac, but I'm powerless to move. Anaconda Woman releases me and whispers, "You must become accountable for the cosmic imbalance."

"Slowly," Sophia cautions, helping me walk, offering me cool spring water from a gourd. "Small sips." I leave my robe on the branch where

Sophia has hung it, and leaning on my *chuchuhuasi* staff, stumble back to the pavilion, falling naked onto my mat, my body trembling, exhausted.

She covers me with the blanket and smooths my hair back from my face. Her hand feels cool on my forehead. "Don't get up just now. You can use the green bucket if you need it, and I will empty it."

My body eases and I don't vomit again, but my grief at losing Lagac doesn't subside. After half an hour, the *maneki-neko* beckons me to the *mesa* again. Somehow I stumble forward. Tingo is sitting trance-like on his platform. Sofia pours me another quarter gourd of the molasses-like *ayahuasca*. The spirits have decided I need another dose.

"Drink," she says. "Take the doctors of the teacher plants inside you."

The medicine unexpectedly calms my stomach. I stumble to my mat where Anaconda Woman lies coiled under the platform, lying in wait to harrow me again.

I point my *chuchuhuasi* staff at her. "Leave me," I say. To my great surprise, she obeys and crawls into the timbers supporting the thatched roof over Tingo's platform.

Sofia helps me lie down, and I splay out on my back, legs akimbo, twitching like a stunned frog in a dissecting pan, vulnerable, and completely exhausted. She covers me and places the *chuchuhuasi* staff next to my body.

A fleeting thought comes into my mind. What if Grandmother *Aya* finds me unworthy, a risible physician with no powers like the Doctors of the Vine? No power like that of Grandmother *Aya* to purge anything that offends her?

I'm burning with fever and throw the blanket off. I'm little more than rape-bait, immobile, a foolish naked old woman chugging roofied drinks at a Green Hell dive bar. Nobody knows where I am and nobody cares.

As soon as the thoughts come, they vanish, leaving no fear or lingering trace. The thoughts are not true, but even if they were, they don't matter. Nothing matters.

Even if Anaconda Woman wishes me dead, it doesn't matter.

"*Ronin* sleeps and does not wish you dead," I hear Tingo for the first time since I took the medicine. I'm not sure he's speaking, but I hear him nonetheless.

Nobody loves me, and it doesn't matter. What the fuck? We all die. None of it matters.

"Grandmother *Aya* loves you and only wants you closer to death to cure you," Tingo says.

"Nobody loves you except Lagac, and he languishes in torment," Anaconda Woman says.

Tingo looks at me with lecherous eyes as I lie here vulnerable. I'm certain he's been lying to me all along."

"It doesn't matter," *Ronin* hisses. "He is a man, after all. Surely the shortcoming is neither his nor yours."

I hear Sofia's voice as in a dream. "I doubt he would take any special notice."

I must disgust her, writhing naked on my platform pining for Lagac. I want to touch myself, but I dare not for offending Grandmother *Aya*.

"It doesn't matter," *Ronin* says. "What can the girl child know of lust and yearning? The shortcoming is neither hers nor yours."

Of course Tingo isn't looking at me with lecherous eyes, and I don't disgust Sofia. Why are these evil thoughts contaminating my mind?

"It doesn't matter," *Metsá Ino* purrs.

"Tingo and Sofia are communing with the spirits. Anaconda Woman is sleeping. Nobody's watching except Grandmother *Aya* and *inos*," *Pedro Bello* says. "You need not be ashamed or afraid."

The jaguars nuzzle me and lick my face. "The doctors of the teacher plants will heal you," *Metsá Ino* says.

Sofia comes to my platform and kisses my forehead. She retrieves the blanket and tucks it tightly around me to ward off the shivering. I'm drenched with sweat and kick the blanket off again. I look at the *mesa*. The objects Tingo has placed there are alive, radiating color and exchanging places with each other. *My maneki-neko* floats toward me, the arm beckoning.

I try to focus on Tingo, meditating and chanting *ikaros* behind his *mesa*. Anaconda Woman has draped herself over his shoulders. She's much smaller now, her skin a shimmering jewel box, her sage-green eyes closed, as are Tingo's. He glows, his skin also flashing jewels, the two of them pulsing together in synchronicity, like the fireflies in the Pasir Ris mangroves.

Tingo opens his eyes and so does *Ronin*. He lifts her from his body and stretches her along the *mesa*.

"*Ronin* is too small to harm us," he says.

He approaches my platform, enveloping me in clouds of *mapacho,* more reassuring than any clothing or blanket. He takes a mouthful of *Agua de Florida* and sprays a fine mist over my body. I feel each of the million flowers clearly, anchoring themselves, taking root, blossoming from my skin—collective realms of them, concrescent gardens, animated lovechildren from the paint pots of Kahlo and Van Gogh, O'Keeffe and Glaser. It's so unexpected and exhilarating. I giggle like a schoolgirl. I have never been so beautiful.

Tingo removes the tapir bone whistle from the *mesa* and blows ear-splitting blasts to the four corners of the world, alerting the spirits. He shakes his *chakapa* over my body, passing from my head to my feet, the rustle of dry leaves like the first *ikaro* I ever heard from a teacher tree.

He returns to his platform behind the *mesa* and motions Sofia to join him, enveloping her in *mapacho* as she lies beside him on the mat. He cradles her in his arms, his beloved child, and sleep comes instantly for them.

I'm passionately awake. Dust motes dance in kaleidoscopic arrays, illuminated by shafts of moonlight spilling through gaps in the thatched roof. My *maneki-neko* floats in a shard of light before me as I lie there, inviting me to follow.

The jaguars are alert now, nudging me off my mat. The three of us follow the *maneki-neko* as it slips through a gap in the roof into the heavens where the stars have rearranged themselves into rosettes like the ones on the jaguars' fur.

I look back and see myself asleep on my platform in the medicine pavilion, billions of miles from where the jaguars and I have journeyed into the jungle. I could not possibly be dreaming.

We're in a clearing in some unfamiliar rainforest, standing before a bonfire. Sparks explode into pink dolphins, piraña, *tsiri* birds, jaguars, blue morpho butterflies, *caimanes*, sloths, tapirs, uakari monkeys with their blazing red bald heads, peacock bass, purple tarantulas with pink toes, marmosets, blue and gold macaws, and countless other creatures I don't recognize.

Ikaros from the exuberant assembly of teacher plants ringing the clearing fill the air, intercalating into the tapestry of animals, creating pointillist eddies, rearranging, resolving into labyrinthine *kené* woven into a cloak draping an ageless body, a crone striding out of the blackness toward me, Anaconda Woman resting on her shoulders.

I am beyond terrified.

"Jessamyn Quilter," she says, her voice shimmering like a polished sword drawn from a block of dry ice. "Have you come to die at my hand?"

I have no answer to her question.

"You may no longer live, Jessamyn Quilter. The evil you have created has unbalanced *néte*. Do you choose to be accountable and die at my hand? Or do you choose for Anaconda Woman to kill you and take the evil inside her as she has done since the beginning of time? What do you answer?"

The choice now seems absurdly simple.

"Grandmother *Aya*. Jessamyn Quilter, whose evil has unbalanced the cosmos, comes to die at your hand."

I don't know why I answered her this way, how I had the courage to answer her at all. I don't know how I have unbalanced *néte,* but if

Grandmother *Aya* and Anaconda Woman declare I have, it's foolish to deny it.

The *chuchuhuasi* teacher tree says I'll not die but become accountable and atone. The jaguars stand with Grandmother *Aya* and have promised to help me. They've given me my *janekon*. I am *ino*. I am of their clan.

Grandmother *Aya* recedes from my vision, leaving empty blackness in her wake. "This is the beginning of death and transfiguration," *Metsá Ino* says, although I can neither see nor feel him. "Come," *Pedro Bello* says, picking me up by the neck like a jaguar cub.

When I awake on my mat in the medicine pavilion, I'm alone. The jaguars have gone. The artifacts Tingo placed on the *mesa* are gone. Only my *maneki-neko*, with his beckoning arm, remains.

Sofia enters the pavilion. "We should bathe and eat," she says. "My father has gone to the village but will return tonight for another *aya* medicine ceremony.

I don't feel as bad as I think I should, given the events of the night, but my heart skips a beat at the thought of a second encounter with Grandmother *Aya* and Anaconda Woman. And my heart aches for Lagac. How can I have doubted he loves me?

Metsá Ino and *Pedro Bello* reappear and are once again at my side as I retrieve my *chuchuhuasi* staff and follow Sofia to the spring. My robe is still hanging on the branch where I left it last night, and I put it on after we have bathed.

Sofia has prepared some vegetable broth for breakfast. I'm starving, but I remember enough to know Grandmother *Aya* will purge even the most benign plant spirits from my body again tonight without mercy, to prepare for my death.

Sofia insists, and I drink a small amount of the broth. I'm resigned to doing as I'm told. It's futile to do otherwise. I'm resigned to death at Grandmother *Aya's* hand. I don't know what comes next. Perhaps nothing.

It doesn't matter. ∎

45

Death

Peruvian Amazon   November 9

Tingo has returned and repurposed his *mesa* for tonight's encounter with Grandmother *Aya*. He's covered it with a different cloth. The *kené* are not as colorful, mostly blue and black with an occasional splash of red.

Some artifacts he used last night are back on the *mesa*—the leafy *chakapa,* the whistle, the bowl of *coca* leaves, the crystals, the bottle of *Agua de Florida* and *mapacho.* I see my *maneki-neko* where it rested, beckoning last night.

"My father has made a fan from feathers of the *kana*, namesake of my *janekon*, the blue and gold macaw," Sofia says, pointing out a fresh addition to the *mesa.* "He honors me," she says with downcast eyes.

"He loves you very much, and you are vital to his work," I say. "No false modesty now. I'm sure Grandmother *Aya* wouldn't have it."

Sofia giggles. "It's just a bird," she says. "Not very special. Like my *janekon*, a 'nice blue and gold macaw.'"

"I don't see the *ayahuasca*."

"My father has it with him for safekeeping," Sofia says. "He would not want evil spirits tempting us to speak with the Grandmother without his guidance."

It's my turn to giggle. "Like we'd want to take that jealous old woman on without his help? Not a chance."

Sofia has tidied up the pavilion, arranged the platforms and their mats, pillows, and blankets. The green bucket at the end of mine is clean and shining, and there's a fresh roll of toilet paper. No need for explanations tonight.

"Let's bathe and prepare for the medicine ceremony," she says. "You should drink some spring water."

We wash in the spring, now glowing faintly with the light of the water spirits, and dress as the sun is disappearing. Night is coming more quickly than I expected.

When we return to the medicine pavilion, Tingo has illuminated the interior and the *mesa* with candles and is meditating on his platform. I recognize fragments of the *ikaro* against fear and the *ikaro* of welcome and homage to jaguars. *Metsá Ino* and *Pedro Bello* flank the mesa, sitting on their haunches.

Tingo has returned the bottle of *ayahuasca* and the gourd to the *mesa*. All is in readiness for my death.

Sofia accompanies me to my platform and kisses me softly on the cheek. I blink back tears as I bask in her tenderness, remembering Lovely and Èlia, Shun and Shantrelle, Eric—my friends from the *Andaman Pearl*.

And Lagac. My wondrous Lagac.

I remove my robe and hang it from a peg next to my platform. Those who are about to die require no clothing, nor do those who are about to be born. I lay the *chuchuhuasi* staff beside me as I recline on the mat and close my eyes, allowing Tingo's chanting to pass through me.

He purifies the *mesa* with *mapacho* and *Agua de Florida*. He blankets me with smoke and spritzes me with a mouthful of the flowery perfume. I'm trying to be brave, but I'm terrified.

He returns to the platform and continues to chant. At last he summons me to the *mesa*. Sofia pours me the measure of *ayahuasca* the spirits have decided I require. I swallow it quickly and return to my mat. The medicine tastes familiar, and that's comforting. I have done this before—there's nothing to fear. I focus on the ever-beckoning *mane-ki-neko* and fall asleep.

I wake with gut-wrenching cramps and hurry to the latrine. Sofia follows as she did last night, singing the *ikaro* against fear. It sounds gentler, more reassuring in her voice than it does when Tingo sings it. When I'm finished, Sofia and I go again to the spring where I repeat last night's upper purging. This time there are no sparkling snakes, just vomit. Nothing out of the ordinary.

I wonder if the medicine is working as it should. Has Grandmother *Aya* abandoned me? We walk back to the medicine pavilion and Sofia straightens my bedding as I lie back on the platform. The jaguars are sleeping now. Tingo and Sofia curl up together on his mat as the candles flicker and die down. I feel very alone.

Suddenly both jaguars leap onto my platform, baring their teeth, hissing. I have never seen them behave this way before, and my skin crawls. Surely they intend to kill me. I pee all over myself.

Metsá Ino disappears and *Pedro Bello* grabs my neck, dangling me from his powerful jaws as if I were prey. He leaps through a crevice in the thatched roof into the blackness.

We're back in the rainforest clearing I remember from last night. He drops me to the ground, and I sit up, my breathing labored. I check my body for damage but find none.

Pedro Bello backs away and stands at the edge of the clearing, his gaze fixing me in place. A dozen more jaguars emerge from the rainforest, ringing the clearing, watching me intently.

The jaguars snarl in chorus. *Pedro Bello* steps forward.

"Jessamyn Quilter, what have you done?"

Metsá Ino crashes out of the rainforest into the circle of jaguars, a man's body dangling limply from his teeth. He drops it at my feet and steps back a pace.

I would scream if I had breath. It's Roderick's body, naked, dead in the same aspect as I "discovered" him on the bathroom floor. The clearing morphs into my bathroom in Massachusetts, identical down to its tile floor on which Roderick's body lies. I'm kneeling beside him on speakerphone.

"911. What is your emergency?"

"My husband's not breathing! I think he had a heart attack. I'm doing CPR."

"Just keep doing that, ma'am. What's your address?"

"It's 1237 Maple Court in Westbury. I can't find a pulse."

Anaconda Woman slithers across the bathroom tile. "Jessamyn Quilter," she hisses, "are you accountable?"

"Yes. Oh god, yes." I look up at Grandmother *Aya*, watching from the firmament. "I killed him. I am accountable for stealing his life."

"You may no longer live, Jessamyn Quilter, since you are accountable for the evil that has unbalanced *néte*," Grandmother *Aya* says. "You are dead at my hand."

There's nothing now but blackness. Void.

I see my body light years away in the medicine pavilion, lying on my platform. Tingo and Sofia are standing over me. Tingo bathes me with *mapacho* and passes the *chakapa* over me, singing the *ikaro* of the "Vine of the Dead."

Sofia touches my head with the macaw-feather fan, flutters it over my body and touches it to my feet. She pulls the blanket up to my neck.

Tingo destroys the silence with the tapir bone whistle, four blasts to the four corners of the world. He returns to the *mesa* and pours *ayahuasca* into the gourd but doesn't offer it to me to drink. Instead, he dips his finger into the brown liquid and paints my face with *kené*, singing the *ikaro* of the *chacruna*.

I am punch drunk, out of body, suffocating in some unrelenting vortex. A blur of pink dolphins swirls around me, but they offer no aid. I hear Tingo's whistle quavering in the background, galaxies away.

Metsá Ino drags me out of the whirlpool, gasping for breath, back to the clearing and disappears. The universe is extinguished. There is nothing but oblivion. I am hovering over the abyss. ∎

46

Transfiguration

R oderick's corpse lies at my feet. The jaguars guard the clearing, watching from a respectful distance. Above me, Grandmother *Aya's* face betrays no emotion, her eyes distant, reflecting starlight and the vastness of *néte.*

Peruvian Amazon   November 9

Roderick stirs. I am no longer gobsmacked by these impossible events. Merely startled. He sits bolt upright.

"What are you doing here?" he demands.

He's his usual prickly, entitled self, even dead. I determine not to indulge him. Before I killed him, I would have answered his question in a way designed to deflect anger. But I no longer care.

"The question is, what are *you* doing here? I killed you and scattered your ashes in the sea," I say, my fingers twitching, balling into fists to keep them still.

So what if he's angry? I'm beyond angry. I'm furious about his arrogance and his usual lack of empathy for what I might feel. I'm also beyond afraid. Fear laced with anger is a dangerous cocktail. I'm both shaken and stirred.

Maybe I'm overreacting. After all, he's dead. And so am I. But I'm unstrung by this immersion into the spirit world, despite knowing Grandmother *Aya,* who has just presided over my death, watches from above, and my jaguars have promised to help me.

Roderick seems oblivious to their presence, or if he notices, he doesn't care. Jaguars can't kill someone who's already dead. I remember my purpose here, tamp down my anger, and swallow my pain.

"I came to atone," I say, my eyes downcast, not fully believing I'm speaking the words but knowing it's what I must do. "To apologize. To tell you how sorry I am. To tell you I understand what I did to you was evil. To tell you how much I wish I had not done what I did. I am accountable, and I need to set the universe to rights."

"Atone for what?

"For killing you."

"I was not aware you killed me."

"How could you not be aware of that?"

"I know only that I am dead. I did not know you had anything to do with it. It's a much less difficult passage than I would have thought, going from life to death. Like being born, I remember nothing about it. How did you kill me?"

"I poisoned your stiffy medicine."

"That was imaginative."

"I took your life, something that did not belong to me."

"Did you get away with it?"

"As far as the world is concerned, yes. It was the perfect murder. But I upset the cosmic balance, and I'm accountable and must atone. I can no longer be the Jessamyn Quilter who killed you and got away with it. That's why I'm here."

"As you please. I know nothing of accountability or atonement. They are of no importance to me."

"Are you not angry with me? I'm furious with you. You took something from me too. You stole my joy and destroyed my passion for life. You tortured my spirit and almost snuffed it out. You pushed DeShawn Williams to kill himself. I killed you for him and to get away from you, from your abuse. I didn't understand, but I do now. Do you not care that I murdered you for what you did?"

366

"No."

"Do you not care that I wish I had killed you years ago? That I'm overwhelmed with guilt for what I've done while at the same time wishing I had done it sooner?"

"No"

"Don't you care I stole many years of life from you?"

"I died when it was my time to die. That's when we all die. When it's our time. The dead don't care what the living did or will do, about your guilt or suffering, about accountability or atonement. The dead care nothing about the living."

"You're not angry?"

"The dead are not angry. We don't know anger or joy. Being dead is something altogether different."

"Do you forgive me, then?"

"No. The dead do not forgive or withhold forgiveness. They do not engage in retribution. The living must sort that out for themselves."

I'm bewildered. I have a passionate interest in retribution and forgiveness. Roderick has none. I must be a different kind of dead than he is.

"Tell me about the dead," I ask.

"There is nothing to tell. Little is different for me between life and death except that the living no longer annoy me. The dead must labor, as the living must, but our labor affects nothing. It makes no difference to the living or the dead, to those who are neither, nor to those who are both."

"What has your labor produced?"

"I have solved the Novikov conjecture. No one will ever know, not even Novikov, who probably isn't dead yet. Even if he is, the dead do not encounter one another. I am alone."

I experience an inexplicable moment of happiness for Roderick. All he has wanted to do since I've known him is solve the Novikov conjecture.

"Congratulations. Has solving the Novikov made you happy?"

"No. Happiness is for the living. I have always known I would solve the Novikov, just not that the solution would come to me while I'm dead."

"What can I do to atone for killing you?"

"Nothing. I know nothing of atonement, but you won't find answers among the dead. If you are finished, other labor awaits me. If you are not, it still awaits me."

Roderick's corpse slumps to the ground. *Metsá Ino* grabs his body, drags it into the undergrowth, and disappears.

Pedro Bello stands guard as the other jaguars return to the rainforest. "What now?" I ask him. "How will I atone?"

"The Jessamyn Quilter accountable for the imbalance in *néte* is dead at the hand of Grandmother *Aya*. The dead cannot atone. The Jessamyn Quilter who lives will find the path of atonement desired by Grandmother *Aya* who cherishes her."

I try to wrap my head around what *Pedro Bello* has just said. I can't.

"You are *ino*," he says. "*Ino* do not need to atone. When *inos* kill, it is right. *Inos* kill to survive. To eat or to escape peril. You killed your unworthy mate because he imperiled you. The cub that came into you by him was also imperiled and chose not to live rather than be born. You sacrificed the joy of other cubs by him to save them from peril. Your sacrifice was the business of *inos*, the sacrifice of purity, nobility, and majesty. The business also of *chamanas*.

"Your dead mate reeks in *Metsá Ino*'s mouth as he returns him to his realm. His foulness remains in all our mouths because all *inos* are part of *ino*. Grandmother *Aya* and Anaconda Woman do not require *Metsá Ino* to be accountable. The Jessamyn Quilter who died at the hand of Grandmother *Aya* was accountable. *Metsá Ino* will find atonement in service to their kind."

I feel a profound sense of loss layered over with a hopefulness I haven't experienced for decades. I'm floored by *Pedro Bello's* next words.

"Your mate will find you soon, *Metsá Ino*. He is worthy of you. Grandmother *Aya*, the mother of the universe, does these things in her own time.

"Now you must sleep, *Metsá Ino*," he says. "*Inos* require lots of sleep."

The dawn approaches as I lie on my mat in the medicine pavilion. Grandmother *Aya* watches overhead, her face serene through the now transparent thatched roof, her eyes reflecting the first glimmerings of sunrise.

"You have done well, *Metsá Ino*," she says. "The balance is restored. The evil within Jessamyn Quilter died at my hand and no longer imperils you. Your path to atonement is the path of the shaman. Purity of spirit, nobility of purpose, and majesty of service.

"The *ino*s, the teacher plants, and wise beings of your kind will be powerful allies. *Néte* will remember your name long after you no longer live in your world."

"Shall I also atone as Jessamyn Quilter who still lives in that world, even as one Jessamyn Quilter is dead at your hand and another is born? Shall I confess to a priest, a police officer, or a judge? Shall I plead for penance or punishment?"

"That is of your choosing. The world knows nothing of the killing. Atonement is the work of a lifetime, and you have much time left. The evil is consumed. Anaconda Woman no longer has pending business with Jessamyn Quilter, but she may be an ally to *Metsá Ino* if she chooses. For now, farewell, Beautiful Jaguar."

She vanishes, in a cloud of *mapacho* and *Agua de Florida*.

At least I think it was her, but I'm no longer certain of anything. As I open my eyes, Sofia is enrobing my body with *mapacho* and Tingo is offering *Agua de Florida* to the four corners of the world.

I dress, we eat fruit and manioc/banana gruel, and we talk quietly about the medicine ceremony. *Metsá Ino* and *Pedro Bello* rest at the edge of the clearing. We sing them the *ikaro* of welcome and homage to jaguars.

"We do not need to visit Grandmother *Aya* again," Tingo says. "We must find lodging for you in the village now that you have completed your *dieta* and medicine ceremonies.

"We have heard Grandmother *Aya* calling you to become a *chamana*. I will teach you what I know, as I am teaching Sofia, since that is what the Grandmother designs for you. The teacher plants will instruct you, as it pleases them.

"We must also consider your return to Iquitos. I have heard they are eagerly awaiting word of you at La Casa Morey. Of course, you will always be welcome in our village, but you may be called to travel more paths than one."

I can't imagine what that means, but I'm certain Grandmother *Aya,* the jaguars, and the teacher plants know exactly what they are doing. And Anaconda Woman. I know better than to second guess any of them. ■

47

Metsá Ino

The arduous work of atonement is made more difficult by the struggle to find the path. The work with Tingo and Sofia has been miraculous. I've learned so much about this rainforest culture and the experiences that nourish it. Beliefs and customs, successes and failures, life and death weave themselves into *kené*, illuminating the tapestry that instructs, interprets, supports, and transforms.

Tingo reminds me from time to time that I bring as much to the rainforest as I take from it. That is sometimes hard for me to accept. Where I fit here, if at all, is still an open question.

In the short time I've been living among these delightful people, I've become a part of their lives and they of mine. The women encourage me, teaching me to paint, embroider, and weave. Spirits have blessed my hands, they say. The same fine motor skills that allow me to stitch up wounds work to my advantage embroidering *kené*.

I have sometimes been able to provide life-saving medical interventions that have been outside the reach of *curanderas,* thanks to Tingo retrieving my medical bag. I wonder if I might teach them something of my craft.

The teacher plants continue to share with me and provide ongoing lessons in humility. Tingo has incorporated me into his *ayuhausca* rituals. I have become a world-class expert on purging. As a physician, I speculate about the visions. I wonder, for example, if they are affected by electrolyte imbalance brought on by the purging itself as well as the properties of the entheogens, the psychoactive chemicals in the plants that put us in touch with the mystical.

As a shaman's apprentice, I believe in entheogens utterly. Shamans and physicians may sometimes see things through differing eyes, but it's foolish to follow one path to the exclusion of the other.

Icing on the cake, the jaguars have been showing me what it means to be *ino*. *Ino* is a state of being, not just the *janekon* of a magnificent apex predator. If humans could behave like *ino*, there would be less trouble in the world, less conflict, and no meaningless violence.

I've been traveling downriver with Tingo on his excursions to the Pink Dolphin Rainforest Lodge and Iquitos. I see the river—the piraña, the *caimanes,* the pink dolphins, the *Victoria Regia* lilies—with the fresh eyes of my heart.

Huanc is always at my beck and call in Iquitos with his gleaming Camry. Luz and Guillermo spoil me at La Casa Morey.

I have begun to write copiously in my journal. I know I have a story to tell even if it's as yet shapeless and incomplete. It won't be the romance novel I contemplated before beginning my journey on the *Andaman Pearl*. It will be something altogether different.

This morning, my computer announces a videoconference request from Shun. It's been too long in coming. I run my fingers through my hair and make myself as presentable as possible.

"Shun! I'm so happy to see you."

"I'm hearing great things about you on the jungle telegraph, Jessamyn. You look amazing. Shantrelle sends her love."

"I've wanted to call you many times, but it never seemed to be the right moment. What do you hear from Lovely and Èlia?"

"Lovely calls us now and then and threatens to subject me to the latest Parisian perversions she has discovered the next time she, Èlia, and Shantrelle get me alone. Èlia's homesick, but she is killing it at the conservatory. They both are. Èlia's family is happy and well, living on the outskirts of Pilpintuwasi around Padre Cocha."

"I miss those young women, but I know they must spread their wings."

"That's what I wanted to talk about. Their agent is so excited about their music he has booked a concert gig at the famous Manaus Opera House in Brazil Manaus a few days from now."

"I just have to see them," I say, unable to sit still. "How far away is Manaus?"

"Only 900 miles downriver from you. You could be there in a leisurely two and a half days by ferry, if everything goes according to plan, surrounded by villagers taking their pigs and bananas to market. I hear it's first come, first served for the hammocks strung across the deck." Shun seems barely able to contain his mirth.

"How long would it take to fly?" I ask, my face the picture of innocence.

"That depends. Anywhere from eighteen hours to a day and change on LATAM airlines, stopping in Lima and São Paulo. Or I could beg my queen for the *Ratu Shantrelle*. The big plane could make the trip in about ninety minutes."

"I remember how much you like begging, you bad boy," I tease him.

"Tell you what. I need to check on business in Lima, and we could stop in Iquitos on the way to Manaus. We can pick you up and whoever wants to come from Èlia's family. We can have one big party like Manaus hasn't seen since the days of the rubber barons."

"That's so exciting, Shun. Do you think we might have room for a couple of extras?"

"Sure. Who do you have in mind?"

"My teachers. Tingo and his daughter Sofia."

"Great. I'll have Ignacio, who you know from Lima, make the arrangements and coordinate with Huanc in Iquitos. We'll ask someone from our São Paulo office to smooth the path for us in Manaus."

"Is Shantrelle coming?"

"She wouldn't miss it for anything. Did I tell you we're having a baby?"

"What! Of course you didn't tell me, you little shit. When?"

Shun giggles. "Shantrelle's about twenty weeks. It's a girl."

"I'm just overwhelmed with all this good news, Shun. I've missed you so much, and yet I've had this feeling you were with me all the time. Will you be spending any time at La Casa Morey? It's a magical place, as you know."

"Unfortunately, no. Press of business and all that, but say hello to Luz for me. If you haven't had her hot chocolate, you must do so without delay."

"You're right. She's a love, and her hot chocolate has become something of an addiction, for me as well as Don Mateo. I dream about it when I'm in the rainforest drinking whatever jungle brew's on offer there."

"Are your jaguars well?"

"I can't tell you what they mean to me. They rarely leave my side, and they drag me to places even you wouldn't believe."

"They're always welcome in Shantrelle's plane."

"I don't think I could go anywhere without them. If I did, they'd find me whenever they wanted. But Shun...what do you hear about Lagac?"

"He's fine. He hit a rough spot after he lost you to Rajaratman and his thugs. He knows you're okay, but he couldn't forgive himself for not protecting you. He quit the merchant marine and went back to live at his father's place in Cebu, but he's in touch with Lovely off and on. Maybe she can tell you more when you see her. Just be aware that she's playing matchmaker, trying to coax him out of his shell."

"That sounds like Lovely. I'll have to speak to her about that."

"Gotta go, Jessamyn. Hugs and kisses, real ones soon, okay?"

"Soon. Very soon. Love to Shantrelle. Bye-bye."

The tears I wipe from my eyes are pure liquid joy. I can't wait to see my old friends from the *Andaman Pearl*. I'll have to badger Lovely for news about her father and the rest of the crew. Especially Lagac.

When I catch up with Tingo, he already knows what's afoot and has told Èlia's family. "Day after tomorrow, right?" Sofia asks.

Why do they always know things like this before I do? The jungle telegraph is nothing if not reliable.

Huanc confirms he'll take Tingo, Sofia, and me to the airport in the Camry, and Ignacio has arranged for a shuttle to pick up Èlia's family across town at Bellavista Nanay.

Early the next morning, Shun waits for us at the airport with the shiny big plane, *Ratu Shantrelle*. Amid many introductions, hugs, and kisses, he shepherds us all aboard like a mother hen. The jaguars have gone on ahead, to commandeer the choice sleeping spots.

None of the rainforest people have ever flown before. All of them join Tingo and Sofia in chanting the *ikaro* for a safe arrival and the *ikaro* against fear. When Sofia learns Shantrelle is pregnant, she sings her the *ikaro* to protect baby in the womb.

Cars are waiting when we touch down in Manaus to take everyone to the Hotel Villa Amazônia in the old town, a block's walk from the famous Teatro Amazonas where we'll enjoy tomorrow's concert.

"Jessamyn," Shun says. "There's something I would like to show you before you settle in." A driver takes the two of us to a heliport a few minutes away. Shun is tight-lipped.

"What's with all the secrecy?" I ask as we pull up to a medevac helicopter, gleaming white with red crosses. "Is something wrong? Someone ill?"

"No. Everything's fine. Don't worry. Have you ever flown in a helicopter?"

"No. What would I be doing in a helicopter?"

He smiles and gestures toward the chopper.

"You'll see. Come on," he says, helping me aboard, giving the pilot a thumbs up. The jaguars squeeze in at our feet. They're not about to miss out on anything that smacks of adventure.

We fly south across the city until we reach the Rio Negro. We follow the river eastward to the confluence with the Amazon halfway to the Atlantic ocean 900 miles away. We hover midway across the water.

"The indigenous people call this the 'Meeting of the Waters,'" Shun says. "The black water is the Rio Negro, and the brown water next to it is the Amazon. They flow alongside each other for another six kilometers before they gradually mix, the Amazon swallowing up the Rio Negro. Amazing, no?" he says as the chopper pilot retraces his path along the southern rim of Manaus.

Shun points out other interesting sights, but I can't imagine he has brought me here just to look at rivers, magnificent though they are. Our flight path turns north again, over the Port of Manaus, and the pilot takes us closer to the water.

Shun points to a large white ship docked at a pier, painted with red crosses on the accommodation and hull. We approach and descend toward the ship's helipad.

"Are we actually going to land on that thing?" I ask.

"Easy, peasy," he says.

The ship looks familiar. I glimpse a jaguar painted on the stern as the chopper approaches and sets down with barely a bump. The ship's name painted beneath the jaguar is *Metsá Ino*, Beautiful Jaguar.

When the rotors stop turning, Shun gets out and helps me down. And it hits me. I know most of the people on deck waiting to greet us. The jaguars bound over to check them out but sniffing no danger they run along, exploring.

"Permission to come aboard, Captain?" Shun asks, grinning from ear to ear.

"Permission granted," he answers. The captain of the hospital ship *Metsá Ino* is Eric Reyes, former second officer of the *MV Andaman Pearl*. Shun takes my arm and escorts me toward Eric who gives me a big hug.

"Welcome home, Jessamyn. We've missed you."

Standing just behind him, grinning like a lunatic during a full moon, is Lagac. He rushes over with a bear hug and a kiss. He has tears in his eyes. I wipe them away and melt into his arms.

The owner's cabin is just as I left it. How did they get my silly *maneki-neko* in here without my knowing it? I'll have a tour of the ship, with its state-of-the-art diagnostic and surgical suites, laboratories, clinics, and hospital later, but now Eric, Lagac, and Shun are filling in the missing pieces.

After the kidnapping and hijacking of the *Andaman Pearl* off the coast of Somalia, Andaman World Marine discovered the treachery within its ranks. Fearing massive liability, they disbanded the crew in Rotterdam and planned to scrap the ship.

Shun and Shantrelle created a Singapore based foundation, *Metsá Ino* Health System, and bought the *Andaman Pearl* for one Philippine peso, less than two United States pennies. They re-flagged her under the Red Ensign of Singapore, transformed her into a hospital ship, and moved her across the Atlantic to Manaus to complete refitting, where she will be a resource in times of disaster from Cape Horn to the Caribbean.

They offered the crew of the former *Andaman Pearl* employment on the *Metsá Ino* in the new world. Captain Bayani declined, retiring to spend time with his wife and teach cello to young musicians in Manila.

They promoted Eric to captain and the handsome junior deck officer to second in command. The cook, the messman, and Lagac remained with the ship whose cargo would soon be more precious than anything it had ever carried.

"Other crew will sign on, pending your approval," Shun says.

"My approval?"

"If you want it, Jessamyn, the *Metsá Ino* is yours," Shun says. "Well, it's really the Foundation's, but you get to do whatever you want as chief medical officer. Or maybe you would rather be the *chamana*. A board seat goes with the offer, so you won't be layered over."

"Yes, of course I want it."

"Good. In that case, we have a few folks waiting next door for a little welcome home reception."

As we enter the saloon, Lovely and Èlia strike up a triumphal march for four hands on the Bösendorfer. Crepe paper garlands and balloons festoon the ceiling and a chocolate ganache cake, decorated with a white fondant silhouette of the ship and the words "Welcome Home, Jessamyn!" grace a table set with nibbles and iced champagne. I haven't had cake for ages, and I'm looking forward to indulging without fear it will upset Grandmother *Aya*. I wonder if the cacao teacher tree might someday teach me her *ikaro*.

Shun saunters over to Shantrelle and stands behind her, hands on the back of her chair.

I cannot ignore demands for a speech.

"Dear friends. Dear, dear sneaky friends."

Polite laughter.

"I cannot tell you what this moment means to me. It's the end, or perhaps the beginning, of a long personal journey. And I promise to bore you with the details over and over as my dotage progresses."

Lovely starts to say something, probably inappropriate, but Èlia shushes her.

"It appears we are being given a chance to embark on a profoundly important mission to bring love and healing to people who might otherwise suffer and die. What greater privilege can we have than that?

"I don't know how it's all supposed to go, and I will be grateful for your wisdom and guidance along the way, but I know I want to do this, whatever this is, more than I have ever wanted anything in my life."

I pause to blink back tears. I imagine myself home at last, in the cabin next door, that I booked so many months ago in Yokohama to begin this voyage. A transit across continents and cultures and circumstances. An ongoing quest to know who I was, who I am, and who I am supposed to be.

"Thank you, Shun. Thank you, Shantrelle. Thank you Lovely and Èlia. Eric, officers and crew, thank you. Thank you all. Thank you, thank you, thank you."

I catch Lagac's eye across the room as everyone applauds. *Thank you too,* I mouth, my hands on my heart.

I can't wait to tour the engine room again with him and thank him in ways only he and I know. The *chuchuhuasi* teacher plant has taught me the *ikaro* to give man's strength and energy to his woman, although I doubt Lagac needs it.

Why are my jaguars flanking him?

"He is your new mate," *Pedro Bello* says. "He is *Metsá Ino.*"

Lovely, Èlia, Shantrelle, and Shun stay behind as Lagac shepherds everyone else out. I hug and kiss them, tears again welling up in my eyes, and listen to them jabber over each other about many things, large and small.

"These two," Shun says, gesturing to Lovely and Èlia, "are staying on the ship, ostensibly to practice and get ready for their concert tomorrow. No sense risking someone leading them astray at some wild party in Manaus. Shantrelle is supposed to chaperone and make sure they get plenty of sleep."

Lovely is still smothering me with kisses. "Stay with us, Jessamyn," she pleads. "Girls' night out!"

"Do you want to stay the night?" Shun asks. "We can chopper you all over to the concert tomorrow, or I'll take you back to the hotel now, whichever you prefer."

"You couldn't get me off my ship right now if you had the entire friggin' *al-Shabaab* army at your back," I say.

"The booking agent has a platoon of security officers aboard to look after those two, so everyone will be safe," Shun says, gesturing toward Lovely and Èlia. "For some reason, he thinks these two are serious artists who might make him rich someday, not just a couple of flighty schoolgirls."

"Be good now, Shun," Shantrelle says. "Can you stay with us too?"

"Unfortunately, no. I need to get back and see that our other important guests are settled and being well taken care of. Èlia, your parents are eager to see you. Lovely, I just heard from Eric that your father and mother arrived about an hour ago. I'll see everyone at the concert tomorrow evening and the triumphal afterparty."

"Shun, a word before you go, please?" I say. "I'll catch up with the rest of you in a few minutes."

The three women retreat to Lovely's cabin across the alley.

"I don't know what to say, Shun. I'm just so overwhelmed."

"I'm happy you are safe with us. And I'm delighted that you will be staying here, in this part of the world where so many need the help you and the crew can provide."

"It's strange. Despite everything going on during my journey I have often thought about poor Mrs. Agarwal, and of course, Mr. Agarwal. I don't know why, but I wonder what his life is like. Is he still in prison?"

"I don't think it strange at all. Both you and Mr. Agarwal are embarked upon journeys of transfiguration. All of us are. I think you called it a 'transit.'"

"Shun, I should confess something to you, something terrible I did before booking passage on the *Andaman Pearl*. Something so terrible I have only just begun to wrestle with the magnitude of my transgression."

"I don't need you to tell me what you were running away from when you left New England, if that's what you have in mind, " he says, "what you are atoning for. I don't doubt your word that it was 'terrible,' but since you already know that what value could I add?"

I look over at the jaguars lying on my bed regarding me with equanimity. If they have an opinion about my awkward attempts to confess to Shun, they don't let on.

"The two of you are of no help at all."

Pedro Bello yawns and closes his eyes. *Metsá Ino* also decides a nap is in order. *Inos* require lots of sleep.

"You must remember I did not arrange for Mr. Agarwal's incarceration to punish him or force him to confess his evil deeds," Shun continues. "I put him in prison to stop him from doing the same thing again.

"He believed Islam mandated him to cause suffering, even death, to his wife. He thought it was right, but it was not. It was evil. If he had not come to understand he was wrong, what would have stopped him from doing the same thing to another woman, damning his own soul in the process?"

"I can't imagine you would behave in any other way, Shun. I'm glad it wasn't me that had the 'opportunity' to teach Mr. Agarwal," I say. "I would have been far less generous."

"I knew you were struggling too, Jessamyn. You know before I make any significant business decision, I do my due diligence. With the *Andaman Pearl*, I arranged for one of my 'spies' to be a part of the crew, as Shantrelle told you, and I investigated everyone aboard and everyone coming aboard, including you. Did you not suspect that?"

"I did, and it terrified me. I wondered if you had discovered my terrible secret? And what you might do."

"Whatever your secret, it is well hidden. All I found out about you was that you were a highly principled, skilled, compassionate physician entombed in a miserable marriage. You are well-liked and respected, unlike your deceased husband who was loathed and feared. It was not surprising you did not fall apart when he died. I assumed you were relieved to be free of his abuse.

"It would not have surprised me to learn you had something to do with his death, but there was no evidence, or even suspicion of that. Except mine."

Did he know? Why didn't he do something about it?

"I have trained myself to be suspicious of events as they seem to be, to look beyond the likely to the possible, even the improbable. You possess the knowledge and skill to engineer your husband's death and shield your involvement from the civil authorities.

"But it is not your way to harm anyone. You have saved countless lives and have never been disciplined or sued for malpractice. There is not so much as a parking ticket on your record to blemish it. If you had anything to do with your husband's death you must have thought you had justification.

"In the end, I tucked all these things in the back of my mind as I did with the background I gathered on the crew and the rest of the passengers. On the *Andaman Pearl,* I watched you live up to your reputation for skill and compassion time and again, with Mrs. Agarwal among others."

My god. He suspects I killed Roderick, and he's decided not to do anything about it. Not only that, but he also doesn't want me to tell him.

"In prison, Mr. Agarwal came to understand the need to atone for killing his wife. His understanding of Islam changed, and he embraced the idea of genuine repentance, assured of Allah's mercy and forgiveness. He is no longer in prison, either in Puzhal or the prison of his own evil. He is atoning and seeking forgiveness day by day, engaging in reparation, doing good deeds to tip the Scales of Justice on the Day of Resurrection in his favor, if even by only the weight of a mustard seed.

"I will listen to your terrible secret, Jessamyn, if that is what you need me to do. If you confess you killed your husband, or something equally unforgivable in the eyes of men, I will acknowledge how painful it is to be overwhelmed by evil. I will assure you of Allah's forgiveness as you repent and balance the scales. Whatever your secret, I believe the hospital ship *Metsá Ino* can be part of your transfiguration."

I am weeping veritable cascades. I shed as many tears as Anaconda Woman must have shed to create the Amazon and all the waters of *néte*.

Shun holds me, kisses my head, and encourages me. "Tears are jewels in the crown of transfiguration," he says. "Cry all you wish, all you must. You can never have too many gems in your crown."

I wipe my eyes with my hand and sniffle. Ever the gentleman, Shun produces a clean handkerchief.

"You are about to work wonders, *Metsá Ino*," he says. "Wonders greater than any of us can imagine. Wonders that will delight Grandmother *Aya* and the teacher plants. Wonders that will be pleasing in the sight of Allah. Wonders that will astonish even the *inos*. You will become legendary among jaguars."

We stand in silence, embracing for a few moments as I compose myself.

Shun gently releases me. "Now, with reluctance, I must leave you in the care of those women across the alley who take such pleasure in mistreating me in exactly the ways I like."

Was Shun ever without a light heart and a twinkle in his eye?

"The chopper will deliver you to the concert tomorrow in plenty of time. We will see you then for the triumphal debut of Lovely and Èlia. Until then, enjoy basking in the love we all have for you.

"Tell Shantrelle she owes me a buck, by the way. She hates to pay up. I told her those two would give a concert on a world-class stage before they graduate from the Conservatoire National Supérieur de Musique et de Danse de Paris. Of course, it doesn't hurt that their agent is on my payroll."

The three women come bounding into the room after Shun leaves. I don't know what they are saying because they're all talking at once.

Lovely is the first one out of her clothes, followed almost immediately by Èlia. Shantrelle and I give in out of fear that if we don't, the other two will simply strip us. Everyone is kissing Shantrelle's baby bump.

383

"Yay." Lovely giggles, popping the cork on a bottle of champagne and uncapping a bottle of Perrier she found in my fridge. "Four butt nekkid ladies, bubbles, and a big ass bed. Fizzy water for you and the baby, Shantrelle. Let's pile in before we freeze in this air-conditioned paradise and talk some shit about anyone we know—including us."

The jaguars find room to snooze at our feet as we pass the bottles back and forth and yack about this and that amid gales of laughter. Nobody is the slightest bit cold. ∎

Finis

Benicia, California
June 6, 2023

We find after years of struggle
that we do not take a trip;
a trip takes us.

JOHN STEINBECK
Travels with Charley

Afterword

This is a time of unparalleled opportunity for writers of debut novels. There are markedly fewer gatekeepers blocking the way and writers have more venues than ever for their work. Readers are beginning to catch on.

A version of *Transit* is serialized on Substack at "Marty Writes Stories" (martymalin.substack.com). It is necessarily somewhat different than the print version because of the unique requirements of serialized writing. But serialization is likely as old as written literature. As such, the serialization of *Transit* is in good company with its forebears, including every novel ever written by Charles Dickens, Dostoyevsky's *The Brothers Karamazov*, Tolstoy's *Anna Karenina*, Dumas's *The Three Musketeers* and *The Count of Monte Cristo*, Melville's *Bartleby, The Scrivener*, Henry James's *Portrait of a Lady*, and The Saturday Evening Post's serialization of Agatha Christie's *And Then There Were None* to drop but a few names.

Serialization of both nonfiction and fiction is enjoying something of a renaissance on Substack. I highly recommend that both writers and readers spend some quality time there in each others' company.

Gratitude

I am grateful to many people who have helped make this debut novel much better than it would otherwise have been. My friends and colleagues of the Benicia, California Novelists Circle deserve special mention: James W. White, Deborah Fruchey, Gregory Montoya, Alethea Morden, David Carrillo, Linda Folk, and Nicky Ruxton. All have read drafts, commented constructively, and generously given of their time and talents. Thank you so much for your experience, wisdom, and encouragement.

I am also grateful for the contributions of fellow writers from Napa Valley Writers First Editions critique group: Sue Kesler, Gary Orton, Michael Wycombe, William Moore, Sarita Lopez, and Rose Winters. I can't begin to convey how much your guidance has meant to me.

Rona Leon, formerly poet laureate of Benicia, was a perceptive and insightful beta-reader. Thank you for your close reading of the manuscript and thoughtful offerings.

Judy Roth is simply the world's best editor. She contributed immeasurably to matters of structure and style and guided me around pitfalls and plot holes I would never have seen without her. That I may have blundered into others is not of her doing. Every storyteller should be fortunate enough to work with her.

Jan Malin, my life partner and wife, created the book design, illustrations and cover art for *Transit*. She critiqued the final drafts of the manuscript and is the creative force behind my publisher Canyon Rose Press. Her contributions are immeasurable.

I would like to acknowledge the influence of the late Arthur L. Kistner, Ph.D. (December 26, 1933 - June 21, 2000), an extraordinary poet, playwright, and professor of English literature who was an invaluable mentor during my undergraduate studies in the 1960s. It was he, when I once naively complained of being bored, who challenged me to write a novel. It took me more than half a century to take him up on it.

Marty Malin

tinyurl.com/martystories
martymalin.substack.com

Made in the USA
Columbia, SC
22 November 2023